By Dennis L. McKiernan

Caverns of Socrates

BOOKS IN THE FAERY SERIES

Once Upon a Winter's Night

Once Upon a Summer Day

BOOKS IN THE MITHGAR SERIES

The Dragonstone

Voyage of the Fox Rider

HÈL'S CRUCIBLE:
Book 1: *Into the Forge*
Book 2: *Into the Fire*

Dragondoom

THE IRON TOWER:
Book 1: *The Dark Tide*
Book 2: *Shadows of Doom*
Book 3: *The Darkest Day*

THE SILVER CALL:
Book 1: *Trek to Kraggen-cor*
Book 2: *The Brega Path*

Tales of Mithgar (a story collection)

The Vulgmaster (the graphic novel)

The Eye of the Hunter

Silver Wolf, Black Falcon

Red Slippers: More Tales of Mithgar (a story collection)

Once Upon
Summer Da

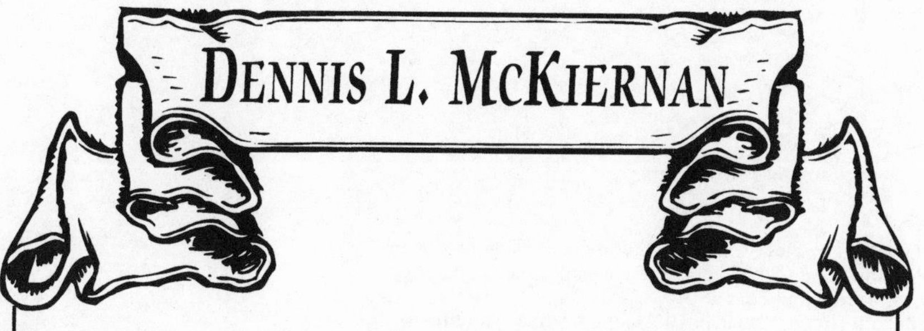

Once Upon A Summer Day

A ROC BOOK

ROC
Published by New American Library, a division of
Penguin Group (USA) Inc., 375 Hudson Street,
New York, New York 10014, USA
Penguin Group (Canada), 10 Alcorn Avenue, Toronto,
Ontario M4V 3B2, Canada (a division of Pearson Penguin Canada Inc.)
Penguin Books Ltd., 80 Strand, London WC2R 0RL, England
Penguin Ireland, 25 St. Stephen's Green, Dublin 2,
Ireland (a division of Penguin Books Ltd.)
Penguin Group (Australia), 250 Camberwell Road, Camberwell, Victoria 3124,
Australia (a division of Pearson Australia Group Pty. Ltd.)
Penguin Books India Pvt. Ltd., 11 Community Centre, Panchsheel Park,
New Delhi - 110 017, India
Penguin Group (NZ), cnr Airborne and Rosedale Roads, Albany,
Auckland 1310, New Zealand (a division of Pearson New Zealand Ltd.)
Penguin Books (South Africa) (Pty.) Ltd., 24 Sturdee Avenue,
Rosebank, Johannesburg 2196, South Africa

Penguin Books Ltd., Registered Offices: 80 Strand, London WC2R 0RL, England

First published by Roc, an imprint of New American Library, a division of Penguin Group (USA) Inc.

First Printing, April 2005
10 9 8 7 6 5 4 3 2 1

LIBRARY OF CONGRESS CATALOGING-IN-PUBLICATION DATA:

McKiernan, Dennis L., 1932–
Once upon a summer day / Dennis L. McKiernan.
p. cm.
ISBN 0-451-46012-X (alk. paper)
1. Princes—Fiction. 2. Quests (Expeditions)—Fiction. I. Title.
PS3563.C376053 2005
813'.54—dc22 2004021892

Set in Trump Mediaeval
Designed by Leonard Telesca

Printed in the United States of America

Once again to all lovers,
As well as to lovers of fairy tales

And to the Chelle we know and love

Acknowledgments

My dear Martha Lee, my heart, for the millionth time let me say I appreciate and am grateful for your enduring support, careful reading, patience, and love.

And again I thank the other members of the Tanque Wordies Writers' Group—Diane, Katherine, John—for your encouragement throughout the writing of this Faery tale.

And thank you, Christine J. McDowell, for your help with the French language. (I would add, though, that any errors in usage are entirely mine. Of course, the errors in English are mine as well.)

Thank you, James C. Grams, for your knowledge of wines and the patter of sommeliers, some of which appears herein.

Lastly, thank you, Grandmaster Tal Shaked, for allowing me to use your chess (échecs) problem in Chapter 37. (A fuller explanation of that specific puzzle can be found in the Afterword.)

Contents

Foreword

Are fairy tales but relics of altogether greater stories that once might have been told, pale remnants of much longer, even epic sagas? To me it seems a possibility. Oh, perhaps not *all* fairy tales are faint echoes of once-mighty shouts, but I think *some* of them surely must be.

You see, what many contend is that most fairy tales are stories from way-back-when, tales that were orally passed from person to person, and so they were unadorned and short and rather easy to remember. And many of them simply were to entertain, while others had a point to be made, whether it be a moral or a truism.

Some of the most beloved stories, those most likely to be passed from folk to folk, were co-opted by religion, and the heroes and heroines were said to be part of a particular religious group, whereas the villains were part of the old order—witches, goblins, trolls, and the like. Hence, these tales were used by whatever religion seized upon them to foster good will or belief, or to recruit. And some of the tales were shortened again to do this, or so I do believe.

But as I said in the foreword of another book *(Once Upon a Winter's Night)*, back when bards and poets and minstrels and the like sat in castles or in hovels or in mansions or by campfires, or entertained patrons as they travelled along the way, surely the original tales were much longer, when told by these "professional" storytellers, than the tellings of the less skilled. And so the bards embellished their tales with many more wondrous encounters than the later, altered—shortened—versions would have them be. After all, in the case of a bardic storyteller, she or he would hold audiences enthralled for long whiles with accounts of love and seduction and copious sex and bloody fights and knights and witches and dragons and ogres and giants and other fantastic beings all littering the landscape of the tale as the hero or heroine struggled on.

And so, I believe it is entirely possible that many of these splendid bardic sagas were severely shortened as the number of bards dwindled, and the people who were left to remember and pass on the tales simply didn't have the oratory skills to tell stories of epic scope. And so they grew shorter and shorter over time as particular portions of a tale went missing bit by bit, until they were pared down to the point where practically *anybody* could tell the story.

For example, were some great bard to tell a grand and glorious tale of the scope of, say, *The Iliad,* or *The Odyssey,* or even *The Lord of the Rings,* and were any one of these orally passed down through the ages from person to person, and if those passing on the tale were "common" folk, I believe the story would have dwindled a bit with each telling. And then, if one far-after day some Grimm brothers decided to write the beloved story down as it had come to be told, it might turn out to be an eight-page fairy tale.

Yes, I admit that's quite extreme, but I simply use it to make a point: that oral tales are difficult to pass on unless they are simple and short and rather easy to recall, or unless the people involved have phenomenal memories.

Thank heavens for writing, eh?

Don't misunderstand me; I am not putting down the fairy tales we've all come to cherish. I love them dearly: from the simplest "Little Red Riding Hood" and "Goldilocks and the Three Bears" and other tellings I heard from my mother and grandmother to the Andrew Lang collections—*The Crimson Fairy Book, The Red Fairy Book, The Pink Fairy Book,* and on through *Orange, Yellow, Olive, Green, Lilac, Blue, Violet, Grey,* and *Brown:* i.e., the spectrum—to the works of more modern writers, such as Dunsany and White and Tolkien (arguably, they were fairy-tale writers though their works are labeled fantasy these days), to some of the works of current writers.

What I am saying instead is I've always felt that many wonders were lost by what I think might be the shortening and altering of each age-old folk and fairy tale to fit a different song from that which the old bards and my Celtic ancestors would sing.

And so, a few years past, I wrote my first "restored" fairy tale (*Once Upon a Winter's Night*) to tell (in a traditional manner and style) one of the time-honored tales as I think it once might have been told. And now here I am again with *Once Upon a Summer Day,* my second "restored" fairy tale. And once more I have chosen a tale that not only is one of my favorites, but is a favorite of people around the world.

And since it is a romance in addition to being an adventure, once more you will find French words sprinkled throughout to represent the "Old Tongue."

By the bye, in my version of *The Blue Fairy Book* this story is but six pages long; the version of the Brothers Grimm is even shorter and probably better known. I thought that much too brief, and, as is apparent, I did lengthen it a bit. But then again, I claim that I am telling the "real" story, and who is to say I am not?

Dennis L. McKiernan
Tucson, Arizona, 2005

And so take care, beware,
for they will seek revenge.

Whisper

There is a place in Faery where eternal summer lies upon the land; it is a region of forests and fields, of vales and clearings, of streams and rivers and other such 'scapes, where soft summer breezes flow across the weald, though occasionally towering thunderstorms fill the afternoon skies and rain sweeps o'er all. How such a place can be—endless summer—is quite mysterious; nevertheless it is so.

Separated from this magical realm by a great wall of twilight is another equally enigmatic domain, a region graced by eternal autumn, and here it is that crops afield remain ever for the reaping, and vines are overburdened with their largesse, and trees bear an abundance ripe for the plucking, and the ground holds rootstock and tubers for the taking. Yet no matter how often a harvest is gathered, when one isn't looking the bounty somehow replaces itself.

Likewise, lying past this realm, beyond another great wall of half-light, there stands a land of eternal winter, where snow ever lies on the ground and ice clads the sleeping trees and covers the still meres or, in thin sheets, encroaches upon the edges of swift-running streams, and the stars at night glimmer in crystalline skies.

And farther on and past yet another twilight border lies a

place of eternal springtime, where everlasting meltwater trickles across the 'scape, and trees are abud and blossoms abloom, where birds call for mates and beetles crawl through decaying leaves and mushrooms push up through soft loam, and where other such signs of a world coming awake manifest themselves in the gentle, cool breezes and delicate rains.

These four provinces are the Summerwood and Autumnwood and Winterwood and Springwood, magical regions in the twilit world of Faery. They by no means make up the whole of that mystical realm. Oh, no, for it is an endless place, with uncounted domains all separated from one another by looming walls of shadowlight, and with Faery itself separated from the common world by twilight as well.

But as to the four regions, a prince or a princess rules each—Alain, Liaze, Borel, and Céleste—brothers and sisters, Alain and Borel respectively having reign o'er the Summer- and Winterwoods; Liaze and Céleste, the Autumn- and Springwoods.

They got along well, these siblings, and seldom did trouble come their way. Oh, there was that difficulty with the disappearance of Lord Valeray and Lady Saissa, and the two curses leveled upon Prince Alain, but Camille had come along to resolve those problems, and everything had then seemed well in order, at least for a while, though there yet was a portent of darker days to come. But at that time joy lay upon the land, with Camille and Alain betrothed, the banns posted, and preparations for the wedding under way.

Yes, all was well in these four realms, or so it seemed.

But then . . .

. . . Once upon a summer day . . .

Out in the gazebo upon the wide lawn of Summerwood Manor, Borel sat and watched four black swans majestically gliding upon the wide, slow-running stream, the graceful birds keeping a wary eye upon the Wolves lying asleep upon the sward, all but the one who kept watch and eyed the swans just as warily, though a predatory gleam seemed to glint in the eye of the grey hunter. A balmy breeze stirred the silver of Borel's shoulder-length locks as he leaned back in the wickerwork chair, his long legs stretched out, his soft-booted feet resting upon a padded footstool. From somewhere nearby came the hum of bees buzzing among garden blooms, and lazy clouds towered aloft in the cerulean sky and cast their quiet shadows down.

How peaceful it was on this gentle day, and Borel closed his ice-blue eyes, just for the nonce, his mind drifting along with the building clouds. How long he remained thus, he could not say, yet there came a muted sound of . . . he knew not what.

Borel frowned and opened his eyes, and then sat bolt upright, for the gazebo was changing, the floor turning to flag, the open sides to stone walls, even as he looked on in amaze. And beyond the windows of the now-stone chamber a seemingly endless number of free-floating daggers filled the air and blocked the light and cast a gloom o'er all.

Opposite from him in the dimness stood a slim young lady, as if in meditation or prayer. Her head was bowed and her long golden hair fell down across the white bodice of her flowing dress. Her delicate hands were clasped together just below her waist. Across her eyes lay a black, gauzy cloth or mayhap a band of shadow, as of a dark blindfold, or so it appeared.

And the lady quietly wept.

Borel stood and stepped closer. "Demoiselle, why do you weep?"

"Aidez-moi," she said, her voice but a whisper. *"Aidez-moi."*

Borel jerked awake and found he was on his feet, and the wind blew hard and moaned through the filigree, the late-afternoon sky dark with the oncoming storm. Then the summer rain came thundering down, and Borel's Wolves took shelter within. And while black swans sought refuge in the overhang of a streamside willow, Borel looked about, seeking . . . seeking, but not finding, even though it seemed there came to his ears an ephemeral echo of a desperate whisper flying past on the weeping air: *"Aidez-moi."*

Colloquium

"I tell you, Alain, it seemed quite real."

Alain sighed. "A stone chamber surrounded by daggers and a blindfolded, golden-haired damsel within?"

Borel nodded. "And she needs help."

They sat in the game room at a small table on which lay an échiquier, the pieces arrayed before them, the brothers only a few moves into the match, for, after Borel had unnecessarily lost one of his hierophants, Alain had asked what was it that distracted him, and Borel had told of the vision.

From somewhere outside came the rumble of distant thunder as the remains of the storm moved away.

"And you think it was a visitation and not a common dream?" asked Alain.

"It seemed totally real at the time."

"And your Wolves . . . ?"

"They were outside the gazebo and sensed nought, or so I deem, for they were not agitated."

"Hmm . . ." mused Alain, running his fingers through his dark hair. "One thing is certain: the gazebo did not remain stone, and perhaps never was. I think if there was a visitation, it was you going to her rather than the other way 'round."

Borel nodded and a silence fell upon the two of them, and once more distant thunder rumbled. Finally Borel said, "If it was but a dream . . . ?"

"Then, Frère, there is nothing to worry about."

"Yet if she is real and in peril . . . ?"

"Then I know not how you can help, for there is not enough to guide you."

Again they fell into silence, but then Alain said, "Let us consult Camille and see what she has to—"

Chirping, a black-throated sparrow flew into the room, and three slender demoiselles followed: auburn-haired, amber-eyed Liaze in the lead; golden-haired, blue-eyed Camille next; pale-blonde, green-eyed Céleste coming last.

Even as Borel and Alain stood, and the wee bird settled on Alain's shoulder, "Aha!" said Liaze. "We thought we might find you two hiding here. But, sit! Sit! We've come to ask about—Why, Borel, you look positively morose on this gloomy day."

Camille gave Alain a light kiss on the cheek, and then looked at Borel and asked, "Why so glum, Brother-to-be?"

"I've had a vision," said Borel.

"Or a dream," said Alain.

Borel nodded. "Or a dream."

"Oh, my, Frère," said Céleste, her face growing somber. She pointed at the large round game table with chairs all about and taroc cards strewn on its surface. "Let us sit, and then do tell us of this dream or vision of yours."

As soon as all had settled, Borel related his vision to them, and when he had come to the end, he once again stated that it might have just been a dream.

Liaze shook her head. "Oh, no, Borel. I think it must have been a visitation, for if it were a mere *rêve* or *songe,* then it would not bother you so."

"She spoke in the Old Tongue?" asked Céleste.

Borel nodded. " '*Aidez-moi,*' she said—'Help me'—and no more. Yet how can I do so when I know not where she is?"

In that moment the sparrow chirped and flew down to the table and pecked at one of the cards.

"Mayhap Scruff has the right of it," said Camille, pointing at the bird.

"What do you mean?" asked Borel, as Céleste reached out and began drawing all the taroc cards to her, and Scruff flew across the room to the échecs table where he had first found the two men.

"Just this," said Camille. "Could we read the taroc, perhaps it has a clue as to what to do."

"Ah, but we are not seers, hence cannot read the cards," said Céleste, as she gathered the last of the deck and began shuffling.

Camille frowned and said, "Lisane can."

"Oui," said Borel. "The Lady of the Bower. Even so, aren't her messages rather vague, hard to interpret until after the fact?"

Camille nodded. "It was only in hindsight that I understood."

"Then," said Borel, "I think she cannot help, for if it is a true vision, then the lady in the stone tower needs help now."

"Perhaps so, Borel," said Liaze. "Yet there is nought you can do until you know more."

"Are you telling me to go about my business and forget the vision?" asked Borel.

Liaze shook her head. "Borel, I think you must follow your heart. Even so, I deem that until you have more knowledge, there is little you can do . . . unless you happen upon someone who knows of a blindfolded lady in a stone tower surrounded by daggers."

A quietness fell in the chamber, and only Scruff across the room and scrabbling among the échecs pieces interrupted the still. Finally Camille said, "Perhaps she'll send you another vision."

As Borel nodded glumly, somewhere in the distance a bell rang.

"Dinner," said Alain, standing.

Céleste set the deck aside and stood as well, as did they all, and started out. Borel paused a moment and cut the cards and looked at the one turned up. It was the Tower, lightning striking the top, men plummeting down among the shattered and plunging stone. Borel sighed and shook his head and replaced the card and then joined the others.

Camille took Alain's arm, and Liaze and Céleste, one on each side, took Borel's, and they all trooped out, and none noticed the board on which the wee sparrow had been scratching and pecking away at the pieces: nearly all were gathered in the center and lying on their sides: spearmen, warriors, hierophants, kings and one queen. On the other hand, the four towers yet sat upright in their corners. And in the midst of all the downed échecsmen, the white queen stood surrounded.

Counsel

"What about the Lady of the Mere?" said Camille, setting aside her spoon. She looked at Alain and added, "Without her aid I never would have found you."

"Lady Sorcière?" said Borel.

"Yes," said Camille. "That is one of her names. Another is Skuld, She Who Sees the Future."

"Lady Wyrd, you mean, one of the Fates," said Borel.

"Another of her names," said Camille. "Regardless, perhaps she can help you with this vision of yours."

"If she is willing," said Alain. "She doesn't come at just anyone's beck."

Céleste nodded in agreement. "It is told that something must be of vital import, else she will not appear."

Borel sighed and shook his head. "I do not think I will disturb Lady Wyrd at her mere unless the apparition comes once again and I am truly convinced she is real. After all, I might merely have had a dream."

Alain looked 'round the table, then took up the small bell and rang it, and servants swept in and removed the soup bowls, and others came with dishes and platters and crystal decanters of red wine and stemmed glasses, and moved about and served, and then quickly vanished again.

Borel held his wine up to the light, as if seeking guidance within its ruby depths. "Besides, I would return to the Winterwood to see if the witch Hradian yet dwells therein."

"Wait, Borel," said Camille. "Did you not propose to Lord Valeray that after the wedding we would get a warband together and run the witch down?"

"Oui," said Borel. "Even so, I would go and see if she yet stays in that cote of hers."

A grim look came into Alain's eye. "Facing a witch alone is perilous. I will go with you."

"No, no, Frère," said Borel, pushing out a hand of negation. "I do not intend to face her unless there is no other choice. Besides"—he smiled at Camille, then turned to Alain again—"you will be needed here to prepare for the wedding." He glanced at Céleste and Liaze and added, "As will you two."

Camille sighed and took her knife to the veal cutlet. "I don't know, Borel. I think you should wait. Hradian is a formidable foe. I agree with Alain: to go alone would be a mistake."

"But I will not be alone," said Borel. "My Wolves—"

"I think they cannot protect you from a curse," said Liaze.

Céleste frowned at Borel. "Heed, Frère: she is a witch and likely to have wards about."

Borel waved a negligent hand then took a sip of his wine, and Céleste expelled her breath in exasperation.

Camille set aside her knife. "From what the Lady of the Bower said, and from what I have deduced, she is a priestess of, or at least an acolyte of, the Wizard Orbane, the one who created those terrible tokens of power—the Seals of Orbane—perhaps in his strongholt on Troll Isle."

"I am told it is no longer called Troll Isle, Sister-to-be," said Borel, grinning, "but L'île de Camille instead, so named in honor of you after your warband slew the Trolls and Goblins and set Alain and the captives free."

"Try not to distract me with flattery, Borel," said Camille, "for no matter the name of the isle, still it once was Orbane's strongholt, and it was there I believe Hradian found several of those dreadful seals. I am certain it was she who gave two of them to the Trolls, and they used them to lay the curses upon Alain. Too, Hradian mayhap used another when she ensorcelled your père and mère. And if she yet has some of them, indeed you will be in grave peril."

"If that be the case," said Borel, "I would rather go alone than subject any of you to the hazard. Besides, I do not intend to confront her head-on, but rather to use stealth and guile, and one alone is certainly more stealthy than the five of us would be. Hence, with nought but my Wolves and me seeking her, I have better prospects of not being noted."

Ignoring Borel's words, Liaze said, "Perhaps we should take Caldor or Malgan with us to counteract anything Hradian tries."

Alain snorted. "Those charlatans? Wizard and seer, pah! I think they could not protect anyone from ought."

Céleste sighed. "Do not be too hasty to name them mountebanks, Brother. They were, after all, trying to negate the effects of two of the seals when they came to lift the curses from you. Remember, Orbane was a mighty wizard—vile in intent, but puissant, nevertheless. It took two of his own seals and most of the Firsts to cast him into the Great Darkness beyond the Black Wall of the World. Hence, those clay amulets are powerful indeed, and not something to be taken lightly. And that Caldor and Malgan failed, along with many others, was perhaps to be expected, though we knew it not at the time." Céleste then turned to Borel. "And as for you going alone—"

Borel held up a hand. "Cease. Cease. I will consider what you have said. But for now, let us forget Hradian, and instead enjoy this fine meal, and afterward retire to the ballroom and hear Camille sing, Alain, too, and then perhaps all of us can round up some of the household and form an orchestra and partners and dance the night away."

"Splendid idea, Borel," said Alain. He stood and stepped to the pull cord and gave it a tug. "Anything to take your mind off this mad plan of yours." Moments later a slender, grey-haired man dressed all in black appeared. "Lanval," said Alain, "please begin recruiting musicians and dancers from among the staff. We're going to have a soirée this eve." As Lanval bowed, a corner of his mouth briefly twitched upward, and he stepped out to gather folk for a spree. When Alain resumed his seat he said, "Besides, Borel, a frolic might well lift this darkness from you o'er that dream or sending you had."

In the ballroom of Summerwood Manor, lords and ladies and maids and lads all engaged in dancing the complex quadrille, and the slow and stately minuet, as well as the prancing rade, and the lively and vigorous caper of the reel. Before and after each dance, Camille sang arias, and she and Alain sang duets—she in her clear and pure soprano, and he in his flawless tenor. And highborn and low- alike all raised their voices in the cascading roundelays. The evening was filled with gaiety and laughter, yet in the early going oft did Camille and Liaze and Céleste and Alain glance at Borel to see if his glum mood persisted. As far as they could tell, he was enjoying the night immensely, and so they cast their concerns aside and gave over themselves to the merrymaking.

Long did the festivity last, and it was in the wee hours when all finally went to bed.

And none were awake in the faint dawnlight, when Borel and his Wolves slipped like grey ghosts through the mist of the morn and across the grounds of Summerwood Manor . . . and up the far slopes and beyond.

4

Summerwood

As he reached the top of the rise, Borel paused and looked back at Summerwood Manor, where ethereal mist twined 'round the great mansion and across its widespread grounds in the silvery light of the oncoming dawn. His Wolves gathered about and pricked their ears and looked intently this way and that, or raised their muzzles into the air, seeking to know why their master had paused, seeking to hear or see or scent what he had sensed. Borel then turned and with an utterance somewhere between a word and a growl, he spoke to the pack, and then, Wolves to the fore and aflank and aft, they all set off at an easy lope through the summer woodland as day washed across the sky.

Into the leafy forest they trotted at their customary pace for long journeys, one they could maintain for candlemarks on end. And long gleaming shafts of morning sunlight arrowed high across the tops of the trees and crept downward with the rising sun. Neither cloak nor vest did Borel wear, for here in the Summerwood the days were warm and the nights mild, and little was needed for comfort. Even so, those garments were rolled atop his pack, along with warmer gear, for Autumnwood lay ahead, with chill Winterwood beyond. Yet for now Borel went lightly dressed, as through the woodland they passed.

All that morn they ran at the easy pace, with small game and large scattering before them or freezing motionless so as not to be seen, while limbrunners scolded down at them from the safety of the branches above. Borel and the pack passed among moss-laden trunks of great hoary trees and wee Fey Folk among the roots or behind the boles or in a scatter of stone looked up from their endeavors as the Prince of the Winterwood and his escort loped by. Across warm and bright fields and sunlit glades burdened with wild summer flowers did Borel and his entourage run, where the air was alive with the drone of bees flitting from blossom to blossom to burrow in and gather nectar and pollen. Butterflies, too, vividly danced across the meadows, occasionally stopping on petals to delicately sit and sip. Hummingbirds *burr*ed through the air and drank of the sweet liquid among floral bouquets, and now and again Borel did see a gossamer-winged sprite playing among the blooms. Yet all this was but glimpsed in passing, for the prince and his Wolves paused not in these burgeoning glades. Instead, they pressed on through forest and field alike, only stopping now and again at sparkling streams to slake their growing thirst.

As the sun rode through the zenith, Borel halted under a broad oak at the edge of a grass-laden meadow, and there he took a cold meal of bread and jerky, while his Wolves foraged in the field at hand for mice and voles and other such ample fare.

After a short rest, again they took up the course, and miles fled in their wake as across the Summerwood they ran, the cool green forest shaded by rustling leaves above, with shimmering golden sunbeams dappling the growth below.

Down into a river-fed gorge they went, the lucid water sparkling, greensward and willowy thickets adorning its banks. From somewhere ahead came the sound of a cascade falling into water, and soon Borel and his Wolves trotted alongside a spread of falls pouring down amid a spray of rainbows into a wide, sunlit pool. Here did they stop to drink of the pellucid mere, and in the glitter a handful of Waterfolk cavorted. Two foot long and nearly transparent they were, as of water itself come alive. Webbed fingers and long webbed feet they had, the latter somewhat like fishtails. Translucent hair streamed down from their heads, as if made of flowing tendrils of crystal. Over and under and 'round one another, darting this way and that they swam, as if playing tag or some other merry game, and though they were completely engulfed in lucid water, still did their laughter come ringing clear above the roar of the cataracts.

Borel and the Wolves, their thirst now slaked, once again trotted onward; and up and out from the ravine they loped and in among the woodland again.

It was nigh sundown when they came to a looming wall of twilight, and this they entered, the day growing dimmer as they went, and then brighter as on through the tenebrous marge they pressed. When once more they reached daylight, they came into a color-splashed forest, the trees adorned in scarlet and russet and gold. There was a nip in the air, for they had left the Summerwood behind and to the Autumnwood had come.

Entreaty

Just after crossing the marge into the Autumnwood, Borel called a halt to the run and set about making a camp 'neath the limbs of an apple tree, its bounty ready for harvest. He put the Wolves to hunting, and shortly there were two coneys spitted above the fire, and several others being consumed by the pack.

Nearby, a patch of wild onions grew along a small rill, and Borel gathered a few of these and washed them clean. He plucked two of the red fruit from above. The apples and onions alike would be replenished overnight, for this was the wondrous Autumnwood, where such things did happen: no matter whether picked, plucked, shorn, or dug, whatever was reaped somehow reappeared when none was looking. Only wild game seemed vulnerable within this forest where falltime ever ruled, yet given the fecundity of such fare—be it furred or feathered or scaled—it would not be long ere whatever was taken came to full fruition again.

Yet Borel did not ponder upon the marvel of the Autumnwood as he set about making his meal, for in this demesne it seemed as natural to him as breathing or eating or sleeping.

Soon the savory smell of rabbit on a spit, with juices dripping into the flames, mingled on the crisp air with the sweetness of fresh apples and the sharp tang of onion. And the Wolves, now finished with their own meals, occasionally turned toward the fire and raised their noses in the air and inhaled the odor of cooking, though for the main they stood alert, with ears pricked and eyes scanning the surround for any sign of intruders.

After consuming the haunches of one of the rabbits, along with the onions and apples, Borel spent some time calling the Wolves to him one by one. He started with Slate, the dominant male, after which he summoned Dark, the dominant female. He then called Render and Trot and Shank and Loll and finally Blue-eye, as he worked his way down through the hierarchy of the pack. As turn by turn they separately came to him, he hand-fed each a bit of cooked rabbit, and he ruffled their soft, clean fur and spoke gently until he had done with the last of the lot.

With words somewhere between utterances and growls, he assigned a watch order, and as two took up station, all the rest settled down, including Borel.

Sleep soon came. . . .

. . . and stars wheeled in the silence above.

But just after mid of night, once more Borel found himself in a round stone chamber, only this time it was deeply shadowed. Again, the slender young damosel was there. With her head bowed, she stood in the dark on the opposite side of the stone floor. In spite of the gloom, Borel could see that her hands were clasped together just below her waist, and an ebon blindfold or a band of blackness lay across her eyes. She was dressed in a sapphire-blue gown with a ruffled white bodice, and dark blue ribbons were entwined through her golden hair; given the utter darkness surrounding her, how Borel could see this he could not say; nevertheless he saw.

Once more, off to either side stood windows, beyond which daggers floated in the air. Only a thin tendril of wan light managed to shine through one of the apertures, so thick were the blades. Borel stepped to that opening and peered up along the meager glimmer. As to its source, he could not be certain, though from its pale silvery illuminance he thought it might be light from the moon. He leaned into the opening for a better look, but daggers darted forward and threatened. Borel stepped back, and the stilettos moved hindward as well, away from the sill.

Even so, Borel yet tried to see past the blades, and he shifted this way and that, attempting to get a glimpse of what lay beyond the sharp poniards hovering so thickly all 'round. And as he moved, so did they, each of them locked in aim toward him. But the only thing he could glimpse that might be outside the beringing dirks was the wisp of light that managed somehow to winnow its way through.

He stopped and stilled his breathing and listened intently, as if to discover something of the world that might lie on the other side of the floating blades, yet all he heard was a faint but persistent squeaking. As to its source, what it might be, he knew not.

Shaking his head, Borel turned and stepped toward the damosel, and as he did so, once again came her desperate plea: *"Aidez-moi,"* she whispered. *"Aidez-moi."* And in that moment she and the stone chamber faded, and Borel awakened to find himself under the apple tree. A waxing gibbous moon shone down through leaves shifting in a faint breeze, and a scatter of pale light rippled upon his face.

Somewhere at hand chirped a cricket.

Nearby, Trot and Shank stood ward, and they both looked toward Borel, sensing he was awake. Slate, too, roused and lifted his head, and he and the ward waited. Yet Borel gave no command, and soon Slate lowered his head and closed his eyes, and Trot and Shank shifted their attention to the darkness beyond the camp.

With a sigh, Borel turned on his side, but it was a long while ere he once more fell asleep.

Autumnwood

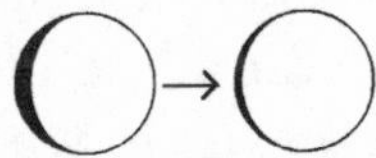

Sleeping but fitfully, at last Borel gave up his attempts at restful slumber and arose just ere the dawntime, and after a meal of apples and a bit of bread left over from the loaf he had taken from the bakery in Summerwood Manor, he and the Wolves set out.

Dawn came and slowly vanished as the sun rose into the morning sky, and its angling light revealed an autumnal forest adorned in yellow and gold and amber and bronze, in scarlet and crimson, and in roan and russet and umber. Through this flamboyant woodland passed Borel and the pack, trotting at the steady pace Borel had set the day before.

In midmorn they came to a long slope leading down into a wide meadow, and a rich stand of grain grew therein. High on the slope stood a massive oak, and 'neath its widespread limbs sat a large man with a great scythe across his knees. As Borel headed for the scarlet- and gold-leafed tree, the man stood and grounded the blade of his scythe and swept his hat from a shock of red hair and bowed.

Borel called out, "Bonjour, Moissonneur."

"Bonjour, Seigneur Borel," the reaper replied as he straightened up and donned his cap. Huge, he was, seven or eight feet tall, and he was dressed in coarse-spun garb, as would a crofter be.

Borel called a halt to the run, and set his Wolves to hunting, though by growled word he forbade them to go into the field of grain, for he would not have any of the wee gleaners within accidentally taken for game. As the Wolves trotted away, Borel turned to the man and gestured to the ground and both sat beneath the autumn-clad oak. "How goes the day, Reaper?"

"The sun rises, passes overhead, and then sets," rumbled the large man, a grin twitching his lips.

Borel laughed and shook his head. "Still the wit, I see."

"And you, my lord," said the reaper, "how fare you?"

"Well, I could say on two legs," replied Borel, but then he sobered. "I have been having strange dreams of late."

"Dreams?"

"Aye, of a demoiselle in some distress, but what that misfortune might be, I cannot say."

"Mayhap instead of a dream, Lord Borel, it is a sending."

"If it is, it is of little use, for I cannot aid when I know not where she is."

"Have you no inkling?"

"She is in a stone chamber, and beyond the windows hover endless daggers."

"Daggers in the air? How can that be?"

"Who knows the ways of dreams, Reaper?"

"A seer, my lord, a seer."

"Aye, you are right, Reaper. Mayhap when I reach the Winterwood, I will consult with one."

The big man nodded. "A wise choice, Lord Borel." He paused a moment and then asked, "And there is no more to this vision?"

"In the dream I hear a cricket chirping, or a squeaking of some sort. Yet it simply could be that somewhere near my place of rest a real cricket sang for a mate."

"Hmm . . ." The reaper frowned. "A cricket does not seem to have a bearing on a maiden in trouble. Perhaps more will come if the sendings continue. On the other hand, if these are not sendings, perhaps there is something of import in recent days that could explain your dream, something dwelling on your mind."

Borel sighed. "The only thing of note is that Alain and Camille are to be married soon, and of late I have been pondering on whether or no I will ever find a truelove as did he. Yet if that has ought to do with this demoiselle of my dream, I cannot say. Perhaps she is nought but a manifestation of my desire, though why I might think of her as being in peril, I know not."

The reaper frowned and said, "Perhaps in your sleep you wish to do a bold deed to win a demoiselle of your dreams."

Borel sighed and turned up his hands.

The reaper shook his head and said, "You have a dilemma, Lord Borel. If it is a sending, then she is real and you know not how to find her. If it is but a dream, then she is not real, and you worry needlessly."

They both sat in silence for a moment, and as the Wolves came trotting back, a brace of rabbits their catch, the huge man sighed and said, "I, too, would like a loving mate."

"Well, I can't give you an adoring bride, Reaper," said Borel, as Shank and Blue-eye each proudly deposited a coney at Borel's feet, "but, as is my custom, I can dress out these rabbits and set them to cook. Would that I could bide awhile and take a share as I normally do, Moissonneur, yet I have far to go and little time."

Borel quickly dressed out the rabbits, and, as the reaper buried the skins and viscera, Borel started a fire and set the game on a spit above.

As the big man took his place to turn the spit, "Adieu, Reaper," said Borel, standing.

The man smiled and said, "Thank you once again, Winterwood Prince, and thanks to your hunters as well. I always look forward to your passing through."

Moments later, Borel and the pack were on their way across the meadow, skirting the edge of the field in which grew oats and rye. And as they trotted onward, scampering alongside but hidden by the teeming stalks, wee giggling elfin gleaners paced them.

Soon the man and Wolves were out of the vale and running among the vibrant trees of the Autumnwood again, and, as before, in seemingly random places did they come upon groves of fruits and nuts and fields of flax and barley and millet and other grains, or they passed through orchards of red apples and golden peaches and purple sloe and fruit of other kind. Too, now and again they veered around plots of loam, the soil bearing beans and peas, leeks and onions, pumpkins and squash, and carrots and parsnips, as well as vines of hops and grapes, or stands of various berries. And none of this largesse seemed to be growing wild. In fact, unlike in the oat-and-rye field where the reaper dwelled, there seemed to be no farmers, no crofters, no sowers, planters, growers, cultivators, harvesters, pickers, or attendants of any kind in the scattered fields and orchards and gardens and other stands. Even so, this was the Autumnwood, where bounty for the dwellers of the Forests of the Seasons was ever present, and anything gathered somehow mystically reappeared when no one was looking.

Yet although these fields and gardens and arbors were scattered throughout this treeland, Borel and his Wolves mainly passed through virgin forest on their run. And as they trotted across the woodland, occasionally others loped or flew alongside—tattooed lynx riders and darting winged folk and other such denizens of Faery—but for the most part, Borel and his Wolves coursed alone.

As the sun crossed the zenith, they came unto a small glade surrounded by great oaks with leaves all vermilion and saffron. Here Borel called a halt, and set the Wolves to forage for their noonday meal, and as they sought mice and voles, or mayhap a coney or two, Borel took his own fare, supplementing his cheese with apples picked in the morning.

Shortly, they were on the trail again, and they passed along deep river gorges and high chalk bluffs and through thickets and mossy glens, the land rising and falling as they went. And whenever they topped crests or went along cliffs, though bright day was upon the land, in every direction afar the vivid woodland faded into distant twilight, just as the remote forest had shaded into silver-grey gloam in the green Summerwood the day before. In fact, in nearly all of Faery, no matter the realm, the view fades into twilight along any bearing one cares to look, clear day or no.

The sun sank toward the horizon, and as dusk came upon the land, Borel called a halt, and once again set about making camp, while the pack set about gathering small game for the evening meal.

That night Borel tossed restlessly, not succumbing at all to deep slumber, but struggling instead on the edge of wakefulness for the fullness of the darktide.

He had no dreams whatsoever.

Late on the second day within the Autumnwood, they came to another looming wall of twilight, and leaving the bright-hued trees behind, they stepped into the gloam, the daylight fading as they went, and then brightening again as they pressed on through, until a gray sky loomed o'erhead, with chill, diffuse light gleaming through ice-laden limbs and glancing across snow, for when they had passed beyond the marge they had come into the cold of winter.

Even so, they continued on, and when darkness finally fell, they made camp in the icy surround, for this was the Winterwood.

7

Winterwood

Though kept warm by his quilted eiderdown bedroll, once again Borel did not fall into deep slumber, but instead was wakeful throughout the darktide. Needless to say, he did not dream, for dreams come to those who pass into deep sleep, a state that completely escaped Borel.

The restlessness of the prince affected the Wolves as well, and they spent much of the night rising and turning about and then settling into the snow again, only to lift their heads at every stir of their master and at every small sound, be it the fall of an icicle or a plunge of snow from a pine or the cracking of rock in the winter cold.

Borel finally fell adoze just ere dawn, yet Loll came and licked his face to announce the coming of the sun and a winter-bright day.

Stiffly, Borel arose and added wood to the remaining few glimmering coals of his fire, and he made strong tea to revive his alertness. Shortly thereafter, he broke camp, then he and the pack began trotting through the Winterwood, with its snow-clad pines and ice-clad deciduous trees barren in their winter dress, trees that in the ordinary world would awake with the coming of spring, yet these trees rested perpetually in the forever winter of this realm. Shrubs and grasses and other plants slept as well, for among the Forests of the Seasons, each woodland was eternal in its aspect: the Springwood was ever burgeoning; the Winterwood ever resting; the Autumnwood ever bearing; the Summerwood ever flourishing. Somehow, these mystical realms seem to maintain one another in concert, each by some numinous means giving unto the whole the essence of that which was needed to remain in a constant state of existence. The Winterwood provided slumber and rest that all such life needs; the Springwood infused all with the vitality of awakening life; the Summerwood gave to the whole the sustenance of coming to fullness; and the Autumnwood spread the fruitful rewards of maturation throughout. Jointly, they ran the full gamut, though each separately remained unchanged as well as unchanging.

And so the realm of the Winterwood slept under blankets of snow and claddings of ice.

And as in any winter realm, within this woodland there were storms and blizzards and gentle snowfalls, days bright and clear and cold or gray and gloomy or dark, days of biting winds howling and blowing straightly or blasting this way and that, of freezings and hoarfrost so cold as to crack stone, of warm sunshine and partial thaws and a bit of melt, and of snowfalls heavy and wet, or falls powdery and dry.

It was a world of silence and echoes, of quietness and muffled sounds, and of yawling blasts and thundering blows.

It was Borel's realm—wild and untamed and white and grey and black, with glittering ice and sparkling snow, with evergreens giving a lie to the monochromatic 'scape—and he loved it most dearly, for never were any two days the same, and never were they different.

And across this icy realm did Borel and his Wolves lope, clots of snow flying from boot and paw alike. And as they trotted, a track left behind, within the ice of the ice-clad trees, and within the ice of the icicles, wee Sprites followed along, some merely to turn and look and note the progress of the prince and his pack, others to somehow shift from ice-clad rock to ice-clad tree to icicles dangling down as they kept pace with Borel or gleefully raced ahead. These were the Ice-Sprites: wingless and as white as new-driven snow, with hair like silvered tendrils, their forms and faces elfin with tipped ears and tilted eyes of pale blue. They were completely unclothed, as all Sprites seemed to be, and they had the power to fit within whatever shapes ice took. And their images wavered and undulated and parts of them grew and shrank in odd ways and became strangely distorted as they sped through the uneven but pellucid layers of frozen water, the irregular surfaces making it so, rather as if they were passing through a peculiar house of mirrors, though no reflections these, but living beings within.

As he ran, Borel glanced at the Sprites and smiled, and thereby acknowledged their presence. For they were of his demesne and subject to his command, though he seldom asked ought of them.

It seems that in all the Forests of the Seasons, wee beings love to pace alongside travellers passing by, though now and again something or someone comes along that causes them to flee in terror. Yet in this case it was Borel and his Wolves running through the Winterwood, and Sprites accompanied them by passing from iced rock to clad tree to coated limb to frozen stream to anywhere ice clung, and they did so without seeming to have to travel the distance between: they simply were here, and then were there, all as if there were no intervening space. And as far as Borel knew, they spent their entire existence within layers of ice.

The sun rose into the clear blue sky above, and tiny gleamings of shifting color were cast from the crystalline snow unto the eye. And across this 'scape trotted Borel and his pack, now and again passing through stark shadows cast by boulder and limb and bole to come again into the glitterbright day. And crows and ravens called through the woodland, for oft did they spend days or even weeks in the winterland. Treerunners, too, chattered and scolded and scampered along barren limbs, for they as well often came through the twilight borders unto this realm. It was as if they were compelled to bring nuts and other fare from the Autumnwood and place these stores in hollows and holes within this cold forest.

As he had done in the Summer- and Autumnwoods, oft did Borel pause at streams and, with Ice-Sprites scattering aside, he would break through the frozen surface and quench his thirst, Wolves at his side lapping. But then he would take up the trot again, and continue on deeper into the snow-laden forest.

He stopped as the sun gained the zenith, and all rested for a while, but before the sun had travelled two fists along its arc, Borel was up and running again.

At times his progress was slowed by deep snow, and often did he break trail for the Wolves, though at other times they broke trail for him. On the prince and the pack ran as the sun fell through the sky, and at last dusk came upon the land, yet Borel did not pause, but kept going.

Night came upon them, and still they coursed onward for a candlemark or so, and in the glow of a luminous full moon rising they passed across the ice of a river and followed a trail up a long slope leading to a great flat atop a bluff overlooking the wide vale below.

As Borel and the Wolves crested the rise, they came into the lights of a great mansion. Yet, unlike stone-sided Summerwood Manor, the walls of this hall were fashioned of massive dark timbers cut square, and its roof was steeply pitched. A full three storeys high, with many chimneys scattered along its considerable length, the manse spanned the entire width of the flat. All along its breadth the windows were protected with heavy-planked shutters, most of them closed as if for a blow. Even so, enough were open so that warm and yellow lanternlight shone out onto a stone courtyard cleared of snow. Atop the high river bluff it sat like a great aerie for surveying the wide world below.

As the prince and the pack crossed the flat and came unto the courtyard, 'neath a sheltering portico great double doors were flung wide, and some ten bundled servants, all men, stepped forth and formed a double line.

Borel and the Wolves slowed to a walk, and as he passed through the short gauntlet all the men bowed, and Borel nodded in return, while the Wolves, noses in the air, tails wagging, scented friends of old. At the head of the line a slender, dark-haired man dressed all in black straightened and stepped forth and smiled. "The Sprites told us you were coming, my prince. Welcome home."

"Arnot," said Borel, acknowledging the steward of Winterwood Manor.

Borel strode inside, followed by his Wolves and then the men, the great double doors swinging to after, and they passed along a short corridor to come to a great welcoming hall. And there assembled were the rest of the of the mansion household—maids, servants, footmen, seamstresses, bakers, kitchen- and wait-staff, laundresses, gamekeepers, and others—men to the left, women to the right, and they smiled in welcome and bowed or curtseyed accordingly.

Borel stepped across the heavy-planked floor to a wide marble circle inset in the wood, within which was a great hexagonal silver inlay depicting a delicate snowflake. As his Wolves gathered about, smelling the air, their tails yet awag for here were many friends as well, Borel said, "Thank you for this warm welcome," and all within the hall applauded his return.

After a moment, to one side Arnot raised a hand, and when silence fell he asked, "What would you have of us, my lord?"

"For my Wolves a fair bit of cooked meat will do, not overdone, mind you, along with a few bones to gnaw," replied the prince. "As for me, I would have a warm bath and a good hot meal and then a pleasant bed, for I have come far these last four days and need a good long sleep."

At these words, and with a gesture from Arnot, the staff bustled off—some to the kitchen, others to Lord Borel's quarters, and still more to the sculleries and other chambers—for there was work to be done.

The prince and his Wolves were home at last.

Turnings

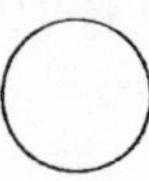

Gingerly, Borel eased into the hot water. Nearby, Gerard, laying out the towels, paused long enough to pour dark red wine into a crystal goblet, and when the prince was well immersed and had leaned back with a sigh, "My lord," said the small redheaded man, and he held out the drink to Borel.

"Thank you, Gerard," said Borel, accepting the glass and swirling the contents about. He took a sip. "Ah, some of Liaze's finest." He set the crystal on the flange of the bronze tub and glanced up at the valet. "I just realized: I'm famished. What does Madame Chef have in mind as tonight's creation?"

"I believe, Sieur, when the Sprites came and said you were on the way, Madame Millé began marinating venison."

"Ah. The dish with the white cream sauce?"

"She said it was your favorite."

"Your mother knows me well, Gerard." Borel took up the goblet again and in one long gulp downed the drink. "Tell her I will be ready in a candlemark or so."

"Yes, my prince," said the manservant. "Will you have more wine?"

"At dinner, I think. But now I just want to soak away the toil of travel."

"As you wish, Sieur." Over a rod on the fireguard Gerard draped a towel to warm it for the prince to use, and placed a washcloth on the edge of the tub and said, "Along with your linens, I have laid out a white silk shirt with pearl buttons and a grey doublet with black trim, black trews with a silver-buckled black belt, and black stockings and black boots. I have also included a crimson sleeve-kerchief. Will they do?"

"Ah, Gerard, you would make me into a dandy. Even so, it will be nice to wear something other than my leathers. Indeed, they will do."

"Very good, Sieur." Gerard took up the empty goblet and the bottle of wine. "I will inform Madame Millé as to when you will be down, and then I shall return to dress you."

As Gerard left the bathing room, Borel smiled and shook his head. *Dress me. Though I always don my own clothes, he insists he must "dress" me.*

Borel settled lower into the hot water, and relaxation slowly eased into his muscles. It was only after long moments that he realized just how tense he had been.

He closed his eyes and leaned his head against the metal slope of the tub. . . .

. . . And in but moments, it seemed, he awoke in water gone tepid to see Gerard standing silently and patiently by.

"Oh, Gerard," said Borel, "Madame Chef will have my hide." As he snatched up the washcloth and soap he looked at his hand and broke out laughing. "My wrinkled hide, that is."

Within a quarter candlemark, with his straight, silvery, shoulder-length hair still damp, he was scrubbed and dressed, and downstairs sitting at the head of a long, highly polished, blackwood table. Quickly, he finished the last of his *apéritif*—sliced mushrooms lightly sautéed in creamery butter. At a signal from Borel, one server whisked away the modest dish while still another server removed the small glass holding a trace of a pale red wine, one that Albert, the voluble sommelier, had called "a refreshing, rose-colored wine fortified with a hint of fruit and a crisp touch of sweet aftertaste—perfect for clearing the palate of any vestige of a previous drink." A third server set a bowl and a silver soup spoon before the prince, and a fourth waiter came in from the kitchen, a great tureen in hand. He ladled out *soupe à la crême de légumes assaisonnée avec des herbes.* When that was done, a fifth server set down a small loaf of bread on a modest cutting board, with a knife in a groove for slicing, and he put a porcelain bread plate to the prince's left, while yet a sixth server placed at hand a dish of pale yellow butter pats embossed with the form of a snowflake. The loquacious sommelier set a new goblet to Borel's right and said, "My lord, I have selected a special *blanc* to stand up to the heartiness of the soup: a full-flavored, substantial white wine with grape and apple aromas mixing well with the mustiness of barrel-aging and culminating in a robust aftertaste."

At a nod from Borel, the sommelier poured a tot into the goblet and then waited as Borel swirled and inhaled the aroma and took a sip and said, "A fine choice, Albert."

Albert smiled and filled the goblet half full.

The meal continued, the soup followed by venison in a light splash of a white cream sauce, with a sautéed medley of green beans and small onions and peas, all accompanied by a hearty red wine poured from a dusty bottle laid down for many years in a cool cellar. As the effusive sommelier put it, "I have selected a red that will enhance Madame Millé's splendid dish, a wine almost delicate in its complex bouquet holding a suggestion of aged cedar, a trace of pipeweed, and a hint of sweet, fragrant leaves of a kalyptos tree. Its rich flavor should spread evenly across the tongue, exciting senses of sweet and bitter equally, followed by a pleasant, drying sensation upon swallowing."

Borel smiled to himself at the sommelier's abundant description, but tasted the wine and said, "Again, Albert, a fine, fine selection," and then he ravenously tore into the meal.

After two full helpings, at last Borel leaned back in satisfaction, the plate empty before him, scoured clean, the last of the sauce sopped up with small chunks of bread.

And then the éclairs were served, and Borel groaned but faced them heroically.

Albert stepped forward with yet another fresh goblet and a

bottle of wine. "A sparkling, bit-off-dry white, my lord. It will enhance the sweetness of Madame Millé's splendid pastry."

Once again Borel nodded his appreciation and managed not one but two of the éclairs.

When that was cleared away, Albert served a snifter of cherry brandy, this from a very dusty bottle Albert held back for special occasions, ". . . a refreshing tartness to clear the palate, my lord. Would you care for some cheese as well?"

Satiated, Borel waved off the cheese, but he took up the brandy and groaned to his feet and headed for the kitchen, Albert trailing after. When the prince entered, all work stopped, and stepping to the fore of the kitchen- and wait-staff came a white-haired man in somber black, and a small woman wearing a chef's hat and a full, white apron over a dove-grey dress. The man in black bowed, as did all the men, Albert now among them, and the woman doffed her hat, revealing red curls, and she curtseyed, as did all the women.

Borel raised his glass on high and called out, "I salute you, Monsieur Paul, Madame Millé, and Monsieur Albert, as well as all who had a hand in the preparation and serving. Never has a finer meal graced Winterwood Manor." Borel then tossed down the drink, much to Albert's dismay, for this brandy was meant to be savored—slowly, and in small sips—else one might just as well guzzle straight from the bottle.

The rest of the staff, however, looked at one another and beamed in pleasure, and then bowed and curtseyed again.

Albert stepped forward, the dusty bottle of cherry brandy gripped tightly, but Borel smiled and shook his head, then set down the snifter on a nearby counter and turned on his heel and headed for his quarters, while behind voices were raised as the staff returned to whatever they'd been doing ere the prince had come: Madame Millé snapping out commands; Monsieur Paul's words less intense; men and women scurrying about.

"Nightshirt, Sieur?"

"No, Gerard."

The valet looked at the bed curtains and shook his head and

sighed. Lord Borel never wanted them drawn good and proper, but instead required them left open—"the better to hear the household" he said, as if at any moment something wicked might come crashing in.

"Good night, then, my lord," said Gerard. "Sleep well."

"So I hope," said Borel, crawling into bed.

Candle in hand, Gerard slipped out the door, taking the light with him, even as Borel eased under the down covers.

It seems somewhat strange, sleeping in my own manor again.

Ah, but it is good to be home.

Two or three days hence, I will head for Hradian's cote and see if there she yet dwells, but for now . . .

Borel fell aslumber ere he could finish that thought.

Long did he sleep, dreaming not at all . . . not at all, that is, until a candlemark or two beyond mid of night. . . .

With stone walls all 'round, beyond the windows Borel could see daggers floating in the air, threatening, ever threatening. A young, golden-haired lady stood across the chamber, her head bowed.

I've been here before, but when?

From somewhere nearby there came a persistent squeaking, though perhaps it was music instead.

"Oh, s'il-te-plaît aidez-moi, mon seigneur," whispered the demoiselle, a band of black across her eyes. *"Il ne reste qu'une lune."*

"What do you mean, my lady, when you say there is but a moon left?"

"Il reste peu de temps, mon seigneur. Il ne reste qu'une lune."

"Time grows short?"

"S'il-te-plaît aidez-moi. Aidez-moi."

"Do I know you, mademoiselle?"

Before she could answer there came a long, low, sustained cry, as of pain or grief or displeasure, and it slowly rose to a shriek, and the stone walls faded, and she was gone, and—

Borel startled awake in the night, a wind wailing about the mansion, and then it fell to a groan. He threw off the covers and stepped into a thin, silvery beam shining through the narrow crack between the two leaves of the shutters on one of the windows. Unclothed and crossing to that window, he lowered the sash and flung wide the hinged planks. A frigid wind moaned inward, bringing him entirely awake, and a bright full moon angling through the sky shone onto the far slope of the wide vale across the frozen river, casting long shadows down the slant.

Help me, she said, and she called me her lord.

Borel gazed up at the argent orb overhead. *And she said time grows short, there is but a moon left.*

Oh, what a stupid question I asked—Do I know you, mademoiselle?—when instead I should have asked where she was.

With the wind whirling up over the lip of the bluff and across the flat and courtyard, and groaning 'round the timbers and eaves, and blustering about the chamber, Borel stood in the aerie that was his mansion and gazed out across the Winterwood, his silvery hair whipping in the blow.

She is real. I know it. Not just a dream but real. How I know this I cannot say, but nevertheless I do. And she is in peril, and there is but a moon left ere something dire comes afoot or awing or aslither or however else it might arrive. I must do something. I must! But what? —Ah, the reaper had it right. A seer. I must consult a seer, a dream seer—a voyant de rêves. *No, wait. Better yet a diviner of dreams—a* devin de rêves*—and the nearest diviner is Vadun, a day beyond the cursed part of my demesne. I will pass by Hradian's cote on the way. Two birds with one stone, or so I hope.*

Of a sudden the wind gusted and banged one of the shutters to and then flung it wide only to slam the other about. Snatched from his musings, Borel grabbed the boards and closed and locked them and drew the window sash. He stood for a moment in the thin beam of moonlight shining inward through the small gap, and then went back to his bed. Yet he did not sleep again that night, his mind atumble with inchoate thoughts, imperfectly formed and vague . . . and in the end quite pointless, for he did not know who she was, nor where she was, nor what hazard she faced. He only knew she was in danger, and time grew perilously short.

Tossing, turning, unable to sleep, at last Borel left his bed just as the moon set and pale dawn graced the sky.

"But, my lord, so soon?" asked the steward. "You are not yet rested from your journey here."

"I must, Arnot. She is in peril, and time is of the essence."

They stood in the armory, Borel buckling on his leather-armor vest, Gerard fussing about, slipping things into the rucksack, while Jules, the armsmaster, handed Borel his gear.

Arnot, however, off to one side, eyed the weaponry all 'round the chamber: swords, halberds, axes, bows, long-knives, shields, bucklers, war hammers, chain, breastplates, and other such arms and armor, all marked with a silvery snowflake. Would that his lord would take up better weapons and protection—a good war hammer, a bronze breastplate, a helm, rerebraces, vambraces, cuissarts, greaves, and knee and elbow guards, as well as a shield—but Borel seemed to prefer to go lightly.

With a sigh, Jules, tall and dark-haired, took up Borel's bow—its grip polished ironwood, its limbs white horn, its bowstring intertwined strands of waxed silk—and turned to the prince. "Perhaps, my lord, it was merely the groan of the wind made you dream so. It was quite fierce last night."

"No, my friend, not the wind, instead 'twas a sending, I am certain. She is real, and somehow we are linked."

"And where do you propose to go?" asked Arnot.

"To Vadun. He is a dream diviner—a *devin de rêves*—and if any can unravel her location, Vadun is the one to do so."

"But, my prince, that means going through the cursed section of the 'Wood, and Hradian lives just beyond the blight. Let me round up some men, and we will go armed with you."

"Non, Arnot," said Borel, taking his long-knife from Jules and belting it on and strapping it to his right thigh. "I would not put you or them in peril."

"Then, my lord, I suggest you swing wide of her cottage," said Jules.

Borel shook his head. "My sire asked me to find out if the witch yet dwells in her cote; you see, after Alain's wedding, then will we raise a warband and run her down."

"But, my lord," said Gerard, the valet's voice tight with stress, "you needn't go nigh; we can send the Sprites to see if she yet resides therein."

"Non, Gerard. The Sprites avoid the cursed section entirely; they fear to go near. And Hradian's cottage lies on the far bound. Instead, I must go."

"Ah, this is a scouting mission then?" said Jules.

"Indeed," replied Borel, turning aside to take up his quiver, hence his gaze did not meet that of his armsmaster nor his steward nor his loyal valet.

"When do you plan on returning, Lord Borel?" asked Arnot.

"Before Alain and Camille's wedding three months hence," replied Borel, slipping the quiver baldric over his head and across one shoulder.

"My lord?"

"If Vadun interprets my dream and it is true, I have but a moon—nay, a day less than a moon—ere the lady must face her peril. At a minimum—twenty-eight days hence—I intend to be with her when that occurs, and I know not how far away lies this stone chamber surrounded by daggers dire. And so, if it takes the full of that time to reach her, and a like amount returning, then I should be back in two moons, well before Alain and Camille's wedding. Yet I hope that I can find her ere the whole of this moon has passed, for I would spirit her safely away with days to spare."

Jules handed the bow to the prince and stood back and examined him, then grunted in satisfaction. The prince seemed ready. But then the armsmaster frowned and said, "My lord, concerning this dream or sending—the daggers may merely be symbolic as to the threat she faces. They could represent an army besieging a palace, or other such encircling hazard. If that is true, you may need a warband or even an army to meet the peril beleaguering this damsel. If so, what then, Prince Borel?"

"I am hoping Vadun can tell me what is needed."

Borel took up his rucksack and stepped from the armory, the three men following. They passed down long corridors to come to the welcoming hall, and thence unto the main entrance and out into the courtyard. And there awaited Borel's Wolves, yipping and yammering and milling about, for they had sensed that another run lay ahead. How they knew the prince would be leaving this day, none could fathom, yet sense it they had, and they were eagerly waiting.

Prince Borel shouldered his rucksack and adjusted the straps to keep it from interfering with the quiver, then he slung his bow by its carrying thong and, with a final adieu to the trio, he set out across the courtyard at the Wolfpace he could sustain all day.

Shivering with the cold, Arnot, Jules, and Gerard watched until the prince passed over the flat and started down the slope beyond, and then with sighs they turned and stepped back into the warm and comfortable halls of Winterwood Manor.

All that day Borel and the pack trotted through the snow and ice, with gleeful Sprites flashing from ice-clad tree to ice-coated rock to the ice of a frozen mere or pond or lake, or of tributaries, be they rivulets, brooks, streams, or rivers. At some of these places, scattering the Sprites wide, Borel and the Wolves would pause and quench their thirst, but mostly they merely passed over the ice and continued on through the snow-laden land.

They rested for a while as the sun passed through the zenith, and then they continued on. And as they ran, the Ice-Sprites coursed with them. Yet toward midafternoon the number of Sprites dwindled and dwindled, until there was but one yet in their company, for they were nearing the cursed section.

Finally, they topped a rise, and downslope ahead stood a tangled and twisted wood, with barren, shattered, stark trees clawing at a drab, overcast sky. All was black and white and gray, no color whatsoever in the land. Even the evergreens were blasted and dead, needles gone, bleak branches broken and hanging lifeless. And there at the verge of this drear and stricken place, the Sprite flashed ahead and took up station on an ice-laden boulder and, with its face twisted in dread, it frantically gestured for Borel to stop, signing that peril lay in the desolate snarl.

Borel signalled that he and the Wolves knew the hazard of this part of the 'Wood, and trotted past the terrified Sprite and into the appalling blight.

Among the twisted trees they went, did Borel and the pack, Wolves running to the fore and flank and aft—Slate and Dark in the lead, Render and Trot to the left, Shank and Loll on the right, Blue-eye bringing up the rear. And all about was gloom and desolation and chill, a drear and silent wood. And now and again one Wolf or another would pause and raise a nose in the air, seeking the scent of peril in the surround, and then lope forward to take station again.

On they went into the fading day, the sky seeming even more drear in this dreadful demesne. Embedded in ice and snow and looming all 'round were harsh gray rock and jagged crags and stripped, barren trees—nought but cracked and splintered and tangled wood—and clawlike branches seemed to reach out to grasp, as if clutching at these insolent travellers who dared to journey within. Yet neither Borel nor the Wolves paid heed as misshapen boughs reached forth with their fingers of twisted twigs as the day drew down toward eve.

And a candlemark or so ere sunset, Slate in the lead trotted free of the tangle, followed by Dark; and then Borel and the flankers—Render and Trot, Shank and Loll—broke out of the snarl, followed at last by Blue-eye.

And just beyond the border awaiting them in an icicle dangling from the limb of an evergreen was an Ice-Sprite. And when Borel had emerged from the gnarl, relief flooded the Sprite's face. It was the Sprite who had accompanied the prince to the opposite side of the blight, and even though terrified, it had waited for them to safely emerge. All the other Sprites had long ago abandoned them, though somewhere farther on, somewhere beyond the reach of the cursed section, they would take up the run again.

Borel signed his thanks to the Sprite, and then—looking first left and then right—he turned leftward and trotted parallel to the tangle.

A horrified look on its face, once more the Sprite flashed ahead, this time to a frozen mere. And it signalled to the prince that menace lay to the fore, for in the near distance sat a small cottage of rough fieldstone, its roof tattered thatch.

Borel paused, and at a growled word, the pack paused as well. As he strung his bow, Borel studied the meager cote, one room at the most. There was no smoke coming from the chimney, and the air was silent.

Still the Sprite frantically gestured. Borel then signalled he knew of the peril and knew what he was doing, and, nocking an arrow, he started toward the dwelling—Hradian's abode—the Wolves yet arrayed to the fore and flank and aft.

The Sprite accompanied them no farther, so strong was its dread, yet Borel and the Wolves went on.

The sun sank lower in the sky.

And then they came to the cote and quietly circled 'round.

There was a single door facing the blighted wood, with a window to either side, and one in the rear as well. Yet the windows were covered with scraped and oiled hide and did not permit Borel to see within.

He looked to Slate and growled a word. A rumble came in response.

No fresh scent; all was old.

Borel stepped to the door. It was latched, yet a simple pull of the string snicked it open. Borel drew his bow to the full, then kicked the door wide on its leather hinges and stood ready.

No one was in the dimness beyond.

Borel stepped inside.

Perhaps the place is abandoned.

He scanned about. A fireplace stood in one corner; a tripod holding a lidded iron kettle dangled over cold ashes. In front of the fireplace sat a three-legged stool. To one side was a table, and hanging from the beams above were pots and pans and utensils. Several rude shelves on a wall at hand held a small number of wooden bowls and dishes and spoons. In the shadows overhead, strings of beans and roots and turnips and onions and leeks and other such fare depended from the joists.

Along one wall stood a cot, and along another wall sat a worktable with several drawers. Just above were more shelves, these with jars of herbs and simples and things that looked like parts of fur-bearing animals and insects and amphibians and reptiles preserved in a pale yellow liquid. On these shelves as well were scrolls and loose sheets of parchment. A half-full drinking bucket, the water frozen, sat on the hard-pack floor nearby, a hollowed-out gourd for a dipper hanging down from the bail.

Relaxing his draw, Borel stepped to the table and set his bow thereon, the arrow beside it. Then he took down a scroll and unrolled it. Whatever it said, he did not know, for it was written in runes unfamiliar.

Another scroll yielded the same result, though the symbols were stranger still. Another scroll and then another he opened, none of which he could read.

Perhaps I will burn these. —No, better yet, take them to Vadun. He is a seer of sorts and mayhap well versed in many tongues.

He unslung his rucksack and set it on the table, and placed all scrolls and parchments within. Then he began opening the drawers, and in the first he found odd instruments of bronze; what they were for he could not say. In the next were powders and what seemed to be lumps of ores, and a mortar and pestle for grinding. The next drawer yielded pressed flowers. Brushing most aside, Borel uncovered a book.

A grimoire?

The sun began lipping the horizon, casting long shadows across the Winterwood.

In the fading light Borel opened the book. It was written in a small, crabbed hand.

No, not a grimoire. Instead it seems to be . . . —Yes, a journal of sorts. Written in the Old Tongue.

Though the writing was difficult to read, still Borel quickly leafed from page to page, skimming.

Of a sudden his eye caught the words *Forêt d'Hiver.* He flipped back a page to the beginning of the entry. Though Borel could read the Old Tongue, still his progress was slow, for the hand was difficult.

"Aujourd'hui, j'ai complété ma malédiction sur la Forêt d'Hiver pour produire sa ruine totale . . ."

Today, I completed the curse upon the Forest of Winter to produce its total ruin, but the forest is too strong and resisted total destruction. Even so, I managed to blight a wide swath between the Springwood and the Summerwood along the shortest route to the common world, hence I deny them an easy journey.

On this same day in an linked act, my elder sister cast a great spell upon Roulan and his entire estate through his daughter Chelle, on this the day of her majority. This vengeance is so very sweet, for Roulan was the accomplice of Valeray the Thief. And now all are ensorcelled and well warded; and since none can find Roulan's daughter—or even if they do, all attempts to rescue her from the turret will fail—then when the rising full moon sits on the horizon eleven years and eleven moons from now—

Startled, Borel looked up from the journal. *Trapped? Turret? Full moon? This has to somehow be—*

From the corner of his eye, Borel noted movement in the bucket near his feet. And there, under the surface of the ice, the Sprite, sheer terror on its face, signalled frantically of oncoming peril. And then the Sprite disappeared.

Borel jammed the journal into his rucksack on the table and snatched up his bow and an arrow. Nocking the shaft as he went, he stepped through the doorway and out into the long shadows cast by the nearly set sun. Alighting in the snow some fifty paces away, Hradian dismounted from her besom, the crone dressed in black, with black lace frills and trim and danglers streaming from her like tattered gloom.

Borel's Wolves stood with fangs bared and hackles raised and growls deep in their chests.

And even as Hradian turned and looked at the cote, Borel took quick aim and loosed his shaft, the arrow to fly straight and true.

Yet even as it flashed through the air, with her index and little fingers of her right hand hooked like horns and pointing at the arrow, and her middle fingers pointed down and her thumb pointed leftwards, "Avert!" cried Hradian at the last instant, and the arrow veered to her left and ripped through her ear as it flew past. Hradian screamed in agony, even as Borel nocked another shaft.

Slate howled, and the Wolves charged.

But Hradian snatched up a talisman on a thong 'round her neck and cried a word and broke the amulet in two, and in a roaring black wind Borel was hurled up and away, his last sight that of the Wolves hurtling at the witch, yet she had mounted the haft of her twiggy besom, and then Borel lost consciousness and saw no more as the black wind bore him away.

Prisoner

"*Mon seigneur, réveillez-vous! Réveillez-vous!*"

Once more Borel stood in the stone chamber, the golden-haired demoiselle opposite, her eyes covered by a dark shadow, her hands held out to him in a plea.

"My lord, wake up! Wake up!" she again cried out in the Old Tongue, adding, "Peril comes down the steps!"

Reaching for his long-knife, Borel looked about, but there were no stairs leading downward from above—only rafters overhead with a conical ceiling beyond. The only steps from this chamber led to someplace below, though what that place might be, Borel did not know.

"My lady," asked Borel, also in the Old Tongue, "peril comes whence?"

"Down the stairs it comes, my lord. Down the stairs. Oh, please, you must wake up!"

Yet confused but gripping his knife tightly, Borel looked about, and still he could see no stairs leading downward from above . . . and yet he could hear footsteps descending. And he—

—opened his eyes to find himself lying on his side at the base of a wall on a cold floor of a shadowy chamber. Across the darkened room, from a door high above, faint light shone along a set of steps angling down the far wall. And bearing a candle and descending tramped two Redcap Goblins, the ilk so named because they dyed their hats in human blood. Some five feet tall they were and dressed in coarse-woven cloth and animal hides. And one behind the other, they stuck close to the wall, for there was no protective railing.

Feigning unconsciousness, Borel tightened his grip on his long-kni—*My blade!*—only to realize that unlike in his dream there was no haft in his grip. Instead he was empty-handed, and 'round his wrists—he chanced a quick glance—he discovered locked shackles. He was cuffed to chains embedded in stone behind.

Borel shifted slightly and set a foot against the wall and then closed his eyes and waited.

The Goblins reached the floor and neared, their bare feet plapping against stone.

They stopped at his side.

Borel felt a finger poke his ribs.

"Well?" snarled one.

"He's lean," replied the other. "Not much fat on these bones. There'll not be much drippin's, and—"

Borel lunged for the Goblins.

"Waugh!" they shrieked and leapt backwards, the tallow candle tumbling to the floor. *"He's awake!"*

Borel now on his feet—*Chank!*—the chains brought him up short, the Redcaps scuttling just beyond his reach.

From the safety of their distance, one of the viper-eyed Goblins said, "Her Nibs di'n't say nothing about this here one being a savage."

"Huah! Di'n't y' see her ear?" said the other, wiping a dangling, gelid string of snot from his overlarge nose onto a well-used sleeve.

"See it? O'course I seen it, what with her screaming about it and all."

"Wull then, likely he's the one who near bit it off." That Redcap covered his own left bat-wing ear with a knobby hand and took another step back from Borel.

Borel growled low in his throat.

The Goblins backed even farther away, then glanced at one another and turned and fled. As they reached the stairs, one of them screeched, "You won't last long when th' big'ns get back 'n' come t'fetch you for the spit."

"Yar, 'n' I'll have y'r boots, too," shouted the other. Then they started up the steps, arguing over which one of them would indeed get Borel's boots. They slammed shut the door at the top, and Borel heard a bar thud into place, or so it sounded. Dim light seeped through a small grille in the door and down.

Borel took up the fallen candle, its guttering flame nearly out. Upright, it caught and began burning steadily again, a thin tendril of smoke rising to the ceiling.

He held the stub high and examined the enshadowed chamber. As much as he could see by the light of the single flame, some fifteen or twenty paces wide and perhaps the same in length it was, with a ceiling mayhap twenty feet above, supported by four evenly spaced stone pillars set in a square. The floor and walls were of cut stone and the ceiling was of hewn timber. Along the wall at his back he could see several more pairs of shackles. Borel frowned. *Perhaps this once was a wine cellar, but now it's a prison of sorts.* Near one of the pillars sat a rather tall and wide three-legged stool, yet the rest of the chamber as far as he could tell held nothing else.

Borel then examined his shackles. They were bronze and thick and clamped tightly about his wrists and required a large key to open. The massive chains themselves were some eight feet long and bronze as well, and they were linked to heavy bronze eyelets set low and deeply embedded in the stone.

Borel carefully placed the candle down and, wrapping the slack about his arms, he sat facing the wall and braced his feet against rock and pulled. Nothing yielded. After several tries, Borel gave up; the cuffs, chains, eyelets, and stone were simply too strong.

Borel then took stock of himself. He yet wore his leathers and boots, but his long-knife was gone. Of his bow and quiver of arrows, there was no sign. *And my rucksack? It yet sits in Hradian's cottage, stuffed with scrolls and Hradian's journal—*

—The journal! It spoke of the curse and the turret and the full moon of her majority. The moon! How long have I been here? How long unconscious? The phase of the moon, where stands it? I've got to get free! Chelle is—

That's her name! I read it: Chelle. It was in the journal: Roulan's daughter Chelle. It has to be Chelle who is at hazard in my dreams.

—My dreams. She cried out that peril came down the steps. I knew it! I knew it! We are in truth linked, for she knew the Redcaps were coming.

Wait! Think! Cease this mental grasshoppering. Chelle is Lord Roulan's daughter. I remember her—a scrawny golden-haired child. Followed me about like a lost puppy, or mayhap the cub of a Wolf. Yet that was a time back, and now it seems she is a lovely mademoiselle.

And Roulan: I know his estates. I must reach them and defend her, take her away to safety ere Hradian's sister's bane falls due. And for that I must escape, and soon; the Redcaps said that when the big'ns get back I won't last long, and if they are what I think they are, then I must be away ere they return. But how?

Again Borel took stock of his situation. Locked in shackles and chained to the wall with no weapons and nothing with which to—

Wait! My leathers. The buckles.

Quickly, Borel undid the lowest buckle of his leather vest armor. He inserted the tang into the shackle keyhole and probed here and there, but the shank merely slid about. Borel removed the shank and held the candle close and looked into the opening and carefully examined the works. Once again he inserted the tang into the gap, and this time he felt it catch. Even so, he could not turn the lock.

I need oil, but where can I— Ah, it's worth a try.

Borel dripped hot wax into the lock, and then again inserted the buckle shank into the keyhole and . . . and . . . and just as he thought the tang would snap—*clack!*—the mechanism released.

The shackle fell free.

Moments later, Borel was loose.

But the candle guttered and went out. Even so, the dim light seeping down from the grille in the door was enough to make out shapes.

Weapon. What can I use as a weapon? Can I pry one out, a loose stone might do, and— Ah, the stool.

Feeling his way through the darkness, Borel located the seat.

Hmm, quite broad, but worn with age. I can break off a leg, but no, instead I'll use the entire thing until something better comes along.

Now to get through that door.

Stool in hand, to the stairs went Borel and up. The steps were wide and the risers high; they were built for a large stride, and Borel took this, along with the size of the stool and the height of the ceiling, to confirm his suspicions concerning the big'ns. Quickly he came to a landing before the door, bronze-bound and heavy-planked and quite tall, twelve feet or so, and four wide. The small grille was inset some eight feet above the floor. Cautiously, he set down the stool and mounted up and peered through the opening. . . .

Daylight shone through a narrow slit along a stone corridor beyond. The corridor itself was empty.

Daylight. It means I have been here overnight at the least. Perhaps even longer. How many days? Where stands the moon? I've got to get out.

Stepping down, he tried the latch and pushed; though it gave slightly, the door did not open, and from the feel of it, indeed it had been barred.

But I was shackled. Why would they bar the door? Ah, perhaps Her Nibs' arrow-ripped ear truly convinced them I am a savage, which means Hradian escaped my Wolves and came personally to see me in chains. Yet that is neither here nor there. Instead, I must get past this door. I wonder: can I somehow reach through and remove the bar if first I remove the grille?

But the lattice was heavy bronze and well anchored on the outside and defied Borel's attempts at prying with a leg of the stool, for he could get no leverage, and the leg itself was too large to wedge into the grillework to give him better purchase.

He was about to start hammering upon the lattice when he heard a door slam. Quickly he stood upon the stool and peered down the corridor beyond.

A Redcap came bearing a bowl and grumbling to himself.

Borel stepped down and took up the stool and stood back against the wall.

A strained grunt and gritted curses, followed by a ponderous scrape of wood on wood, signalled that the bar was being lifted. A loud thunk followed, and a dragging. And then the latch rattled and the massive door swung wide, and, stooping over and picking up a bowl of gruel and muttering—". . . them that wants to fatten up the prisoner ought to fatten him up themselves, 'n' I says we doesn't wait for the big'ns, but spits him ourselves, 'n' . . ."—the Redcap moved through the doorway and onto the—

Borel stepped out from the shadows and, with a two-handed swing, slammed the Goblin with the stool, the force of the blow shattering the seat as the Redcap smashed into the wall, to rebound and pitch over the edge and plummet to the stone floor below and land with a sodden thud.

And all was silent but for the wooden bowl clattering down the steps, gruel flying, and finally that stopped as well.

Borel listened. . . .

There seemed to be no alarm.

Stepping into the hallway, he examined the remains of the stool. Tearing off a leg for a cudgel, he placed the rest back on the staircase landing, then closed the door and took up the heavy wooden beam—*Too unwieldy for a weapon*—and dropped it into the brackets. *Perhaps they'll think that all is well with the door shut and barred.*

Club in hand, Borel slipped down the corridor, pausing momentarily at the stone slit. A short way below lay a narrow ledge, the edge of a cliff, a long sheer drop down a rock face, a river wending past at the bottom, reeds thick along the banks. Perhaps he could free-climb down could he get through, but the slit was too strait for him to do so.

On went Borel, and he passed a door to the right. Perhaps the very door that the Redcap had come through. But Borel went on, looking for—*Ah, a corridor leading away from the precipice. Surely the entrance into this holt lies opposite that fall.*

Along this new corridor he went, passing more doors, some closed, others open, leading into chambers with overlarge tables and chairs and other such. *The big'ns, no doubt.* He passed stairwells leading up and down, and these he ignored, for it was the main entrance he sought, a way out, and from the sight he'd glimpsed through the stone slit, he reasoned he was on the ground floor.

From ahead he heard voices squabbling, and cautiously he crept forward to come to what looked to be a step or two leading down into a broad hall.

In the chamber, three Goblins squatted—

Knucklebones! They're playing knucklebones.

—their attention completely on the game. All were armed: one with a saber, another with a wicked dirk, and the third with—

My long-knife. That one has my long-knife.

Great double doors stood just beyond where the Redcaps bickered.

The way out, I deem, for this can be nought but an entry hall.

Of a sudden as two Goblins cursed, the third jumped up and danced about and shouted in glee. "I gets th' boots, th' boots. They're mine, they're mi—" His words chopped shut, for he was looking directly at Borel, and for just a moment none moved, but then the prince charged, club raised.

"Waugh!" shrieked the Redcap and turned to flee even as the others looked up and 'round and screamed and leapt to their feet, the one with the long-knife scrabbling at the haft to draw it. But before he could even get a grip, Borel, roaring, smashed the cudgel into that Goblin's skull. Blood and bone and gray matter sprayed wide as the Redcap flew sideways to crash down dead. In spite of being armed, the other two took to their heels, but Borel did not follow. Instead he retrieved his long-knife and scabbard from the dead Goblin.

Quickly he strapped on the weapon, and, long-knife in hand, stepped to the great double doors. He opened the rightmost one, only to see three monstrous Trolls striding up the steps to the building from a walled courtyard beyond.

The big'ns!

He slammed the door to, and looked about for a bar. A huge one for these main doors lay nearby, entirely too heavy for him to handle in the time given.

Back across the entry chamber he sped and up the two steps to the hallway he knew, and just as the front doors opened, he ducked into a stairway leading up.

Perhaps I can let them pass, and then get out the d—

Goblins shrilled—*The Redcaps! The ones who fled*—and the massive, ten-foot-tall Trolls grunted in response.

Without hearing more, Borel turned and ran up the steps.

One flight and 'round a sharp turn, then two flights, three flights—he lost count.

But he came to a large door at the top. He pressed his ear to the panel to hear—*Nothing.* Cautiously he turned the handle. The door was unlocked. Quietly, he opened it. Beyond lay a cluttered chamber. On the far wall was another door like the one he had just entered. Quickly he stepped inside and eased the door shut behind. Yet there was neither a bar to barricade it nor a way to lock it. He turned and looked about. The chamber seemed to be a storeroom of sorts, where the Trolls and Goblins stashed plunder taken from victims.

Rope. Rucksacks. Clothing. —My bow!

Sheathing his long-knife, quickly Borel took up the bow, and nearby lay his quiver and arrows, and he looped the baldric over his head and one shoulder, and slung his bow by its carrying thong.

If I escape— No, when *I escape, I'll need gear.*

He grabbed up one of the packs, and as he stuffed various goods within—tinderbox, flint, steel, bedroll, rope, a cloak—he saw a massive, bronze, three-pronged grappling hook lying on the floor, or perhaps it was an anchor; he could not tell which, it was so large. He glanced at the far door, the one he had not yet opened.

If there is a window beyond—

He grabbed a pair of gloves and slipped them on, then took up several ropes and the rucksack and hefted the hook.

Quickly he glanced 'round.

Nothing else to take? Borel smiled, for he espied a three-cornered hat. He tried it on. It seemed a good fit.

Borel stepped to the far door and set his goods down and drew his long-knife. He then removed the tricorn and pressed his ear to the panel and listened. All seemed quiet, but for the faint sound of a buzzing insect. Slowly he opened the door and peered within.

Beyond was a chamber with tall windows open to the outside air. The room itself was completely empty but for a table on which sat a golden cage—rather like a birdcage—and inside with his back to Borel sat a tiny, diaphanous-winged Field Sprite, its face in its hands, its sparrow-brown hair falling about its shoulders as it wept silently, while an agitated dark bumblebee darted about the aureate bars.

Borel sheathed his weapon and replaced his hat and took up his goods and moved them within. Inside, there were wall brackets and a heavy beam to bar the door. Quickly he set the beam into place, then started across the chamber.

As the prince moved inward, the Sprite sprang to its feet and backed away. Pulling itself up to its full, just-under-two-inch height—"Have you come to torture me?" cried the wee being. "I warn you, I am armed!" Yet from its complete lack of clothing it was clear the Sprite bore no weapons at all.

Borel replied, "No, tiny one, I have come to set you free." With a great smile on his face, he stepped toward the small prison.

But the bumblebee darted at Borel, and as the prince took a swipe at it, the Sprite yelled, "No! Don't hurt her! She is my friend and my guardian."

Borel backed away, and the bee returned to the cage, and the Sprite seemed to talk to it, though whatever sound, if any, the wee one made was beyond Borel's hearing. In moments the bee lighted atop the small jail, and it turned to face Borel, its faceted eyes sharply gleaming.

"It's all right, now," said the Sprite, beckoning Borel forward.

Borel stepped to the table, and now, close up, he could see that the Sprite was male. Moving slowly and with the bee watching, Borel drew his long-knife and easily pried open the tiny door.

On his glittering dragonfly wings and laughing in glee the Sprite flew free and up and around the chamber, the bee following.

Yet in that same moment, from beyond the barred door Borel heard muffled voices and heavy footsteps coming inward.

The Trolls!

"We must flee!" cried the Sprite.

His heart pounding, quickly Borel stepped to a window and looked out . . . and down . . . and groaned. He was back at the rock face with its sheer drop down to a river, only now he was five storeys higher.

The door behind rattled, and then there came booming shouts.

With the Sprite and the bee buzzing about in distress, Borel knotted ropes together in haste, and, even as the door thudded under massive blows, he tied on the large, heavy hook and lugged it to the window. He set two prongs of the huge grapnel against the edge of the sill and gathered up the great armload of rope and tossed it over. Down it plunged and down, yet whether or not it reached the ground at the base of the bluff, the prince could not see.

Boom! . . . Boom! . . .

The door juddered beneath hammering jolts.

Grabbing the pack and tossing it out the window as well, "Time to go," he said to the Sprite, taking up the line.

Boom! . . . Doom! . . .

Borel passed the rope between his legs and rightward 'round and up across his chest and over his left shoulder and down his back. Then he stepped to the sill and, making certain that the hook was well set, he turned about and backed over the edge. His last sight of the door was that of stone dust sifting down from one of the brackets. And then he began a swift rappel.

With his right hand at the base of his spine and gripping the rope and controlling his descent, and his left above, loosely holding the lead for balance, down he went, the line slipping through his gloved hands. Down he slid and down, pausing only to work his way past the knots.

"Oh, hurry, hurry," cried the Sprite, darting about alongside, the bee trailing, "else something dreadful will hap, I just know it."

From above there came a sharp crack and the banging of a door slammed wide.

"Faster!" cried the Sprite.

Still Borel slid downward, the rope slipping through his upper hand and 'round his leg and up across his chest and over the shoulder and down his back to his other hand, friction burning, so swift was his descent.

As Borel neared the bottom, far above a huge face peered over the sill. Then the rope gave a jerk, and suddenly went entirely slack. And with the Sprite screaming, Borel fell, the massive, three-pronged grappling hook plummeting down behind, its now-deadly tines aglitter as it plunged toward its victim below.

10

Flight

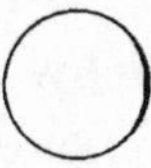

At the base of the bluff, Borel crashed down on a steep, precarious slope of scree; and pebbles and sand and gravel and shale and rocks and boulders and slabs roared down in a great rock slide, Borel tumbling amid all. *Blang!* Behind, the huge grapnel struck a boulder and bounded into the air, spinning, tines flashing like great whirling talons as it lunged after, the tied-on rope whipping violently in great spiralling arcs. "Look out! Look out!" shrieked the Sprite, darting this way and that, the bumblebee following, yet there was nought Borel could do as down he pitched amid a great spill of rock, the massive hook now overtaking in its wild and deadly swirl. And as the slide and Borel slowed—*Blang!*—again the huge grapnel struck another boulder and caromed wildly and passed over the prince, its great spinning talons slashing nought but empty air as it hurtled onward. And then Borel slid to a stop, a few pebbles rattling on past, a large slab sliding by.

And even as Borel staggered upright and the Sprite cried out, "My lord, you are safe," the tumbling, whirling juggernaut of a grapnel hurled on, snapping the rope taut to violently jerk Borel from his feet and wrench him plowing down through scree the remainder of the slope ere both hook and prince came to a stop.

With the Sprite anxiously hovering nearby and the bee orbiting 'round, Borel lay for long moments, trying to collect his thoroughly addled wits and wondering if ought was broken.

"My lord, are you dead?" asked the Sprite.

"Ungh," replied Borel, cautiously moving, feeling of his limbs and fingers and ribs, grimacing now and then as he probed.

"Oh, good, you are fine," said the Sprite, settling on a nearby rock, the bee alighting as well. "For an instant I thought you killed."

"I feel as if I have been slain," replied Borel, bloody and bruised and wincing as he removed the three-cornered hat, which incredibly had somehow managed to stay on, and he touched a great knot even then swelling on the back of his head.

"My lord, we must away," said the Sprite. "The Trolls are like to pursue."

Borel eased the tricorn back on his head and, groaning, slowly got to his feet. Moving with care, he untangled the rope from 'round his torso. "See you the rucksack I tossed over the sill?"

"I will look," said the Sprite, taking to wing, "though we must away soon." Off he darted, the bee following.

Borel examined his bow, finding it fit—neither horn nor ironwood nor silken string were any worse for the wear—though most of his arrows were broken or missing; only three survived intact, yet he retained all six of the ruined ones for their heads and fletching. His long-knife as well had come through unscathed, though the scabbard was now freshly scarred. As for Borel himself, he was thoroughly battered, and blood seeped from a handful of scrapes, but his leathers had protected him from the worst of his tumble among the rocks, and, but for one knot, the cocked hat had saved his head. Even so, amid all the other hurts, he knew he would have a great long bruise running from his crotch up across his chest and over his shoulder and down his back where the entangled line had been jerked taut by the runaway grapnel.

Borel made his way down the last few feet of the slope, dragging the rope after. And then coiling it as he went, he made his way to the hook, where he untied the last of the line. A few yards ahead lay reeds, growing in the muddy shallows of the river, its far bank perhaps a quarter mile away.

The Sprite came flying back. "I did not find your rucksack, my lord; I'm afraid it's buried under the slide, though there is a rock-laden cloth of some sort lying nigh."

"Where?"

"I'll show you, my lord."

Following the Sprite, Borel painfully made his way up the slope of rubble, where he found the cloak he had packed in the rucksack, but no sign of ought else. He unslung his bow and quiver and took up the garment and slipped it on, and found a brooch hidden in the collar to fasten it with. The Sprite flying well above called out, "Boats, my lord. I see some boats. Perhaps you can use one to escape the oncoming Trolls."

"Whence the Trolls?" asked Borel.

The Sprite pointed, and Borel saw two Trolls tramping along a sloping way wending across the nearly plumb face of the cliff, a handful of Goblins trailing.

"No doubt they want their meal," growled Borel, slinging his bow and the quiver. "Which way the boats?"

"Yonder, my lord," said the Sprite, again pointing.

Borel groaned. "Toward the place where the Trolls are heading."

"Yes, my lord," said the Sprite.

"Then let us go," said Borel, and he haltingly made his way to the bottom of the scree and took up the coil of line and began hobbling in the direction indicated, following the flow of the river.

And the Trolls continued on downward.

And the Sprite and the bumblebee flew ahead of the prince and headed for the cache of boats.

In the distance the Goblins began yelling and pointing. They had spotted Borel making his way downstream along the riverbank.

The Trolls hastened. . . .

"Hurry, my lord," urged the Sprite.

Grunting against the pain, Borel limped faster.

"This way," said the Sprite, his bee buzzing ahead.

More swiftly went the Trolls, and more swiftly went Borel.

Now prince and bee and Sprite came to a bend in the river, and the reeds grew thickly there.

"Into the water, my lord; all are hidden within."

Borel splashed in among the reeds, and he came to a half-sunken boat, its bottom stove in.

Another boat and another he found, all broken.

"Is this as they all are?" he asked.

"Oh, my lord, I am sorry," said the Sprite, darting from craft to craft, "but they all seem smashed."

"Is there nought afloat?"

The Sprite flew higher, even as Borel could hear shouts and thudding footsteps nearing.

"A raft, my lord, here is a raft!" cried the Sprite, flying back to lead the way. "Oh, hurry, please hurry."

Now flitting down among the reeds so as not to be seen, the Sprite led Borel to a large log float with steering sweeps fore and aft and rafting poles adeck, a reed-free channel to the river lying ahead. Throwing his coil of recovered rope onto the raft and untying the float's mooring line from a post deeply driven into the bottom, Borel pushed. The craft did not move, for it was mired in the mud.

"Oh, hurry, my lord, they draw near."

Straining, gritting his teeth, and heaving to the limit of his strength, Borel managed to break the float free of its mud-bottom anchorage, and even as he heard Trolls splashing into the water among the reeds, searching, and Redcaps ashore calling to one another, he shoved the raft out and away, pushing it along the channel. At last he won past the reeds and into the slow-moving current, and he clambered up over the end and grabbed a pole and thrust toward midstream.

"There he is," shrilled a voice, and Borel turned to see a Goblin on the high bank and pointing.

And as the ten-foot-tall Trolls bellowed and splashed through the reeds in pursuit, Borel poled with all his might, the long, heavy shaft finding purchase against the bottom. Thrust, lift, set, thrust, lift, set, thrust . . . time and again, and all the while the Sprite screamed, "Oh, faster, my lord, faster, faster! Oh, my lord, my lord."

The Trolls broke free of the reeds, and Goblins ashore shouted in glee and sprinted downstream.

And then the float reached swifter water, and yet the howling Trolls came on, now but a handful of yards away.

And still the Sprite shrieked in fear for Borel.

Realizing that unless the river got deeper, the Trolls would reach the raft, Borel dropped the pole adeck and strung his bow. And even as he nocked an arrow, one Troll grabbed the aft sweep.

Sssthock! The shaft pierced the Troll through the eye.

The monstrous being screamed and pitched over backwards, slain, water closing over his massive body. The following Troll, waist-deep, roared in fury and pressed faster through the flow.

Borel nocked another arrow and drew the shaft to the full. Once more he loosed—*Sssthock!*—and took the Troll in the throat.

Gggh! Choking, grabbing his gullet, the Troll fell sideways with a splash, to rise up and fall again and disappear into the current.

Borel nocked his last good arrow and aimed toward the Redcaps ashore pacing the raft, and they screamed in terror and turned and fled.

Exhausted, Borel slipped the arrow back into his quiver and slumped down on the logs.

"I thought you were a goner for certain," said the Sprite, landing adeck, tears streaming down his face.

"So did I, tiny one," said Borel, removing his quiver and setting it aside, then dragging the coil of rope over to use as a pillow. He reclined on his back and looked up at the high blue sky and sighed and said, "So did I."

The bumblebee landed as well, alighting on Borel's chest. Controlling his urge to slap, the prince looked at the wee dark insect and began to laugh as the flowing river bore them away downstream.

River

Of a sudden, "The moon!" cried Borel, and he lurched upright to a sitting position, upsetting the bee, who took to wing and buzzed away to land on the handle end of the fore steering sweep. "Where stands the moon?"

"My lord?"

"What is the phase of the moon?"

The Sprite frowned then said, "Tonight it will be two days past full, Sieur."

"Ah, good," said Borel, painfully groaning as he lay back down. "Then I haven't lost a great deal of time."

The Sprite flitted to land on Borel's chest, there where the bee had once been. He plopped down and, elbows on knees and his face in his hands, he sat looking at the prince.

Borel smiled and said, "Have you a name, tiny one?"

"Yes, my lord.'Tis Flic." The Sprite stood and sketched a bow and then resumed his seat and said, "And you, Sieur?"

"I am Prince Borel of—"

"Of the Winterwood?"

"Yes, Flic. It is my demesne."

"Oh, I've always wanted to see the Winterwood, but Buzzer would go dormant in the cold, and so might I."

"Buzzer?"

"My companion," replied Flic, pointing at the bee yet perched on the fore sweep.

"How came you to be in that cage, Flic?"

"The goblins captured me in a fine net and took me prisoner."

"To what end?"

"I am a Sprite of the fields, and the Trolls tried to force me into having my friends—the bees—make honey, every last drop of which the Trolls would take to baste their fare. I refused, of course, for I cannot think of a more heinous crime than making slaves of bees. Regardless, the Trolls said that when I got hungry enough, then I would obey. They tried to starve me into submission, but they hadn't counted on Buzzer feeding me. I thought, though, that I would never get free, be a prisoner forever, yet you came along and, well . . ."

They drifted downriver in silence for a while, the unguided raft slowly turning in the current, and then Flic said, "And you, Prince Borel, how came you to my rescue?"

"I was escaping, Flic, for I was to be one of those whom they would baste with honey."

A horrified look came over the Sprite's face. "You mean they were going to *eat* you?"

Borel nodded. "Spitted, roasted, and consumed."

"Oh, my, that might be a crime even worse than making slaves of bees."

Borel grinned. "Perhaps."

"Is that their customary fare? —Trolls and Goblins eating people, I mean."

Borel nodded. "Whenever they can come by such, I ween."

"Oh, my. Well then I am glad that I didn't have the bees give them honey."

A frown came over Borel's face, and he glanced back in the direction of the cliff. "Hmm . . . By the number of shackles in the prison where I was held and the count of the craft they've hidden in the reeds, I deem they waylay river travellers."

"Oh," said Flic. "That's why all the boats were . . ." His voice trailed off, but Borel knew what he meant.

"Someday," said Borel, "after I complete the task I am on, I'll have to take a warband to that place and clean out the nest of its vipers."

Again they drifted along without speaking, but then Flic said, "Yet tell me, Prince, how came you to be in their clutches in the first place, and what is this task you are on, and what does the moon have to do with ought?"

" 'Tis quite a tale, Flic, not long in the telling, and it seems we do have time. You see, I've been having these dreams, and there is a witch named Hradian. . . ."

"And so you always see this lady, this Demoiselle Chelle, in a stone chamber?" asked Flic.

"Yes. That is the way of it. We seem to be linked, and always I find myself there, and likewise she seems to know something of where I am, else she wouldn't have warned me of the oncoming Goblins."

Flic stroked his chin. "Next time you find yourself in that chamber, why don't you take her somewhere else? Somewhere out of that chamber. Perhaps down those steps you spoke of."

"Dreams are strange, Flic. It's not as if I can control them."

"Ah, but you can, Lord Borel, to some extent, that is."

"How so?"

"A seer once told me that if in the midst of a dream I somehow discovered I was dreaming, then I could change the dream to an extent."

"Hmm . . ." mused Borel. "And you think I can in some way use this knowledge?"

"Indeed, Prince Borel, for can you guide your dream, perhaps you can turn the conversation in a way that will aid you in your task."

"Maybe so," said Borel. "Yet tell me this: just how would I go about discovering I am dreaming?"

"Ah, there is the rub," said Flic. "What is required is some sort of trip or trigger or stratagem that will let the dreamer know he is dreaming. In your case, I suggest you fix on something extraordinary about the setting—say, the band across her eyes, or better yet those strange, floating daggers—so that when you see them you can then become aware that you are in a dream and take steps to guide the dream into channels other than the one you find yourself in."

"And how do I do that, Flic?"

"I'll tell you what I was told: when you settle down to sleep, try to fix the triggering sight—say, the daggers—in your mind, and the thought that when you see them you will know you are dreaming. If successful, you can then change the dream."

"Have you ever done this, Flic? —Guided your own dreams?"

"Well, no. But you see, I've never had a need, never found myself in a dream as important as yours. I mean, after all, perhaps by guiding your dream and speaking with the demoiselle, she can aid you in setting her free."

Borel sighed and said, "I cannot promise I will succeed, nevertheless I will try. Yet it seems to me that I have a larger problem than guiding my dreams. You see, although I have been to Lord Roulan's estate, at the moment I do not know where we are, hence I know not where his lands lie from here, and yet I must get to them ere the full moon comes again."

Flic frowned and said, "What are his gardens like?"

"What?"

"Lord Roulan: what kind of flowers does he grow?"

Though he was lying down, Borel managed a shrug. "I don't know. Besides, what has that to do with ought?"

"I believe we can take you there," said Flic, glancing at Buzzer.

Surprised, Borel sat up, nearly dumping Flic. But the Sprite took to flight and settled atop the stanchion of the aft steering sweep. Holding out a hand of apology, Borel said, "Know you where Roulan's estate lies?"

"Nay, my lord, I do not, but mayhap Buzzer does."

Borel frowned. "Your bee knows of Roulan?"

"Nay, Prince, but mayhap she knows of Roulan's gardens."

"His gardens?"

"Aye. You see, unlike most bees, Buzzer is not deterred by twilight borders, and she wandered into Faery from the mortal world quite long apast, and she has been here ever since. She has plundered more blooms than anyone can count, and when it comes to flowers, she remembers where blossoming fields and beds lie. And so, all I need from you is a description of Roulan's gardens, and if Buzzer has been there, well . . . So again I ask, what kinds of flowers does Lord Roulan grow?"

Borel turned up his hands. "It has been long since I was there. Besides, I do not know much of flowers, for I am of the Winterwood, where flowers are all but nonexistent."

"Regardless, Prince, this is important if we are to aid you. So try to remember."

Borel closed his eyes, attempting to visualize Roulan's estate. "I don't . . . um— Oh, wait, I do remember a strange little flower. Clumps of green leaves, three to a stem straight from the ground, and several tiny blossoms on separate stems."

"Clover, my lord?"

"I don't think so." Borel held out a hand and spread his fingers wide. "Unlike the nubs of clover heads, I seem to recall that the flowers had petals straight out that went all the way 'round."

"How many petals?"

His eyes yet closed, Borel said, "Five, six, seven— Ah, I do not remember."

"What color?"

Borel sighed and shook his head. "Yellow, I think— No, wait, pink. Chelle—she was but a child at the time—plucked a blossom and held it up saying, 'Pink as my lips.' "

"Pink as your lips?"

"No. Pink as hers."

"Ah, then. Three leaves on a stem, growing in clumps, tiny pink blossoms, most likely with five petals if I have guessed right: shamrock, I think. Not exactly rare in Faery, yet not common either. Even so, shamrock alone is not enough to go on."

Borel opened his eyes. "I recall something else, Flic. Chelle also had a flower in her hair, a rose, I believe, white with a pale pink tinge."

"Good. Pink-flowering shamrock and white roses with a faint blush. What other blossoms were about?"

"I don't recall any others."

"None at all?"

Dejected, Borel shook his head.

"Do not despair, Lord Borel, for there are yet ways to explore."

Borel looked up. "Such as . . . ?"

"What fruit did you eat while there?"

"None I recall. Oh, we did have a blackberry torte, but I think that's not exactly—"

"Fresh blackberries, or preserves?" Flic interjected.

Borel closed his eyes and frowned, then said, "Was it fresh-picked that day? Yes. I remember now. We spent part of the morning plucking them from a rather large patch of briars. Chelle's mouth was stained purple, for she ate one of every two she gathered."

"You seem to recall much of Demoiselle Chelle, Lord Borel," said Flic, grinning.

"I found her quite a nuisance," said Borel, opening his eyes and smiling. "Even so, she was very bright. Yet that is neither here nor there. What else would you ask concerning flowers?"

In that moment, Buzzer came winging to Flic, and agitatedly flew about the Sprite. How they conversed, Borel could not say, but Flic looked startled and peered downstream and said, "Prince Borel, Buzzer says there is noisy water ahead. I think she means rapids."

"Rapids?" Grimacing in pain, Borel stood and peered downstream.

The river narrowed and the banks grew higher and the current grew swifter, and from 'round a turn in the flow he now could hear a distant roar. Even as he hobbled aft, Borel glanced at the single undamaged arrow he had left, and then the line, and shook his head; rope was entirely too weighty for an arrow to bear; besides, the nearest shore was yet some hundred or so paces away, and any trees still farther. Taking up the sweep, he pulled for the closest bank. The rear of the float swung sideways.

Borel stepped to the front sweep and again hauled for the shore. The raft swung about once more, this time opposite, though it did not come closer to land for, with a fore and aft sweep, it was meant to be steered by two oarsmen, who, pulling together, could have reached either bank at will.

Using the sweep, Borel stopped the slow-turning spin and oriented the float so that one end was aimed toward the shore, the banks ever steepening, and then he used the sweep in a fishtailing fashion as a sculling oar. But the raft was ponderous and progress slow; surely it would not reach land in time.

Borel took up one of the poles and thrust against the deep bottom, but the shaft went in nigh its full length, and he got little purchase, and the ever-swiftening current now had the raft in its grip, and Borel's efforts proved futile.

'Round the bend they went and, ahead between rising walls, Borel could see rapids falling away, their end beyond seeing past a distant turn, the roaring white water crashing among and over great boulders.

"Ah, Mithras," he groaned, "more rocks."

He took up his bow and slung it across his back by its carrying thong, and then he looped his quiver over his head and across one shoulder.

"Lord Borel, what will you do?" cried Flic above the oncoming roar.

"There's nought I can do but ride it out," shouted Borel.

"Oh, if you could only fly," cried Flic, hovering, Buzzer orbiting.

"Indeed," muttered Borel, and he grabbed the aft sweep stanchion and held on tightly as the raft plunged into the thundering rage.

Reft

Down the long slope hurled the river to roar and shout and rend the air with the thunder of water storming apace, as it crested and rolled and broke over hidden barriers and smashed around great rocks to leap and fall crashing, only to hurtle into the next barrier and the next and the next. And amid the crests and troughs and rolling swells came the raft, lurching this way and that as it smashed into rocks and spun about, completely ensnared in fury. "Look out! Look out! Oh, my lord, look out!" cried Flic, flying above and followed by Buzzer, though Borel, clinging tightly and thoroughly drenched, heard nought but the bellow of a river run amok as the craft pumped and smashed over roiling, roaring billows; yet e'en had he heard the cries of the Sprite there was nothing Borel could do. Again and again the raft leapt up, to pause, and then to plummet back to the water; and Borel was jolted and jarred each time the timbers smacked down or crashed into or over a rock. Time after time Borel was knocked to his knees, but he held on tightly to the stanchion and lifted himself up before the next massive hammering crash. And the foaming river water funneled this way and that through gaps amid the great rocks and whelmed the float into jut and boulder and slab, and it began to disintegrate, as one after another the slender thwartwise struts broke in twain, and the logs began to separate.

The turning, pitching, fragmenting craft bucked and plunged and bashed downriver, the outermost logs breaking away, the innermost ones separating . . . and then the bulk of the raft smashed into a great midstream crag and pitched Borel off and into the chaos, the furious water tumbling him this way and that and hammering him into rock and stone and down into gravel and then hurling him back up through the water again to toss him into the air, only to reach up and drag him down and plunge him under once more, great logs and shattered timbers tumbling before and after.

Hacking, coughing, spewing water, Borel crawled out from a great, wide eddy pool to collapse ashore amid rounded river rocks a furlong or so below the last of the rapids.

Battered and bruised, he lay there panting, completely ignoring Flic's entreaties of, "Are you all right, my lord?" and "I thought you drowned, my lord," and "Is anything broken, my lord?"—the Sprite fretfully flitting about and hovering momentarily only to begin flitting about again.

Buzzer, on the other hand, said nothing, but puttered among the nearby flowers ashore as she gathered nectar and pollen.

Finally, Borel groaned and rolled over and stared at the sky.

"My lord . . . ?" said Flic, now alighting on a broad blade of a single cattail reed standing alone amid the river pebbles along the shore.

"I think I would have been better off to have been spitted, roasted, and consumed," said the prince at last.

"Oh, my lord, certainly not," said Flic.

Bracing himself against the pain, Borel sat up, sucking in air through clenched teeth. He turned to the Sprite. "Flic, within the last candlemark or so, I have been shackled in a prison, been poked and prodded by Redcap Goblins, fought my way free just in time to fall down the face of a cliff to nearly be buried by a rock slide and almost be slain by a runaway grapnel that then jerked me off my feet and dragged me through even more rocks;

I have been chased by Trolls and barely escaped only to be slammed into boulders by an angry river and all but drowned. So, when I say that I would have been better off had I been— Ah, *zut!* My long-knife. It's gone."

Flic looked at the empty scabbard yet strapped to Borel's right thigh, then said, "But you still have your bow."

Borel hauled the weapon 'round and examined it. It was undamaged. Next he upended his quiver. Nothing came out but water, his last arrow and the remains of the broken ones gone, swallowed by the rapids.

"And your hat," added the Sprite, pointing at the shallows, where, caught in the eddy, the tricorn, half-submerged, slowly circled.

Groaning, Borel painfully stood, then, cursing at the river, hobbled out into the wide swirl and fetched the sodden hat. Water streaming, he slapped it onto his head. Flic began giggling, and Borel smiled, then winced, for his right cheek was bruised.

Clk! Clk! Borel, unclothed, sat by the fire and struck a stone against a shard of flint, shaping a primitive knife. His damp leathers and cloak and silks—shirt and undertrews and socks and linens—now nearly dry, hung on nearby shrubs, and his boots sat at hand.

Perched on a twig of one the shrubs, Flic nibbled on a grain of pollen.

Chk! Clak!

"Tomorrow, Flic, I would have you and Buzzer find a flower called 'viburnum.' Its blossoms come in small white clusters and—"

"I know viburnums, Prince Borel," said Flic, sighing and rolling his eyes and silently appealing to Buzzer, the bee turning about on a nearby leaf to settle down for the evening. "After all, I *am* a Field Sprite."

Borel grunted, and—*Clk! Tkk!*—continued to knap flakes from the flint.

With Flic's help, the prince had found an outcropping of the stone, and had collected some pieces and then had made camp nearby. Using the carrying thong of his bow and the bow itself and a slightly hollowed rock cupped in his hand to steady a straight stick, he had spun the point of the wood against a piece of dry bark laden with dead grass to start a fire in a ring of stone on a wide patch of bare ground he had cleared. Nursing a glow into a small flame and carefully feeding the tiny blaze with more grass and then dried twigs and finally dead branches, he at last had a campfire. He had then used the very same carrying thong to set a clover-baited snare on the trace of a trail at the edge of the woods a distance away. Returning to the fire, he had doffed his togs and draped them on nearby bushes, and had then taken up a suitable knapping rock and had begun shaping one of the larger fragments of flint into a primitive but sharp-edged stone knife. And while he was setting the fire and doffing his clothes and had begun chipping flint, Flic and Buzzer had flown back upstream to see if the remaining Troll and Goblins were following; they were not. Flic and Buzzer had returned and the noontide had turned to midafternoon, and it in turn had drifted into evening.

Flic frowned. "I say, Lord Borel, you being the prince of a demesne—the Winterwood—where flowers do not bloom, how came you to know of the viburnum?"

Borel glanced at his bow and then at the Sprite and said, "The viburnum plant, with its long, straight stems, is also known as arrowwood, and I need arrows, else I might just starve out here in the wilderness."

"Ah," said Flic, "I see. Too bad you don't live on pollen and nectar and honey as do Buzzer and I, though I must admit, it would take many, many blossoms to feed you, my lord, perhaps an entire field."

"It would indeed," said Borel, chipping away at the stone. He held up the flint knife and examined it. Grunting in satisfaction, he laid it aside and then began tapping away flakes from another shard of flint, fashioning an arrowhead. "Too, I might need a number of shafts to rescue the Lady Chelle."

"Oh," said Flic. "I had forgotten." He glanced at the bee, now adrowse in the twilight. "But I'm afraid we'll have to wait for the morrow ere we see if Buzzer has ever plundered Lord Roulan's gardens. Yet this I ask: if Buzzer knows nought of those beds and blooms, which way shall we go then, my lord?"

"Would that the Fates smile down upon us," said Borel, "but if not, then we follow the river, for streams are thoroughfares of commerce, and can we find a hamlet or town alongside, or even a croft, someone therein might know." Borel glanced at the scrapes and darkening bruises over much of his body, especially his arms and legs, and he had a long, narrow discoloration running from his crotch 'round his thigh and up across his chest and down his back, there where the rope had snapped taut. "Yet travelling will be a bit slow, hammered as I was by rock and rope and river. But as sore as I am, worse yet I am stiffening, and I fear on the morrow I will be even more afflicted. Nevertheless, we must set out, for the moon does not halt in her journey, her face ever changing, and time diminishes for Lady Chelle."

Borel continued to chip away at the shard of flint, Flic watching in silence, and moments passed. Of a sudden there came a whistling squeal in the near distance, and Borel grinned and took up his flint knife and grunted to his feet. He hobbled away to the snare, and took from it a coney, and shortly had it dressed out and spitted above his campfire. He rolled up the rabbit skin and set it aside.

As his meal cooked, Borel continued to knap flint, though occasionally he turned the makeshift spit. And by the time the coney was ready, the prince had managed to fashion three sharp points for arrows. "Now all I need are shafts from the arrowwood plant. As for fletching, I'll cut a bit off the bottom of my shirt and make rag tails."

He pulled the spit from the fire and tore off a haunch and offered some to Flic, but the Sprite looked on in dismay and refused. "I neither kill nor eat dead things, my lord. Hummingbirds, though, eat mosquitoes and gnats, and at times both butterflies and bees feast on meat. Even so they are all my friends: butterflies, hummingbirds, and bees."

Borel frowned and glanced at Buzzer and paused in thought and then said, "Are all bees your friends?"

"Well, I do not know all bees, Prince, but those I've met are quite friendly."

"Could you ask them to search for Roulan's estate or even for Lady Chelle? I mean, could you ask the bees in concert to look for her? Send messengers out and have all bees search? Or the hummingbirds, for they are swift?"

Flic shook his head. "Were it like in some stories, where a mythical ruler of all bees—or one of all hummingbirds—is repaying some favor, perhaps then it could be done. Hummingbirds, my lord, they keep to their nests and fields, and are quite territorial, and squabble o'er certain stands of flowers. They do care for their mates and brood, yet I know of none who cooperate with any others. And I know of no sovereign they have. But they do migrate, and perhaps they will have seen a turret with daggers about in which a demoiselle is trapped. I will ask those we come across.

"And as to the bees, some are solitary but most live in individual swarms, each with its own queen, and queens are quite jealous of one another, and oft there are wars between colonies. Hence, for bees throughout Faery to go on a quest is but an amusing tale told to younglings, or so I do think. Besides, I remind you, my lord, bees are loath to cross the twilight borders, Buzzer being an exception. No, in this task, if we are to rely upon a bee, it has to be Buzzer who leads the way."

"I see," said Borel, returning to his meal. He took a bite and chewed awhile and swallowed, then said, "I suppose the same is true of ants, eh?"

Flic smiled. "Most likely. Oh, one might convince a queen of a single colony of ants or bees or the leader of a school of fish or a flock of birds or a pack of animals or the like to send the entire group on a search within their own territory, but for creatures of a single kind—or even creatures of different kinds—to go throughout all of Faery on a hunt to repay a favor, well . . . that would be quite extraordinary; it might even require the gods themselves to intervene."

Borel nodded and sighed and finished the remainder of his meal in morose silence.

As the nighttide deepened, Borel hobbled down to the river and washed his face and hands, then returned to camp and donned his now-dry clothes. He refreshed the fire with two more logs and, as the moon, two days past full, climbed into the sky, he wrapped himself in his cloak and settled down upon a bed of grass.

"Remember, my lord," said Flic, "should you see daggers afloat in the air, you are in a dream."

Borel grunted in acknowledgement and swiftly fell into an exhausted sleep.

As Borel's breathing deepened, Flic watched. Then he took to wing and began searching by moonlight for blossoms and mosses and herbs most rare.

13

Turret

The slender demoiselle stood across the chamber from him. She was dressed in a sapphire-blue gown with a white bodice. Her golden hair was twined with blue ribbons and white. Borel frowned, for there was a shadowy band across her eyes.

In the Old Tongue she said, "There is less than a moon remaining."

Something tugged at Borel's mind, something elusive, and then it was gone. "What do you mean, mademoiselle?" he asked, also in the Old Tongue. "Less than a moon till what?"

"I do not know, my lord. Yet something terrible looms, and you must help me, please." She reached out toward him.

The prince crossed the floor and took her hands in his and felt the trembling of them. "I will aid you, my lady," said Borel, and he raised her fingers to his lips and kissed them.

Even though frightened by whatever might threaten her, shyly she turned her face aside.

Thinking that he had embarrassed her, Borel released his grip and took a half step back, yet she reached out and caught one of his hands in hers and held tightly.

"I must escape," she said.

"Escape?"

"From this tower, this turret."

Again an ephemeral thought fled across Borel's mind, yet ere he could catch it, it was gone.

"And it seems you must find me and help me get free," she added.

"But I am here," said Borel, frowning in puzzlement. "I *have* found you."

"Indeed, you are here," said the demoiselle, "yet you have not found me."

"Why say you this?" asked Borel. "Can you not see I am here? Yet you tell me I have not found you?"

"I know not why it is true," said the lady. "Nevertheless it is."

Borel looked about the chamber. There were windows open to the air, and a stairwell going down, and there was a faint squeaking sound, though perhaps instead it was music. He moved toward one of the windows, and as he stepped away, she reluctantly released his hand, her fingers trailing against his.

The loss of her touch overwhelmed Borel, and he turned back and reached out and took her hand in his. "Come."

"We cannot get out that way," she replied.

Borel looked. Things hovered beyond the sill; things solid and dangerous and in shadows. What they might be, he had no idea, for they were too deep in the dark. Once more a critical thought skittered on the edge of revelation, yet again whatever it was escaped his grasp. "Then, my lady, if we cannot get out that way, we will go down the steps." He started toward the stairwell, her hand firmly in his.

"No!" The demoiselle gasped and pulled back, and she tried to drag him hindward.

Borel turned and looked at her. "My lady?"

"Oh, my lord, not down the steps. Something dreadful lies below."

"Something dreadful? What?" Borel reached for his long-knife. It was gone, his scabbard empty.

Of a sudden he was covered with bruises, and he felt as if he had been battered by all the hammers of the Gnomes.

Nevertheless, weaponless, he released her hand and hobbled toward the stairwell.

"No!" cried the demoiselle. "I will not let you go!"

In that moment the chamber vanished, and Borel awakened with a start to find himself lying on a grassy bed, a whisper of distant rapids wafting through the moonlit woodland upon a gentle breeze.

Beeline

"Zut! Zut! Zut!" cursed Borel, hammering his fist into the ground. "How could I have been so stupid?"

"Stupid, my lord?" The Sprite sat nearby sorting through plucked blossoms and buds. Beside him were several small piles of mosses and herbs.

"Ah, Flic, you told me to concentrate on seeing daggers so that I would know that I was in a dream, and I simply fell asleep without doing so."

"Do not chastise yourself overly, Prince Borel. I understand it takes several tries . . . or so I was told."

Borel growled a response and then groaned to his feet and stumped away to relieve himself. Then he hobbled to the river and drank deeply. Upon returning to the camp, as he placed more wood on the fire he said, "What are you doing, Flic, this sorting of flowers by moonlight?"

"My lord, you need to treat your injuries, else the going will be slow. The herbs are for a paste to rub into your bruises, the juice of the moss for your scrapes, and can we think of a way, the blossoms to make a tisane to treat your soreness. We should make the tisane first."

"A tisane? A drink for my aches and pains?"

"Aye," said the Sprite.

"Then we'll brew it in my hat," said Borel, pointing to the tricorn.

"Your hat, my lord?"

"Indeed," said Borel, groaning back down onto his grassy bed. "On morrow morn. But for now, I need rest."

"As you wish," said Flic.

In moments, the prince fell into a deep and dreamless sleep.

When Borel awoke in the early light of dawn, he had stiffened up in the night, and he was slow to rise. Once on his feet, he looked to see Flic asleep and curled on the leaf next to Buzzer. The bee, however, was awake, yet she remained still by her ward.

Moving with difficulty, Borel added more branches to the yet-glowing coals of the fire, and blew up a blaze, and when the flames were well caught, he took up his tricorn and hobbled to the river and scooped up a hatful of water and drank his fill. He then selected a number of rounded river rocks, all nigh the size of a chicken egg. These he took back to the fire and placed them among the burning branches. Back to the river he stumped and again filled the tricorn with water, and back to the camp he limped.

Then he groaned down with his back to a tree and ate leftover rabbit, while with his flint knife he scraped away at the coney skin and waited for Flic to awaken.

As the sun rose, so did the Sprite. "We'll need two washed-clean, fairly flat rocks," said Flic, "though if you can find two slightly hollowed, that would be even better. One on which to crush the moss to paste; the other to squeeze the juice from the herbs. We'll also need a couple of rounded river rocks to do the crushing. But as to making the tisane, we'll need water and a way to heat it."

"The water is in my hat," said Borel, "and the way to heat it is in the fire."

Flic glanced at the fire. "Ah, I see. But how will you fetch them out from the flames?"

Borel hefted his flint knife and pointed at a nearby young tree. "I'll cut a forked branch."

"Then, my lord, while Buzzer and I break fast, you gather what we need."

After cutting the branch from the limb and trimming it to suit his purpose, Borel took up his quiver and the scraped rabbit skin and hobbled down to the river, where he thoroughly wetted down the hide and rolled it tightly and dropped it into the quiver. Then he found two flat rocks slightly hollowed to act as mortars and two round ones to act as pestles. As he limped back to the camp, Flic flew alongside and pointed and said, "Buzzer has found a stand of viburnum at the base of that steep hillside just across the field."

"Splendid," said Borel and, gritting his teeth, he hobbled on, while Flic sped back to the blossoming field to continue his breakfast.

When Flic and Buzzer returned to camp, Borel donned one of his gloves and slid the fork of the cut branch under a hot rock and dropped it into the water in his hat. Shortly, with his gloved hand he fished that rock out and put it back into the fire, and scooped another one in. In less than a quarter candlemark the water was bubbling, and Flic said, "There is too much. Pour a bit out . . . say, half."

After Borel had done so, the Sprite dropped a selection of different blossoms into the liquid.

"Stir it, my lord."

Borel used his forked stick to stir the blossoms 'round and 'round and under. After long moments of doing so, Flic said, "Let me see."

Borel stopped, and the Sprite stuck in a finger and tasted. "A bit more stirring, Prince."

Twice more Borel stirred and twice did Flic taste, and at last he said, "Drink it all, Lord Borel, in one gulp if you can."

The tisane was quite bitter, the heat of the liquid making it even more so, but Borel squinched up his face and swallowed the whole of it.

Borel shuddered with the aftertaste and set the tricorn aside, and Flic grinned at him and said, "Now for the moss and herbs."

* * *

With Flic working on the places Borel could not see or easily reach, they washed his scrapes with the juice of the herbs and smeared a thin film of moss pulp over his bruises. As Borel eased back into his silks and leathers, Flic said, "We'll do this every morning for a threeday, and then you should be quite well."

"Three days, that's all? After the beating I took?"

"Yes, my lord."

"I need your recipes, Flic. There are many who can benefit from this."

"I'm afraid, Prince Borel, they are not my recipes to give. You will have to ask my queen."

"You have a queen?"

"Indeed."

"Hmm. I never knew. Regardless, when the time comes, I will ask her. But for now we have a demoiselle to find." He glanced at the bumblebee. "Does Buzzer know of Lord Roulan's gardens?"

"Please, if you would, smooth out a patch of ground, my lord, a place not too close to the fire. One the size of your hand will do."

Borel squatted at the edge of the cleared ground and smoothed over the loam.

Flic flew down to the bare patch, Buzzer following. Flic looked at Borel and said, "Shamrock with pink blossoms, white roses with a pink blush, and blackberries, right?"

Borel shrugged but nodded.

Flic sank to his knees and somehow spoke to the bee, and Buzzer began a peculiar wiggling, buzzing dance, Flic paying rapt attention. Back and forth in a straight line the bee wriggled, pausing now and again to thrum her wings. And then Buzzer began dancing in a different direction, and again and again she buzzed and wriggled and paused. Once more and again and several times thereafter she changed the course of the dance, each on a separate tack. Finally, Flic turned to Borel. "Buzzer knows of a number of places with all three things, some closer than others, but all of them quite far. Is there ought else you can tell me? Other flowers? The lay of the land? An orchard? A lake? Anything?"

"The manor with its gardens sits in a dell along with a small lake," replied Borel. "A league or so beyond the mouth of the vale a river flows, a town upon its banks."

Again Flic conversed with the bee, and Buzzer took up the dance once more, now wriggling and buzzing and pausing, this time in a single direction.

"Good," said Flic. "She has it narrowed down to a definite place, though it is across several marges of twilight. Still, it may be that this is not Lord Roulan's estate, but one very much alike."

"It isn't as if we have another choice," said Borel, groaning to his feet.

Using his hat and river water, Borel quenched the fire, and made certain it was out. He then placed the various work rocks, the shards of flint, the arrowheads, the moss, and finally the blossoms into his quiver, all cushioned from one another by layers of grass. He slung his bow by its carrying thong, and slipped the quiver over his head and across one shoulder and said, "Let us first stop by the arrowwood and then be on our way."

Borel cut and trimmed some ten shafts from the viburnum stand and shimmied them down through the layers of grass and blossoms and moss and skin and flint and rocks. He looked at Flic and nodded.

Flic spoke to Buzzer, and the bee flew up and 'round.

Flic said, "She's sighting on the sun."

How the Sprite could tell was a mystery to Borel, yet the prince did not question Flic's word.

And then Buzzer took off in a beeline, heading straight up the steep hill.

Borel groaned, but followed after, Flic no longer flying but riding on the prow of the tricorn. By the time the prince had limped to the top, Buzzer had flown back to see if anyone were truly following.

The way was rough and the going slow and often did the bee return to make certain the prince was yet on course, and it seemed Buzzer was somewhat impatient and vexed. Flic assured the bee that indeed they really meant to go to the place Buzzer had remembered. And then Flic laughed and said to Borel, "Buzzer says that we could go much swifter if you would simply give up this walking and fly instead."

Yet at times they came to an obstacle Borel would have to go around—a bluff, a ravine, or the like—the prince cursing all rocks and his bruises and soreness, saying that were he in better health these barriers would be but minor impediments. At these places Flic would take to wing and find a place Borel could manage, and whenever such a detour took them significantly off course, Buzzer would take a new sighting and then streak away.

Occasionally they would cross a glade wherein flowers bloomed, and at these places they would pause while Buzzer gathered nectar. "Flying takes a good deal of vigor," said Flic, "hence, much nectar is needed."

During several of these pauses and with his flint knife, Borel fashioned his arrows: trimming the shaft to length, nocking one end, notching the other; cutting a thin strip of rabbit hide. And when they came to a stream, he wetted the thong and stretched it taut, and then set the base of the flint arrowhead in the notch of the shaft, and tightly wrapped the thong about shaft and base both.

Flic looked on with interest. "Why do you wet and stretch it, Lord Borel?"

"It will shrink when it dries, Flic, and thereby strongly clinch the head to the shaft," said Borel, grunting as he forcefully tied off the thong. "Too, the sun will cure it a bit as it dries."

When that one was well cinched, Borel took one more arrowhead and set it in the notch of a shaft, and as he wrapped another thong about, he said, "Tell me, Flic: this dance that Buzzer did, how does it speak of flowers and directions and distances?"

Flic grinned. "It is something I learned from honeybees and taught to Buzzer. You see, when scout honeybees find a source of nectar and pollen, they return to the nest and use the dance and buzzing to tell other members of their colony which way and how far to go."

Borel grunted and then said, "The dance the direction, the buzzing the distance?"

Flic clapped his hands. "Exactly so: direction with respect to the sun; distance with respect to the hive, or, in this case, from where the dancer dances."

As Borel cinched tight the thong, he said, "You tell me you taught this to Buzzer, yet didn't she already know?"

"No, my lord. Except for Buzzer, bumblebees do not use the dance at all. But when I explained it to her, she adopted it right away."

In that moment Buzzer came flying back, and they took up the journey again.

Taking advantage of these pauses for Buzzer to feed, by the time twilight fell, Borel had trimmed out all of his shafts, but only three had arrowheads. Those three had silken tails instead of fletching to aid them in flying true.

And with one of these new-made shafts, Borel had brought down a grouse to dress out for his meal.

As the sun set and the day came to an end, they set camp in sight of a twilight border lying ahead. Yet, battered as Borel was, they had gone but some fifteen miles altogether throughout the whole of the day, much to Buzzer's disgust.

Even so, even though it was well short of Prince Borel's usual pace, still it was fifteen miles closer to a vale where grew pink-petaled shamrock and blushing white roses and thorn-laden blackberry vines, a place where a slender young demoiselle would be found. . . .

. . . Or so did Prince Borel hope.

15

Poniards

Again Borel used his bow, the carrying thong, and a slightly hollowed rock cupped in his hand to steady a straight stick to spin against a piece of dry bark laden with dead grass to start a fire. And soon the grouse roasted above the flames, and Borel knapped out a flint arrowhead and started on another.

"How do you manage that, my lord prince?" asked Flic.

Borel looked up and frowned.

"The shaping of the stone, I mean," said Flic.

Borel shrugged and held up the piece he was working on. "Flint has what I would call a natural direction for shaping, and all one need do is carefully chip with the grain instead of across, else the piece will be ruined. Precise sharp raps with a knapping stone break small flakes away from the flint and leave a matching hollow behind." Borel grinned. "The trick is to gradually strike away everything that isn't the arrowhead."

As Borel continued chipping out the second point, he said, "Hummingbirds, butterflies, and bees are your friends, Flic, but who are those that pose a threat to you?"

"Various creatures that slither and crawl and walk and fly."

"Such as . . . ?"

"Meat-eaters for the most: spiders, snakes, shrews, some

birds, some insects such as praying mantises. Oh, and now I can add Goblins and Trolls."

"Yet you carry no weapons?"

"Buzzer protects me well," replied Flic, glancing at the bee, sleeping on a nearby leaf.

"But not at night, it seems," said Borel. "What if a night-hunting creature comes upon you when you are aslumber?"

"Buzzer and I deliberately select a place where something moving on the branch or across the leaves will cause enough of a tremble to waken me, and should that happen I would then take up Buzzer and fly away," said the Sprite. He pointed at the clear sky above Buzzer's resting place. "And we sleep where there is no overhang for a spider to come dropping down by thread, or other such to leap upon us from above."

Borel nodded and then said, "Even so, Flic, at first opportunity I will get for you a weapon that you can wield. The brooch of my cloak has a long silver pin which will suit you fine as a sword. Yet I must find a way to fashion a hilt and cross guard to make it into a proper blade."

"Hai!" said Flic. "Then Buzzer won't be the only one with a sting, eh?"

Borel laughed and continued to chip away flakes of flint.

The point fashioned at last, Borel paused in his crafting long enough to eat the entire grouse, insufficient as it was, and then fashioned two more arrows, using flint heads bound to the shafts with thongs of rabbit hide, and though he now had grouse feathers he instead cut silken strips from his shirt and tied them to the arrows as tails to aid them in flying true.

Finally, he washed his face and hands at a nearby mere and drank deeply, then added more wood to the fire and bade good night to Flic and settled down for the eve, telling himself over and again to look for daggers in his sleep to know he was dreaming. He was yet mumbling of daggers when he drifted away.

"What is it you do, my lord?"

Borel looked up from the great arrowhead he now fashioned. Across the chamber stood a slender, golden-haired demoiselle dressed in sapphire blue and white. There was something strange about her eyes, as if a dark band lay across.

"I need a great arrow to slay Trolls," said Borel.

"Trolls, my lord?" She glanced at the stairway going down. "I think there are no Trolls herein."

Borel set aside the great melon-sized knapping rock and struggled to shove the massive piece of flint from his lap. After a moment the tiny arrow point tinked to the floor. Borel stood. "The Trolls are at the door, and we must escape out the window." Hefting the great loop of rope over his shoulder, Borel stepped to the sill to see . . .

. . . Daggers! Now what . . . ? —Wait! I am in a dream!

Borel dropped the rope and turned to the demoiselle.

"My lady, are you Chelle, daughter of Lord Roulan?"

"Yes, my lord, I am. And you are . . . ?"

"Prince Borel of the Winterwood."

"Oh, Borel, my love, are you here to help me escape?"

Borel found himself back at the window, the rope and grappling hook in hand. Even as he set the tines against the sill, the daggers darted forward. Borel stepped back.

Daggers! I am in a dream. Why didn't I remember?

The hook vanished along with the rope.

Borel stepped close to Chelle and took her hands in his and looked closely into her face.

"My lady, where are you?"

"Why, here in the turret, Borel. And please, stand not on formality; you may call me by name."

"And where is this turret, Chelle?"

Chelle frowned. "On my father's grounds."

"Ah, good. Then I am on my way to find you."

"But you are here, Borel. You have found me."

She doesn't remember what she told me when last I was here. 'Tis the vagary of dreams.

"This is but a dream, Chelle. Somehow we are linked."

Chelle looked about. "A dream? Linked? I do not understand."

"Neither do I, Chelle. Nevertheless it is true. Do you not recall warning me of the oncoming Goblins, and telling me I must waken?"

Hesitantly, Chelle nodded.

"At the time I was in a prison, unconscious, and you came to me then. —Or rather, I came to you, for it was here in this chamber you cried out the alert that Goblins were coming down the stairs. I wakened in time to fend for myself. Hence, we are dream linked."

"Are you telling me that I am at this moment asleep?"

"Yes, Chelle. We both are."

Of a sudden, the room began to waver, and in spite of trying to hold on to the moment, the chamber vanished, and Borel awakened.

Yet sore, he painfully lurched to his feet and stumped away from the camp and relieved himself. Then he stepped to the mere and jerked to a halt, arrested by anxiety, for upon the mirrorlike surface floated the moon, now some three days past full.

16

Gnome

"She called me her 'love.' "

"Mayhap you merely wished it to be so, Lord Borel. After all, it was a dream."

The prince fished the rock from the heated water in his hat and dropped in a stone fresh from the fire. "No, Flic, I do not dictate what she says, nor does she control my words. Instead, she named me her love, and yet I know not why."

"Well, you did say she followed you about when you were on Roulan's estate."

"Indeed, she did. Even so, she was but a child."

"Nevertheless, Lord Borel, that could have been when she forged this link with you as well as the ardor she expressed for you."

"Ah, Flic, at that age it would have been puppy love at best."

"If you say so, my prince. Still, dreams are strange and unpredictable things—some are omens, others are true, and some are simply flights of fancy. Yet you say she is now a lovely demoiselle, and so I think more able to forge bonds of love. Would that I could be so fortunate as to have someone I love and someone who loves me."

"You have never been in love?"

"No, my lord; only liaisons."

Borel sighed. " 'Tis the same with me."

Borel removed the last rock from the now-bubbling water. Flic dropped blossoms in, and Borel stirred with his forked stick. Shortly, after Flic's approval, he drank the tisane all in one gulp. It did not seem as distasteful as it had yestermorn. Even so, a frisson ran the length of his spine. Setting aside the tricorn, Borel next turned to his makeshift mortar and pestle and began crushing moss. As he did so, he glanced at the nearby twilight border. "I wonder what lies beyond?"

"More flowers, I imagine," said Flic, smiling at Buzzer.

"I hope the going will be easier today," said Borel.

"Less painful, you mean?" asked Flic.

Borel shrugged.

"It should be," said Flic, "for you are healing quite well."

Borel peered at his exposed skin. " 'Tis true my bruises have turned from black to yellow. Even so, I am yet tender, and I ache now and again. And I am hungry. The snare caught nothing in the night."

Flic grinned. "Perhaps we'll come upon a meal beyond the marge."

"One can only hope," said Borel. He looked at the result of his handiwork. The moss had turned to slime. "Is it ready?"

Lightly touching it, the Sprite tested the sludge between thumb and forefinger and said, "Oui, Prince."

They smeared a thin film upon each of the bruises. When that was done, Borel began crushing herbs for the juice, and a short while later his scrapes had been treated.

He donned his clothes and after quenching the fire he took up his goods and strung his bow and readied an arrow. "Let us hope something lies beyond I can fell and eat."

Buzzer took to wing and sighted on the sun and then flew in a straight line into the twilight margin, Borel following, Flic again riding upon the prow of the tricorn.

Through the twilight they went, the day growing dimmer as they pressed on, and then lightening again as they came to the far side, where Borel groaned, for they had come into a high mountain valley with towering peaks all 'round. If Buzzer flew up and across a mountain, then this day would not be easier after all.

As Buzzer circled 'round and took a bearing, Borel gazed about at the place they had come into, seeking to see if ought was familiar. Whin grew on the land, and aspen groves dotted the hillsides. Streams tumbled down from high mountain snows, with groves of silver birch clustered along the flow. A long vale stretched out before them, sloping up toward a distant pass.

Borel sighed and said, "I've not been here before, and so I still do not know where Lord Roulan's estates lie."

"Fear not, Prince," said Flic. "Buzzer knows the way."

Even as the Sprite said that, along the rising length of the valley arrowed the bee toward the col.

Panting in the thin air, Borel trudged up the long slope, wending this way and that among the thick hells of gorse, doing his best to avoid the thorny evergreen shrubs, with their sharply pointed leaves and solitary deep yellow cuplike flowers.

"See, I told you that there would be blossoms on this side of the marge," said Flic.

Borel growled, but said nought.

"And you say the chamber just vanished?" asked Flic.

"What?" said Borel.

"Your dream, the chamber, it vanished?"

"Yes," said Borel, pressing through a place where the furze spread too widely for him to go around. "When I told her we were both asleep and dreaming, that's when it went away. I tried to hold on to the chamber, but it faded and then was gone, and I woke."

"You could not control it, eh?"

"No."

Flic pondered a bit as Borel trudged on upward.

Far ahead, Buzzer passed through the col and disappeared downward beyond.

Finally, the Sprite said, "I think it is because it is her chamber and not yours, hence it is hers to control. Perhaps when you told her you were both in a dream, the reality came as a shock and she withdrew, and that's why the chamber vanished. You will have to gently dance 'round her predicament to perhaps discover how she came to be where she finds herself."

Forgetting that Flic was on the prow of his tricorn, Borel sighed and shook his head. "Hoy!" called the Sprite as he was nearly pitched off.

"Sorry," said Borel. "I was just thinking if it upsets her that much to know we are dreaming, mayhap I should not try to ask her any more about her predicament."

"Hmm . . . Perhaps you are right, Prince," said Flic. He rode in silence for a while but then said, "There is this to consider, my lord: you must remember that if you are aware you are dreaming, you control aspects of the vision. Perhaps you can change the setting. Take her somewhere she can forget her troubles, and then seek answers."

"How would I do this?" asked Borel. "I cannot take her out through the windows, and she refuses to go down the steps."

"I do not know," replied Flic. "I just know that as long as you and she remain in that chamber, you do not control the setting."

Again Borel sighed and shook his head, but Flic was holding on to the upturned brim of the tricorn and remained well seated.

On up the slope Borel went and passed through the col, and then strode down the far slant, the way easier, for the whin mustered less thickly upon the land on this side of the notch.

Of a sudden Borel paused and said, "I hear the sound of an axe, I think . . . or perhaps that of a hammer."

Faintly upon the air came a distant thwack, and after a moment, another . . . and another. . . . And in the distance among a stand of evergreens—

"Look, a thin tendril of smoke," said Borel, pointing at the grove.

"I see it as well," said Flic, taking to wing. "I'll scout ahead."

"Take care, my friend," said Borel. "It could be more Goblins and Trolls."

"Or something worse," said Flic. "I will be wary of nets and such."

With that the Sprite flew down the slope and toward the distant copse.

On downward strode Borel, his steps not as faltering as they were yester, for Flic's flowery potion and mossy salve and juice of herbs seemed to have alleviated much of Borel's woe, his soreness but a dull aching rather than a collection of sharp pains. Even so, he was not yet up to running, not yet capable of the Wolftrot he could maintain throughout a full day. And so, gaining the benefit of two applications of Flic's medications, Borel strode on the edge of discomfort, rather than hobbling along in acute hurt.

Buzzer came flying back, apparently to make certain that this walking two-legs followed. Not finding Flic in Borel's company, the bee agitatedly flew 'round and about Borel's head, then alighted on the brim of the hat, then flew again, and landed again and flew and landed and flew.

"He's gone on a scouting mission," said Borel, and he pointed at the grove. And still smoke drifted into the air from the center of the trees, and still there came a periodic thwacking.

Buzzer flew down before Borel's face and hovered somewhat menacingly.

In spite of the bee, Borel continued to stride forward, and Buzzer turned and flew a short distance, then hovered again directly in Borel's path. "I tell you, Flic's gone on ahead," said the prince, once more pointing.

When he reached Buzzer, Borel stopped and held out a hand, palm down, and then slowly raised it up underneath the bee, until she had no choice but to land on his hand or fly.

She landed.

Borel moved his hand to his tricorn, and Buzzer walked off and onto the hat. Then Borel strode on toward the grove.

Some moments later, Flic came flying back; he was giggling. Buzzer flew up and about the Sprite, seemingly overjoyed at the wee one's return. But then the bee buzzed angrily, as if admonishing Flic for worrying her so.

They both landed on Borel's tricorn, and as Flic stroked the bee, Borel said, "Well?"

"You must go into the grove, my lord prince." Again the Sprite broke into giggles.

"And what will I find?" asked Borel.

"Oh, I would not wish to spoil the surprise," said Flic.

"Flic, I would rather enter the coppice knowing what is there than be surprised by a danger dire."

"My prince, I was gone as long as I was because I flew throughout the entire grove, seeking peril, and I assure you there is no danger lurking within."

With that the Sprite would say no more, and Borel strode on to the stand of evergreens and, nocking an arrow, he cautiously walked within, following the sound of the rapping and the fragrance of woodsmoke, and then he heard cursing.

He came upon what looked to be a very small, one-room log cabin, perhaps no more than four foot high, its wee, leather-hinged door standing ajar. The rapping and cursing came from beyond the tiny dwelling.

Not wishing to leave danger lurking behind, Borel stooped down and took a quick look within the small dwelling. No one was inside. Cautiously, he worked his way about the lodge and toward the oaths, the Sprite on the tricorn with his hand pressed to his mouth to keep from laughing aloud, though now and again a giggle did escape.

Borel came to the back corner, and he drew his arrow to the full and stepped 'round. There behind the cabin knelt a small Gnomelike man, two foot tall at the most, a tiny axe in one hand, a small, blunt wedge of wood in another; using the flat of the blade, he was trying to pound the poorly tapered block into an entirely too-narrow, lengthwise crack in a large log in which his long white beard was trapped nearly all the way up to his chin.

Flic broke out laughing in glee.

At this sound—"Are you girls back again? Are you girls back again?" snarled the little man, unable to turn about to see for himself. "Go away! Go away!"

"Nay, Sieur," said Borel, smiling and relaxing his draw. "We are no girls. —Or rather, only one of us is female."

Upon hearing Borel's deep voice, the little man jerked and tried to—"Ow!"—swing 'round to see, but his beard was caught, and a goodly number of strands tore free as he tried to look behind. "Now see what you made me do," he cried. "Oh, my beautiful beard."

Laughing gaily, Flic flew up and across and lit on one end of the log, and the Gnomish man's undersized eyes widened at the sight of the Sprite. Then Buzzer lit nearby.

"Oh, oh," cried the little man, "kill the bee, kill the bee, else I am certain it will sting me."

Flic gasped in horror. "Kill my friend? Why you ugly little man. You deserve to remain stuck."

"Now, Flic," said Borel, even as the Gnome began to cry, "I am certain that he is merely frightened, and had he known Buzzer is a friend, he wouldn't have said such a thing."

"Oh, oh, are you going to leave me trapped here forever?" asked the small man.

"No, no," said Borel, "I will help you, Sieur." The prince slid the arrow back into his quiver and stepped to the opposite side of the log, where he unstrung his bow and slung it across his back.

Before him, Borel saw a rather homely Gnome, with a nose much too large for his face, and eyes much too small, and a very wide mouth running nearly from one overlarge ear to the other.

At the sight of the prince, again the wee man's eyes widened. "You're not going to cut my beard, are you? That's what the girls did. Cut my beard. It took years to grow out to its now magnificent length."

"No," said Borel. "I assure you, I will only cut your beard if nought else will set you free."

"Oh, no," moaned the Gnome, great tears forming and running down his cheeks and nose and splashily dropping onto the bark.

Borel knelt down and examined the log, the crack, and the beard. "Give me the axe," he said.

"Oh, no, you're going to chop my beard off," whined the Gnome, and he tried to hide the axe behind his back.

Sighing, Borel reached across and took the axe from the wee man. "Have you a hammer, a mallet?"

"Y-yes. In my cottage."

Borel frowned and looked at the oak-hafted axe, more of a hatchet in size, being just slightly longer than a foot in all. "Never mind," he said and took up a billet nearby. He set the cutting edge of the small axe into one end of the split well away from the Gnome's beard, and then with the billet he hammered the bronze blade into the crack, widening it. In moments the Gnome was free.

"Oh, thank you. Thank you," said the wee man, standing up to his two-foot height and stretching, while at the same time keeping a wary eye upon the bee. He tucked the end of his foot-long beard into his belt and said, "I've little to pay you with."

"I ask for no pay," said Borel, "though a meal would be splendid."

"As you wish, my lord," said the Gnome, "though it will take me awhile," and he rushed away toward the back door of his cabin.

"It would also suit my friends," Borel called after, "if you have a bit of honey as well."

"Yes, yes," called the wee man over his shoulder, and into the cabin he went.

Borel looked about, and then wrenched the axe from the log and, in spite of his lingering aches, he began splitting the wood in twain.

Borel had laid aside nearly a half cord of wood by the time the Gnome returned, the small man staggering under a steaming tray piled high with honey-baked beans, several wee slabs of black bread slathered with butter, a number of small rashers of well-cooked bacon, and a tiny bowl holding perhaps a spoonful of honey.

"Just as I was trying to wrench my axe out of that log," said the Gnome, now sitting on the ground before Borel, "a gust of wind blew me down on it at the very same time my axe came free and the crack snapped shut on my beard."

Also sitting on the ground, *"Mmm . . ."* said Borel, his mouth full of beans and bread.

"By the bye," said the Gnome, "my name is Hegwith. And you would be . . . ?"

"He is Prince Borel of the Winterwood," said Flic, licking sweetness from the tip of one finger, while beside him Buzzer lapped at the small dish of honey. "And this is Buzzer, my guardian"—Flic shot a glare at the Gnome—"and not a bee to be swatted nor trifled with. And I am Flic, Sprite of the Fields."

"Prince Borel?" said the Gnome, looking up at the man.

Still chewing, *"Mmm . . ."* replied Borel, sketching a seated bow, then scooping up another mouthful of beans, using the Gnome's soup ladle as a spoon.

Hegwith stood and bowed to the prince, and then seated himself on the ground again.

"How came you to believe we were girls coming to cut off your beard?" asked Flic, dipping his finger into the honey again and then licking it clean.

"Well, this isn't the first time my beard has been caught in a crack, and for that I think some evil witch or the like has cursed me. You see, awhile back and at a place far from here, I got my beard caught in another split in a log. Two young girls came along, and to get me free they snipped off the very tip of my beard. I'm afraid I was rather ungracious, seeing as how my marvelous beard had been virtually destroyed. I'm rather vain about it, you know.

"In any event, not a week went by when again my beard got caught in a crack, and as fate would have it, again came along these same two girls. And they cut off even more of my beard. This time I cursed at them, for now it was even worse than before.

"Finally, when my beard got caught the third time around, and this same pair of girls came by, I promised them treasure if they would set me free without snipping off more of my beard. They readily agreed, and, well, wouldn't you know, they took the treasure and ran away, leaving me with nought but a small pair of scissors." Tears filled the Gnome's eyes. "I had to cut my own beard. My very own beard."

Borel shook his head in commiseration, but Flic laughed in glee. "Clever girls. I say they well earned that treasure."

"What do you mean?" sobbed the Gnome. He took out a red kerchief and noisily blew his nose, but continued to weep over the loss of part of his beard.

"Why, they kept their promise, Hegwith," said Flic. "By leaving the scissors, they gave you the means for you to get free without they themselves cutting your beard." Again Flic broke into gleeful laughter.

"Yes, but I had to cut it myself," wailed Hegwith above the Sprite's giggles. "At least if they had snipped it off, I would have them to blame and not myself."

Borel sopped up the last of the honey-baked beans and popped the bread into his mouth.

Drawing in a shaky breath and stifling his tears and blowing his overlarge nose once more, Hegwith looked up at the prince and said, "At least you, my lord, didn't chop off my beautiful beard. And for that I am grateful."

"Had I had to cut it off," said Borel, "it would have been at your chin."

"Oh, my," said Hegwith, clutching his beard, and he burst into tears again.

"My lord, I see you travel light," said Hegwith. "Do you live nearby?"

"No, Hegwith. I have not much gear, for I lost nearly all of my goods when I was captured by Trolls, and then again during my escape."

Startled, Hegwith blurted, "Trolls? Where?" The Gnome looked about in panic.

Borel pointed back up the vale. "Past the twilight marge, and over hills and through woods to a distant river and then upstream past rapids; altogether some fifteen or twenty miles hence."

A look of relief passed across Hegwith's face. "For a moment I thought they might be nearby. Yet you escaped them, you say?"

Borel nodded.

"What did you lose?"

"Lose?"

"Your goods. When you were captured and then escaped."

"Oh, it's not important. Just a rucksack and a tinderbox and provisions, as well as a small kit for fletching arrows and other such things. Yet that is neither here nor there. Instead let me ask you this: do you know of Lord Roulan? Where his estates might be? We are on a desperate mission, and it is vital we get to his lands."

Hegwith shook his head. "I'm sorry, my lord, but I do not know of him. Would that I did, but I don't."

Borel sighed and then pointed ahead and said, "What lies along the vales we follow?"

"Meadows. Flowers. Streams. Coppices. All the way to the next border, some twenty-five miles hence. But there are no estates along that path."

"What lies beyond the next twilight marge?" asked Flic.

"Oh, you don't want to go there," said Hegwith, pushing out both hands, as if to stop any movement in that direction. " 'Tis a terrible mire—hideous bogs and quags; why, I nearly drowned when I passed through, back when I fled from the hag who wanted to steal my—um, er, harrumph, and those horrible girls who cut my beard. Regardless, there is muck without bottom and quicksand and leeches and snakes and other dreadful things, things that slither and plop and wriggle and . . ." Hegwith's voice trailed off, his face squinched, his gaze lost in ill memories.

"Blossoms?" asked Flic.

"What?"

"Are there blossoms, flowers, within the swamp?"

"Why, I suppose so. Yes, I remember. Many flowers hanging from trees, altogether quite beautiful. Others were growing up out of the muck. And some of those filled the air with the odor of carrion, as if some animal had crawled within and had become trapped and died, the stench of putrefying meat rather dreadful."

Flic looked at Borel. "Then, my lord, I think that is where Buzzer is headed, for the flowers of a mire are rich in nectar."

Borel shrugged and hitched to his feet, for sitting had stiffened him up. "If it lies along Buzzer's route, then there's nothing for it but that we must follow."

The prince slung his bow by its carrying thong and said, "I thank you for the tasty meal, Hegwith. It filled up the empty spots in my hollow stomach. But now we must go, for our mission is dire and the moon sails on and stays her course for no one." He turned to the Sprite and the bee. "Flic, Buzzer, 'tis time to fly."

At a signal from Flic, Buzzer took to wing and flew up and 'round, sighting on the sun, and then she arrowed away. Flic flew up to the prow of Borel's tricorn and settled down. Borel sketched a bow to the Gnome, then turned and strode off through the evergreens, and Hegwith watched them go. Just ere they disappeared from sight, the Gnome called out, "Thank you for setting me free without cutting my beard."

Hegwith stood a moment in thought, muttering "What has the moon to do with ought?" Then he looked at the axe and the crack in the log and at the cord of wood Borel had split and laid for him. His eyes widened and he glanced once more in the direction that Borel, Flic, and Buzzer had gone, then turned and rushed into his tiny dwelling, where he opened a trapdoor and climbed down into the mine below. There he took up a maul and began pounding on the bedrock, his rhythmic hammerings sounding very much like signals.

"Nought but liaisons, eh?" said Flic.

Borel frowned and then brightened and said, "Ah. With the fair sex you mean?"

Now Flic frowned. "Fair sex?"

"Women," said Borel. "Females. Ladies. Mademoiselles and demoiselles. *Femmes fatales*."

"Oh, I see," said Flic. "Yes, they are who I meant."

"Oui, liaisons is all I have had with members of the fair sex," said Borel.

Flic sighed. "Me, too. Ah, but as I said before, I wish I had someone to love and someone who loves me."

"A lady Sprite, eh? Someone from the fields?"

"That would be my choice," said Flic, "though I suppose a Woodland Sprite would do."

Borel frowned. "There's a difference?"

"Oh, indeed. A great difference. They live in the woods, you see, whereas I and my kind live in the fields."

Borel strode forward several steps before asking, "Are you of a size: Field Sprites and those of the woods? Do you more or less resemble one another?"

"Um, yes," said Flic.

"Then why would there be any problem in such a union?"

Flic pondered a moment. "Well, I, uh . . . Hmm. I suppose we could live in the woods some of the time and in the fields at others. That or live in a field on the edge of a woodland."

Borel smiled. "What of living in a woodland on the edge of a field?"

"Hmm . . ." Flic mused. "I suppose that would work as well, though surely the other way 'round is better."

Borel laughed. "It never occurred to me that where one lives might keep lovers apart. I would think that the important thing is whether or no one has found his truelove and she has found him. Then from that moment on, they would seek to overcome whatever obstacles lay in their way so that they could be together."

Flic fell silent, and Borel strode on, following the path that Buzzer flew, the bee keeping to the vales rather than flying up over any of the mountains hemming them in.

At times Borel waded streams and rivulets and deep flows. At other times he trudged up long slopes, or down. Through laurel hells he went, and groves of aspen and birch. Whin oft stood in his way, and this he passed 'round when he could, or pushed through when he could not. Stony ways he sometimes followed, or whisked among tall grasses springing forth from rich loam. Yet no matter the terrain, always there were flowers along the way: Buzzer's larder.

And as Borel strode and Flic rode and Buzzer flew, the prince and the Sprite talked of the mysteries of amour and ardor and passion and affairs of the heart, and they both bemoaned the fact that each had yet to find his very own truelove.

They were yet in the high mountain valleys when they came to the wall of twilight marking the border into the next realm of Faery. And as the sun set, hearkening to the words of Hegwith the Gnome, they set camp in a coppice this side of that marge and planned on passing through and into the mire the next morn.

Altogether, they had gone some twenty-seven miles that day, for with the ministrations of Flic's medicines, Borel's hurts had considerably eased.

Once again Borel knapped flint arrowheads as he sat beside the fire. He had seen no game that day, and so he would be without meat for his meal. *Had I my loyal Wolves, I would set them on a hunt. I do hope they escaped Hradian's wrath.* Though he had not felled game, he had managed to dig up a tuber—something akin to a parsnip—from one of the meadows, and Flic had assured him that certain grass grains were nutritious, at least to grazing animals, that is, and so whenever they had passed through thigh-high grass, Borel had plucked and chewed the heads. And so he roasted the tuber and knapped flint, while he and Flic spoke of liaisons and love and lovers.

That eve, when Borel settled down to sleep, Flic reminded the prince that he needed some way to change the setting of the turret, should he happen to find Chelle in his dreams again.

Yet Borel did not know how to do such a thing, and even as he concentrated upon remembering that daggers meant that he was dreaming, still the quandary of how to escape the stone chamber lurked on the edge of his thoughts.

Dance

"My lady, what is it across your eyes?"

"There is something across my eyes?"

"A dark band."

"Then I know not what it might be, my prince, for I see you clearly, and you, my love, are just as I remember."

Borel took her hand and bowed and kissed her fingers. As he straightened, he glanced about the deeply shadowed chamber. The room was round and seemed somehow vaguely familiar, as if he had been there before. The walls were of stone, and the floor of wood, as was the conical ceiling above. To one side, stone steps led downward to somewhere below, and there were windows opening out onto—

—Daggers! Floating daggers! I am in the dream.

"My lady, I must get you away from here."

"How, Lord Borel? The windows are warded, and something dreadful lies down below. It isn't as if we have a magical doorway to lead us to safety."

Magical doorway?

Flic's words echoed in Borel's mind: "*. . . you must remember that if you are aware you are dreaming, you control aspects of the vision.*"

Again Borel looked about. *Perhaps in the deepest shadow opposite the stairwell.* He closed his eyes, concentrating, and when he opened them again— *There!*

"My lady, if I have done this right, I have a surprise for you. If you please." Borel offered Chelle his arm.

Hesitantly she took it, and Borel led her to the hidden door in the wall, and when he swung it wide—

—Music and gaiety filled the air, and they entered a large chamber full of people waiting their turn to dance the minuet: the women in silks and satins, their long, flowing gowns of yellow, of peach, of lavender, pale jade, deep red, of puce and rust and umber, and of white. Chelle was the only one wearing a gown of sapphire blue and white. The men were arrayed in silken tights and knee hose and buckled shoes, with doublets and waistcoats and silken shirts and ruffles galore, their colors in darker shades than those of the women, but running throughout the same range. Only Borel was dressed in leathers. And violins and violas and cellos and a harpsichord sounded out the stately air, while a single pair in the center of the floor gracefully paced out the courtly steps.

"How utterly wonderful," breathed Chelle.

"My lady, does this suit?"

"Oh, yes," replied Chelle, a glorious smile lighting her face, though the dark band yet remained.

And she and Borel moved in to take their place among the elegant circle of waiting couples—

"Where are we?" asked Chelle.

"In Summerwood Manor. Here it was I last danced."

"Who is the man in the mask?" asked Chelle.

"My brother, Alain," said Borel.

"And his partner?"

"Camille, his truelove."

"Why does he wear a mask?"

"He is cur—" Borel frowned. "No, wait. He *was* cursed, but no longer."

Of a sudden the mask vanished, yet none in the gathering seemed to notice that ought had changed, not even Chelle.

The music segued into an interlude, and amid applause Alain

and Camille stepped to the edge of the floor, and from across the circle Alain gestured to Borel. All eyes turned toward the Prince of the Winterwood.

And as the violins and viols and cellos and the harpsichord continued the interlude, "My lady," said Borel, stepping onto the dance floor and bowing to Chelle and then straightening and holding out a hand to her.

Chelle smiled and curtseyed, and then took Borel's hand and he led her to the center of the floor. And as the prince and his lady took position, the musicians played an introductory refrain, followed by the dignified air of the minuet.

And while all those about them watched and waited their turn, Borel and Chelle moved in time to the moderate tempo, the stately court dance one of small steps and erect posture and deep curtseys and bows and hand-holdings and pacing side by side while facing one another. And they turned and drew close and then stepped apart, and struck the requisite poses, the whole of it having an air of restrained flirtation.

"It is called the kissing dance, Chelle," said Borel, smiling mischievously.

"I know, my lord," said Chelle, a rising blush touching her cheeks.

"Fear not, my lady, I will not embarrass you in front of these guests."

"Oh," said Chelle, her voice falling.

As they continued the dance, yet effecting the various postures and carriage, Borel said, "I would not have you be a mere liaison, Chelle."

"And I would not be one, Sieur," replied Chelle, a hint of coldness in her response.

"Ah, my Chelle, do not take me wrong," said Borel. "I find I am strongly drawn to you, and it is more than mere desire."

"Oh, Borel, I have loved you ever since I first saw you," said Chelle.

"You were but a child then," said Borel.

"I am no child now," replied Chelle, again a blush gracing her cheeks.

Borel's blood raced and his heart hammered in his breast, threatening to escape. And of a sudden he and Chelle were stepping out the dance in the center of an enormous floor, the ring of spectators still all 'round but now furlongs away.

And Borel leaned down to kiss her and Chelle raised her face to meet him, and in that moment the music slipped into the interlude, and all the spectators suddenly appeared right at hand, applauding.

Borel and Chelle sprang apart, and Chelle, blushing furiously, hid part of her face behind the fan that suddenly appeared in her hand, while women in the circle about them clapped and smiled and whispered to one another, and the men slapped their hands together and looked at Borel and grinned their approval.

Borel led Chelle from the floor and they resumed their place among the bystanders, while another couple took the center.

The music again segued from an introductory refrain to the dance, and Borel leaned over and murmured, "I apologize, my love, I should not have been so bold."

"I am not sorry, my lord," said Chelle, her fan rapidly whisking back and forth, as if to cool her face.

As the couple on the floor minced through the steps of the minuet, Borel said, "How came you to be in the turret?"

The walls of the hall in Summerwood Manor began to turn to stone, and Borel clutched Chelle's hand and cried out, "No, no, my love, there are more dances to dance and things to say!"

And the stone faded and became wood once more, and Chelle looked up at Borel and, though he could not see them behind the shadowy band, he knew there was fright in her eyes.

No one else seemed to have noticed ought.

The music changed, and Prince Alain announced they would begin the *contredanses*.

Dancers formed into squares and stepped out the intricate but lively footwork of the cotillion, and then that of the quadrille, with its handful of complex figures, each with its own vigorous tune. And some of these dances again turned upon flirtations, where couples frequently switched partners and hands were held and cheeks were kissed and long lingering looks were exchanged with much touching and swinging about, though every time Borel traded partners it was always Chelle with whom he next danced.

Then came the longways dances, where the men arrayed themselves in a line facing the women in a like line opposite, partners directly across from one another.

Here the music was lively, sprightly violins showing the way, and various partners took turns dictating the mode of the dance, the others following in whatever pattern the leaders had set, sometimes dancing a lively romp down the center, at other times weaving in and out of the lines or circling 'round the outside, and when each couple reached the far end they took a place there and stood still while those following romped or reeled or wove past in a dancing game of follow the leader. When Borel and Chelle's turn came to set the pattern, Borel called out, "The Dance of the Bees!" and then he and Chelle flapped their arms as if they were wings and wriggled and buzzed down the center of the lines, and then ran back and wriggled and buzzed down the center again, Chelle laughing gaily in between her buzzings, men and women in the long lines laughing and clapping and waiting their turn at becoming bees.

After this merry and vigorous dance, Alain called a halt for both dancers and musicians to rest. And as Borel led his demoiselle through the wide double doors and out into the garden beyond, he looked up to see the moon four days past fullness, and of a sudden they were back in the turret, Chelle gazing at the thin beam of moonlight shining against the floor.

"There is less than a moon left," she said in the Old Tongue—

—And Borel awakened in a camp next to a twilight border to hear small footsteps scurrying away in the night.

In Summerwood Manor, both Alain and Camille startled awake.

"I had the strangest dream," said Alain.

"So did I," said Camille.

They looked at one another, eyes widening.

"A dance?" asked Alain.

Camille nodded.

"Borel?" asked Alain.

Again Camille nodded.

"A demoiselle with a dark band across her eyes?" asked Alain.

"Oh, yes, Alain," replied Camille. "How can this be?"

Alain shook his head and replied, "I think, my love, the more important question is: what can this possibly mean?"

18

Torrent

As the footsteps scrambled away, Borel bolted upright and gazed through the moonlight in the direction of the sound, but there was too much underbrush to see ought. Snatching up his bow, ready to string it, the prince jumped to his feet; still, he saw nothing. Then he whirled about and breathed a sigh of relief: Flic and Buzzer slept peacefully upon the broad leaf they had taken to as their bed. Borel knelt and added wood to the fire, and in the growing blaze, he examined his meager belongings to see if anything had been stolen: nothing had. But he found in addition to his goods a tiny rucksack, and within were several small bags, and these he cautiously examined: in one there was oatmeal; another contained strips of jerky; a third one held a loaf of black bread, the same as the Gnome had served; the fourth and final bag held several coins, silver and gold among the coppers. Furthermore, there was a small jar of honey, a coil of line, a tiny pot of glue, a packet of thread, a small tin pot with a bail, and a tinderbox with flint and steel and fine wood shavings.

Borel called out through the darkness in the direction the footsteps had fled: "My thanks to Hegwith!"

Jolted awake, Flic sat up and rubbed his eyes and said, "What's all this shouting about?"

By firelight, Borel examined the ground. "We've had visitors in the night, by the look of the tracks perhaps three altogether. They left gifts."

"Gifts?"

"A jar of honey for you and Buzzer. Some provisions and other needful things for me."

"No good deed goes unrewarded," said Flic, yawning. "Or is it instead no good deed goes unpunished?" He glanced at the moon, then lay back down and said to the sky, "It looks as if there is a goodly part of the night left, my prince. Me, I'm going back to sleep. You had better sleep as well; perhaps there is yet time to meet the demoiselle of your dreams."

"I already did," said Borel. "We danced."

"Danced? In the turret?"

"No. In Summerwood Manor. You see, I stepped through a hidden door and into the ballroom."

Flic did not reply.

Borel looked up to see the Sprite curled against Buzzer in his sleep.

"We had a merry time," continued Borel, faintly smiling and speaking to himself. "And I called her 'my love.' "

"You what?" said Flic, as he and Buzzer broke fast, lapping at a dribble of honey inside the upturned lid of the jar.

"I called her my love," replied Borel.

"Well, do you love her?"

"In my dreams I do."

"Ah, dreams are wild, and anything can happen therein," said Flic, licking honey from his finger. "I mean, it seems as if there are no restraints on what one will say and do in a dream: give your heart to someone; engage in liaisons; in one moment be here and in the next instant there; conquer your worst enemy; flee from the most insignificant thing; grow to giant size; and other such. Oui, you might confess a desperate love to someone you know—or even a total stranger—when ensnared in a dream, but what matters is how you feel when awake."

Borel frowned. "I don't know how I feel. Oh, I think she is

quite splendid, but as to love . . . Flic, she was a child when last I actually saw her, and that is hard for me to dismiss. But in my dreams, she is a lovely demoiselle."

"Perhaps her dream image is misleading, Borel," said Flic. "Perhaps it only shows what she would like to be, rather than what she is."

Borel nodded and stirred the blossoms in the water in the tin pot hanging from the spit above the fire.

Flic said, "Let me see."

Borel stopped stirring and lifted the pot free and set it before the Sprite, and Flic dipped in a finger and tasted. "It is ready."

Taking a deep breath, with his gloved hands Borel raised the pot to his lips—"Ow! Too hot!"

"Let it cool a bit," said Flic, licking more honey from his finger.

Borel stood and took the pot to the stream and set it within, letting chill water cool the metal. In moments he raised it to his lips and drank the full of the yet-warm tisane without pausing. This day it seemed bitter and sweet at one and the same time, and Borel sucked in air between clenched teeth and a tremor ran down his neck and back.

Then he half filled the small container with water, and returned to the fire and set the pot to boil.

He took up his pestle rock and began crushing the last of the moss, turning it to sludge. By the time he and Flic had slathered a thin film of the slime over his faintly discolored bruises, the water in the pot was bubbling. Borel tossed in a fistful of oatmeal, and as he crushed sap from the last of the herbs, he occasionally paused to stir the gruel.

They daubed the herbal juice onto Borel's nearly healed cuts and scrapes, and then he dressed and broke his fast with oat porridge, using two fingers to scoop it into his mouth.

"Any need to keep the mortars and pestles?" he asked, tilting his head toward the rocks.

"No, Borel, we are finished with the treatments."

"Good. No use in lugging extra weight." He took another two fingers of oatmeal and chewed without gusto and swallowed and said, "I am sorely tempted to sweeten this with honey."

"Feel free, my lord, for Buzzer and I can live long whiles on nectar alone."

Borel shook his head. "No, tiny one. You and Buzzer need good sustenance. Besides, what I have is nourishing enough, even if it is not tasty." He scooped another portion into his mouth and barely chewed before swallowing. He glanced at his bow and said, "Perhaps today I will bring down some game."

As Borel used the Gnome-given rope to belt on the wee rucksack, Buzzer flew about and took a heading, then darted into the twilight border. Borel followed, Flic riding on the prow of the tricorn. They passed into a dimness growing darker and then lighter again, and they emerged into a downpour, a dismal swamp all about.

Nearby, Buzzer clung to the bottom of a limb, and when Borel emerged, the bee flew and alighted on the underside of the tricorn-hat brim.

"She can't fly in this storm," said Flic, the Sprite swinging down to land on Borel's shoulder to take shelter 'neath the brim as well.

Borel turned and strode into the twilight to emerge back in the high mountain vale. "What can we do?"

"Wait for it to stop," replied Flic.

"Can Buzzer take bearings in the rain?"

"Not in that downpour."

"Can you ask Buzzer if it's straight through we need to go?"

"Smooth out a patch of ground," said Flic.

Moments later, Buzzer was doing her wriggle dance, with Flic paying close attention. Borel smiled, remembering the dance he and Chelle had performed. Finally the Sprite said, "If you can pass straight through the mire to the opposite side and the border beyond, she can take a new sighting. But listen, if you are too far off the line, we might end up someplace altogether different, and she might not be able to find the vale with the pink-petaled shamrock and blushing white roses and thorn-laden blackberry vines . . . that is, until she comes to a known place, in which case she can fly from there onward."

Borel nodded, for the twilight borders of Faery are peculiar. A person might cross a given marge at one place and find a pleasant land, whereas crossing that same marge at another point could lead to a dreadful realm. And in some places, one can cross and lop days of travel from the journey, yet just a furlong or so away from that crossing another passage through could add leagues upon leagues to the trek. Hence, one had to be careful of one's bearings when venturing athwart the twilight walls of Faery, else a planned destination might elude one altogether. Usually, when one found this to be, he crossed back over, moved along the border one way or another—from feet to furlongs to leagues—and then passed through again, hoping to arrive where he wished.

Borel sighed and shook his head. " 'Tis a mire yon, where one can easily get deflected and off track. I'd rather not gamble. We'll wait it out."

And so they waited, impatient Borel repeatedly crossing through the twilight wall, each time discovering the downpour yet raged.

As he waited, he fetched from his quiver the grouse feathers and the thread and the glue provided by his visitors in the night; and he fletched arrows, plume trims replacing the cloth tails. Too, he knapped flint arrowheads, and fitted the rest of the arrowwood shafts. And in between knappings and fittings and fletchings, he crossed over, only to curse at the torrent and then return to the vale.

When night came on, the rain hadn't stopped, and Buzzer fell dormant in the dark. A short while later, Flic curled up next to the bee.

"Ah, *zut!*" said Borel. "There's nothing for it but that we must wait for morn."

And so he set his snare in a distant trace and added wood to the fire, and then settled down to sleep.

Garden

"Chelle, my love."

"Yes, Borel."

"I have in mind another surprise for you."

A smile lit Chelle's face. "A dance?"

"No."

"If not a dance, what?"

Borel laughed. "If I tell you, it won't be a surprise."

"Oh. Hmm. Yes, of course. Then let us be gone, my lord, for I would see this surprise."

A fleeting grin crossed Borel's features, only to be replaced by a somber mien. "I must warn you, though, if I do this rightly, then when we step through this door I believe there will be a moon in the sky"—Chelle gasped, but Borel squeezed her hand in reassurance—"and I do not wish you to be alarmed and flee back to here."

"My lord, the moon, there is less than a moon left."

"I know, Chérie, and I am on my way. I will be here ere then."

Chelle stiffened her spine and said, "I will face the dwindling moon with you at my side, my sweet Borel."

Borel smiled, then turned toward the door and closed his eyes and stood a moment in deep concentration, then opened them again. "I think all is now ready, Chelle," he said and offered her his arm, and when she took it he led her across the turret floor to the enshadowed door and opened it to find—

—A moonlit garden, rife with blossoming flowers, white stone pathways wending throughout. Vine-laden arbors graced the grounds, some with deep purple grapes ripe for the plucking, others with grapes of golden-white or rouge-red. Ivy flowed across the soil and up trellises, and a gazebo stood on the bank of a slow-running, crystalline brook.

"Oh, my," said Chelle, "how splendid. Chrysanthemums, hibiscus, and, oh, spider lilies, red ones and white ones, too. And there is white stonecrop. Oh, the flowers, the flowers, how rich this garden is. Whose is it?"

"It belongs to my sister Liaze. We are in the Autumnwood, her principality."

"Well, it is a wonderful garden, Borel, and I thank you for bringing me here."

Borel nodded but said, "I know little of flowers, for my demesne is the Winterwood, where ice and snow rule, though at times, when it thaws a bit, a winter crocus blooms."

They strolled down the stone pathways, Chelle now and again stopping to inhale the fragrance of a particular blossom.

"I need to know what flowers grow in your own gardens, Chelle," said the prince.

"Don't you remember, my lord? I gave you an extensive tour when you visited."

"Chérie, I think at that time I was more interested in the afternoon hunt your father had planned. As for the tour, well, I merely recall a skinny girl chattering away."

"Was I, am I that much of a pest?" said Chelle, lifting her face toward his.

"I think you will always distract me," said Borel, and a long, lingering kiss left both of them breathless. Reluctantly, he released her, and they continued their stroll.

"Chrysanthemums and roses and various wildflowers," said Chelle.

"What?" said Borel.

"Chrysanthemums and roses and various wildflowers," said Chelle. "They are what grow in my gardens."

Borel's heart sank. "Shamrock? Have you shamrock?"

"Shamrock?"

"I seem to recall you showed me shamrocks. 'Pink as my lips,' you said."

"You remember that?"

"I do."

"I was trying to get you to notice my lips, my best and perhaps my only feature back then, though my mother seemed to favor my smile, and my sire my eyes."

"Ah, yes, your eyes," said Borel. "Would that I could see them."

"Can you not?"

"No, Chelle. There is a darkness covering them."

"A darkness?"

Borel nodded.

Chelle frowned. "But I see perfectly well."

" 'Tis a mystery, then," said Borel. "One that we will resolve when I come for you."

Again Chelle frowned, as if trying to understand what Borel meant. Finally she shrugged and said, "Oh, yes, we do have shamrocks, and they have pink flowers."

Feeling relieved, Borel said, "White roses with a faint blush?"

"Mm-hm," said Chelle, as she leaned down to smell the bloom of a crimson mallow.

Now even more confident, the prince asked, "Have you blackberry brambles on your estate?"

"Oh, yes. Don't you remember we went blackberry harvesting when the hunt was called off?"

"I remember your mouth was stained purple," said Borel.

"Well, it is not purple now," said Chelle, turning to face him.

"No, my love, it is not," replied Borel, and, laughing, he swung her up and about and lowered her until their lips met in another lingering kiss.

When he set her to the ground, she fanned her face and reddened under his gaze, and as if to draw attention elsewhere, she gestured about and said, "I understand the Autumnwood has a peculiar power."

Borel grinned and nodded. "Each of the Forests of the Seasons has its own peculiar power. In the Autumnwood, it is the season of eternal harvest. Here, let me show you." Hand in hand, Borel led Chelle to a nearby arbor, one bearing purple grapes. He said, "Note which bunch I pluck, say, this one dangling through this particular trellis opening." Borel reached up and picked the cluster, and he offered the grapes to Chelle and said with a grin, "Make your mouth purple, my love?"

Chelle laughed and popped in a grape, and offered one to Borel. Smiling, he reached out to take it, but she shook her head and lifted the fruit to his lips and said, "I understand the way to a man's heart lies through his stomach," and she slipped the grape into his mouth.

Borel chewed, seeds and all, and swallowed and softly said, "You need not feed me, Chelle, for you already have my heart."

He wrapped her in his arms and again they kissed, and as they did so, she let fall the grapes.

Yet nestled, "Oh," she said, and she glanced aside at the dropped bunch. "See what I have done."

Borel laughed and released her and stepped back. "Fear not, love, there are plenty more where they came from. In fact . . ." He pointed above.

"Oh, my," said Chelle, looking at the dangling cluster. "Can it be?"

"Yes, love. The Autumnwood has replaced the clutch we picked."

Chelle turned and looked out on the moonlit garden. "What of the flowers?"

"Should we pluck a blossom, then it would reappear on its stem when none was looking."

"Oh," said Chelle, a bit crestfallen.

Borel frowned. "What is it, Chérie?"

"Then nothing changes in the Autumnwood? All things plucked replaced?"

Borel nodded.

"How sad," said Chelle. "Wonderful, but in the end quite sad."

"Why do you say so?" asked Borel.

"I repeat," said Chelle, "nothing changes. All is static. Forever fixed. Even this garden is frozen in its display." Chelle turned up her hands and sighed. "It seems to me that such an existence must eventually become quite dull."

In silence they strolled to the gazebo by the stream, and as they took a seat in a swing, Chelle said, "What of weeds? Do they return when plucked? If so, then how does one care for a garden?"

"Weeds are burned, my love, or dug out entirely. Anything destroyed by fire is not replenished. To plant a garden in new soil, one has to either burn whatever was standing—burn it in place—or completely uproot whatever was there."

"Oh. I see. Well, then, what of root crops—tubers, parsnips, onions, and such? If you harvest them—uproot them—do they not return?"

"If you unearth one normally," said Borel, "always does some part of it—perhaps a minuscule part, a bit of hair root or stem or such—remain within the soil, and the vegetable returns."

"Oh," said Chelle. "Then you do not have the pleasure of turning over new soil, tilling, planting, hoeing, tending . . . getting your hands in dirt and watching things grow, and then enjoying the fruits of your labor. You see, for me and many others not only is there delight in seeing a garden or field in its fullness, but there is also joy in all the steps it takes to bring such a thing about. And so, to have a never-changing realm, a realm without seasons, well, it seems quite sad to me."

A thoughtful look on his face, Borel nodded but said nothing, for until this very moment he had not considered the Autumnwood anything other than a place of everlasting harvest.

They gently swung to and fro without speaking for long moments, the only sound that of the brook murmuring past and the rustle of leaves in the faint breeze. But as the silvery light from above crept across the garden, Borel glanced at the waning moon and said, "Tell me this, my love, how do you know that there is less than a moon"—of a sudden they were back in the enshadowed turret—"left?"

Her voice trembling in dread, "Rhensibé told me," whispered Chelle, and the stone walls began to waver, and there was nought Borel could do to hold on to the dream.

20

Mire

"Rhensibé? She said 'Rhensibé' told her?"

"Yes, Flic," said Borel, scraping the hide of the marmot snared in the night, the dressed-out carcass roasting over the fire. "Know you anyone by that name?"

"No," said Flic, licking honey from a finger. "Perhaps it's a friend of hers, or on the other hand mayhap a foe."

Borel scraped for moments without speaking. But then he nodded and said, "Chelle was quite frightened when she named Rhensibé, but whether it is because Rhensibé is vile or because time grows shorter, or both, I cannot say."

"Last night the moon was five days past full," said Flic, dipping a finger back into the honey. "That leaves a fortnight, a sevenday, and a threeday ere it is full again. Plenty of time to reach the vale and somehow win through the ring of daggers, whatever they might represent."

"Only if we are heading to the right valley," said Borel. "Although Chelle did confirm that pink-petaled shamrocks and blushing white roses and thorn-laden blackberries grow on her sire's estates, I just hope that Buzzer has been there."

"There's a good chance she has, my lord," said Flic. "After

all, it has the right blossoms and lies in a vale with a small lake and with a river nearby."

Buzzer arrowed back through the twilight wall and landed next to the Sprite. After a silent conversation of waggles and postures that Borel could not interpret, Flic said, "She tells me that it is not raining in the mire. Even so, it is cloudy, yet she can still take a bearing and fly the course. We can only hope the storm is on the way out, and rain stays its hand."

"As soon as this marmot is done, we'll leave," said Borel. "I cannot take a raw carcass into the swamp, else we'll be covered in pests."

"Humph," grunted Flic, as Buzzer took station at the jar lid, the bee lapping up sweet honey therein. "Raw carcass or no, we'll be plagued by pests regardless."

Borel nodded but made no reply.

"By the blossom, how are you feeling?" asked Flic.

"Surprisingly well," said Borel. "It seems my bruises and cuts and scrapes are all gone."

"No surprise to it," said Flic. "Did I not tell you that three days would see you hale?"

Borel smiled. "You did, my friend, and for the treatment I thank you. Without it I would yet be hobbling about in pain. And I still intend upon seeing your queen and obtaining the secret of those curatives from her."

"Mmmm," said Flic, his mouth full of honey.

With his flint knife, Borel tested the marmot and then turned the spit again, and resumed scraping the hide.

"Is she still in love with you?" asked Flic. "—Chelle, I mean."

"It seems in my dreams we are both in love with one another," said Borel.

"A passing fancy?"

"No, Flic, I know now I am truly in love, and I think she is the one I have been searching for all my life. I can only hope that she feels the same when we are not dreaming."

"But you've only known her for, what, a fortnight or so?"

"Nevertheless . . ." replied Borel. He held up the hide and examined it closely, then wetted it down and rolled it up tightly and stuffed it into the wee rucksack.

"Well," said Flic, "twice now you have managed to take control of the dreams. This thought of yours to create a 'magic door' to change the setting was rather clever of you."

"It was Chelle who gave me the notion," said Borel. "Else we'd still be trapped in that turret."

Again Borel tested the marmot. "Ah, I think we can leave just as soon as I break my fast." He wrenched off a haunch and began eating.

As he chewed, he managed to say around mouthfuls, "Chelle said something I had never thought of before: that the Forests of the Seasons are fixed, static, and each one in and of itself has no seasonal change. She likes to till and plant and watch as her gardens grow and come to fruition. If we were to plight our troth, would she eventually hate my demesne?"

"My lord," said Flic, "you could always visit places where change is the rule. Too, can you devise a way to provide her with a place in the Winterwood where she could plant a garden and watch it change, watch it grow, then she might be content with such."

"A greenhouse," said Borel. "I could furnish her with a greenhouse."

"What is that?" asked Flic.

As Borel explained what a greenhouse was, Flic frowned and *umm*ed and *err*ed and *ahh*ed throughout and wondered why anyone would choose a glass-enclosed garden over one in an open field. The prince finished the leg of marmot and cleaned himself up and packed away his things, as well as the jar of honey. He then strung his bow and said, "Swamps at times are perilous, and I should be set for such." He turned to Flic. "Ready?"

"Ready," replied the Sprite, and at a silent signal, Buzzer took flight and headed into the twilight border.

They emerged from the crepuscular wall and into the swamp, the leaves adrip with water yet runnelling down from the bygone storm. In the damp air, Buzzer circled up and 'round and took a sighting on the sunglow seeping through the overcast, and then she flew into the environs of the mire, with Borel following, Flic riding in his now customary place on the prow of Borel's tricorn.

Into the bog strode the prince, even as gnats and biting flies and mosquitoes began to swarm about.

"Oh, my, this won't do," said the Sprite, and he launched into the air. He hovered a moment before Borel's face and said, "I will fetch something to deal with these dratted pests," and then darted away, while Borel, taking a sight on landmarks along the line set by Buzzer, pressed ahead.

Slogging through ooze, onward went Borel, now and then splashing through stagnant, green-scummed water, while all about large hoary trees—black cypress and dark swamp willow, and other such—twisted up out of the muck, looming, barring the dim morning light, their warped roots gnarling down out of sight into the slime-laden mud. A greyish moss dangled down from lichen-wattled limbs, like ropes and nets set to entangle and entrap the unwary. In spite of the morning chill and the dripping water all 'round, a faint mist rose up from the quag, reaching for, clinging to, clutching at, and swirling about those who would seek to pass through. In the surrounding saw grass and reeds, unseen things plopped and splashed and splatted, and snakes slithered from drowned logs into the torpid water, and now swarms of bloodsuckers filled the air like a grey haze.

Slapping at those that landed on his exposed skin, Borel paused long enough to don his gloves, and now only his face and ears and neck were bare. He slogged forward, keeping to his line of travel, taking new sightings when warranted to keep on a straight-line course.

Bearing what appeared to be a large, dark, and somewhat rotted toadstool, Flic came flying back, his entire face twisted in revulsion. And as he neared, a terrible stench filled the air. "Here, my lord, crush this and smear it wherever they bite."

Borel mashed the toadstool between his gloved hands, and a greenish mucus oozed out, and he gagged on the putrid stench.

"I am like to lose my breakfast," he gritted between clenched teeth. "What is this dreadful thing?"

"Blackstool," said Flic, gagging as well.

"I think I prefer the bloodsuckers," said Borel, gazing at the nauseating mess in his hands. Nevertheless, he wiped the viscous, snotlike gel over his face and ears and neck, nearly retching as he did so. He offered some to Flic, and the Sprite slathered his entire body with the toadstool phlegm.

And with their faces twisted in revulsion, on into the environs trod Borel, both man and Sprite swathed with the stench of blackstool to repel the ravenous mites. Oddly enough, Buzzer herself seemed unaffected by the malodor.

As the day wore on the sky slowly cleared, and the heat became oppressive. Clouds of swarming pests flew all about, and at times Flic would have to find more blackstool to keep the insects at bay. Yet now neither man nor Sprite noted the horrible stench, for as Borel said, "I think my nose is dead, slain by your cure, Flic."

The bog itself was a veritable maze of water and mire and land. Frequently did Buzzer return to keep them on course, for often Borel had to backtrack to get around some obstacle—quicksand, deep muck, fallen trees, snag-laden pools, and the like—but at times he had no choice but to wade through the scum-laden waters; and he would emerge with leeches clinging to his leathers, razor mouths clamped tight to the hide, attempting to suck away his life, but failing. Borel scraped them away with his stone knife, grateful that they didn't strike blood and draw even more pests into the frenzied mass swirling all about.

Slowly the clouds above parted, and the sun crept up into the sky and glared down upon the swamp, the mire steaming in response; and it seemed as if the air itself became too thick, too wet to draw a clean breath. The marsh heaved with gasses belching from slimy waters, bubbles plopping, foul stenches drenching the air. And Borel had no idea how far he had come, nor how far there was left to go. Yet he pressed onward, following the bee, for he had no choice but to push on through if he were to reach the place where grew pink-petaled shamrock and blushing white roses and thorn-laden blackberry vines.

As the sun reached the zenith, Borel paused to give Buzzer and Flic some honey, and to take some jerky for himself, and only the stench of the blackstool permitted the trio to eat, for insects swarmed even more thickly here in the heat of the day. And then Buzzer took to wing, and Borel pressed on, his thirst held in check by sips of water from leaves adrip, for he would not drink from the torpid sloughs of the mire.

It was midafternoon when the quag began to repeatedly quake, rhythmically, as if jolted and then jolted again and again and again, with measured regularity.

"What is it?" asked Flic.

"Something this way comes," said Borel. "Something large."

"I will see," said Flic, and he flew up and away as Borel continued following the beeline.

Long moments passed, the jolting of the ground getting heavier with each quaking thud, as of something enormous striding across the bog. Of a sudden Flic came winging, panic on his face. "My Lord Borel, you must hide! You must hide!"

"What is it, Flic? What comes?"

"I do not know, my lord, but all creatures flee before its steps, and yet it remains unseen, though its passage is marked by great gouts of splashed water and the bending away of boughs. And even though it is not visible, it is gigantic, for at times whole trees fall in its path, as if smashed down and crushed merely for being in the way. Oh, my prince, you must hide."

In that moment, the quaking stopped, and there came through the air a great snuffling, and then—*Thd-d-d! . . . Thd-d-d! . . .*—the massive steps resumed, now drawing closer.

"Oh, hide, my lord, it has caught your scent!" cried Flic.

"How does one hide one's scent, especially when covered with blackstool?" said Borel, and then he knew. And he stepped back to a great, wide bog hole he had passed 'round but moments before and waded into the putrid sludge until he was waist-deep; and great bubbles sluggishly rose to the surface and splatted open, reeking of the sulphurous stench of weeks-old rotten eggs.

THD-D-D! . . . THD-D-D! . . . The massive steps neared, and louder came the great snuffles.

High above, Flic darted back and forth and screamed, "Look out, my lord, oh look out, look out!"

And the trees before the quag hole bent aside as something unseen and unseeable pressed through—

THD-D-D! . . .

—and stopped—

—and snuffled—

—and silently Borel took a deep breath and submerged completely.

Long did he stay down, and he knew the monster stood somewhere above, turning its unseen head, if it had one, this way and that, snuffling, taking in air, trying to catch his scent. And Borel's lungs began to burn, to cry out for air, his diaphragm pumping uncontrollably, seeking to breathe in anything, air or not.

And just when he knew he could hold out no longer—

THD-D-D! . . . THD-D-D! . . . THD-D-D! . . . THD-D-D! . . . thd-d-d! . . . thd-d! . . . thd! . . .

—the unseen monster moved away, the jolting quake of its steps diminishing with every stride.

Borel surfaced and—*Ghhhuh!*—took in a great lungful of air and stood panting, drawing in the stench of rotten eggs with every sweet breath taken. And as he wiped his eyes free of quag, Flic came flying down.

"Oh, my lord, that was so close. I thought you gone for certain."

"Flic, my lad," said Borel, as he waded out from the sludge and sat down on the sodden shore, "although I appreciate your concern, it does little good for you to shriek 'look out, look out' when there is nought I can do."

"My lord?" said Flic, puzzlement on his features, "I was screaming?"

Covered with muck and mire, Borel began to laugh so hard he fell over backwards.

In that moment Buzzer came flying back to see what was the delay, and Borel pointed at the agitated bee and laughed all the harder.

As he made his way toward one of the stagnant pools, Borel noted the tracks of the creature, though, in the mire as they were, much mud and silt had oozed back into the depressions, and even as Borel looked on, the spoor vanished altogether. Whatever the monster had been, it had walked upon massive feet, yet whether it was beast or fowl or something altogether different, Borel could not say. The prince shook his head and said, "Here is something I hope never to meet face-to-face, unseen or not."

He went to scum-laden waters, where he sloshed about and ducked under to rinse the quag-hole muck away, and, after picking off the leech that had fastened to his cheek, he washed out his quiver and rinsed off the arrows. Somewhat cleaned of the muck, Borel resumed the trek, and biting, stinging insects swarmed about, the cloud of them maddened by the odor of blood seeping from his leech-wounded face. But then Flic returned with another blackstool, and the swarm was held off by the putrid stench of the snotlike salve.

And the day pressed on, and the sun slid down the sky, until long shadows fell across the bubbling, steaming mire. And as twilight came on, they still hadn't reached the far margin, and Buzzer came flying back and settled on Borel's hat.

"My lord," said Flic, "Buzzer says night comes and it is time to sleep. She has settled in for the eve."

"But we're not at the border yet," said Borel. "Can she not fly until we reach it?"

"Non, my prince, 'tis the way of bees."

"Then we will gamble," said Borel, "for I would not spend a single night in this swamp, most especially this one, with its unseen monsters lurking."

Lining up landmarks along the beeline, Borel slogged onward. And as the dusk deepened, ghostly blobs of light rose up from the swamp in the oncoming night and drifted among the waterlogged boles of dark, looming trees.

"Will-o'-the-wisps," said Flic. "Follow them not, for they would lead you to a watery grave."

"Corpse lanterns they are," murmured Borel, and he waded onward by the light of the stars, for the waning moon was not yet risen.

With both Flic and Buzzer sound asleep in the turned-up brim of his three-cornered hat, it was nigh mid of night when Borel reached the twilight wall. Exhausted, he pressed on through the marge to emerge into a broad grassland, the plants waist-high and slowly nodding in the wind. He took no steps onward, for had he strayed from the line, they would need to pass back into the mire once more for Buzzer to locate the way; and given the vagaries of twilight borders, a misstep in either direction could lead them to an entirely different place. And so, as the half-moon rose o'er the distant horizon, Borel flattened out a great swath of grass right next to the looming dark wall. Then with the Gnome-gifted thread, at the edge of the trodden area he bound together the tops of a great number of still-standing stalks and carefully set his hat with its precious cargo over the tip of the living sheaf, where ground-dwelling shrews and such could not get at them. Finally, yet slathered with the snotlike gel of blackstool, giving off a horrid stench that should drive most creatures away, he stretched out nearby and lay his head down to sleep.

21

Majority

"And where are we now?"

"In the Springwood, Chelle."

"Oh, my, it is so marvelous."

In the angling light of the stars and the risen half-moon Chelle looked out over a burgeoning forest, a realm where the gentle air of midspring wafted among newly leafed-out trees, a place of color so vivid that even in the wan glow shed down from above still she could see new life agrowing.

Chelle stood on the crest of the knoll onto which the hidden door had opened, and she slowly turned and breathed in the scent of the woodland, some sproutlings fresh and full of new promise, some trees old, their roots reaching deep, their great girths moss-covered, their branches spread wide and interlacing with others. Oak, she could see, proud and majestic, and groves of birch, silver and white; maple and elm stood tall, with dogwood and apple and wild cherry blossoms filling the air with their delicate scents.

Borel led her downward and in among the boles of old growth and the reed-thin saplings of the new. And among the roots running across the soil, crocuses bloomed, as did small mossy flowers, yellow and lavender and white. As they passed among the trees, now and again Borel pointed above, and there aroost were drowsing birds—chickadees and finches and sparrows alike. Somewhere nearby and hidden in bracken, a small stream burbled and splashed, as if singing in the night as it danced on its way to the shores of a distant sea. And there was a nip in the air, as of snow hidden away 'neath enshadowed ledges, lingering, clinging, desperately resisting a final melt.

Hand in hand, Borel led Chelle past the great bole of a huge elm and over a series of stepping-stones across a brook, the bourne singing its rippling song as it tumbled o'er pebbles and rocks. Toward a crepuscular wall they went, the twilight looming upward in the night.

"I thought you might like a glimpse of the mortal world, Chérie," Borel said as he came to the fringes of the marge.

"Will that not make us old and withered?" said Chelle, frowning but unhesitant.

Borel laughed. "Only if we stay overlong there. Yet I propose but a brief look."

Into the twilight border they went, the half-moon dimming as they strode therein, then brightening again as they began to emerge.

They came forward into a springlike forest, the air nippy, water runnelling as of snowmelt. Wild cherry and dogwood and other flowering scents filled the night.

"Hmm . . ." said Borel. "I think we somehow got turned about, for we are in Céleste's demesne again."

"Céleste?"

"My sister. The Springwood is her principality."

"Ah, I remember."

Borel shook his head and wheeled 'round to face the border again. "Come, Chelle. We will see the mortal world yet."

Hand in hand they strode into the twilight wall, only to once more emerge in the Springwood.

After two more tries, Borel gave up. He led Chelle into a wildflower glade, saying, "Mayhap, Chérie, the only way we can be together as we are is to remain in Faery."

Chelle knitted her brow. "Be together as we are? What do you mean, my love?"

Borel took a deep breath and then slowly let it out. The last time he had told Chelle that they were both dreaming, she had fled away, the dream dissipating, and he had wakened in regret. "Did I ever tell you of the day of my majority?" he said.

Chelle did not seem to notice he had changed the subject. "No, Borel. Was it a happy time?"

"Indeed."

"Then say on, my love."

"Ever since I was but a wee babe," said Borel, "among my friends I have always had Wolves as my companions."

"Wolves? But aren't they wholly vicious? Quite dangerous? Killers all?"

"Oh, no," said Borel, smiling. "I think tales of such are to frighten small children, and they carry this fear ever after."

A bit of a frown graced Chelle's features, and she said, "I did not know."

Borel grinned. "Would you like to see my Wolves?"

"Oh, yes," said Chelle.

Borel closed his eyes and stood a moment, and then opened them again. "There," he said, pointing.

Like shadows slipping among the trees, silently came the pack. Chelle drew closer to Borel and gripped his arm, yet she did not blench.

Tails awag, out from the forest trotted the Wolves and, yipping and fawning, they gathered 'round.

Borel squatted, and Chelle, holding on, of necessity was drawn down as well.

"This is Slate," said Borel, ruffling the big male's fur. "And here is Dark, his mate." Borel reached over and stroked her head. "And then we have Render and Shank and Trot, as well as Loll and Blue-eye."

Laughing, he fended off their licks, but Chelle seemed unable to do so, and she let go of Borel's arm and petted and stroked and hugged, her silvery mirth ringing as they gathered 'round and lapped her face and nuzzled her and took in her scent.

After moments of fondling the pack, Borel stood, and Chelle rose to her feet alongside. With a word from the prince, the

Wolves settled, most lying down, all but Trot who took station as ward. Chelle turned and embraced Borel there in the field of wildflowers and said, "Oh, my darling, they are quite splendid. Until now, I thought Wolves savage beasts, yet I see—"

Borel tilted her face upward and kissed her deeply. Then he clasped her tightly against him, his blood pounding in his ears.

Chelle held on to him fiercely and murmured, "I love you so, my Borel."

They stood without speaking for a moment, savoring the closeness of their embrace, and nought but the gentle breeze *shush*ing among the petals of wildflowers disturbed the stillness.

"I can hear your heart beat," whispered Chelle, her ear against his breast.

"It's a wonder it doesn't fly out of my chest," said Borel, "along with my soaring spirit."

Chelle laughed and broke away from his embrace, and whirled about as if dancing. Wolves' heads came up and cocked this way and that in curiosity at this gyrating behavior, and Chelle broke into peals of laughter, and she rushed to Dark and dropped to her knees and hugged the Wolf about the neck. Then she sat and looked up at Borel. "Oh, my prince, I love them. And they have been with you since you were a child?"

"Yes, Chérie," said the prince, and he settled down beside her. "My sire, Lord Valeray—you met him when we came unto your own sire's estate—anyway, my père thought I had an affinity for them when he saw me with a cub, I but a babe at the time. And so, he gathered this pack, cubs all, back then, and we grew to fullness together.

"Just ere I reached my majority, he asked me which of the Forests of the Seasons I would claim as my own. You see, I am the firstborn of his get, and so he gave me first choice.

"I and my pack, we visited each of the woodlands in turn, and together with the Wolves, I chose the Winterwood. For therein at times is a breathtaking silence, and running free through the snow is a joy I had not thought would ever be rivaled—that is, until I found you.

"And so, on the day of my coming of age, at the gala thrown

I announced my decision, and I have never regretted my choice, nor has the pack.

"Ah, what a wonderful day that was: we danced and ate and drank, and gifts were exchanged and songs were sung; games were played, and favors given, and promises made and kept.

"Oh, Chelle, the day I attained my majority is one I will never forget."

They sat in silence for a moment, and then Borel reached out and took Chelle's hand and kissed her fingers. Then he looked into her face, her eyes yet concealed behind a shadowy band. "What of your day of majority, Chérie? Was there dancing and joy?"

"Oh, indeed," replied Chelle. "It was just today, you know. All of us were gathered—my père and mère, our guests, my friends, and the staff—and the music soared, and we danced and sang and played at croquet and archery and quoits and games of blind tag and the like. My sire had invited some special friends, those who had aided in a struggle long past. Feylike they were, and they came to me and said that I had attained all they had wished for in a daughter of such a brave man—beauty and grace and joy and other such things, they claimed, though I am but an ordinary girl.

"And, oh, the party was gay and bright—"

Of a sudden, Borel found they were back in the shadowy stone turret.

"—and then Rhensibé came."

Chelle began to weep, and even as Borel stepped toward her, the walls began to waver, and—

—he awakened in a grassy field with dawn upon the land and the waning, slightly gibbous moon yet above.

In the Winterwood, Wolves startled awake, and Slate sprang to his feet and howled, and the others stood and joined him, all muzzles raised to the sky.

In his chamber, Arnot, steward of Winterwood Manor, awakened and leapt from his bed and rushed to his window. He threw open the sash, and looked out to see the Wolves milling about and calling, as if seeking someone lost.

To Arnot's right another window was flung wide, and Gerard, valet to Prince Borel, looked out upon the same scene.

And in that very moment, with Slate in the lead, and Dark and Render and Shank and Trot and Loll and Blue-eye following, off in the direction of the Springwood they sped, with clots of snow arcing high into the air from their flying feet.

Gerard looked at Arnot, his unspoken question unanswered, for neither man knew what had gotten into the pack, although they feared the worst, for the Wolves had returned five days past without the prince, and none at the manor knew ought of what had occurred.

As to the prince himself, he had gone on a mission to find someone he had dreamt was in peril, and whether or no he was yet on that quest and had merely sent the Wolves back . . . well, again none could say. Gerard and Arnot both thought it unlikely that Borel would leave the pack behind unless he had no other choice.

And so, they had assembled an armed search party, and it had marched away just two days gone—first to Hradian's cote, and then to the dream-seer Vadun beyond—and no word had yet come from them.

And even as steward and valet closed their windows, onward sped the pack, Wolves running through snow and toward the Springwood and a particular wildflower-laden glade, for surely the prince and his lady were there. After all, the pack entire had just moments before been at that place . . . or so to them it seemed.

22

Stone

"Rhensibé again?"

"Oui. Rhensibé again, Flic. And even as Chelle said the name, the dream began to fade, and there was nought I could do to stop it."

Flic frowned and looked up at Borel. "And she gave you no hint as to what or who this Rhensibé might be?"

"Non." Borel took another bite of cold marmot meat.

Buzzer landed next to Flic and began a waggle dance. After a moment, the bee stepped to the jar lid and began lapping honey. Flic dipped a finger into the sweetness and licked it off.

"Well?" said Borel around a mouthful of marmot.

"You are to be congratulated, my prince," said Flic. "Buzzer says we are not too far off the line. How you managed to hew to the course while wading through the swamp with nought but the light of stars to illume the way, well, that was quite a feat."

Borel laughed. "Flic, my lad, I used those same stars to guide my feet. —And speaking of swamps, is there a stream nearby where I can wash this putrid blackstool slime and the other foul leavings of that wretched mire from me?"

Flic shoved two fingers of honey into his mouth and then

said, "I'll look." Up he flew to a great height, and then arrowed off on an angle to the twilight wall behind. Buzzer continued lapping sweetness from the jar lid, though it seemed to Borel that Buzzer's eye facets remained locked upon him.

Just as Borel finished the last of the marmot meat, and Buzzer the last of the honey in the lid, Flic circled down. "There is a small thicket in a low spot yon, a mere therein. I believe it's large enough to be a bath for you, my lord."

"Ah, good." Borel capped the honey jar and packed away their meager belongings into the tiny, Gnome-given rucksack, which he then belted by rope to his waist. He strung his bow and took up his quiver and said, "Let us away."

And with both Buzzer and Flic riding the tricorn, off toward the thicket Borel marched, Flic pointing the way.

"We still do not know whether this Rhensibé is friend or foe," said Flic, as Borel strode through the hip-high grass, some stalks of which were topped with tiny blue flowers.

"Given Chelle's fright, I think Rhensibé is a foe," said Borel.

"Mayhap not, my lord," said Flic. "Rhensibé could merely be a bearer of ill tidings, and one should not blame the messenger for the message. But then again, perhaps you are right and Rhensibé is a foe, or a dreadful beast, a savage monster, or even a dumb brute."

Borel shook his head. "Not a dumb brute, Flic. Recall, Chelle said it was Rhensibé who told her there was but a moon left. So, no matter what or who this Rhensibé might be, he or she or it can speak. —Heed, my tiny one, we can speculate all day and still be no closer to the pith of it. When we reach Roulan's estate, then will we learn the truth."

"Perhaps so, my lord. Perhaps so. —Ah, there is the thicket."

With himself bathed and his leathers wiped off as best he could, Borel made ready to go. As the prince stepped from the thicket, Buzzer flew up and sighted on the sun and then shot away. Borel sighted along the beeline Buzzer took, and in the distance afar, he could see foothills rising up into the flanks of a low range of mountains, their sides green with foliage in the midmorn sunlight. Borel's heart beat a bit faster, for he seemed to recall that such forest-clad slopes lay behind Roulan's lands.

Taking up the Wolftrot he could sustain all day, he started toward a particular mountain peak along his line of sight.

Flic, jouncing but a bit on the tricorn prow, said, "Can you talk while you run, my prince?"

"Oui. It is how my père taught me to gauge my rate. 'Trot at a pace at which you can just carry on a running conversation,' he said, 'and then you will know you are at nigh the fastest clip you can keep to nearly all day.' "

"Ah, good," said Flic, "for I would ask you this: what is this 'majority' you spoke of?"

"It is a holdover from when humans lived only in the mortal world," said Borel, "and concerns the status of having reached full legal age, with attendant entitlements and responsibilities. It means one has the right to make his own choices, to go his own way, and on his own to decide what to do with his life. Yet it also means that one has obligations to fulfill to his kindred, his clan, his realm. Some also call it the coming of age."

"And when might that be?" said Flic.

"It is that point in time when a person becomes an adult," said Borel. "In the mortal world, it can be fifteen years for some, twelve or thirteen for others, or eighteen, or even twenty-one."

Flic laughed. "In the mortal world it sounds as if time is as irregular as it is here in Faery."

"Oh, no," said Borel, jogging 'round a small stand of trees. "What it really depends on are the needs of the culture; in some, majority arrives earlier than others. I would have been twenty-one in mortal years when I came of age. For my sisters, eighteen."

"Hmm . . ." said Flic. "I wonder what it would be in my case."

"Who knows, my lad," said Borel. "In Faery, a millennium can pass in but a single day, and a thousand or more days in but a single year."

Flic frowned and scratched his head and tried to imagine what a mortal year might be, and Borel jogged on, sighting on the crest of a particular mountain to hew unto the line flown by a special bee.

As the sun reached the zenith, it seemed they were no closer to the foothills and mountains, but distances can be deceiving in the realms of Faery. Even so, the thigh-high, blue-flowered grass of the plains had vanished arear, and now Borel loped across a lowland, turf and peat aground. Borel paused on the bank of a flowing rill and laid out some jerky and the honey jar, dribbling a bit of the golden sweetness into the lid. As Borel took a bite of the dried meat and chewed, and Flic dipped fingers into the sticky fluid and licked it away, Buzzer returned annoyed by the delay, but settled down to sip beside the Sprite.

Flic looked up at Borel and said, "Have you made love to her in your unfettered dreams?"

"Eh?"

"I asked if you and Chelle had yet made love in your unfettered dreams."

"Do you mean, have I bedded her?"

"Oui," said Flic, a Pixyish grin on his face.

"Non."

"Non? Why not? It is only a dream, and anything can happen in a dream."

"Flic, if it were an ordinary dream, then whatever happens happens. But this dream is not ordinary, for it is a dream she and I share. And in it I know I am dreaming, but she does not. And though I control aspects of the dream, I would not force myself upon her. You see, I do love her, and when or if we ever lie together, it will be a matter of free choice on both our parts. But for now, I am the only one who truly has free will, who truly is not subject to the heedless whims and wild emotions of a dream, and so I have not made love to her, and will not until she and I both choose to do so. Perhaps it will never be, but if it does so happen, then it will be when we meet in the flesh."

Flic burst out giggling, and when Borel raised a questioning eyebrow, "Meet in the flesh, indeed," gasped the Sprite, and giggled all the harder.

"Ah, Flic, you know what I mean," said Borel, smiling in spite of himself.

They ate without speaking for long moments, and then Borel said, "Let me tell you a tale."

"Oh, good! I love stories," said Flic. Then he frowned and added, "Unless they're bloody. This isn't a bloody one, is it?"

"Non. It is quite mild, my wee friend."

"Well, not too mild I hope. I mean, an Ogre getting smashed to a pulp and squirting out in all directions, well that's all right. Or a seven-headed Giant getting each of his heads chopped off, that's acceptable, too. Gushing blood, if it comes from Goblins and the like, that I wouldn't mind. Or ropelike guts spilling out from a gleaming sword cut, or sprayed wide from a swung axe, I find that quite to my liking, and—"

"Wait, wait," said Borel, flinging up a hand, "just what do you mean when you say you don't like bloody stories?"

"Oh, well, you know," said Flic, shrugging one shoulder, "like, say, a bee getting smashed . . . or a Sprite. Now *that* would be entirely too bloody."

Borel fell over backward, laughing, and Flic cried, "Well, it would be, you know!" And in a huff, the Sprite hitched around sideways to the laughing prince and crossed his arms and jutted out his chin, a glaring pout on his face.

Buzzer merely kept lapping at the honey.

Finally, Borel sat back up, and he held out a hand of apology to Flic, the Sprite to snort in response and turn his face ever further away.

The prince sighed and took another bite of jerky. He chewed a moment and swallowed and said, "Once upon a time there was a king in the West—that means duskwise—who heard of a princess of surpassing beauty and wisdom in the distant East—dawnwise. It was said that this princess had made up her mind that she would never marry unless the man who asked for her hand could answer her question. Her father decreed that if a suitor was unsuccessful then his head would be forfeit and would rest on a pike outside the city gates. So far, many a man had tried, but all had failed, and all had died at the hands of her cruel sire, which pleased him much, for this way he would not lose the wisdom of his daughter in his rule of the kingdom."

Borel paused and took another bite of jerky. The scowl had left Flic's features the moment he heard of heads on pikes; even so, he yet remained with his face turned away from the prince. After a moment, Borel swallowed and said, "The king in the West, intrigued by this story, went to see for himself. He rode his gallant steed over many miles, crossing burning deserts, climbing snowy mountains, swimming deep rivers, and faring o'er endless plains, but at last he found himself at the gates of a great city in the East wherein it was said the princess dwelled. And outside the portals on hundreds of pikes, some with blood yet dripping, were impaled the heads of hundreds of would-be suitors, all who had failed to answer one simple question."

Again Borel paused for a bite of jerky, and at mention of blood yet dripping, Flic had turned completely 'round and now faced Borel, eagerly awaiting the next part of the story.

"The king from the West then entered the city and rode his horse to the palace, where he dismounted and approached the guard and asked to pay his respects to the king in the East as well as to his daughter. Learning from the guard that this petitioner was a powerful king from the West, the king in the East bade him to enter, and all the courtiers and advisors made way, and into the audience chamber the Western king strode.

"There on a throne of her own near her sire's chair of state sat the princess, the most lovely creature the king from the West had ever seen. For her part, the princess was taken by this handsome man, and once again she regretted the pledge she had made in a fit of pique so long past, a pledge that her cruel sire would not let her rescind and who enforced the consequences with the keen edge of a headsman's sword."

Borel paused, and Flic demanded, "What happened? What happened?"

After another bite and a long chew, with the Sprite fidgeting about and barely able to contain himself, Borel went on:

" 'I ask for the hand of your daughter,' said the Western king, and all the courtiers gasped, and tears welled in the eyes of the princess, for she knew what fate awaited those who failed, and she would not have this man die on her account. And so she warned him that no man could answer that which she asked.

"Nevertheless, the Western king insisted, and so she had no choice but to pose the question to him."

Borel took a bite of black bread and chewed, while Flic jumped to his feet and demanded, "The question, the question, what was the question?"

Borel smiled and chewed and Flic huffed and dithered from foot to foot, and finally the prince swallowed.

"And so, the Eastern king called his headsman to the chamber so that there would be no delay when this latest suitor failed. And when the black-hooded man entered bearing his great curved sword, the king turned to his daughter and bade her to pose the question.

"Sighing, the princess, her voice as lovely as that of a lark, again begged the Western king to reconsider, but he insisted, for she was even more lovely and wise than he had ever dreamed. And so she posed her question: 'What is it that women want?' "

Borel paused once more, and Flic screamed, "The answer, the answer, what was his answer?"

Borel smiled and said, "Have you forgiven me, Flic?"

"Yes, yes, but I must have the answer! Tell me now or I will burst!"

"Oh, well," said Borel, "we can't have you bursting all over the place. Buzzer might take ill to such a thing, and I would not have her enraged."

"Then tell me!" shrieked Flic.

"Why, what would your own answer be, my tiny friend?"

Flic flung his arms wide and shrilled, "How would I know? How would *anyone* know? Isn't that the mystery of the ages?"

"Indeed it is, Flic, but you see, the Western king knew the answer."

Flic hopped from foot to foot and demanded, "And . . . ?"

"The Western king simply bowed gracefully to the princess and said, 'My lady, what all women want is to be masters of their own fates.'

"Tears of relief sprang into the eyes of the princess, and she turned to her sire and said, 'As you know, Father, that is the answer I am seeking.' "

Flic's mouth flopped opened in surprise. "That's it? That's the answer to the mystery of the ages?" Then he knitted his brows together and plopped down and peered at the ground and said, "How utterly simple. I never would have thought of that."

"The tale is not yet done, Flic," said Borel, "for an even more perilous challenge lay ahead for the Western king."

Flic's head jerked up. "What? Not done? Something more perilous?"

"Indeed," said Borel.

"Well, then tell me, tell me."

" 'That is the answer I am seeking,' said the princess. But her sire ground his teeth in rage and slammed his fist to the arm of the throne, and he growled and said, 'Bah! Indeed he has guessed the answer to *your* question, but now you must pose to him the dilemma *I* set.' And all the court gasped, for they did not know there was a second response needed to win the hand of the princess, for no one else had ever gotten this far.

"Once again tears sprang into the eyes of the princess, this time tears of sorrow, for at last here was the man she had dreamed of—young and handsome and wise and a king in his own right. Nevertheless, she assented to her sire's demand, and of a sudden she changed into the most repulsive creature anyone could imagine. Members of the Eastern court fell in swoons or ran away screaming or dropped to the floor begging for mercy. Yet the Western king stood staunchly and said, 'Speak the dilemma, my lady.' And the monstrous creature croaked, 'I will take on this form half of the day'—and she changed back into a lovely maiden—'and this form the other half. You can have me at your side during the daylight marks as a lovely companion, lending your court elegance and wisdom, but in your bed in the nighttime marks you will have me as this'—and once again, she changed into the horrid monster. 'Or you can have me at your side as a hideous thing in the daylight hours, sending all in your court screaming away'—she shifted again to the beautiful princess—'but in your bed you will have me as you see me now. And so, if we are to marry, which will it be?' "

Borel paused again, and Flic said, "Oh, my, oh, my, what a dilemma that truly is. Which did the king choose?"

"Were you in his place, Flic, how would you choose to respond?"

Flic's face twisted in an agony of indecision. "Loathing by day and allurement by night? Or allurement by day and loathing by night? Oh, oh, oh, Prince Borel, I simply could not choose."

"Exactly so," said Borel, smiling, "you have hit upon the answer."

Flic's eyes flew wide. "I have?"

"Indeed, for the Western king said, 'Either way I would love you, my darling, and so the choice is yours.'

"The beautiful princess laughed and ran down the steps to the Western king and threw herself into his arms and said, 'Then I choose to keep this form both day and night.' But her enraged sire shouted in fury, for the Western king had again responded correctly. And, black in the face, the Eastern king leapt up from his throne and hurtled down to the headsman and grabbed the great curved sword, and as he raised it to slay them both, of a sudden he clutched at his head and screamed and fell dead of wrath at their feet.

"And so, the Western king and the Eastern princess became rulers o'er two lands: one in the East, one in the West, and they lived in happiness the rest of their lives."

Borel fell silent, and Flic said, "I never would have thought of either of his answers, Lord Borel. I didn't know what women want, and I certainly couldn't choose between day and night." He looked up to see Borel smiling faintly, one eyebrow cocked. Flic sighed and said, "You told me this story for a reason, didn't you."

As he packed away their goods, Borel nodded and said, "I did at that, my friend. You see, just as the Western king knew that women need to make their own free choices—and that's what the tale is all about, making free choices—so do I know that as well. In the dream we share, Chelle is somehow ensnared, and so I think she has little choice concerning what occurs. But as for me, I do have choices, and I will not force them upon her, no matter that it is just a dream. And when we set her free, awake or asleep, it will be the same."

Borel stood and looked toward the foothills and the mountains beyond and said, "Time to go."

Buzzer flew up and 'round and then arrowed off toward the range. And Borel, with Flic riding on the prow of the tricorn, loped o'er the land after.

It was late afternoon when Borel swam and Flic flew across a meandering river and came in among the hills. And although they had passed scattered farmsteads here and there, still Borel had not veered from the course set by the bee. When they reached the distant bank, Borel could see at an angle upslope a league or so away the mouth of a narrow vale. It was the dell of Lord Roulan's estate, or so he believed.

As he redonned his clothes and took up his belongings from the driftwood log he had used in making the crossing, Borel said, "At last, my friend, thanks to you and Buzzer, we have come nigh the goal. Yon leftward upstream and well beyond that distant croft lies the town I remember, and at the top of this long slant is the vale of Roulan's manor and gardens." He shouldered his quiver and said, "Yet now we must deal with the daggers, whatever they might be."

"I will scout ahead, my prince," said the Sprite, "and seek out hidden dangers, and warn you of peril, should there be any."

"Well and good, Flic. Yet 'ware, for hazard may lurk unseen."

Flic darted up and up, gaining height before winging toward the dell.

Borel continued his Wolftrot, angling up and cross-slope, the mouth of the vale ever nearing. In less than half a candlemark he had drawn almost even with the gape, but Flic had not yet returned, and a feeling of foreboding gnawed at the edges of Borel's mind, for surely the Sprite should have been back by now.

And so the prince nocked an arrow and slowed as he reached the shoulder of the ridge forming one side of the valley.

And then he heard weeping, and rounding the turn he came upon a desolate Flic sitting high upon a boulder, Buzzer at hand. As Borel stepped close, the Sprite looked up, tears in his eyes. "Oh, my prince, Buzzer says this is the place, but we have flown the entire length, and there is no manor, no gardens, no pink-petaled shamrock nor blushing white roses nor thorn-laden blackberry vines. There is nothing at all." Once more Flic burst into tears.

His heart pounding in dread, Borel stepped forward and 'round the shoulder of the ridge and gazed down the full of the dell, his eyes seeing nought but a bare stone vale, as if the land had been stripped down to raw bedrock, with nothing else whatsoever therein.

23

Black Wind

Stunned, Borel stood long moments staring into the stone valley. Finally, he said, "Perhaps there is a glamour on this vale to fool any would-be rescuers." With arrow set to string, the prince walked into the barren dell, its surface hard and rough, solid, uneven. Down the center he walked, on a line along which he remembered Roulan's manse to be, and if this place were enspelled, then soon or late he should collide with the mansion. Deep into the vale he strode, all the way to the end, and no unseen manor, gardens, trees, or blackberry briars did he come upon.

Yet he was convinced that this was the place wherein such things should be, for this was Lord Roulan's dale, of that he was certain.

But now it was nought but bare stone, nought but bedrock, the entire valley stripped.

Despairing of ever finding Chelle, he stood long moments in dejection, his head bowed, his heart in despair. But then he straightened his shoulders and turned on his heel and strode back toward the mouth of the dell.

When he came to Flic and Buzzer he said, "There is yet a fortnight, a sevenday, and part of one ere the moon rises full. We will find her yet. Let us go to the nearest farmstead and speak with the crofter. Perhaps it is common knowledge what has happened herein."

Flic dried his eyes and silently spoke to Buzzer, and they took station on Borel's tricorn.

Down from the stone vale Borel strode, following the trace of a road, now overgrown with weeds and grass, as if no cart, no wagon, no horse had traversed it for years, and by the time they came upon the farm and its dwelling, the sun lay low in the sky and cast long shadows o'er the land.

Out to one side and slightly back of a thatch-roofed cottage stood a coop for chickens. Beyond the coop sat a small byre, a single cow within. Fields of crops stretched away left and right and aft. Even as Borel passed through the gate and stepped toward the doorstone of the house, he heard the ringing of a bell—likely a dinner bell—and off to the right he saw a man carrying a hoe walking through a bean field toward the humble abode, a brown dog racing ahead and barking.

As the man got closer, Borel called out a greeting, and in the cote a window curtain was pulled aside and a ginger-haired woman peered out and then withdrew. Moments later the door opened, and the woman stepped onto the stoop at the same time the dog arrived, its hackles up. Snarling, it stood between Borel and the woman. *"Brun, se taire!"* she commanded the dog, but the animal continued to gnarl. Then Borel growled a word, and the dog whined and promptly sat down just as the man came and stood beside the woman, and they both sized up this stranger. When their gazes fell upon Flic, their eyes flew wide in amaze, and the woman managed to say, "Oh, my, a Sprite. A Field Sprite. Have you come to bless our farm?"

"I would be pleased to do so," said Flic, "though I've not done such before."

"Well, don't just stand there, Maurice," said the woman, elbowing the man. "Invite them in. Invite them in. They've come to bless our farm." And then without waiting for him to do so, the woman stepped past the dog—"One side, Brun"—and said to Borel, "We've supper on the table, all but the biscuits, and I can easily set two more places." She took him by the arm and pulled him in through the door, Maurice following.

They came into what appeared to be a well-kept, three-room cottage—the main room taking up perhaps half the interior, the kitchen to the right along one wall, and a single bedroom to the front on the left, a workroom adjacent to the rear, these two chambers with a loft above.

"And who might you be, Sieur?" asked the woman as she drew Borel inward, then stepped away toward a cupboard.

Ere Borel could respond, "He is Prince Borel of the Winterwood," said Flic. "And I am named Flic, and this is Buzzer, my friend and guardian."

As Borel gave a slight bow, the woman's mouth fell agape. But she quickly rallied and called out to her husband who was standing just behind Borel, "Take off your hat, Maurice, for a prince has brought a Field Sprite with his bee to bless our farm."

"Monsieur Maurice," said Borel, turning to the man and acknowledging him.

The man doffed his hat, revealing a bald head, which he bobbed, and managed to say, "My lord."

Borel turned to the woman. "And your name, Madame?"

The woman giggled and blushed and awkwardly curtseyed. "Charité, my lord."

"Well, Madame Charité, it has been some time since I've had a good hot meal, and I thank you for it."

"Lord Prince Borel," said Charité, "it is nought but biscuits and sausage gravy and onions and string beans."

"Ah, Madame Charité, *biscuits avec de la sauce aux saucisses, avec des oignons et des haricots verts, c'est magnifique!*" said Borel.

Charité beamed, and then turned to Flic and said, "Sieur Flic, I'm not familiar with Field Sprite fare; what will you have, you and your bumblebee?"

"Buzzer will take honey," said Flic. "As for me, I think I'll try a biscuit, if you please."

"Slathered with butter and honey, they're right good," said Maurice. He walked away and set the hoe in the workroom, his hat atop the handle, then turned to the prince and said, "And you, Sieur, I have a bit of wine cooling in the well. Would you have some?"

"Indeed," said Borel, grinning.

Maurice pulled out the chair at the head of the table and said, "Have a seat, my lord, while I go fetch the bottle."

Borel shook his head, and drew a chair along one side of the board and sat and said, "I'll not take your place as the master of the house. The side of the table will do."

A smile swept over the face of the crofter, and he flushed with pride. "As you wish, Sieur. As you wish." He stepped through the back door and out.

"Brun," said Borel, and the dog came meekly, its tail low but wagging. Borel spoke a few gutturals to the dog, and lifted the tricorn from his head and said to Flic, "He now knows you and Buzzer are friends."

"Good, I was wondering," said the Sprite, and he stepped off the hat and onto the table, Buzzer following.

"My lord," said Charité, her eyes wide in startlement, "you speak the language of dogs? Are you a *magicien*?"

"Non, Madame, no magicien am I, though I do speak a bit of Wolf, and dogs seem to know what I mean. My sire tells me that long past all dogs were Wolves."

"My, my," said Charité, "who would have known?" She peered into the brick oven and said, "Ah, good, the biscuits are ready."

"I speak Bee," said Flic.

Maurice came back in with the wine.

Maurice frowned. "Thirteen, fourteen years past, I can't say exactly. Reckoning time in terms of the mortal world, well, it escapes me." He spoke in a near whisper, for Flic was asleep on the table next to a biscuit slathered with honey and butter, the whole of it entirely too much for him to consume but for a small portion. At his side Buzzer dozed.

"Maurice was never very good at it," said Charité, her own voice low. "Now, me, I think it was perhaps closer to twelve years agone, or just under. It was the day of the big doings up at the manor, for it was when the duke's daughter, Michelle was her name, came into her majority."

"Michelle?" said Borel.

"Indeed, my lord prince," said Charité, "though everyone I know, from castle to town to farm, has called her Chelle since she was but a wee babe."

"Michelle . . . my Chelle. I see. —But tell me, what came about? How came the vale to be nought but stone? What would cause such?"

Both Maurice and Charité made warding gestures, and Charité looked about to see if ought were lurking in the shadows and, finding nothing, said in a whisper, "Something wicked, that's what." And husband and wife looked at one another and nodded.

"We don't go up there," said Maurice, and again he made a warding gesture.

"As mortals would reckon it, not for nigh these twelve years," added Charité, her own warding gesture joining his.

Borel frowned, and counted on his fingers, then said, "Could it have been eleven years and ten moons past?"

Maurice shrugged, but Charité nodded and said, "Could be."

"Ah, that's when the Winterwood was cursed, and on that same day . . ." His words fell to silence, and then he said, "It was some twenty years ago when I and my père were here visiting Lord Roulan; I know it was then, for within a year he and my mère vanished."

"Vanished?" said Maurice.

"Oui. They were enchanted and gone for nearly nineteen years altogether, but now they are back, discovered by my soon-to-be-sister-in-law Camille who found the way to break the enchantment."

"There's a story here for the telling," said Maurice, replenishing Borel's cup of wine.

"Perhaps someday I will," said Borel, nodding his thanks, "but let me see if I am right.

"Chelle would have been about ten at the time Père and I

were at Duke Roulan's manor twenty years back. And so, when another eight years passed, then she would have reached her majority. I believe that would have been nearly twelve years ago—eleven years, ten moons, and a handful of days to be exact."

Maurice turned up a hand, but Borel said, "It all seems right, if I have correctly reckoned the mortal years."

Borel looked to Charité for confirmation, and she nodded, then stood and stepped to her bedchamber and came back to the table, bearing a kerchief, which she used to cover Flic. Next to him, Buzzer shifted, but didn't waken, the bee dormant for the night.

"Tell me," said Borel, "what happened that day?"

"Well," said Maurice, "Charité and I, we took two of these very chairs to the yard and sat and watched as the lords and ladies and their attendants all rode past on their fine horses or in their splendid carriages, all heading up the road toward the manor. Brun was a pup at the time, and he was quite excited by all the doings going by."

"Tell him about the Fey ladies on the horses with silver bells," said Charité.

"I was just getting to it," replied Maurice. He turned to Borel and said, "As Charité says, there were a number of Fey ladies on horses bedecked with silver bells that rode past, the ladies laughing together as if sharing a great secret."

"They were magical, I think," said Charité. "Fairies or some such I would guess, what with their silky gowns flowing in the wind and such, the silver bells all achime. I believe they were the same ones who attended the birth, though we didn't see them at that time."

"The birth?" said Borel.

"Oui, of the duke's daughter," replied Charité. "It is said that Fey women came then."

"Regardless," said Maurice, "there was many a rich lord and lady went past, as well as the Fey Folk with their tilted eyes and golden hair and delicate ways."

There came a lowing from without, and Maurice said, "Oh,

my, what with all the talk, I forgot to milk Madame Vache. I will go do it now." Maurice stood and added, "Much like that day, I was milking when it happened."

"When what happened?" asked Borel.

"Why, when Charité called me to come and see," said Maurice. "When I stepped out from the byre, Charité screamed and pointed up toward the duke's vale, and I turned and looked." Maurice's eyes widened in memory, and he thumped the table and said, "And that's when the great black wind came, and the valley turned to stone; either that, or the entire dell just up and flew away, dirt, plants, manor and all."

Jolted awake by the thump, "Hradian?" asked Flic, sitting up and rubbing his eyes, the Sprite hearking back to the story Borel had told him. "I mean, with a black wind and all, it seems the same sort of thing to me."

"No, not Hradian," said Borel, grimly, "but her sister instead. I deem this is her curse, the one I read of in Hradian's journal."

"Could Hradian's sister be this Rhensibé?" asked Flic.

"Mayhap," said Borel.

"Rhensibé?" hoarsely whispered the crofter, and both he and his wife made warding signs.

24 Moonlight

"They say she's a *sorcière,* this Rhensibé," whispered Charité.

"Oui. In town there are some who claim she has some sort of grievance against the duke," said Maurice, "or she did, until the valley turned to stone."

"You know this for a fact?" asked Borel.

"Well, rumor would have it be so," said Maurice.

Charité nodded her agreement and said, "I think someone—perhaps one of those Fey ladies—anyway, someone said—'round the time of Lady Chelle's birth I think—that Rhensibé's rancor against the duke goes back to a distant time."

Flic looked at Borel. "What was it Hradian wrote in her journal about her sister?"

Borel took a deep breath and intoned, " 'On this same day in a linked act, my elder sister cast a great spell upon Roulan and his entire estate through his daughter Chelle, on this the day of her majority'—"

Maurice and Charité gasped, and Maurice said, "Ominous words, them."

"That great spell had to be the black wind," said Flic. "But we interrupted you, Lord Borel. There was more."

"Oui," said the prince, "there was more. 'This vengeance is so very sweet, for Roulan was the accomplice of Valeray the Thief. And now all are ensorcelled and well warded; and since none can find Roulan's daughter—or even if they do, all attempts to rescue her from the turret will fail—then when the rising full moon sits on the horizon eleven years and eleven moons from now . . .' " Borel paused, then added, "That's as far as I read in the journal ere Hradian came."

"And Hradian is . . . ?" asked Maurice.

"A witch," replied Borel. "A very powerful witch."

Maurice and Charité nodded and looked at one another, and Charité said, "Another sorcière."

"Like Rhensibé is said to be," added Maurice.

"Perhaps sisters," said Flic.

"They must have had a pact," said Borel. "My sire and the duke were both cursed, all for what they did during the struggle against Orbane."

"Orbane!" exclaimed Maurice and Charité together, making warding signs. And Maurice pled, "Oh, Lord Borel, speak of him no more, for we would not sear our minds with thoughts of that foul magicien nor have his name uttered in this house. It might draw him here."

"But he is cast out," said Borel, "banished to the Castle of Shadows beyond the Black Wall of the World."

Both Maurice and Charité moaned in fear, and from under the table, Brun whined, the dog sensing his masters' dread. Charité said, "Oh, my lord prince, we will not hear any more, else he himself is likely to appear." And she grabbed Maurice by the arm and together they fled to their bedchamber and slammed the door to, and left Brun sitting without and whimpering.

The dog looked over his shoulder at Borel, seeking reassurance. Borel growled a word or two, and Brun settled down.

A moment later, the door opened a crack and Brun jumped to his feet. Through the gap a blanket was tossed into the main room, and Charité called, "Sieur, you may sleep in the loft," and she slammed shut the door again, abandoning Brun. The dog came to Borel and looked up at him, and the prince reached down and stroked the animal's head.

From outside, there came a persistent lowing, and Borel and Flic heard the slide of a window sash. Borel looked at Flic and said, "It is Maurice. He's gone out through the window to milk the cow."

Flic yawned and said, "Speaking of windows, would you open that one a bit?"

"Ah, yes, fresh air," said Borel.

"Or something of the sort," said Flic.

As Borel stepped to the sash and lowered it, the jamb sliding into the recess below, Flic lay back down near dormant Buzzer and pulled the kerchief to his chin and yawned and said, "Good night." Then he grinned and added, "Pleasant dreams."

"Good night," said Borel, and he took up the blanket and climbed the ladder to the loft. And even as Madame Vache out in the byre quit bellowing now that Maurice had come to relieve her of her milk, and as Brun took station under the table and turned 'round several times before flopping down, Borel fell fast asleep.

In the faint breeze, water lapped softly against the shore. The just-risen half-moon cast a long glimmer of light across the rippling surface. "I thought we might take a stroll by this lakeside," said Borel.

"Oh," said Chelle. "I was rather hoping this night I would see the Winterwood."

"Perhaps another time, my love," said Borel. "You see, I would rather take you there when I find you at last."

Chelle laughed. "But I am not lost, my lord. Must we play hide-and-seek ere you show me your demesne?"

Borel's laughter joined hers. Still, he did not dare say more, else she might wrench them both back into the turret, wherever it might be. He closed his eyes a moment, and then opened them again. "I think there is a small skiff just past this stand of reeds. Would you join me in a row?"

"Oh, yes, my Borel. I would."

Borel frowned a moment. "Ere we go out onto the water, I need to ask: can you swim?"

"Indeed," said Chelle, and of a sudden she stood unclothed on a bluff above the lake, her golden hair gleaming in the moonlight, her firm young breasts high, her aureoles pale, her narrow waist gracefully flaring into slim rounded hips tapering down to her long slender legs, a golden triangle at her cleft. Borel's breath shuddered inward, for she was splendid. Laughing, she dived outward and down into the pellucid waters of the lake.

Borel found himself naked beside her, his blood pulsing, a fire in his loins, and in the water he took her in his arms and kissed her hungrily as they sank below the surface, his erect manhood pressing against her—

No! I cannot do this!

Borel wrenched himself awake, and he groaned softly in his desire. Yet—*Great Mithras, what have I done to Chelle? Is she trapped in a place of my making? I must return to that dream. I must!*

Borel tried to will himself to sleep, yet he could not force slumber, and he lay with his mind racing, wondering, anxiety gnawing at his viscera, his breath rasping in disquiet.

This will never do.

Down from the loft he clambered, and as he crossed the floor he glanced at the table—*Flic is missing. Buzzer is here, but Flic . . . ?* Borel looked at the open window, moonlight shining in. *Mayhap he has gone outside to relieve himself.*

With Brun at his side, Borel stepped into the yard, his mind yet churning in turmoil, his gaze irresistibly drawn toward the mouth of Lord Roulan's vale. He glanced at the waning half-moon, now risen some four fists above the horizon—*Two candlemarks past mid of night*—its light angling across the slope and foothills above and the mountains beyond.

Shaking his head, he turned and walked out to the byre, Brun running ahead. Madame Vache stood inside adoze.

Yet Borel couldn't keep his mind off his beloved, and he looked once more at the vale. *Not only might she be cast adrift in a dream of my own making, but somewhere in Faery, or mayhap not, she is lost to me as well, and I need to find her. And there are but some twenty-one days until the moon is full again. Oh, Michelle, my Chelle, where are you?*

Then Borel saw a faint glitter flashing through the air . . . nearing. *What can that . . . ?*

He watched as it drew close, a tiny flickering luminescence, or perhaps moonlight glancing off—

Wings! It is Flic.

The Sprite sped toward the stead, and then veered toward Borel. Now Brun saw the glimmer, and he set up a din at this strange—

"Brun," said Borel, and then a guttural word, and the dog immediately stopped.

Flic flew down and alighted on Borel's shoulder.

"I thought it would be worth a look," said the Sprite, "yet I found it unchanged, nought but stone." He sighed in dejection and said, "I was wrong."

"Wrong about what, Flic?"

"I've heard tales of enchanted people and places and things that only reveal their true form or can only be seen or only show up in moonlight. It seems Lord Roulan's estate is not one of those. Either that, or perhaps this moon is simply not full enough for the vale to appear."

25

Adieu

"You flew over the vale?"

"Yes, and along it, too. I went there to see if all would reappear in the light of the moon. And as I said, it did not."

"Ah, then, that's why you had me open the window. Why didn't you tell me what you planned?"

"I didn't want to raise any false hopes," said Flic. He sighed and added, "Would that my own lifted hopes had been realized, yet they were not. —But you, Lord Borel, what are you doing out and about?"

"My dream got away from me," replied Borel. "I'm afraid I might have stranded Chelle in a place of my making."

"How so?"

"I nearly did that which I said was unprincipled: bed her on the whim of a dream. When I realized what I was about to do, I wakened. And so she may be—I don't know where—lost in my dream as well as in reality."

"Gracious me," said Flic. "Well then, you're just going to have to go back to sleep and rescue her from the quandary of your making."

"I tried, Flic, but sleep now eludes me. That's why I am out in the night, trying to achieve a measure of serenity so that I can fall aslumber. But my mind is racing helter-skelter, and stillness of my spirit eludes me. What I need is"—Borel turned about, searching—"Ah, I see."

Borel stepped to a woodpile, where an axe stood embedded in a upright stump. "Fly, my friend," he said. "Labor will tire my body and perhaps my mind."

"As you wish, my lord," said Flic, and he launched himself from Borel's shoulder and into the air and flew 'round the cottage and in through the open window.

Borel wrenched the axe free from the chopping block and took up a billet. "Step back, Brun," he said, adding a guttural, and the dog moved away.

Shortly, the night air was filled with the sound of hewing as Borel split logs and stacked wood. Maurice drew aside the curtain on the bedroom window and peered out, then he turned to say something to Charité as he let the fabric fall back.

The moon had risen another two fists when Borel embedded the blade of the axe once more into the chopping block. He sat long moments in the cool air while gazing at the moon, and then went back into the house, Brun following. Into the loft he crawled and lay down to sleep, yet he tossed and turned fitfully, and did not dream again that night.

"My lord prince," said Charité as she fixed a great breakfast of eggs and sausage and warmed up the biscuits, "I want to apologize for our fearful behavior last eve. You may call us foolish for being in such dread over . . . er . . . um . . . the magicien who shall not be named, but strange things happen in Faery, such as the duke's valley turning to stone and such. And so, we know firsthand, do Maurice and I, that terrible things can come about when sorcières and magiciens and other such are involved, to say nothing of strange creatures, like Trolls and Ogres and Goblins and—"

"Madame Charité, give it no second thought," said Borel, "for you are right in fearing Orb— pardon me, in fearing the magicien who shall not be named."

"Well, Maurice and I, we just thought it best to not tempt fate," said Charité.

In that moment, Maurice came through the door, Flic riding on his left shoulder, Buzzer on his right, another bucket of milk in hand. "Madame Vache, she seems full morning and night," he said as the Sprite and the bee flew to the table. "It means more butter and cheese and curds to sell in town . . . and buttermilk," he added, as he covered the pail with a cloth and set it by the churn.

"The cream, it's quite delicious," said Flic, and glanced at Buzzer. "And she agrees."

"Good morrow, Monsieur Maurice," said Borel.

Maurice bobbed his head and returned the greeting and said, "I thank you, my lord, for setting aside a goodly amount of wood."

"Did I wake you? If so, I am sorry. I was working out a problem."

"A problem, my lord?"

"Yes. You see, I thought that I had reached an impasse, a cul-de-sac, but as I wielded your axe, I realized I hadn't. At least, not quite. I will go to the town and see if there is something of truth to the rumor you spoke of, something that might send me on my way. Perhaps I can find someone therein who knows ought of Lord Roulan and Chelle, or where this Rhensibé might dwell."

"Oh, my lord prince," said Charité, as she ladled out great spoonfuls of eggs and slid sausages onto Borel's plate, " 'fi were you, I wouldn't have ought to do with Rhensibé. But as to perhaps finding Lord Roulan's estate and the duke and his daughter—assuming the vale and all were carried away by that black wind—well, that's a noble goal, and we wish you good fortune in that."

Her eyebrow cocked, Charité looked at Flic and slightly lifted her platter of breakfast fare, but he waved her off, saying, "None for me, thanks. I'm full of rich cream from Madame Vache, and so is Buzzer."

"As you wish, Sieur Flic," Charité said, and she spooned out eggs and sausage to Maurice, while he passed the biscuits to Borel.

Charité looked at wagging-tail Brun and said, "You can have what's left over, Monsieur Dog."

* * *

"Come look!" called Maurice.

Borel placed four copper pennies on the table, and then took up his bow and stepped through the back door to join Maurice and Charité.

They stood behind the cottage and watched as Flic and Buzzer flew over the fields of crops and the byre and cote, over the pond and well, and over the green pasture where Madame Vache grazed contentedly. They could hear the Sprite calling out something or mayhap even singing, Buzzer's humming wings accompanying Flic. Yet what the Sprite cried or sang, they could not quite hear, though it was definitely lilting words of a sort, mayhap in a language unfamiliar.

Finally, Flic and Buzzer came spiralling down and landed on Borel's tricorn, and Flic said, "There, I've blessed your entire stead, Monsieur Maurice and Madame Charité. What good it'll do, I cannot say, for I've not done such a thing until now."

"Oh, Sieur Sprite, we thank you, we thank you," gushed Charité happily, beaming in gratitude. She elbowed Maurice in the ribs, and he humbly added his own thanks as well.

Borel made a slight bow and said, "Madame, Monsieur, I thank you for your hospitality, and if I am ever back this way, Maurice, I will tell that tale of my père and mère's enchantment and how Camille managed to dispel the glamour. But now we must hie to the town, for Chelle is entrapped somewhere and I would set her free." Borel then turned to Brun and spoke a word or two, gutturals mixed within, and the dog seemed to take heart, and his tail curled up o'er his back.

Charité rushed into the cottage and then came running back out, a cloth sack in hand. "There's biscuits and boiled eggs and dollops of honey in a jar and apples and cheese and a bit of salted bacon. I wouldn't want you to go hungry on your way to town."

"Mother," said Maurice, "town is but a half a morn away, and I am sure they won't starve ere they get there."

"Well, you never know, Maurice," snapped Charité. She turned to Borel and her voice softened. "What with enchantments and magiciens and sorcières and Fairies and other such strange things on the road, you never know."

Borel tied a length of rope to the top of the bag and looped the improvised sling over his head and across one shoulder. Then he raised Charité's fingers to his lips and kissed them, she to simper coyly. Then the prince shook hands with Maurice and turned on his heel and stepped 'round the cottage and through the gate and set off down the trace toward the river gleaming in the distance, Maurice and Charité following him to the fence and calling out their adieus, proud Brun barking his own farewell.

Borel strode onward; after a while he looked back to see Charité scattering grain for the chickens, and Maurice in the bean field plying his hoe.

"What was it you called out as you were flying about and blessing that stead?"

"Oh," said Flic. "I was merely singing an old song about the richness of the land and the luxury of the rains and the goodness of those who husband the crops and care for the beasts and tend such. Whether you can call that a blessing, well, I couldn't say. And whether or no it will do ought whatsoever . . . hmm . . ." Flic shrugged a shoulder and fell silent and Borel strode on for the river crossing, he, too, saying nought, for he knew nothing of blessings either.

In later days and thereafter, though, it would be said by those who should know of such things that Maurice and Charité had the most fertile and prosperous farmstead in the realm, no matter the seasons or weather.

"Do you really think that someone in town might know something of Rhensibé and where Lord Roulan's estate might be?" asked Flic.

Borel shrugged. "Perhaps. Then again, mayhap we can find one of the Fey Folk that Maurice spoke of. If they are truly Fey, then they might know of something that will give us an inkling as to where to go next."

"Perhaps," said Flic. "Yet if I were you, I'd be careful of what Fey Folk say."

Borel broke out in laughter.

"What?" said Flic.

"Oh, Flic, my innocent. Don't you realize that you are as Fey as any? Should I be wary of your words?"

"Humph!" snorted Flic. "I should say not. After all, I am not speaking of Sprites and such, but of the *true* Fey Folk."

"*True* Fey Folk? And just who might they be?"

"Well, um, er . . . oh, I know: Fairies, that's who. Those and—" Flic's words jerked to a halt, but then he whispered, "Oh, my, perhaps that's one of them now."

Flic pointed, and just ahead on the riverbank sat a crone, mumbling to herself and picking at her considerably long nose.

As Borel drew near, she whirled about and screeched, "Where have you been! It's quite late you know, and I can't wait here all day."

26

Wyrd

"Madame," said Borel, "are you speaking to me?"

"Of course, you fool," snapped the partly bald, scraggly-gray-haired, warty-headed crone, the old lady dressed in filthy rags, wooden-soled sandals on her dirty, misshapen feet, the shoes held on by half-rotted leather straps across her insteps. "Do you see anyone else here?"

"I am here," said Flic. "I am someone else, and so is Buzzer."

"Pah!" sneered the wrinkled hag. "You little pip-squeak, you can't carry me across the river, while this big lummox of a man can."

Flic frowned. "Pip-squeak? You call me a—?"

"You wish me to bear you across, Madame?" said Borel, interrupting Flic.

"Have you no ears, or are you total a dolt? Didn't I just say so?"

"Leave her be, my lord prince," said Flic, now thoroughly irritated. "Let the old fool wade."

"Is that food you've got in the sack?" queried the snaggle-toothed crone. "I smell food, and I am hungry."

"Indeed, Grandmother," said Borel. "Let me offer you some." He unslung the cloth bag from his shoulder and untied the rope and held the sack out to the old woman, its top open. "What will you have?"

She snatched the pouch from his hands and began wolfing down biscuits and cheese, and drinking honey straight from the jar.

"My lord," cried Flic, "take it back from this old beldame, else she'll gobble it all up."

The hag clutched the sack to her bosom and turned away from Borel so that he couldn't easily grab it from her.

As she cracked open a boiled egg, Borel said, "She's hungry, Flic, and I can always hunt, and you and Buzzer can always sip nectar."

"Bu-but, she's eating it all!" exclaimed Flic.

"Nevertheless," said Borel.

'Round a mouthful of apple, and over her shoulder, the crone snarled, "Swat that little pest. Swat the stupid bee as well."

As Flic, thoroughly infuriated, hissed in rage, Borel said, "Non, Madame. Flic and Buzzer are my friends and my guides and my allies. I'll not do them harm, nor shall you."

"Friends? Guides? Allies? Ha! Then you are a fool thrice over," sneered the hag.

"My lord," gritted Flic, the Sprite seething, "let me set Buzzer upon her, and then we'll see just who is the fool."

"Non, Flic," said Borel. "She is old, and a bee sting might kill her."

"Good riddance, then," growled Flic, but he made no move to carry out his threat.

The crone turned and shoved the sack back into Borel's hands. "Now carry me across," she demanded.

Borel peered into the bag. Only the salted bacon and an empty honey jar remained.

Borel sighed and retied the bag and looped the sling over his head and across his shoulder again, then he turned to the old woman and started to pick her up in his arms.

"You fool!" she screeched, "you might drop me that way. Instead I will ride on your back."

"Leave her," screamed Flic, "the ungrateful old witch that she is."

But Borel sighed and turned his back, and the crone climbed up, complaining about the quiver and bow and rope slings and the Gnome rucksack belted to Borel's waist all being in the way. But finally she was in place.

Flic would have none of this, and he and Buzzer took to wing.

"Well, are you just going to stand there all day?" snarled the crone, a gust of her breath nearly gagging the prince.

Following the trace of the road, into the river stepped Borel, the ford wide and slow-running. Up to his ankles, his shins, his knees rose the water as he bore the old lady across, she breathing at his ear, a miasma of foulness swirling forth from her snaggletoothed mouth. And with every step she seemed to grow heavier . . . and heavier . . . and then heavier still.

Up to his thighs rose the water, and the crone screeched that her feet were getting wet, and she climbed higher, her knees gripping his waist.

Onward waded Borel, while Flic circled above and shouted that the prince ought to simply dump the whining old hag. So what if she drowned, it would serve the ancient carp right.

And still she seemed to get heavier with every step.

"My shoe!" screamed the crone. "You've made me lose my shoe! Get it! Get it!"

Borel looked and saw the wooden-soled sandal drifting toward an eddy. "Madame, it is merely a *sabot*, a wooden clog, and easily replaced."

"No, no, it's my shoe, and your fault that it is floating away! Get it! Get it now!"

"Dump her!" shrilled Flic. "Let her bob along after it, or better yet, let her sink out of sight, never to be seen again."

Sighing, Borel turned and waded after the sabot, the water deepening, the crone on his back and screaming at him that she was getting wet. Finally, Borel overtook the shoe and, waist-deep, he waded for the shore, while the hag on his back screeched, "Get me out! Get me out! I am like to drown!"

"Let her!" shrieked Flic, flying above, Buzzer circling alongside. "Let the old harridan drown!"

With the crone squalling and Flic screaming, at last Borel reached the far bank and trudged up out of the water.

The hag scrambled off his back, but held on to Borel while standing on the one foot still sandal-clad. "My shoe," she demanded, "put my shoe on my foot!"

"Throw it back in the water instead," shouted Flic.

With her yet holding on, Borel knelt and she raised her hammertoed, broken-nailed, dirt-encrusted, bunion-laden foot to receive the worn and wet sabot. And as he slipped it on, her foot became slender and graceful, and the shoe turned to silver. And even as Flic gasped and cried, "Oh, my," Borel looked up to see not a withered crone, but instead a graceful silver-haired, silver-eyed demoiselle of surpassing beauty, arrayed in a silver gown.

And above the sound of the river and just on the edge of hearing, it seemed he could faintly detect the sound of a shuttle and loom, as if someone nearby were weaving.

"Lady Wyrd," he said yet kneeling, and she canted her head in assent.

"Lady of the Mere," he added, and once more she acknowledged the name.

"Lady Sorcière," he said, and again she nodded.

Finally, he said, "Lady Skuld," and she smiled.

"I am known by many names, Prince Borel," she said, "those among them." She turned her silver gaze toward a nearby frond on which Flic sat, his face in his hands, Buzzer at his side. "Sieur Flic," she said.

Flic mumbled, "Didn't I tell you, Lord Borel, when we first saw her waiting on the bank of this river that she might be one of the Fey? Well, she is, she certainly is. Too bad I didn't listen to me."

He dropped his hands from his face, and stood and bowed. "My Lady of the Yet to Come, I apologize for all I said. Had I but known—"

Skuld laughed, her voice as silver as her hair and eyes. "Ah, my Flic, I must play my games." She turned to Borel. "You,

Sieur, you did very well, for ere I can aid, a favor must be given, and you were tested sorely." She held out her hand to him.

Borel stood and bowed and said, "My lady." He took her hand and kissed her fingers.

"Ah me," she said, smiling, "are you trying to turn my head?"

"No, my lady, though I would ask you for guidance in the quest I pursue."

"I know your quest, Lord Borel, and it is worthy."

"Will you help me, Lady Wyrd? I need aid, for I know not where my Chelle lies, nor where lies the manor of her père, and there is little time left."

Skuld sighed and said, "My sisters and I are bound by a rule: no answers of significance or gifts of worth can we give to anyone without first a service of value being rendered to us—which, in my case, you have certainly done, bearing me across the river as you did."

"Um, begging your pardon, my lady," said Flic, "but he gave you food as well."

"Indeed, he did, and that's two *beaux gestes*," said Skuld. "Even so, my sisters and I, we cannot grant favors until a riddle we ask is correctly answered, and even then our answers will be couched in mystery."

"My lady," said Borel, "any answer is better than what we now have . . . and to be fair, I know the riddles you and your sisters asked Camille, as well as their answers. Too, I know the answer to the riddle of the Sphinx."

"Honorable," murmured Skuld. Then she turned and looked at Flic and smiled. "Do you fly in races 'gainst other Sprites?"

"Oh, yes, and I'm quite good at it," said Flic, beaming.

Now Skuld turned to Borel and said, "Here then is my riddle:

"Were Flic in a Spritely contest
To see who was most fleet of his Kind,
But in some manner unknown to him
He had fallen behind—"

"What?" Flic started to protest, but Skuld threw up a hand to stop him—

"But through a furious burst of speed,
He passed the Sprite in second place,
Where then would our sprightly Flic
Now be in this incredibly fast race?"

"Oh, I know, I know!" cried Flic, jumping up and down on the frond, Buzzer bouncing beside him.

" 'Tis not yours to answer, Flic," warned Skuld.

Again she turned to Borel, and he said, "Flic would then be second."

Skuld grinned and nodded. "Well answered, Borel."

"What?" cried Flic. "Second? But I passed that one. Why not first?"

Borel smiled and said, "Flic, my lad, when you pass the second-place Sprite, you have not yet passed the one who is first, hence, you would be second."

"Oh," said Flic, his face falling. "I thought I would have been in first." Then he sighed and said, "It's a good thing it wasn't my riddle to answer, for I seem to be no good at it. I mean, I didn't know what women want, nor could I choose between night and day, and—"

"Flic, you are a valuable member of this quest," said Borel. "Again I say, without you and Buzzer, I wouldn't be here."

Flic grinned and said, "That's true. Besides, it wouldn't have been but a moment before I would have passed that Sprite in first place anyway."

Both Borel and Skuld laughed at Flic's cockiness, but Borel then turned to Skuld. "My lady . . . ?"

Skuld smiled. "Ah, yes. Aid."

She pondered a moment and then said: "Heed me, Borel:

"Long is the journey lying ahead.
Give comfort to those in dire need,
And aid you will find along the way,

Yet hazard as well, but this I say:
Neither awake nor in a dark dream
Are perilous blades just as they seem.

"And this I will add for nought: you must triumph o'er a cunning, wicked, and most deadly steed to find the Endless Sands."

Borel frowned, taken aback by her answer, and he said, "My lady, I do not under—"

But in that moment the persistent sound of the loom swelled, then vanished as did Lady Skuld.

27

Riverbend

"She's gone," said Borel.

"Vanished into thin air," said Flic, his mouth yet agape. Then he scowled. "Isn't it just like fate to strike unexpectedly and then as quickly disappear and leave the victim—or beneficiary—to deal with the consequences?"

"You are right, Flic. None knows when the Fates will come and go, nor whether they might bring good or ill." Borel sighed and shook his head. "But this I wonder: whenever they speak, why can't the Fates—the Ladies Wyrd and Lot and Doom—ever answer straight out? Why must they always couch their words in riddles?"

"I don't know," said Flic. "However, my prince, it seems to me that Lady Skuld *did* tell you something of worth."

"Oui, she did. She spoke of finding the Endless Sands, whatever and wherever they are, yet she did not say what might be there."

"Whatever it is, my lord," said Flic, "it surely will help in the quest."

Borel frowned. "Endless Sands . . . they're in many a childhood tale, but I know not where they are. Do you?"

Flic shook his head. "Non."

"What about Buzzer?"

"I'll ask."

After a moment, Flic said, "She has flown over sands, but they were not endless. Besides, I think that something called the Endless Sands would not have flowers abloom."

"Well, then," said Borel, "we'll seek another way."

"My lord," said Flic, "Lady Skuld did tell you what must be done to find them: you must triumph o'er a cunning, wicked, and most deadly steed. Hmm . . . perhaps you are to slay some terrible monster."

"I think not, Flic, else she would not have called it a steed. I think I am meant to ride it, perhaps to tame it and even ride it to those Endless Sands, wherever they are."

"That could be," said Flic. "Tell me: do you know how to ride?"

Borel sighed and nodded and said, "Not as well as my brother Alain, but I have spent time ahorse in saddle."

"I think you are not likely to have a saddle on a cunning, wicked, and most deadly steed. And it might not be a horse at all, but, rather, as I said, some terrible monster, a fell beast of some sort—a Gryphon or Wyvern or even a Dragon."

Borel took a deep breath and slowly let it out. "You might be right, Flic. But come, get Buzzer and let us be off and discover what we can in the town. It could be that someone there knows of the Endless Sands or can otherwise aid us with Lady Wyrd's rede. As for you and me, we can ponder as we trek."

And so, with Flic and Buzzer riding the tricorn, Borel set out along the meandering river, heading for the community lying upstream a league or two off.

As Borel strode townward, Flic said, "What about that verse she spoke. How did it go?"

Borel intoned:

"Long is the journey lying ahead.
Give comfort to those in dire need,
And aid you will find along the way,
Yet hazard as well, but this I say:

Neither awake nor in a dark dream
Are perilous blades just as they seem."

"Well," said Flic, "we've already journeyed far and no doubt have farther to go. And you've given comfort and found aid, and I am sure that will continue. And there has been hazard along the way, and, as things are going, there will likely be more. As to the blades—"

"I think Lady Wyrd was referring to the daggers surrounding the turret," said Borel.

"Oui," agreed Flic. "I believe she has simply verified what we suspected all along—that the daggers aren't daggers at all but rather represent some other peril, such as terrible guardians or even an army. We won't know what they really are until we find the turret."

"Oui, Flic. But here is the true riddle as I see it: just why did Lady Wyrd speak the verse at all?"

"Your meaning, my lord?" asked Flic.

"Why did she utter those particular words, when all it told us was how we already act and what we already know or suspect?"

Flic frowned and shrugged a shoulder. "That is certainly a riddle, my prince, yet who can comprehend the ways of the Fates?"

Even as they passed dwellings on the outskirts of town, Flic said, "You know, at first I thought I should have seen that the crone was not what she seemed, and that I should have detected the glamour. But after she revealed her true self, I realized that her bewitchments would always utterly defeat my Fey sight."

"Fey sight?" asked Borel.

"Oui. I can at times see when something is not what it seems. Oh, if the glamour is strong enough, it defies my vision. Or, if the being is powerful enough, again I am helpless to see . . . as was the case with the invisible monster in the swamp."

"But you can see through some glamours?"

"Oh, yes. But not all. And sometimes when I do not see what I expect to be there, then I think an enchantment might be involved—either a spell so strong that my sight cannot penetrate it, or that it is truly gone. In the case of Lord Roulan's dell, I did not see what I thought should be there, yet when you walked its length, I knew it wasn't merely hidden. Then I thought that during the day it might be absent, but at night moonlight might make it materialize, yet I was wrong." Flic shook his head and said, "Pah! Most of the time having Fey sight is not an advantage this way or that."

Borel smiled and said, "I would think in the case of Lady Wyrd, she can deceive the best of *any* vision, Fey sight or no."

Flic laughed and said, "Indeed, my lord, indeed."

Using a bit of the Gnomes' coinage, Borel took a room in the Running Stag, the best of the three inns in Riverbend, a rather modest and sleepy town. As Borel signed the register, the clerk eyed the Sprite and then the bumblebee, both of them beside Borel's hat on the counter. The clerk turned to Borel and said, "Are you certain, Sieur, the bee is well behaved?"

As Flic huffed, Borel said, "Indeed, she is. Of course, should someone try to swat her, then she will not be bound by manners."

"Oh, perhaps I'd better warn our other three guests as well as the staff, then."

"I should say so," said Flic, drawing himself up to his full naked two-inch height. "Else they'll have to deal with me."

"I would add," said Borel, that the bee is quite protective of her charge."

"Her charge?" said the clerk.

"Me," said Flic, grinning. "Swat me at your peril, Sieur."

"Oh, my goodness," said the clerk, holding out a key to Borel. "I'll be certain to warn all."

As Borel took the key he said, "And your baths are . . . ? —Oh, and I will need my leathers cleaned, and a robe."

"Indeed, Sieur."

"This, too," said Borel. "Have you a jeweller in town, and a weapons shop? And a place where I can get a good rucksack and supplies?"

"No jeweller as such, Sieur," said the clerk, "though there are a few brooches and rings and other like items over at the milliner's. Jewellers, you see, arrive in the spring, peddling their wares; the milliner, she always takes extra on consignment. As for weapons, our blacksmith has a few knives and such; if he has not what you wish, he can easily make it. The dry-goods store is two streets over."

"Ah, yes, milliner," said Borel, looking at Flic. "Perfect, for she will have pins and needles. Which way the milliner? Blacksmith, too?"

The clerk gave directions, and then told Borel the baths at the inn were out back.

Even as Borel turned to go, a town crier stepped into the lobby and loudly called out, "Another man drowned! Another man drowned! A crofter from a stead beyond the White Rapids found floating under the red bridge by a passing goose girl." The townsman then hurried back out to the street to herald the latest news.

"Oh, Mithras," said the clerk, "three drownings in the last three weeks, and that's the second one this week alone. Will those farmers never learn to respect the river?"

"Three altogether have died by drowning?" asked Borel.

"Oui, Sieur," replied the clerk. "As I said, three in the last three weeks."

"Has anyone investigated?"

"The constable. He went up there to the White Rapids and looked about."

"These rapids are . . . ?"

"Terrible," said the clerk. "They lie some two or three leagues upriver. I mean, on a quiet night, like most nights around here, you can sit on the veranda and hear them roar. They're not anything like the rest of the Meander."

"So the constable went up there?" said Flic.

"Oui. It was after the second death, but he found no sign of foul play."

"Still, three in three weeks sounds somewhat suspicious," said Borel.

The clerk shrugged. "Nevertheless, the constable, he said there just wasn't anything to see."

Borel frowned and looked at Flic, but the Sprite turned up both hands. He stepped onto the tricorn and said, "Let us away to the tubs."

With Flic and Buzzer aboard, Borel took up his hat and headed for the door to the baths. Just as he reached it, the clerk called after, "Though there were quite a number of hoofprints."

Borel turned and said, "Hoofprints?"

"Up beyond the rapids. That's all the constable found. There's a wild horse running amok 'round those parts that's been destroying crops and raising havoc at night."

Flic gasped and swung down to Borel's shoulder and said, "Lady Wyrd knew. She knew! That's what she meant."

Borel nodded and intoned, " 'You must triumph o'er a cunning, wicked, and most deadly steed.' "

"A Pooka," said Flic. "Oh, Borel, she was speaking of a Pooka. There's a Pooka beyond the rapids, and it is drowning men."

28

Interlude

Borel said, "We should go right now and—"

"Oh, no, my lord," said Flic. "Pookas are night creatures. Besides, you don't even have a good blade."

"I have this one of flint," said Borel, pulling the stone knife from his belt.

"I think you will need a better one, my lord; Pookas are quite perilous, you know . . . one of the Dark Fey . . . unseely. And so you need something better than a piece of flint to threaten him with, but not to kill him."

"Not that I was planning to, but why not kill a Pooka?"

"If you kill a Pooka, my lord, you will be forever cursed."

"Very well, Flic. I'll get a long-knife at the blacksmith's. Then we'll go."

"My lord prince, it is yet midmorn, hence we have most of the day for you to not only purchase a weapon, but also supplies and goods for the long journey Lady Wyrd said lies ahead of us. Hence, I think we should spend the day in town acquiring what we need. After all, we know not exactly where the creature might be, other than perhaps in the vicinity of the White Rapids. Once we get there I can fly in the night and find him."

"All right, Flic, all right. I yield. We do have time. Let us first to the baths, and while I soak I would have you tell me all you know of Pookas. Perhaps an idea will occur on how to triumph o'er this cunning and wicked and most deadly steed."

Borel gave over his leathers to the attendant for cleaning, and his linens for laundering, and then he eased his trim frame with its long, lean muscles down into the great copper tub full of hot water, where he lathered and rinsed his shoulder-length, silver-cast hair, then lathered and rinsed his body; and the silver-sheened hair on his broad chest tapered in a vee down across his flat stomach toward his narrow hips and to his groin to meet the same silvery tone, though there it was perhaps a bit darker. He then settled in to soak. As he did these things, Buzzer watched from a towel rack, while Flic sat on the side of the tub and spoke of Pookas:

"They're also called Phookas and a number of other names, none of which are to be confused with Pwcas—a name that sounds the same, but is spelled differently—who are really Bwcas, a kind of a Goblin, but usually helpful rather than vile.

"Anyway, Pookas are of several natures: some are merely out for a lark, while others are a bit more destructive, and still others are on a rampage."

Borel grunted and said, "It seems as if the one beyond the rapids is on a rampage."

"Oui," said Flic, "for it is killing men, rather than merely swooping them up for a terrifying ride through bogs and briars and such and then dumping them in muddy ditches or quag holes."

"That's what I've heard of Pookas," said Borel. "They are tricksters, and they fool people into thinking they will go on a pleasant ride when instead it is quite the opposite. But that is all I've heard of them. This one, though, the clerk said, destroys crops and raises havoc at night."

Flic nodded and said, "Oh, yes, my lord, Pookas do such things. In the night it roams the countryside and tramples crops and tears down fences and scatters cattle and sheep and other such. Why, they even say that should a crofter's fowl—chickens and geese in particular—merely catch sight of the creature, they entirely stop laying. Too, they can cause livestock to sicken or sour their milk or cause a number of other wicked mischiefs."

Borel frowned. "It would seem that if the Pooka were doing most if not all of these things, the constable would know that it's not merely a wild horse running amok."

"Perhaps none in this town nor in the steads 'round have ever heard of Pookas."

"Either that," said Borel, "or they are afraid to acknowledge that one of the Dark Fey is responsible for the killings."

Flic knitted his brow. "Perhaps the Pooka was wronged by someone herein, or wasn't given its due."

"Its due?"

"Aye. At the end of the harvest, long strips of standing crops are left behind by the reapers specifically for the Pooka. It is his share."

"And if the crofters do not do such . . . ?"

"Then the Pooka rampages," said Flic.

"Ah, then, perhaps here we have the motive for this destruction," said Borel.

"Even so, my lord, it does not justify murder."

"No, it does not. But tell me, what else is there about Pookas? If we are to stop him, I need to know."

"Well, Pookas are also shapeshifters: most of the time they take the form of dark horses with burning yellow eyes, but they've also been known to become huge and hideous and hairy Boglemen, sometimes with goats' heads and horns, at other times they become great black goats in full. Pookas can also transform into a variety of enormous birds: vultures, eagles, crows, ravens, and the like, all with wingspans as wide as a barn, they say, however wide that might be.

"Oh, and there is this: they say Pookas are nearly impossible to kill, but should someone do so, he and all his kith are cursed forever. Not only that, but wherever a Pooka might be slain, great storms rise up, especially along seacoasts and waterways and lakes. Too, wherever the Pooka dies, the land for leagues about is blighted for a hundred years or more. That is what I have heard, my lord. Whether it be true, I cannot say, though I do believe it to be so."

"Then I shall not try to kill the Pooka," said Borel. "After all, we need its aid, or so Lady Wyrd implied. —Is there ought along those lines?"

"Indeed," said Flic. "Though it be rare, it is said they sometimes help people by prophesying or giving guidance."

"Ah, then, this is why Lady Wyrd uttered what she did," said Borel. "We must get the Pooka to give us aid." Borel frowned and looked at Flic. "Tell me, how does a Pooka do so? —Give aid, I mean."

"Why, my lord, it speaks," said Flic, turning up a hand.

"In a human voice?"

Vexed, Flic snorted and said, "And in the voice of the Fey, too."

"Sorry, Flic, I didn't mean to omit the Fey."

Borel then stood and, dripping, stepped from the tub and took up a towel from a shelf rather than from the rack where Buzzer rested. As he dried off he said, "And just how are we to stop this rampage and gain the guidance we need?"

"By riding him until he submits, my prince, and perhaps by giving him his due."

"Has anyone ever ridden a Pooka to submission?"

"Just one, I think: a man—a king of the Keltoi, I believe—but I don't recall his name. There was some trick to it. If I can remember how it was done . . ."

"I hope you do, my friend," said Borel, now donning a robe. "For Lady Wyrd says I must triumph o'er a cunning and wicked and most deadly steed, and every trick will help."

Even as Borel looked about for the attendant, the man appeared and said, "Your clothing will be ready ere the noontide, Sieur."

"Good," said Borel, "Just in time for a midday meal."

After eating, Borel, with Flic and Buzzer riding his hat, went to the dry-goods store, where he purchased a bedroll and a rucksack and a good length of rope, to add to his Gnome-given things. Next, he stopped in the farmers' market and bought supplies for the trail, including another jar of honey. With his rucksack full and the bedroll atop, he went to the smithery, and though the metalworker had no blade on hand to fit Borel's longknife sheath, if the lord would only leave it behind, the blacksmith promised he would have a keen, proper-sized bronze blade within it by morn.

As they left the smithery, Borel sighed and said, "Perhaps we'll go after the Pooka this night, and come back for the blade in the morn."

"My lord, I would have you go armed with a good bronze blade rather than the one of flint."

"So would I, Flic, yet the moon does not pause in her path, and I would not tarry one moment longer than necessary."

"Lord Borel, take it as an omen that your blade will not be ready till the morrow. Besides, I would scout the place ere we go, else we will be in unknown territory with peril about. And we yet have a fortnight and seven till the moon rises full."

Borel sighed. "Again, perhaps you are right. You need to scout, and we need to go fully armed. And speaking of weapons, let us hie to the milliner's."

"Weapons? The milliner's? Why so?"

"You will see, my wee one."

In the small shop on a side street—Marie's Millinery—Borel examined a silver needle, one just the size to fit Flic as a sword.

"Demoiselle, have you a silver sequin?" he asked.

"Oui, Monsieur," replied a *fille* who had just begun to blossom, she the daughter of the milliner. At a table to one side sat her mother, fixing ribbons to a hat.

"A sequin that is not holed?" asked Borel.

"Oui," said the daughter.

"Ah, good. And I see by your sign without that you make minor repairs to jewellery."

"Small things. Nothing major."

"Can you puncture this sequin in the very center with the silver needle, and then slide it up to the eyelet and fix it in place?"

"What's that for?" asked Flic.

"Your needle will act as an épée or a foil, and the sequin as a bell," said Borel.

"A bell?"

"A guard for your hand," said the proprietress, looking up from the beribboned hat.

"Madame, you are familiar with épées?" asked Borel.

She nodded. "Although I am known as the Widow Marie, a mere milliner, I am well acquainted with fencing blades. My Renaud—bless his departed soul—was a maker of fine épées and foils for going out into the world, as well as fine rapiers. He even made a colichemarde or two."

"Colichemarde?" said Flic.

"The ancestor of the épée," said Marie. "For you, though, my tiny Sprite, I would suggest an épée."

"Why not a colichemarde or a foil?" asked Flic.

"A foil, I think, is not stiff enough," said Marie, "and a colichemarde is a bit on the heavy side for one as small as you."

"Ah, then you know what it is I want for my wee friend?" asked Borel.

The proprietress stood and stepped to the counter. She eyed Flic, and glanced askance at Buzzer, and then said, "Sieur, I think a finer choice than a needle would be a silver hatpin or, better yet, a man's scarfpin; they're a bit sturdier, less likely to snap. Of course, I'll need to remove the ornamental head; it would just get in the way. And with the bell fixed in place and the grip properly wrapped with my finest silver thread it will be a weapon worthy of this Sprite."

At Borel's assent, she selected several of her scarfpins and held each up next to the Sprite, finally selecting the one that best fit his stature.

"He will need a baldric," said Borel.

"A matter of a few strokes of needle and thread and a ribbon," said the milliner. "Step here, Sprite; my daughter will take your measure." She turned to the demoiselle. "Renée, *s'il-te-plaît.*"

Even as the mother passed through an archway to a back room, "But, Mère, he's naked," said the daughter.

"Demoiselle Renée, it's not as if I am going to ravish you," said Flic.

Though she reddened, the demoiselle laughed and said, "Wee little thing as you are, I do not feel threatened."

"Ah, *ma chérie,* I might surprise you, for I am Fey."

"Oh!" Renée exclaimed in startlement and backed away.

With an eyebrow raised, Borel looked at Flic, and the Sprite laid a finger alongside his nose and gave Borel a slow wink.

"Fear not, Demoiselle," said Borel, grinning. "I will protect you."

Somewhat assured, the young lady stepped to the counter once more and, reddening again, began to measure the Sprite for a baldric.

"Will this interfere with my wings?" asked Flic. "I do need to fly, you know."

"Perhaps a belt would be better," said Borel.

"A sash about the waist," called the mother from the room beyond. "We can fashion a scabbard as well."

Blushing furiously, the daughter wrapped a thread as a gauge about Flic's tiny waist, trying to see what she was doing while at the same time trying not to look at Flic's maleness. Despite their manifest disparity in size, under the blushing demoiselle's gaze, Flic, grinning, began to respond.

"Oh, my," blurted Renée, and quickly she pinched the thread at the right length and pulled it free and turned her back to the Sprite.

In that moment the mother stepped in through the arch, the scarfpin free of its bauble and with a pierced silver sequin affixed as a bell.

Flic's response vanished.

"Though it is not quite ready, let me see how this fits," she said, and handed the miniature épée to the Sprite.

Flic took the tiny foil in hand and, eyeing the silver shaft, said, "It has no edge."

"It is meant to stick, to impale, not to cut," said the Widow Marie.

"Ah, like a bee sting, then," said Flic, glancing at Buzzer. "I like that."

To judge its fitness to his size, Marie had Flic strike several poses. She closely looked at the grip and Flic's grasp of it, then held out her hand for the weapon and said, "It seems to suit you well enough. Come back in the morning. It will be ready by then."

As he gave over the foil to her, "My belt, too?" asked Flic.

Glancing only sideways at the Sprite, the daughter nodded.

"I need to get a mate," said Flic, as they emerged from the millinery. "I mean, after all, she was fifty times my height."

"More like twenty-seven or -eight," said Borel, grinning, "and much too young for you."

Flic laughed.

"What?" asked Borel.

"Never let it be said that I don't like tall girls," replied Flic. They both laughed, but Flic sobered and said, "I repeat, I need to find a mate."

"Someone to love?" asked Borel, a smile yet on his face.

"That would be fine, but at least someone eager for passion," said Flic.

"Ah," said the prince.

As Borel strode on toward the inn, Flic said, "You know, since neither of us will be properly armed until the morning, I think I'll just fly out to the fields and flit about the flowers for a while."

Borel broke out in a guffaw, and said, "Luck, my little man."

Flic and Buzzer took to wing and gained altitude, then shot away, following the river upstream. Borel watched until they were out of sight, then turned and continued on his way to the inn. Once inside, he settled in to a dinner of roast beef and scallions and bread, all washed down with a hearty dark beer. *After all, if I fail with the Pooka, this just might be my last good meal.*

Borel sat out on the veranda and sipped an unpretentious after-dinner brandy and watched a number of people on the street hurrying home or running errands or strolling leisurely to somewhere. Nearby, the Meander River flowed past, and when the air got still Borel could hear a distant rumble, as of water hurtling apace. *The White Rapids, no doubt.* As the sun set and twilight drew down, Flic and Buzzer had not yet returned. Borel raised his glass to the deepening lavender sky and said, "May you have found what you seek, Flic, my friend, be it a lasting love or nought but a brief liaison."

He watched as a horse-drawn wain trundled past and over the bridge and away. All fell quiet after, but for the faint grumble upstream. Borel downed the last of his drink and stood and trudged into the inn and up to his chamber, where he opened a window for Flic to use, should the Sprite come flying back, though since Buzzer was with him it was not likely he would return till morning, for the bee fell dormant when night drew its spangled dark cloak across the sky.

Borel shed his garments and settled down to sleep, his thoughts meandering much the same as the river flowing past.

Tomorrow . . . Tomorrow . . . Tomorrow we shall seek a cunning and wicked and most deadly steed and I shall try to triumph o'er him. If I fail—Borel jerked awake, his heart hammering. *Nay! I will not even consider failing, for Chelle's life depends upon me.*

Slowly Borel gained calmness, and he turned on his side and watched through the window as the night darkened and stars appeared one by one.

Chelle, my Chelle, where are you now?

And then Borel slid into sleep.

29

Idyll

"Oh, Chelle, my love, I am so happy to find you here," said Borel.

"Trapped in this turret?" said Chelle, frowning and gazing about in spite of the shadowy band across her eyes. "How can you be happy over that?"

"Oh, Chérie, I am not happy to find you trapped; it's just that when last I saw you it was in another place, one that I left abruptly, and I was afraid you might be lost, and I would never find you again."

Once more Chelle frowned, this time in concentration. "I do not recall where last I— Were we in water?"

Borel took a deep breath and let it out. "It was at a lake. We were going for a row, but you went swimming instead."

"Ah, yes. Then suddenly I was here and you were gone, Borel. What happened?"

"Would you like to take that boat ride now?" asked Borel, steering away from that specific dream and the talk of dreams in general. "There is an isle I would take you to."

"Oh, yes. A row to an isle would be splendid."

Borel frowned in concentration and then offered his arm to Chelle, and together through the door they stepped, to find themselves high on a grassy slope leading down to the shores of a lake. Above, the moon—just under half full and waning—shone in the starry sky. A small pier jutted out into the water, a skiff afloat at its end. As they strolled toward a dock, Chelle said, "It has been awhile since I last went boating. The Meander flows near my father's manse, and there is a small lake in our vale."

"I know," said Borel. "I fished in your lake."

Letting go of Borel's arm, Chelle swung about and faced him and grabbed both of his hands and walked backward, tugging him after. "Did you catch anything?"

"I think not," said Borel, smiling. "Oh, wait . . . a small one I threw back."

"Yes, because I pled for you to do so," said Chelle, grinning. "Do you not remember?"

"Hmm . . . I think there was something about it being a magic fish and if I spared its life then one day I would be repaid sevenfold."

"You *do* remember," said Chelle, stopping abruptly and raising her face to his.

Borel took her in his arms and pulled her close and kissed her. She pressed her body against him, and his heart began to race and his blood roared in his ears. It would be so easy to—

No! I cannot take advantage!

Borel withdrew and held her at arm's length.

She looked at him, her head canted as if in puzzlement, yet with the shadowy band across her eyes he could not be certain of her expression, though it seemed there was a slight frown upon her forehead.

"Ma chérie," he said, dissembling, trying to gain control of his heart, "you are so very beautiful."

She smiled and released his hands and curtseyed. "Why, thank you, Sieur."

He grinned and bowed and reached out and took her hand and kissed her fingers. Then he straightened and said, "Demoiselle, your boat awaits."

Chelle turned. "And this isle you are spiriting me away to . . . ?"

"Beyond the argent mist, my love," said Borel, pointing.

Out in the lake a silvery haze shone in the half-light of the moon. Past the vapor a vague silhouette loomed, as of close-set trees standing tall in the night.

"Let us away then, my sweet Borel."

Hand in hand, they strolled toward the pier, and Borel said, "Tell me, my love, have you ever heard of the Endless Sands?"

"In children's tales," she said.

"Know you where they lie?" said Borel.

"Non. Should I? Are they even real?"

"Perhaps, ma chérie."

"Why do you ask?"

"Just curious," said Borel as they reached the dock. "Oh, here we are."

Borel handed her into the boat and to the reclining seat in the bow, and then he sat upon the mid thwart, and, facing her, he pushed the oars to propel the craft, rather than using a pull stroke.

As the dip and press and lift and swing of the oars caused ringlets to expand in ripples and swirls to spin away, Chelle trailed her fingers in the crystalline water, and Borel smiled and said, "Mayhap you will catch a fish come to nibble upon you."

Chelle grinned. "Do you think?"

"Perhaps the very same fish you had me cast back in," he replied.

"Oh, then it might take my entire hand," said Chelle, "for surely it is grown large by now."

Even as she said it, a great whorl formed nearby, and Chelle—"Oh!"—jerked her hand from the water.

Borel frowned. *'Tis a dream where anything can occur, sensible or no.*

Without pausing in the beat of his oars, Borel said, "My love, take care, for this is a fey lake, full of strange phenomena and oddities. We should not tempt fate, hence I shall no longer speak of catching fish."

"And I shall no longer trail the bait," said Chelle, laughing.

Into the silvery mist they glided, and the moon dimmed and

then brightened again as they passed through. And they came to a cypress-ringed isle, the trees close together and growing right at the water's edge, their great roots reaching out and down into the lake as if drawing up water to drink. And the faint fragrance of cedar filled the air.

Working the skiff between two of these giant conifers and into a tiny cove, Borel beached the craft. He handed Chelle out of the boat, and arm in arm they made their way inland to come to an open glade overflowing with wildflowers.

"Oh, my Borel, it is beautiful," said Chelle, interlacing her fingers with his. "What a wondrous place, this isle."

She pulled Borel toward the center of the glade, stopping now and again to stoop at a particular blossom and inhale its fragrance. And as they worked their way inward, Chelle paused and gasped and said, "Oh, look, two Sprites. But what are they doing? Fighting?" She stepped closer, drawing Borel after. "No, not fighting, instead they're— Oh, my." Blushing furiously, Chelle turned her back and looked into Borel's face, and then, yet flustered, turned away from him.

Ah, me, I said it before and it bears repeating: 'tis a dream where anything can occur, sensible or no.

Of a sudden, Chelle turned back to Borel and pulled him to her and kissed him passionately, and he returned her kiss in kind, his senses overwhelmed with fervor. And she pulled him down among the flowers.

And then they were unclothed, and he kissed her lips and neck and the palms of her hands and her stomach and her breasts, and she moaned with desire. And Borel, and Borel, and Borel—

—jerked awake, as Flic and Buzzer came flying in through the window in the dawn, the Sprite crying, "I remembered! I remembered!" And grasped in his hand were three very long, thick hairs trailing after.

Pooka

As Flic settled down on one of the bed knobs and Buzzer on a candlestand, Borel stumbled out from the bed and across the chamber to a basin and ewer. Flic eyed the naked prince and said, "Well, I see *you* were having an exciting dream."

"Oh, Flic, I almost did it again."

"Did what again, my lord?"

"Took advantage of Chelle in my dream."

"You mean you nearly bedded her?"

Borel splashed cool water on his face and took up a towel and dried. "Yes. I nearly bedded her, there in a field of flowers."

"Sounds fitting," said Flic.

One eyebrow arched, Borel looked at the Sprite.

Flic said, "To deflower her among the flowers."

Borel snorted and stumbled back to the bed and flopped down and said, "Ah, Flic, you don't understand."

"Don't understand what?"

"Courtship."

"Pish!" exclaimed the Sprite. "I don't know what it is with you humans. Dillydallying about as you do and calling it courtship. It's just a waste. We Fey . . . or at least we Sprites, we make love to see if we fall in love. If not, then it is just a pleasurable liaison, whereas if we do find our truelove, then we've lost no time dancing about and hemming and hawing and such."

Borel shook his head. "But, Flic, we humans engage in courtship to get to know one another, to see if we have common interests and common dreams, to see if there is something about the other that draws or repels. In other words, to see if we are compatible in likes and dislikes, in desires and loathings, in longings and aversions, in interests and tediums."

"Again I say: Pish! There's plenty of time to discover that afterward," said Flic.

"Tell me, my wee friend," said Borel, "just how long do your trueloves last?"

"Oh, sometimes whole days, other times weeks—"

"Days? Weeks?" said Borel. "And you call it true love?"

"You didn't let me finish, my prince," said Flic. "Fleurette and I, we both think our love will last for years upon years, if not forever."

"Fleurette?"

"Oh, didn't I tell you about her?"

"No."

"Well. I met the most wonderful Sprite: Fleurette. She is splendid, and we are deeply in love. But I told her that I was on a quest, and that just as soon as it is done, then I would return."

"And you met her . . . when?"

"Oh, yesterday. Out in the fields. I told you where I was going. Don't you remember?"

"And you are deeply in love, you say?"

"Oh, yes. Deeply."

Borel broke into chuckles, and Flic huffed in vexation. "Well, I am!" declared the Sprite.

Borel's chuckles turned to laughter, but he waved a hand of apology even as he was guffawing.

Flic turned his back and crossed his arms, the three long, thick hairs yet in his grip and dangling down from the top of the bedpost to nearly touch the floor. "Well then, Monsieur Scoffer, just maybe I won't tell you what else happened last night," he announced, his nose in the air, the Sprite quite miffed.

Borel finally mastered his laughter, and soberly he said, "Ah, Flic, I am sorry. I think I was laughing to relieve the stress of my near-violation of Chelle. Will you forgive me?"

"Humph," snorted Flic, still facing away. "I told you you should go ahead and bed her, dream or no dream. It would allay the strain."

"Ah, but, my friend, though by your lights we humans may be pixilated, we are not Fey, and so—"

Flic broke out in laughter and turned around to face Borel. "Pixilated?"

Borel smiled. "Daft. Mad, crazy, foolish, stupid for carrying on courtships."

Flic nodded. "You are." Then he sighed and added, "But I suppose that's a penalty for being human."

"Or a reward," said Borel.

"Well then I'm glad I'm Fey," said Flic.

"I will not hold that against you," said Borel, grinning. Then he sobered and said, "I hope you harbor no ill will because I laughed at your ways."

Flic said, "Aah, I cannot hold a grudge 'gainst you, my lord."

"Flic, my lad, I think you cannot hold a grudge against anyone."

"Oh, no, my lord. There you are wrong, for I can and do have hard feelings toward those Trolls and Goblins who captured me."

"Ah, then, the exception to the rule," said Borel, grinning.

"I suppose," said Flic.

"By the bye," said Borel, "what were you screaming when you came in through the window, and why in Faery are you grasping those, those—what are they—four-foot-long hairs?"

Flic's face lit up and back and forth he waved the hand holding the hairs, causing sinuous ripples to undulate down the strands. "He did it by having an Elf weave three of the Pooka's tail hairs into an Elf-made rope."

"What are you talking about? *Who* did what?"

"That king of the Keltoi, the one who prevailed over a Pooka. He had an Elf weave three Pooka hairs into a rope and then used the rope—perhaps to fashion a harness, though I don't exactly remember that part—anyway, he used the rope in some manner to make the creature submit. You see, I remembered the legend at last."

Borel's eyes widened in hope. "And you think we can do the same?"

"Indeed, my lord, and you can master the Pooka, for these are hairs from his tail." Of a sudden, Flic's countenance sank, and he glumly said, "But I don't think there is an Elf hereabout, and we don't have an Elf-made rope."

"Wait. Wait," said Borel. "Those are hairs from the Pooka's tail? *Our* Pooka?"

"Oh, yes. Last night my sweet Fleurette upon hearing of our quest told me where the Pooka might be, though she wouldn't go there herself. Pookas terrify her, you see, and so she simply keeps away from them. But I went, and there he was. And as the Pooka was rampaging about some poor crofter's stead, his tail brushed against one of the old splintery posts of the fence he was tearing down, and some of it wedged in a split—rather like the Gnome's beard, you see, only this was a jagged notch, rather than a crack—and when the Pooka galloped away, there they were, three long hairs. Anyway, the moment I saw them, then I remembered the tale of the king and how he mastered the Pooka."

Enthused, Borel leapt up from the bed and began throwing his clothes on. "And you think this might actually work?"

"Well, I suppose you could say they were given freely, which I think adds to the power, but as I say, if we had an Elf and an Elf-made rope—"

"A moment, Flic. Are you saying we need a rope into which to weave the three Pooka hairs?"

"Oui. Wasn't I clear about that?"

"I thought maybe you were saying we only needed to braid the trio together as a rope unto themselves."

"Oh, non The Elf who told me the tale said the king used an Elf-made rope and had an Elf weave the three hairs within that rope."

"Ah, I see."

"But, my lord, as I say, we have no Elf-made rope nor an Elf to weave the hairs within."

As Borel donned his socks he said, "Ah, Flic, you are one of the Fey—surely as good as an Elf—and as for a rope, we have one that is Gnome-made. I think that will certainly do."

"Really?"

"Really." He pulled on his boots and stood and lightly stamped to settle his feet within.

"But I don't know ought of how to make a harness," said Flic, "if that's how it was done."

"Don't worry," said Borel, sliding his silk shirt over his head. "I do."

"Well, whatever the harness, you have to deceive the Pooka just to get it on. And it has to be one that will make him submit, and I think you must make him submit immediately, else he will ride you to death."

"The simplest submission harness is a jaw rope, and one of those should cause the Pooka to yield," said Borel, buckling on his leather jacket. "I think I can slip it in and over in less than a wink, can I get him to open his mouth."

"Jaw rope?"

"Oui. In the lower part of the jaw of a horse there is a gap between the nipping front teeth and the grinders aft—it's where the bit rides—and if I can slip a simple noose into that breach and 'round his lower jaw, I'll have him."

"But this is a Pooka, my lord, a Dark Fey, even a Démon, and certainly a shapeshifter. It might not have a gap where an ordinary horse would. Or it might shift shape into that of the Bogleman, and simply bite through the rope."

"Hmm . . ." said Borel, now dressed. He sat back down on the bed. "Perhaps you'd better tell me how this king of the Keltoi caused his Pooka to submit."

"I don't know that, my lord."

"Well then, why the three tail hairs? What would that have to do with ought?"

"I can only guess about that."

"Then guess away, Flic."

"All right, my lord. Let me ask you this: have you heard of the power of three?"

"I think so," said Borel. "It has to do with heart and body and soul, doesn't it?"

"Well, some think it means those three, while others think it means mind and body and spirit, and still others think it means three sorcières working together, while some reject that and choose three different things altogether. But no matter which, my understanding is if you have three things from someone or something—oh, not of their belongings but rather of their physical self, such as are these hairs part of the Pooka—then you can create a thing—an amulet, an image, a doll—a thing that will then make a connection with that someone or something. Whether this created thing is used for good or ill is up to the one who made it, or rather the one who possesses it.

"That is what I was told and it's all I know concerning the power of three. But as to just how a trio of his tail hairs woven into our Gnome-made line can gain mastery o'er this Pooka, I cannot say, though it means the resulting rope will have a power-of-three bond with the creature."

"Well, then," said Borel, "perhaps I don't need to tie the rope to the creature to be linked to him. —Oh, wait, you say the king of the Keltoi used his as a harness?"

Flic frowned and said, "Maybe it was a harness; I'm a bit hazy on the details."

"Hmm . . ." said Borel, "then I'll need to do something similar, for as long as the rope is tied to the Pooka and as long as I can hang on to the rope, I will be linked to him, not only in a physical way but perhaps in a mystical one as well. Mayhap it will mean he cannot throw me."

"Perhaps, Prince Borel. On the other hand, maybe the rope with his three hairs in it will prevent the Pooka from shapeshifting. If so, then you will merely have to master the creature as you would a horse."

"A wild horse," said Borel.

"A cunning and wicked and most deadly horse," said Flic.

"Ah, well, a lower-jaw rope then is my best chance," said

Borel, "for such a thing has been used in the past to make even the most savage horse submit."

"If you can get him to open his mouth," said Flic.

"We'll think of a way," said Borel, standing. "I'm hungry. How about you?"

"Well, I suppose I could do with a bite. Buzzer, too."

"Come, let us to break our fast and scheme of ways to master the Pooka."

"How does a horseman get a wild horse to open its mouth for a lower-jaw rope to be slipped on?" asked Flic, as he picked at a portion of biscuit and dipped the resulting bit into honey. "—Oh, not that such a trick can be used on a Pooka, for they are not horses but are Dark Fey instead and smarter than most humans. Still, perhaps a trick can be done in a similar manner."

Borel said, "At times, one man strong enough, or several men working together, can grab an unruly horse about the head and force it down and slip the rope in place."

"My lord, here we are dealing with a—a Démon," said Flic around his mouthful of honey-soaked crumb, "its strength beyond measure, and I think such a trick will not avail here."

Borel rolled a rasher of bacon up in a piece of bread and shoved it into his mouth and chewed awhile. Finally, he said, "At other times a carrot or a piece of sweet apple or other such will get an unruly horse to open his mouth, and so food is used to trick the creature."

"My lord, I think a Pooka too wily to be fooled by mere food," said Flic, picking off another crumb of biscuit. He looked at the bee and said, "What if I have Buzzer sting him, say on the lip? —Oh, no, that won't work, for it will be at night. —But wait, when I get my épée, I can jab him there."

"I think that would just cause him to toss his head and then trample me," said Borel. "But there must be a way to fool him."

"Once more, I say, he is a Démon and clever," said Flic. "Though I am quite dull-witted, my lord, surely you are smarter than he is."

"Perhaps not," said Borel, "for you are no more dull-witted

than I, and—" Of a sudden Borel's eyes lit up. "Dull-witted! Oh, Flic, you have hit upon it!"

"I have?"

"You do say he can talk and therefore understand speech?"

At Flic's nod, Borel said, "And he is very clever, for he deceives men into thinking they are out for a pleasant ride when it is anything but. Well then, here is the nub of it: if he would have me ride, in me he will have met the most dull-witted creature in the whole of Faery." Borel grinned and added, "Flic, my wee friend, thank you for the idea."

Flic shrugged and said, "You're welcome, my lord, no matter what the idea is."

After breaking their fast, with Flic and Buzzer riding atop Borel's tricorn the trio set off for the smithery. As they fared along the way, Borel said, "To get this plan of mine to work, we will first have to find the Pooka."

"Oh, that's no problem," said Flic. "I know where it lives."

Borel stopped. "You do?"

"Didn't I tell you?"

"No."

"Oh, me. What with my meeting Fleurette and falling deeply in love and finding the three hairs and all, perhaps I'm the one who is pixilated."

"But you say you know where it lives?"

"Oui. You see, after working the three hairs loose from the splintery fence post, I followed the Pooka on its rampage, but as dawn neared, and as the night came to a close, it made for the river and entered it right in the midst of what are surely the White Rapids."

"And . . . ?"

"And nothing, my lord. You see, the Pooka is a water creature, and it either lives in a body of water—the ocean, a lake, a river—or it hides away inside a mountain, probably in an underground pool. *Our* Pooka lives under the rapids during the day, and comes out at nightfall. We will merely need to get there before darkness."

"Easily done," said Borel, moving ahead again. "I just hope my scheme is as simple to accomplish as it is for us to reach the torrent."

When they came to the forge, the smith had just finished honing Borel's new blade. With a final swipe and then a wipe of a cloth, he sheathed the weapon—a keen, double-edged bronze long-knife with a needle-sharp point—and handed it to the prince.

As Borel drew the blade from the scabbard, the man said, " 'Ware, Sieur, for 'tis finely whetted to a razor's edge. You'll have no trouble shaving with it." Then he grinned and added, "Or with gutting Trolls, I'll warrant."

Borel smiled and held the long-knife up in the light and said, "Well, Smith, I hope not to meet a Troll to gut, yet I thank you for the warning."

He slid the blade back into the sheath; the fit was perfect.

"Nicely done," said the prince. He handed over the agreed-upon fee, the coins from those gifted by the Gnomes, and belted the scabbard and strapped it to his right thigh.

Next they went to the milliner's, where the scarfpin sword waited, along with a tiny green belt fitted with a wee buckle made of silver wire, and affixed to the belt was a tightly wound coil of silver wire the length of the blade to act as a minuscule sheath. As Flic and Borel examined the tiny weapon, the Widow Marie said, "Since you will be using this against foe—or so I did assume—I filed it so that it has a three-sided, fluted blade, just as would a genuine épée."

"Épées have three-sided blades?" said Flic.

"Oh, yes, little master," said Marie. "It gives them strength while at the same time allows lightness. A good weapon with which to go out into the world and meet dangerous foe. You see, to face perils you either need a cutting blade or one with a very sharp point. And I think you too wee to wield an edge that cuts—such as a rapier—for that takes a bit of strength, and since you seemed to favor a bee sting—a jabbing weapon—an épée is best for you."

"A good choice, Madame," said Borel. "Better than a limber

foil, and I see that you have well wrapped the grip against slippage, and fashioned a small pommel as well."

"I also shaped it for the Sprite's grip," said the widow, "and I fixed the bell in place with silver-wire collars and a bit of crucible-melted silver as solder."

"Well done, Madame," said Borel, inclining his head.

"And the belt . . . ?" said Flic, smiling at the daughter Renée.

Renée refused to look directly at the Sprite, and instead cast a sidelong glance at him as she said, "Sieur Sprite, please note the silver-coil sheath has a keeper to secure the épée in place so that it won't fall out as you, um, flit about. A simple flick of the thumb will set the épée free."

"Superb, Demoiselle Renée," said Borel.

Renée blushed before Borel's penetrating, ice-blue gaze, but she said nought.

"Well, try it on, my lad," said Borel.

Flic, a wicked grin on his face, said, "Demoiselle Renée, would you care to fasten my belt 'round me?"

"Non!" said the daughter as the widow choked back a laugh.

"Ah, me," said the Sprite, and he took up the belt and buckled it about his waist. The fit was exact, though there were additional holes for expansion. Borel handed him the silver-bladed épée, and Flic flourished it about, and then slid it into its silver-coil scabbard. He frowned a moment, but then discovered how to slip the keeper in place.

"There, how do I look?" said Flic, strutting back and forth.

"Ah, *très bon!*" said the widow, glancing at Borel and winking. "The very picture of a gay blade."

And even Renée looked, for she could not resist seeing just how well her handiwork suited the Sprite. Flic turned toward her and struck a full frontal pose, and Renée threw up her hands in exasperation, and Flic struck another stance. At this posture, Renée burst out in titters.

"What, ma chérie? Do you find me amusing?" said Flic.

Renée only giggled all the harder, though she did turn away.

Flic stepped toward Buzzer and said, "Well, Madame Buzzer, now we both have stings."

Borel then said to the milliner, "My lady, we need a needle that will fit these." He drew forth the three Pooka hairs. "We must weave these three into this rope." Now he drew out a length of the Gnome-made line from another pocket.

Marie said, "Ah, in my daughter's hands it will take but a trice."

"Madame Marie, I think this is something Flic must do," said Borel.

"But I could use instructions," said Flic. "Perhaps Demoiselle Renée could guide the work while I actually perform it."

A small smile graced the corner of Marie's mouth, and she said, "Most certainly, for she has a finer hand than I. Renée, *s'il-te-plaît.*"

"But, Mother, he is still naked!" protested Renée.

"No I'm not," retorted Flic. "I'm wearing a belt."

"Though to me it was rather like my épée, we used a silver needle," said Flic, "once Marie discovered what it was to be used for. She said silver has wondrous properties for dealing with things of ill intent, and a Pooka is certainly that."

"And how did you and Renée get along," said Borel, grinning. "Did she, um, get a rise out of you?"

Flic smiled, but shook his head. "Oh, no. She's a rather nice girl, once you get to know her. I think we became friends as she showed me how to slip the needle and the Pooka-hair 'thread' through the plait of the Gnome rope. When I told her we were depending on the power of three, she had me weave the three hairs in three separate spirals up and about the line, exactly three turns each, and always making certain to keep them an equal distance apart from one another, even though they twisted 'round the rope. It practically made me dizzy, but she said patterns are important, and if it made me dizzy, then think what it would do to the Pooka. We chatted about this and that while she guided and I worked. —Say, did you know that her father Renaud was in Lord Roulan's manor when the black wind came?"

"Ah, then," said Borel, "perhaps the Widow Marie isn't a widow after all."

Flic frowned. "Your meaning?"

"Just this: since Chelle is yet alive, then there is a chance that others within the manor are alive as well. Of course, that presupposes the vale was carried up and away by the wind, rather than being turned to stone."

"Ah, even so," said Flic, "if there is a chance the others survived . . . Perhaps I should fly back and tell—"

"Oh, Flic, I think it better to not get anyone's hopes up in case I am wrong."

"Very well, my lord," said Flic.

They sat a moment without speaking, and then Flic said, "What about the constable? What did he say when you told him of the Pooka?"

"He was shocked, to say the least. He wanted to get an armed party together and run down the beast."

"Did you tell him that anyone who killed a Pooka would be cursed forever, and that the entire area would be blighted?"

"Oui," said Borel. "I also told him that I had a plan to rid the area of the Pooka, and he was most glad to hear it."

"Well, my prince, let us hope your plan works, whatever it is."

Two candlemarks before sunset, Borel and Buzzer and Flic set off upriver, the Widow Marie and Daughter Renée and Constable Moreau the only ones to see them off.

As Borel strolled along the trace of road paralleling the bank, Flic said, "Tell me, my lord, you say that you must court a woman and get to know her before you know whether she is really your truelove, right?"

"Oui," said Borel.

"Well, then, what of love at first sight? Do humans not experience such?"

"Humans oft fall in love at first sight," said Borel.

"What of courtship then, my lord?"

"Then, Flic, it is very swift," said Borel.

"Ha! No different from Fey, eh?"

Borel laughed, but made no reply.

After a moment Flic said, "If you insist upon doing it,

haven't you been courting Chelle and she courting you in your dreams?"

"Although it appears that way, Flic, I think one cannot truly court in a dream unless both sleepers are aware they are dreaming, and even then I wonder. You see, dreams are ephemeral, and though in this case I am aware in the dream that it is such a thing, Chelle is not, and therefore is subject to its whims, both during the dream and afterward. Hence, when she wakes, just as with any dream, courtship or no, she might not remember it at all. She might also be an entirely different person awake from what she is asleep. As I said before, in dreams inhibitions are greatly muted, and one can profess love for a total stranger and believe it to be true, and yet upon awakening will know such a thing to be entirely false.

"And so, my friend, I think it is only in our waking life that we might know of true love . . . and even that is not certain, for true love seems to be rare, as wonderful as it is."

Flic snorted and said, "Humans: the hoops you jump through to find a mate. Me, I'd rather be a Sprite. Besides, I've found my truelove, though I've only known Fleurette for a brief part of a single day."

Borel strode on upriver, both he and Flic pondering the oddities of the other's Kind, each *knowing* the "one best way" for trueloves to find one another.

And the farther Borel walked, the louder came the rumble of the raging water ahead, until at last—with the sun setting and twilight drawing across the land—they came to the long, steep slant of the White Rapids, where the river narrowed and roared between sloping stone banks to thunder over rounded boulders and great jagged crags and slabs of rock as it plunged down the perilous incline.

Above the thunder of water hurtling apace, Flic said, "There, by that big rock—yes, that one there—that's where the Pooka submerged."

Borel strode up the slope and stopped opposite. "Here will I wait, and when night falls, here will I become a fool."

"Remember, my prince, whatever else you have in mind, make him submit immediately."

"Oui, Flic, I will try."

Flic took to wing, Buzzer with him, and the Sprite hovered before Borel and said, "As soon as I get Buzzer settled, though she will be asleep in the night, I will return to watch over you, my lord."

Borel shook his head. "Flic, for my plan to work, the Pooka must think I am alone. Any suspicion that I am with others, and he will become chary and thwart what I have in mind."

Flic frowned in exasperation but said, "Oh, very well." He looked about and pointed toward a tall sycamore nigh. "I will remain hidden high in the branches unless you are in great peril, in which case Argent and I will come to aid."

"Argent?"

Flic patted the épée at his side. "My silver stinger. Renée named it so. It is a formidable blade, and all such require names."

"Oh, Flic, I would rather you stay completely out of it. I don't want you to get injured."

"Nor would I see you hurt," said Flic, his chin jutting out stubbornly.

Buzzer, orbiting about, sensed the tension and flew to hover at Flic's side before Borel's face. At this redoubtable show, Borel smiled and said, "Very well, Flic, you may come to my aid, but only in the extreme."

"Hai!" cried Flic. "I'll stab him in the eye."

With that, the Sprite flew to the high branches of the sycamore, Buzzer following.

And Borel stood alone upon the bank and waited, the thundering rapids falling further into shadow as twilight slid across the sky, dragging the train of dark night after.

And as the first stars began to appear, up and out from the furious churn came a sleek, black horse with a long flowing mane and tail, and cruel, sulphurous yellow eyes.

And Borel, his tricorn askew and pulled down to the point where his ears stuck out and his forehead all but vanished, began trudging upslope along the stone bank and singing a tuneless air, his hands worrying a short length of slender line. And he took no note of the dark steed, ebon as night, standing but fetlock-deep in the midst of raging white water, though the bottom itself was fathoms down, the savage rapids having no effect whatsoever upon the jet-black beast.

And the raven-dark creature trotted through the fury and made its way toward the shore. When it gained the bank, it paced after Borel, a seemingly oblivious fool. And when it reached this unaware dupe, it paused at the man's side and softly nickered.

Yet Borel continued to sing tunelessly and plod on.

The Pooka snorted, and trotted ahead and stood across the simpleton's path.

Borel collided with the horse, and looked up. "Oh, my. A horse. Are you lost? So am I."

The Pooka presented itself, inviting the imbecile to mount.

"Um, um . . ." Borel dithered from foot to foot. "What do they say? What do they say? Ah, yes: always look a lost horse in the mouth before you take a ride. Yes, that's it; I am sure that I've got it right. So, my gone-astray steed, I am going to look into your mouth, and then I'll go for a ride."

But the simpleton, the nit, the ninny, he began walking toward the Pooka's hindquarters, mumbling stupidly about having to look in the horse's mouth.

The Pooka turned about and faced this fool.

"Now, now, Sir Lost Horse, I do need to look into your mouth. I am certain I have to see your teeth before I can go ariding with you."

Once more the tomfool dullard started for the rear of the Pooka, and once more the Pooka turned 'round to face the gull.

"Listen to me, Lost Horse, I cannot ride unless I have a look in your mouth."

For the third time the idiot human plodded toward the creature's hindquarters, and, snorting in exasperation, the Pooka whirled to face the goose of a twit. And this time it showed its teeth.

"Oh, my, silly me, are these what I'm—"

In a flash and before the Pooka could react, Borel jammed the loop into the Pooka's mouth and 'round the lower jaw and into the gap and jerked the slipknot tight, and leapt to the creature's back and grabbed the mane and hauled hard against the rope.

A piercing scream of pain and rage rang through the night, for the Pooka had never before been fooled, and never before felt such pain.

And it leapt into the river and submerged, for it would drown this fool.

Borel barely had enough time to take a breath as they plunged into racing water, and he held the mane tightly in his left hand and hauled with all his might on the Gnome-made line.

And again the Pooka screamed in pain, but it dove for the bottom.

And the current buffeted and hammered at Borel, but he held on and haled back against the line, jerking again and again.

Yet he needed to breathe, but there was no air, and his diaphragm pumped, trying to take something into his lungs, be it air or not.

Screaming in agony, the Pooka raced through the water as if it were nought but ephemeral atmosphere, and, just as Borel knew that he would of a certainty drown, back onto the shore and into the woods galloped the creature. Borel breathed in great gulps of blessed air, even as the Pooka raced across the ground and crashed through thickets and slammed up against trees and rocks, trying to knock this deceitful person from its back.

But Borel hung on to the mane as well as the Gnome line, and he slid from side to side to avoid the boles and boulders and such, and he hauled hard against the rope.

"Submit!" cried Borel. "Submit!"

But the Pooka was strong and stubborn and enraged, and in spite of the pain it galloped on.

Of a sudden it transformed into a monstrous, hairy Bogleman with the head of a black goat. And it bit down on the line and shrieked in agony, for, with the three Pooka hairs woven throughout the rope, it was as if it were biting itself.

"Submit, I say!" cried Borel, even as the Pooka reached for the line to tear it from its own mouth. But Borel leaned back and threw all of his weight as well as all of his strength against the rope.

"Eeyagha!" shrieked the Pooka, and it flung its hands wide and became a great dark vulture and took to wing.

Up it flew and up, skreighing in agony, the rope through the vulture's beak, Borel hanging on and fiercely haling back on the line and shouting for the Pooka to submit, while the slipknot clenched tighter and tighter.

Yet the Pooka did not give in, but instead it rolled over and over in the air, trying to shake loose its tormentor, trying to make him plummet to his death 'gainst the ground far below. Yet the only thing that fell away from the Pooka was Borel's long-knife, for earlier, on a run through a thicket, the keeper had jolted free, and now as the Pooka repeatedly spun upside down the weapon slipped loose from its sheath and tumbled away, bronze glittering against the starlight to vanish in the night.

Above his own shouts for the creature to yield, Borel became aware of Flic shrieking. The prince looked over his shoulder and against the starry night sky he saw the tiny Sprite, swift as an arrow, overtaking the great black bird. And as Flic neared he cried out, "My lord, my lord, if he goes much higher, the air will get too thin for you to breathe and you will lose your strength and swoon."

Now Flic drew his épée, and—"Yahhh!"—he dove at the head of the monstrous scavenger and stabbed him with Argent, the vulture to *skraw* in related hurt.

And Borel hauled hard at the rope, and agonized screams filled the sky.

Again and again, Flic stabbed at the hideous bird, and again and again Borel jerked at the rope and called for the Pooka to yield, and at last the creature began spiralling downward.

It landed in craggy mountains and transformed into a huge black goat, and it began dashing its flanks against icy crags and pinnacles and massifs and hurtling in great leaps and bounds up and down sheer slopes and across deep chasms. And Borel shouted at Flic to stay back, else the Sprite might be smashed between creature and stone.

Borel hung on and wrenched the jaw loop even tighter and shouted for the creature to submit, but still the Pooka screamed in agony and rage and slammed into rock and ice, but Borel held on and slipped from side to side to avoid being crushed. Now the black goat leapt down the vertical steeps of the mountain toward the vale below, landing in a series of bone-jarring jolts in an attempt to dislodge this vile human from its back. And Borel, exhausted and battered, knew that he had not the strength left for another transformation and wild ride. And even as they reached the vale and Borel was certain the creature would win, the Pooka transformed back into the black steed with its sulphurous, burning yellow eyes, and it stopped and stood still, trembling, its sides heaving as it moaned in pain.

And then, its words muted by the rope 'round its jaw, it said, "What is it you wish, O Man?"

31

Exaction

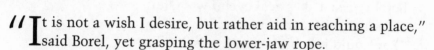

"It is not a wish I desire, but rather aid in reaching a place," said Borel, yet grasping the lower-jaw rope.

"Where, then, is it you wish to go?" said the Pooka.

"The Endless Sands," said Borel.

"Endless Sands?"

"Oui," said Borel. "A desert of sand stretching forever, or so the tales would have it be."

The Pooka snorted. "I am a creature of the water. What would I know of deserts?"

Borel gave the rope a tug. The Pooka moaned and cried out, "Spare me, my lord, for I am telling the truth. I know nothing of any Endless Sands."

"He is of the Dark Fey, my prince," said Flic, waving his silver épée. "He might be trying to trick you, to trick us. Let me jab him with Argent, and then he'll tell the truth."

Borel shook his head and said, "Non, my friend, I would not have you prick him, at least not yet."

"Oh, pox!" said Flic, clearly disappointed.

"Pooka," said Borel, "the Lady Wyrd sent me to master you, and so I have, and you will—"

"Skuld?" asked the Pooka. "Skuld sent you after me?"

"Indeed," said Borel.

The Pooka shuddered and said, "Then, my lord, I must speak the truth, and I have: I know nought of the Endless Sands."

"My lord, please let me jab him," said Flic. "Argent will puncture his lies."

"Sprite," said the Pooka, "I swear by the Lady Skuld, I am telling the truth."

"I believe him," said Borel, "for none can tempt the Fates by taking their names in vain."

Flic frowned and sighed and sheathed his épée and said, "Well . . . if he truly does not know, and since Lady Skuld sent you to triumph over him, perhaps you are to keep the Pooka as your mount."

"*Je vous en prie,* non, my lord," said the Pooka. "Oh, please, I beg of you. Were you to take me as your mount I would die."

Borel raised a skeptical eyebrow. "Die?"

"I cannot withstand the sun."

"You could ride him at night," said Flic.

"Do not heed the Sprite, my lord," said the Pooka, "for every nighttide as dawn draws nigh I must return to water ere the sun rises, and water may not be at hand if I serve you as a mount."

"Well, then," said Flic, "if that be the case, I say let him die in the sunlight, for he is a murderer."

"No, I am not," said the Pooka.

"What of those three men who drowned?" asked Borel.

"They were foolish enough to pursue me," said the Pooka. "In spite of my warnings, nigh dawn they chased me into the rapids and were caught in the flow. I was helpless to aid them, for the sun was then rising."

Borel frowned. "If I cannot use you as a mount, and if you know not where the Endless Sands lie, then why would Lady Wyrd send me to master you?"

The Pooka said nought, but Flic volunteered, "Perhaps it is as she said: to give aid to those in need, and the steads back nigh the rapids are certainly in need of relief from this Dark Fey."

"Non, my friend," said Borel. "Recall what she actually uttered: 'You must triumph o'er a cunning, wicked, and most deadly steed to find the Endless Sands.' "

"Skuld said that of me?" asked the Pooka.

"Oui," replied Borel. "Hence you must know of the Endless—" Borel's eyes widened in revelation. "Ah, wait, you must know of them or know of someone who does."

"My lord, it is as you say, for although I do not know of these sands, I do know of someone who might."

"And that would be . . . ?" said Flic.

"The King Under the Hill," said the Pooka.

"Oh, my," said Flic. "Someone even more dangerous."

"More dangerous?" said Borel.

"More dangerous than the Pooka, my lord," said Flic.

"Nevertheless," said Borel, "I would speak to this King Under the Hill. Where will I find him, Pooka?"

"I do not know, my lord," replied the Dark Fey.

Borel yanked on the lower-jaw rope.

"My lord, my lord," cried the Pooka. "I swear, I do not know, but I know of those who do."

"And they would be . . . ?" said Flic.

"The Riders Who Cannot Dismount," replied the Pooka, groaning in pain. "They would know, for the king himself cursed them."

"And where can I find these riders?" said Borel.

"They frequently pass through the Glade of the Mere," said the Pooka. "And *that* I can show you, for therein lies a water refuge."

"Then let us go," said Borel.

"Wait, my lord. What of Bu—what of our bee?" said Flic, the Sprite unwilling for a Dark Fey to know any of their names, not even the common ones.

"We must fetch her," said Borel. "I would not abandon our companion." He leaned forward and said to the Pooka, "I would have you fly back to the rapids, where we have a friend awaiting, and then take us to this Glade of the Mere."

"It is a long flight, my lord," said the Pooka, "and if you could just loosen the clench of this rope even if only a bit."

"No, no!" cried Flic. "It is a trick, and remember, he is a cunning and wicked and most deadly steed."

"I remember, Flic," said Borel. "Non, Dark Fey, I will not loosen the clench by as much as an iota until we are delivered unto the Glade of the Mere."

"Very well, my lord," said the Pooka, and he transformed into a giant eagle and took to wing, Borel holding on to feathers and the rope and locking his knees firmly against the eagle's flanks.

With Flic now standing in the prow of Borel's tricorn and hanging on tightly to the brim, and with Borel on the eagle's back and hanging on just as tightly, over the land they flew, starlight gleaming in rivers and lakes.

The eagle was swift, and soon they came to the White Rapids, where they landed beside the Meander, though in this part of the river it did not meander at all.

Flic flew up into the sycamore, and in moments came flying back, sleeping Buzzer in his arms, the Sprite rather struggling in flight, for the bee was nearly as big as he. Somewhat disturbed by the movement was Buzzer, and her wings trembled, but Flic silently spoke to her, soothing and calming the bee in the night.

On the tricorn Flic landed, and when he and Buzzer were well settled, at a signal from Borel the giant eagle took to wing, and up it spiralled and up, and then shot off toward the mountains. Long did it fly, league after league, and through several looming twilight walls of Faery, passing over farm fields and inlets; above long stretches of tundra, where herds of antlered animals grazed; over stretches of snow and ice; above vine-laden jungles; over villages and towns; over open prairies with shaggy beasts standing asleep in the night; and across other realms as well.

Finally, even as the waning crescent moon rose into the sky, above a great forest flew the eagle, now slowly gliding down through the air until at last it spiralled 'round and 'round to come to rest nigh a small lake in an open glade.

There were no riders on horses within.

"Here is the only place where I know the riders come," said the Pooka, even as it shifted back into the form of a dark horse with sulphurous yellow eyes.

"There's no one here," said Flic, his hand moving to the hilt of his épée. "Perhaps this is just a trick."

"No," said the Pooka. "Did I not swear on Lady Skuld?"

"Well, there's that," said Flic.

"Pooka," said Borel, "a vow taken in the name of Skuld is one not to be broken."

"Indeed, my lord," said the Pooka, his voice yet laced with pain.

"Then, ere I loose you, " said Borel, "there is a pledge I would have you make, a vow—"

"Oh, my lord, loose me now," said the Pooka, "loose me now. I will swear the vow when I am free of this agony."

"No, no!" cried Flic.

Borel said, "I know, my friend: he is a cunning and wicked and most deadly steed."

The Pooka sighed. "What is this vow, my lord?"

"Ere I tell you the vow," said Borel, "three men died because of your rampages, Pooka. I ask you, what would be a fitting punishment?"

"None, my lord," replied the Pooka. "They did not give me my due, and I justly destroyed their fences and gave some of them a ride. They themselves are responsible for their own deaths, for they chased me into the rapids, trying to kill me, but instead got caught in the flow and drowned of their own accord. Hence, no punishment is warranted."

"Hmm . . ." mused Borel. "Your rampage against them is still not defensible. Even so, they tried to murder you."

"Yes, yes, murder me," said the Pooka. "That's absolutely correct. That's why no punishment or vow is due."

"Not so," said Borel. "Here is what I would have you swear on the names of Skuld, Verdandi, and Urd—"

"All three Fates, my lord?"

"Yes, Pooka, all three. A more binding oath I cannot imagine."

The Pooka sighed and said, "Yes, my lord."

"Here it is then," said Borel: "You must altogether leave the realm of the White Rapids and never rampage on men again—"

"Not rampage? But they did not give me my due."

"Pooka!" snapped Borel. "What you name as getting 'your due' is nought but obtaining by threat that which you desire. It was not yours to begin with, and you did nought to earn it—no labor nor services rendered. And so would I have you swear."

"My lord," said the Pooka, "if I cannot rampage against men, then what, pray tell, will you allow?"

Borel sighed. "I would have you act as your more gentle Pooka brethren: you, like they, can take men for wild rides and dump them in muddy ditches and quag holes, just as long as they will not die or sustain any but superficial injury."

"My lord, I cannot merely—"

Borel gave a yank on the jaw rope.

The Pooka moaned and said, "Though you yourself are obtaining by force and threat that which you desire—an offense you accuse me of—I will take your oath."

"Have him also swear to leave us unharmed," said Flic. "You, the bee, and me, my lord, for I do not trust him."

Borel nodded. "You will swear by the Ladies Skuld, Verdandi, and Urd all of these things I—we—demand."

The Pooka sighed and spoke the oath, as elaborated upon and administered by Borel.

At last Borel dismounted. And he loosened the lower-jaw rope and set the Pooka free. With a sigh of relief the Pooka worked his jaw and lips, feeling of them for residual hurt. But with the three Pooka hairs now out of his mouth, miraculously it seemed there was none. And the Pooka said, "My lord, you fooled me by playing the dolt even better than any third son could, and I applaud you for it. You were too clever for me by far. Yet heed: never again will I be duped by such a trick or even one closely linked."

Borel smiled and said, "All I ask of you is to keep your oath, Dark Fey."

"Oh, that I will do, else who knows what the Fates would have in store for me?" The Pooka shuddered and added, "Perhaps they would assail me with even more of your kind."

With that the Pooka transformed into a great bird and flew away in the starry moonlit night.

32

Legend

After settling Buzzer on a selected leaf, Flic turned to Borel and said, "What now, my lord?"

Borel hobbled about, laying a fire, for he was sorely battered from his wild ride. "Now, Flic, we wait," he replied.

"For the Riders Who Cannot Dismount, eh?"

"Yes, though why they cannot is a puzzle, except the Pooka said they were cursed by the King Under the Hill. And speaking of the king, what is it about him that makes him even more dangerous than that Dark Fey?"

"Because, among other things, he can lay curses," said Flic. "Too, it is said that on a whim he keeps people prisoners for thousands of summers merely to dine with him. It seems time runs at a different pace within his hold."

"Ah, well," said the prince, "I'll try to avoid each of those things."

"Well, if he gives you any trouble, you might— My lord, your long-knife: it's gone!"

"Tumbled away in the night, Flic," said Borel, "when the Pooka was the vulture and rolling over and over. I could not spare a hand to try to catch it, hanging on as I was. Yet even had I tried, I think I would have only cut myself."

"You needed a keeper for your blade," said Flic, "like my Argent has."

"The sheath has a keeper, Flic, but when the Pooka ran through thickets and smashed against trees and such, it must have come loose. Regardless, it lies somewhere lost. Perhaps one day someone needing a weapon will come across it."

"Perhaps," said Flic, stretching and yawning and settling down beside Buzzer. "Besides, I was going to say you could use your long-knife should the King Under the Hill give you trouble, but I think with his power to curse someone, it's better that you don't." Again Flic yawned.

Borel lit the campfire and, groaning a bit, settled down to a meal of jerky and hardtack, after which he stepped to the mere and took a deep drink and replenished the waterskin he had purchased in Riverbend. Then he cast another branch upon the fire and turned to bid Flic good night, but the Sprite was sound asleep.

"Good evening, ma chérie," said Borel, determined this time to control his heart, with its lusty urges. He was back in the turret surrounded by floating daggers.

"My Borel," she replied, smiling and curtseying. "Where are we off to tonight?"

Borel frowned in thought and then smiled and said, "I think to a place that once held peril, but now does not."

"Ah, a mystery, I see," said Chelle. "Lead on, my lord."

Borel offered Chelle his arm, and together they stepped into the shadows and through the hidden door to emerge on the stone bank of the White Rapids. And the air thundered with the roar of water hurling furiously down the long slope of the run.

"Oh, my, what a beautiful fury," said Chelle, raising her voice to be heard above the churn. "And you say peril was here?"

"Oui, and recently at that."

"What kind of peril?"

"A Pooka. Have you ever heard of such?"

"Oh, yes," said Chelle. "My père often told me of the king of the Keltoi and his wild ride."

"What?" said Borel, and he shook his head. "I should have asked you of the legend."

"The legend of the king and the Pooka?"

"Oui," said Borel. "I heard of it from a Sprite, but he did not know how the king prevailed."

"Would you like to know? It will cost you a fee."

"A fee?"

"A kiss," said Chelle.

"Gladly," said Borel, and he took her in his arms and they kissed long and lingeringly. Finally he backed away and said, "A splendid fee, my lady, joyously paid, but now I would have that tale. Yet let us find a place a bit quieter."

Upstream they strolled, until the rumble of the rapids faded and the wide Meander slowly slid past. They came to a mossy bank, where they settled down to talk.

"Now about this Keltoi legend . . ." said Borel.

"Pookas," said Chelle. "They are rather dreadful night creatures, though in the legend there seems to be only one instead of the many my father believes are in Faery. What do you know of them?"

"A bit," said Borel, "but not the legend."

"Did you know they can assume many forms?" said Chelle.

Borel nodded but did not interrupt, for he was entranced by Chelle's lilting voice, which was both soothing and exciting at one and the same time.

"The most common of which are goats, Boglemen, giant birds, and horses," said Chelle. "But they also can take on the forms of bats and horrible things right out of a nightmare—some of which might jump out at you in the dark." Chelle smiled. "Or so my père said."

She pointed at the moon. "It is said that sometimes in its bird form it swoops up a man and flies to the moon and abandons him there, though I think that merely a tale for children.

"It is also said that in one of its nightmare shapes it leaps onto a person's back and claws at him, and the only way to dislodge it is to pray or to say a blessing. Of course, should the person not do these things, death of fright will occur."

Borel cocked a skeptical eyebrow, but again remained silent.

Chelle grinned at him and went on: "The most common shape the Pooka takes is that of a black horse with burning yellow eyes. And it can run swifter than an arrow, and does so. Again it is said that as a dark steed it snatches up men—drunkards especially—yet in this case it doesn't go to the moon, but instead takes them for fearful rides before dumping them into a bog ditch.

"It is a water creature, haunting rivers and lakes and the sea, and it sometimes carries men to their death by drowning."

"That I most assuredly know," muttered Borel, and when Chelle looked at him in curiosity, he motioned for her to continue.

"Sometimes on long voyages the sailors will see in the night a black steed galloping o'er the waves after, and then they know something terrible lies ahead—a reef, a shoal, pirates, or such—and so they become fearful and change course."

Chelle paused and leaned over and kissed Borel, and it was some time before she began the tale again.

"There was a king of the Keltoi whose land was plagued by a particular and quite cruel Pooka, who had caused the deaths of many of the king's subjects—by drowning, by fright, by being hurled from a cliff, or by having their bones crushed by its powerful kicks. And no matter which road or river or field a person walked, the Pooka could be met anywhere. It was as if the creature claimed the realm as his own, when instead it was that of the king."

"Do you remember his name?" asked Borel.

"The Pooka or the king's?"

"The king's," replied Borel.

Of a sudden Chelle laughed. "I don't know why I asked that, for neither the Pooka's name nor that of the king do I recall." Then she frowned in concentration, trying to dredge up from her memory either of the names, but finally she sighed and shrugged her shoulders. "I seem to remember it was a name similar to yours, though I am not certain of that at all."

"I think it matters not," said Borel. "Please do go on."

"First, my tale-telling fee, Sieur," said Chelle, and she leaned over for another kiss.

Her lips were so soft and her breath sweet, and he felt there was no better place for her than in his arms. And he held her and inhaled her fragrance, his blood hammering in his ears. And he kissed her again and this time he began to harden, and—

Borel gently disengaged and murmured, "Ah, Love, please go on with the story."

Chelle sighed but nodded and said, "Well, the king set out to deliberately find this Pooka and master it. Now somehow the king had gotten hold of three of the Pooka's tail hairs, and he wove them together—"

"He didn't have them woven by an Elf into an Elf-made rope?"

"Oh, no," said Chelle. "At least not the way my père tells it. You see, I think if they had been woven into a rope, that would have muted their power, and the king would have had an even more terrible time of it."

Borel groaned but said, "I'm sorry for interrupting you, Chérie. Please go on."

"First my fee," said Chelle.

Again they embraced. Again they kissed. And again Borel began to respond. But Chelle laid her head against his chest and said, "I can hear your heart, my love. It beats like a horse agallop . . . or mayhap a Pooka arun."

They sat quietly, the river murmuring past, the rapids afar rumbling, and then Chelle said, "The king plaited the three hairs together, and then went looking for the terrible Dark Fey. When at last he found the creature—in the form of the black horse, I add—he looped the braided Pooka hairs about the creature's neck and leapt upon its back. The moment he did so, the plait became a rope of steel, and steel being a form of iron, and the Pooka one of the Fey, it screamed in pain, in agony, for iron was against its skin.

"Still it was enraged, and off it ran, taking the king on a harrowing ride and trying to throw him, but the king hung on and let the Pooka run to exhaustion. And when it was defeated, the king made the Pooka swear never to harm another man."

Chelle stopped and looked into Borel's eyes, her own unseen behind the shadowy band. "Isn't that a wonderful tale, my love? Not that it likely happened, for who but a drunk or a fool would dare ride a Pooka, regardless of a three-hair charm?"

Borel burst out laughing, his face turned to the sky, and he finally answered, "Who but a fool, indeed?"

Chelle twisted 'round to lie back against him, and she looked up and smiled and said, "Kiss me, my sweet Borel, for I have given you the tale you desired."

"Oh, my love, I desire more than a mere tale," said Borel, and he embraced her and leaned down and—

"My lord, wake up, wake up!" cried Flic. "The riders have come, they've come!"

Groggily, Borel opened his eyes to see Flic holding his own head and groaning in pain.

"Wh-what did you say?"

"The riders have come, my lord, and I must leave, for they bear iron—dreadful, aethyr-twisting iron."

And with that, Flic flew up and away, Buzzer following, as into the Glade of the Mere came men ahorse in cavalcade.

33

Riders

Into the glade came the riders on horses, some nine men altogether, all armored in what appeared to be light chain shirts, and armed with bows and spears . . . and swords hung at their sides. And they stopped on the far shore of the mere as if to let their horses drink, yet none did, and not one of the riders dismounted. And they seemed to be arguing among themselves, and so they took no notice of Borel as he made his way 'round and toward them. But their voices carried well o'er the water, and he heard what discord lay among the men.

"My lord, my lord," cried one of the riders, his voice tight with distress, "we are on an endless ride, for the cur will ne'er jump down of its own accord."

Borel frowned. *Cur?* And as he neared he saw that one of the riders held a small dog across his saddlebow.

And the man with the dog said, "Chevalier d'Strait, you must not give up hope, for surely someone can solve our dilemma. Think of the others who felt as you do, for they are now gone. Think of your horse as well."

"But, my lord king, there is nought left in the mortal world for us to return to," said the first man, the one named by the king. "I would join my wife and child in the Beyond."

At this, other of the men set up a clamor, some crying out *No!* while some nodded in agreement.

As Borel came up to them, he noted that although the arms and armor seemed solid enough, the men themselves as well as their horses seemed pale and wan and not quite real, as if they had somehow grown tenuous.

Borel frowned. *Perhaps they are spirits, even specters, though the sun is up, which would seem to belie any contention of them verging onto ghosthood.*

"It is within my power to command you, d'Strait, to list to me and not do this thing. Yet it is my fault we are as we are, and so I will not forbid you. Instead I beg of you to—"

"Enough, my king," the chevalier cried out in agony. "Debate is useless; all is hopeless." And he swung his leg over his saddlebow and leapt from his horse. And the moment his feet touched the ground his flesh withered and fell away, as did that of his horse, and their bones clattered down, but then turned to dust.

Men cried out, as did Borel, and some began to weep, and a whirl of air spun among the ashes, as if something were seeking some essence within.

And now Borel stepped in among the mounted riders, and he knelt at the side of the wind-stirred mound, where all that was left behind were ash and dust and aged and cracked tack and tatters and shreds of cloth, along with rust and timeworn splinters where arms and armor once had been, but for the hilt of a sword jutting out from the desiccated heap.

"Mithras, receive him," said Borel, and he passed his hand over the ashes in a sign of blessing.

Borel stood and turned to the others and said, "Now I understand why they call you the Riders Who Cannot Dismount."

Mastering his grief, the man with the dog upon his saddlebow asked, "And you are . . . ?"

"I am Prince Borel of the Winterwood in Faery," replied Borel, bowing.

"And I am King Arle of the mortal realm," replied the man, canting his head in acknowledgement. "And these are my men, what remains of them."

Borel glanced from man to man, and each had nought but desolation in his eyes. Then Borel looked at the ashes. "I take it he was not the first."

"The fifth," said Arle.

"Here is a story to be told," said Borel. "Perhaps I can help, for Lady Wyrd, Lady Skuld, She Who Sees Through Time's Mist, she sent me to aid others, and perhaps receive aid in return."

"Skuld sent you?" said the king, as if mulling over what he had just heard, and his men shifted about in their saddles and looked at one another, a bit of hope in their eyes.

"Indeed, my lord."

"And she said we might help you in turn?"

"Oui, my lord."

"And what is it you want?" asked Arle.

"To find the King Under the Hill," replied Borel.

At this, all the men gasped and made warding signs and cried out in a great clamor that he must not seek the King Under the Hill.

Arle held up his hands for silence, and when it fell he said, "Prince Borel, you must stay away from the King Under the Hill, for it was he, the High Lord of the Fey Folk himself, who cursed us to be the Riders Who Cannot Dismount."

"That I understand, my lord, for such did the Pooka say."

"Pooka? That dark creature?"

"Oui. He was the one who told me to seek you out to find the King Under the Hill."

"I think they be in league," called one of the riders, "the Pooka and the King Under the Hill. Both are black of heart."

"Nevertheless," said Borel, "I must find the High Lord, for my truelove's life depends upon it."

King Arle sighed. "Ah, me, if that be the case . . ." He frowned and said, "But first I would tell you our tale, and then you will see whether or no you still wish to seek out that king." He looked at Borel for consent.

"I will listen," said Borel, "yet I am determined."

King Arle nodded and said, "This then is the way of it:

"I am monarch of a mortal realm bordering on Faery—or perhaps I should say, I *was* monarch there. Regardless, one day I decided to go on a hunt, and twelve of my chevaliers were eager to accompany me."

"*Dix et trois,*" said one of the riders. "Unlucky thirteen."

Arle sighed and ruefully nodded. "Unlucky thirteen indeed we were."

The king remained silent for moments, and Borel thought he might not continue. But then Arle said, "We had no intention of riding into the realms of Faery, but up jumped a white stag. We sounded the horns in glee and gave keen pursuit. Yet into the twilight border he ran, and for such a magnificent creature we would ride into the very Realms Of Perdition, were he to run that way—or so we told ourselves.

"And thus into Faery we raced, hot on the trail of the White Hart, though one of us, d'Strait, I believe, said such creatures were enchanted and to beware.

"Yet I would not easily yield such a trophy, and after him I galloped, all twelve of my chevaliers following, for they would not abandon me in dread Faery.

"Over hill and dale we ran, and through many of the looming twilight borders, the White Hart just out of range of bow shot, and just a bit faster than our steeds, though every time it stopped to rest, again we caught up.

"And just ere dusk, it fled into a large opening 'neath a dolmen sitting atop a hillside, light pouring out from below, and we pursued, and found ourselves not only in Faery but also in the very Hollow Hills of the Highborn Ones, a gala in full swing.

"But when we came riding into their midst, they fled before us, and down corridors and passages and ways unknown. As to the White Hart, he was nowhere to be seen.

"But then the King Under the Hill stepped from a side hall and welcomed us, though there was a pained look upon his countenance. Yet we did not understand why . . . until it was entirely too late.

"But as I say, the High Lord welcomed us, and offered us food and drink and quarters overnight, for darkness was even then descending.

"We gladly accepted his hospitality. And though we were mostly shunned, still, women of surpassing—even ethereal—beauty served us food and drink, though they did not linger in spite of our entreaties."

Borel said, "You ate their food and drank their wine?"

"Yes," replied Arle, glumly, "for ten days running."

"Ah, then, that does not bode well, my lord."

"Indeed, it did not, for when we mounted up and made ready to depart, the High Lord came and said, 'For ten days herein you have eaten our food and drunk our wine and so when you return to your own world you will find a thousand mortal years have passed.'

"We were aghast at hearing such a dreadful thing, for all those we had known and all things we had owned were now crumbled unto dust. Yet that was not the last of our torment, for the King Under the Hill said: 'Hear me, you did pursue me, for I was the White Hart who fled, and this by itself is enough to bring woe upon you. Further, you brought the Agony of Iron into our midst, and for that alone you are cursed. Take this dog, 'tis a gift the like of which I have given to many,' he said, 'to the peril of those receiving.' And he placed it on my saddlebow, where you see it now. And he further said, 'And unless and until it leaps down of its own will, you must not dismount, else it shall be to your doom, for in the moment you set foot to ground, you will become wholly mortal, and, even though you might yet be in Faery, all of your years will catch up with you.'

" 'How can this be, my lord?' I asked, and then he told me that as time is reckoned in the mortal world, for every day we stayed within his hill and ate his food and drank his wine, one hundred mortal years had passed, hence, for the ten days we had been within his hall a thousand years had elapsed all told. And he said that when we return to the outside world, all will have changed, and we will no longer know anyone nor will anyone therein know us. And my realm would now be ruled by strangers, if it yet existed at all.

"We were devastated, and we rode out from under that dolmen and have been riding throughout the realms of Faery ever since . . . riding for years untold." Arle held up a ghostly hand and said, "And each day we fade a bit more, and we are shunned by those in towns, for they fear us, given our ghastly state. And so we avoid them altogether, and have no companionship but our own. Ah, zut! There will come a day when we and our mounts will be gone altogether, be nought but empty armor riding upon unseen steeds."

Arle sighed and gestured at the pile of ashes. "And so, you see, if we dismount, then of a sudden we are a millennium old, and fall into complete ruin.

"Five of my men have perished, for they could not bear what they were becoming, nor could they forget what they had been and what they had lost, d'Strait just the last of them."

King Arle fell silent, and Borel looked at the dog and said, "You say the dog must jump down of its own will?"

"Oui," replied Arle.

"This then is my bargain, King Arle," said Borel. "I will tell you how to break the curse, and you will tell me how to find the King Under the Hill."

King Arle said, "Prince Borel, even if it is as you say—that your truelove's life is at stake, the King Under the Hill is not to be trusted."

"Nevertheless, I insist," said Borel.

King Arle looked at his men, and for the first time saw that they now had hope in their eyes, and he turned to Borel and said, "Very well. From here to reach the King Under the Hill you must go across three twilight borders always in the direction where the sun sets and only in that direction and do not deviate; then, beyond the third border, look for the hills, and amid them find the one with a great dolmen on top; at dusk a hole like a cavern will open within the dolmen and light will shine out. Down a steep slope twisting 'round within you will find the King Under the Hill, for therein is where he dwells.

"This I would offer, were we ordinary men: that you mount up behind one of us and we would take you there; yet we are not commonplace men, and as long as we are cursed, it would mean that you yourself perhaps would take on that curse were you to ride with us as we are; and so we can only lead you to that place."

"Thank you, my lord," replied Borel, "but I have no need to be led, for I have an unerring guide who takes her direction from the sun. Instead I would have you break your curse and find your way to your goal, whatever it might be, once the curse is done."

"Say on, Prince Borel," cried one of the men. "Tell us how to lay aside this bane."

"The dog, is it male or female?"

"Male," replied Arle.

"Then here is the way of it," said Borel. "Ride to the nearest town where people abide, no matter their fear of you, a town where many dogs do dwell. Find a bitch in heat, and surely will your dog leap down of its own accord to mate with her."

The king looked at his men in amaze and they in turn at him. "How simple," breathed Arle. "How very simple." He turned to Borel. "Surely, my prince, this is the solution. We are deeply in your debt."

"No more than I in yours," replied Borel, bowing.

"My Lord Borel," said one of the men, reining near, "take care, take care, and beware this High Lord. Eat not his food nor drink his wine nor cross him in any manner. Take no iron into his realm, else you will find yourself in dire straits."

"I heed and thank you," said Borel. He stepped back a pace or two and called out, "Now go, for you have a curse to break."

At a signal from King Arle, all the men wheeled their horses and into the forest surround they rode, and just ere they vanished from sight among the trees, a horn sounded in gratitude and farewell.

Borel strode around the mere and began to break camp, drowning the remaining coals of his fire with water and then replenishing his waterskin. As he strapped on his rucksack and slung his bow and shouldered his quiver, Flic and Buzzer came flying back.

"Well . . . ?" said the Sprite.

"Come," said Borel, we must go to where I spoke to the riders, and then Buzzer need take a sighting and guide us toward the exact place where the sun sets, for three twilight borders hence is where the King Under the Hill dwells. I will tell all as we fare about the mere."

And so Borel strode and Flic and Buzzer rode to the opposite side of the mere, and Borel told of what the men had done and what they had said, and when he reached the far side he pointed out the pile of ashes and rust and aged tack and tattered cloth and timeworn splinters that had once been a man and a horse and their accoutrements.

Flic said, "A dreadful fate, yet he and the others pursued the White Hart and brought the Agony of Iron into Faery." Then the Sprite frowned and asked, "What I wonder, though, is what do the riders and their horses eat, how do they sleep, and when they have to relieve themselves, how do they, um, go?"

Borel shrugged his shoulders and said, "I didn't ask."

Flic groaned in frustration.

"Come," said Borel, "we've more important things to do than to worry about the daily lives of the riders. Tell Buzzer what it is we want. Go directly to where the sun sets, Arle said, and no deviation."

Flic sighed and, with Buzzer, flew to the ground. Somehow Flic spoke to the bee, using that silent language of theirs. After a moment the bee did a short waggle dance, and Flic replied. Finally, Buzzer took to wing and sighted on the morning sun, and then shot off at an angle.

Flic flew to Borel's tricorn. "She wanted to know if you would be any faster. I told her no, and in fact perhaps a bit slower, after your Pooka ride. Next chance we get, I'll see if I can find flowers for another tisane or two; I mean, given your ways so far, it seems you are certain to suffer damage again."

Borel smiled and nodded distractedly, for his gaze was locked upon the hilt jutting out from the pile of ashes and rust. "All blades are not what they seem," he murmured, and he bent down and took hold of the sword and lifted it free. It came up in its decrepit sheath, and as ash and dust drifted down he drew out the weapon, and the scabbard, baldric, and edge alike crumbled, and all that was left was the hilt and a short, jagged piece of rusted blade.

"Does this bother you, Flic?"

"Non," said the Sprite. "Only iron in a near pure form twists aethyr enough to pain the Fey. That or steel. It seems the blade you have in your hand—including its tang—is wholly rust and it is no more hurtful than the ore from which it comes."

"Good," said Borel, and he sheathed the jagged remainder in his empty long-knife scabbard.

"Well, are we going to stand around all day?" asked Flic.

Borel barked a laugh and began his loping Wolftrot, following the beeline Buzzer had flown.

34

Events Past

Through the forest they hastened, Buzzer awing, Borel afoot, and Flic aseat on the hat. Past great old oaks they went, and across flowering glades, and up and down wooded slopes, some steep, others not. Through streams Borel splashed, ever following the course set by Buzzer. In less than half a candlemark, his soreness from yestereve's harrowing ride upon the Pooka diminished to the point that Borel's lope was nigh his usual rate.

And they came upon a wide glen, wherein a herd of Unicorns—of silver-sheened grey and pearlescent white and lightly brushed gold—did graze, and they scattered before Borel as he loped across, and they fled into the woods.

"Oh, my," said Flic, "so beautiful they are. See how they run: so graceful."

Borel paused and watched, for even in Faery Unicorns are rare, and to see an entire herd rarer still. Soon these single-horned, cloven-hoofed, nimble creatures passed from view, running as they did among the trees. When the last one disappeared, Borel took up again his own run.

"Much nicer than the Pooka, eh?" said Flic.

"Oui," replied Borel, and then added, "Speaking of the Pooka, perhaps I should have asked Chelle about him before going after that Dark Fey."

"How so?" asked Flic.

"In my dream of last night I asked her what she knew of Pookas, and she related to me the legend of the ride of the king of the Keltoi. It seems he had a much easier time of it than did I."

"Did she tell you the tale? If so, I would have you refresh my own memory."

Borel said, "Her version had no Elf weaving three Pooka hairs through an Elf-made rope. She said that twining them thus would mute their power."

"I wondered about that," said Flic. "But, you know how Elves are: they tend to insert themselves into all manner of stories . . . at least the several Elves I've met do."

"Ah, then that might account for the difference," said Borel.

"If Lady Chelle's telling had no Elf-made rope," said Flic, "then how did the king use the three hairs?"

"He merely made a charm by plaiting them together," said Borel, "thereby making them into a cord. Hence, their power was not muted, and all he had to do was ride the Pooka until it became exhausted."

"Did the Dark Fey shift shape?" asked Flic.

"I think not," replied Borel.

They came to the brink of a short drop to a mossy bank. "Hold on, Flic," said Borel, and without waiting for an answer he sprang down. But the moss was slick and Borel nearly lost his balance. Flic was thrown from the hat and took to wing, but as soon as Borel gained his footing, the Sprite returned to the tricorn and settled in.

"Next time, my lord, a wee bit more warning would help," said Flic.

Borel merely grunted and continued his lope.

"Also, my lord, it certainly won't do for you to twist an ankle."

Again Borel grunted, but said no words.

After moments, Flic said, "By the bye, woven together into a cord, I would think three hairs alone not strong enough to subdue one of those Dark Fey. How did the king use them?"

"He merely looped them around the neck of the Pooka and leapt upon its back," said Borel. "The instant he did so, the three hairs turned to steel, and so they were strong enough."

"Feh, my lord. That Pooka hairs could change into steel or into *any* form of iron is but a flight of fancy, for the Pooka is of the Fey, and iron is an anathema to him, to us, to all Fey. Such a thing simply could not be."

"Strange things have been known to hap in Faery," said Borel, "and if Pooka hair did turn to steel, it could be among the strangest."

Neither spoke for a while as Borel continued to lope, and Buzzer continued to fly, the bee keeping to the line where she knew the sun would undoubtedly set. But finally Flic said, "Unless and until we meet that very king of the Keltoi, I think we'll not know the truth. Regardless, Prince Borel, you did ride that Dark Fey to submission, magic cord or no."

Borel said nought as he ran on.

They stopped for a meal in the noontide: Flic and Buzzer lapping honey; Borel chewing jerky and hardtack. And as they sat, Flic said, "Tell me of Valeray and his friend Roulan and what they did to make Rhensibé angry."

Borel looked at the Sprite. "Are we to assume Rhensibé is Hradian's sister?"

"I think it most likely," said Flic.

"If that be so, then here is the way of it: Hradian and her sister—if it is Rhensibé—were acolytes of the dark magicien Orbane, the most terrible of all the Firsts. —Did I mention that Camille has a notion how Faery came to be?"

Flic shook his head, *No*, and Borel said, "Camille believes that long past the Keltoi bards told tales that were so entrancing that the gods themselves became enamored of the stories. So, after hearing of Faery, they created it, and initially they populated it with folk from the tales. And whenever one of the Keltoi bards spoke of someone of a new Kind—a Kind the gods had not before heard of—they made that Kind manifest in Faery. Hence, Raseri the Firedrake and Adragh the Pwca—and others who were first of their Kind—became Firsts in Faery. And so, too, was Orbane a First—a terrible magicien as told by the Keltoi bards.

"And Orbane and his acolytes caused much trouble throughout all of Faery, until the Fates themselves stepped in and through riddles told other of the Firsts if nought were done there would come a day when Orbane would be the ruin of Faery and the mortal world as well."

"Why would the gods create someone so horrible?" asked Flic.

"I think for the adventures he would cause," said Borel, "as good folks and the Firsts tried to overcome him."

"Ah, I see," said Flic. "Please go on with the tale."

Borel nodded and said, "After the Fates gave warning, many of the Firsts formed an alliance, and they took cause against the magicien. Yet even with all of their powers, Orbane was still more powerful.

"But then an oracle among the Firsts said that Orbane could only be defeated by his own hand, and so Valeray, my sire—a considerable trickster in his time—was chosen to find a way to discover the means by which this could be done.

"Disguised as a soothsaying crone, my sire inveigled his way into one of Orbane's many castles—he had several, you see, one of them on an isle far in the sea, another on a mountain crest high above the land, still another mid a stormy lake, and yet others scattered throughout Faery.

"Regardless, my sire—as a soothsaying crone—went to one of these holts: a castle on a bald hill in the midst of a dark forest. Therein the crone met the witch Nefasí, one of the acolytes, and—even though my sire knew the magicien was not within—the soothsayer asked for an audience with Orbane. When Nefasí asked why, the crone replied she had a dreadful message to give to the dark one.

"Nefasí told the old crone that Orbane was elsewhere, but that she herself would receive the message from her and pass it on to Orbane.

"The old soothsaying crone agreed, but she insisted that they go to a place of protection—a place of power and transmutation—ere she would divulge the message dire. And after wheedling and haranguing, at last Nefasí consented.

"Accompanied by well-armed Troll guards, by winding ways and up stairwells and past many rooms—ways and wells and rooms my observant sire committed to memory—Nefasí took the aged soothsayer into Orbane's own alchemistry chamber, where a pentagon of protection was permanently inscribed upon the floor. There did Nefasí cast a spell, one that temporarily rendered the Trolls deaf and mute, and then told the old soothsayer to speak. And so, surrounded by unhearing and unspeaking guards, with both sitting at a table within the pentagon, the crone divulged the message: 'Orbane will be defeated by his own hand.'

"At these bodeful words, Nefasí's gaze flicked briefly toward a small locked chest sitting atop a table, a chest my sire clearly noted. Nefasí asked if there were more to the sooth divined, and the crone shook her head. Nefasí rewarded the soothsayer with a single gold piece and sent her on her way.

"That very same night, my sire scaled the outside wall to the alchemistry room, and he picked the lock and found within the chest two clay amulets—Seals of Orbane—and he wrapped them well and stood in the window and, using a sling, he cast them to Roulan who was waiting at the edge of the woods. Then down clambered my father, and soon he and Roulan were riding agallop to the waiting Firsts. Yet even as Valeray and Roulan passed through that dark forest, they were seen and recognized and pursued.

"They managed to reach the Firsts, and the enemy was routed.

"Later, the Seals were descried for what they were, and the two were used to cast Orbane into the Castle of Shadows beyond the Black Wall of the World, where he remains still."

Borel fell silent and Flic said, "Oh, my, but what an adventure. Is that the end of Orbane?"

"I think not," said Borel, "for the Fates did tell Camille that events were afoot and Orbane might be set free, and if so, he planned to pollute the River of Time itself."

"And what does Hradian have to do with such?" said Flic.

"Along with unnamed sisters, she is one of Orbane's acolytes," said Borel.

Flic nodded and said, "Ah, then Nefasí and Rhensibé and Hradian might be sisters three."

"That is my thought as well," said Borel, standing. "Yet we are not certain at all whether this be true, and speculation alone is not proof."

Borel then looked at the bee. "We should be on our way. Is Buzzer done?"

"Oui, my lord," said Flic, "and so am I."

Borel repacked the rucksack and made ready to leave, and Buzzer took flight and sighted on the sun and shot away. Borel set his hat upon his head, and Flic took the prow, and away they went, following the beeline once more.

All the rest of the day Borel loped, and just ere sunset he broke free of the forest, and across a grassy field stood a wall of twilight, where Buzzer awaited. "Here be the first of three borders of which King Arle spoke," Borel said, and into the marge he jogged, and when he and Buzzer and Flic emerged on the far side, they came into a savanna stretching away for as far as the eye could see. In the distance a great herd of some sort of beasts were agraze on the veldt.

As darkness fell, Borel made camp within a stand of spiny acacia, the thorn-laden trees a bit of protection against wild predators, though perhaps not all.

35

Soaring

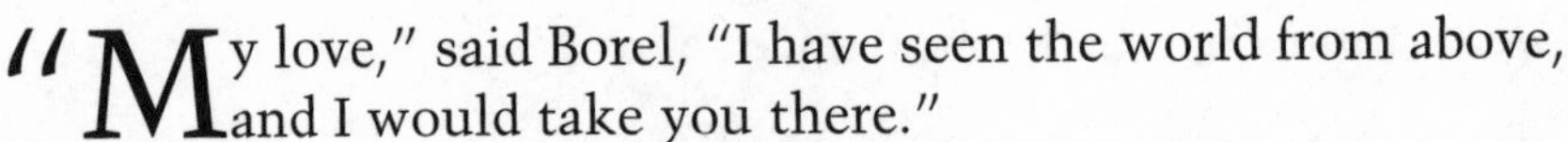

"My love," said Borel, "I have seen the world from above, and I would take you there."

"Are we to go to a mountaintop?"

"Something much better, ma chérie."

Chelle smiled. "Then let us away."

Hand in hand they stepped through the enshadowed door and out onto a broad, windswept ledge upon a looming mountainside. Snow shone white on the crest above, wooded slopes lay darkly on the flanks below, the trees leading down to a deep forested valley, where a glint of a river hinted at its existence in the light from the waning moon, a thin crescent in the sky. To their right a torrent of meltwater thundered onto the ledge and then cascaded on downward into deep shadows 'neath.

"It is beautiful up here," said Chelle. "But I thought you said we were not to go upon a mountain."

"This is but temporary, Chérie," said Borel, stepping behind her and clasping her in his arms. "Here comes our mount now." And he pointed, and silhouetted against the starry sky came winging a Great Eagle.

"Do not be afraid," whispered Borel.

"I'm not," said Chelle, and she pressed Borel's arms tighter about.

With a graceful turn the mighty bird glided down to settle upon the broad shelf, and then stepped 'round and to the verge and waited. "After you, Chérie," said Borel, and he handed her up to sit on the eagle's back, and he took seat behind.

"Away," he called to the eagle, and the raptor leapt from the ledge and flew into the air.

Up they soared into the night sky and out over the forest below, the mountainside falling away as eagle wings stroked atmosphere.

"Oh, but how splendid," cried Chelle, enraptured. "Would that we ourselves had wings."

High over the terrain they flew, and they left the woodland behind, and far below they could see farm fields looking much as would an échiquier, squares awaiting échecsmen—spearmen, hierophants, kings, queens, towers, and chevaliers all that were lacking.

They flew over campsites, some with small fires ablaze, others with nought but ruddy coals aglow, still others dark. Over lakes they soared, some with night fishermen casting their lures. Wild horses ran across plains, and then in the sky beside them a vee of honking geese flew by heading for a place only they knew.

"Oh, my Borel, how did you ever—?"

Of a sudden the air shuddered and jolted, and Borel—

—woke to a thunder and rumble and a juddering of the ground.

He sat up in the dawn as hundreds of strange wild beasts like an engulfing, dark flood raced past the acacia grove, but whether running from or to, Borel could not say.

Somewhere in a distant aerie, a Great Eagle awakened disturbed.

36

Veldt

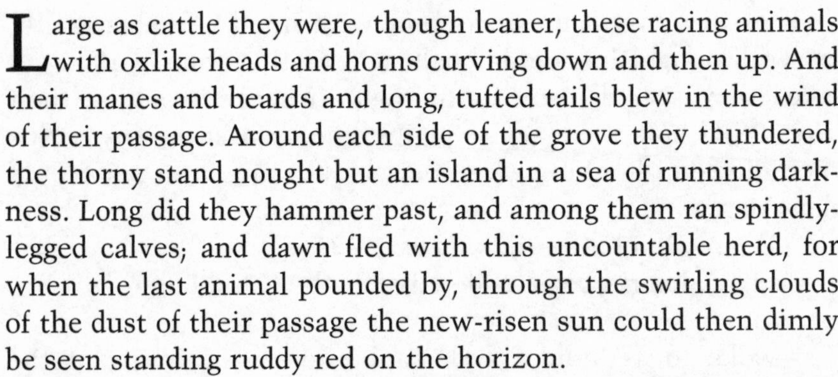

Large as cattle they were, though leaner, these racing animals with oxlike heads and horns curving down and then up. And their manes and beards and long, tufted tails blew in the wind of their passage. Around each side of the grove they thundered, the thorny stand nought but an island in a sea of running darkness. Long did they hammer past, and among them ran spindly-legged calves; and dawn fled with this uncountable herd, for when the last animal pounded by, through the swirling clouds of the dust of their passage the new-risen sun could then dimly be seen standing ruddy red on the horizon.

Flic, upon the very top branch of the tallest acacia, with Buzzer just below, called out, "What were they, or, rather, what are they?"

"I don't know," said Borel, "I've never seen such before."

"Well, they numbered in the thousands, I think," said Flic.

"More like in the tens of thousands," replied Borel, "if not ten times even that."

Long did Borel watch as they receded, while the whirling motes blew away on the wind, then he turned and peered the way they had come; in the very far distance down through a shallow, league-long swale and up the gentle slope beyond, he could just make out a group of ocherous beasts crouching 'round something, as if tearing at a victim and feeding.

Borel strung his bow.

Then he sighed and turned to the camp and said, "Come, let us break our fast and then be on our way."

All day Borel ran across the savanna, passing large herds of grazing animals: some were dark-and-light-striped, others dun and cream, or brown and white, or black and brown. Once Borel paused to watch a spotted cat of some sort run with amazing speed to haul down a small but agile deerlike creature. And then he took up the run again.

They stopped in the noontide to take a meal nigh a broad pond. And when Borel stepped down to replenish his waterskin, he did so quite warily, for opposite and watching him one of the tawny hunters lay in wait.

After the meal, Borel took up the Wolftrot again, oft passing through herds of widely scattered animals, and for the most part they seemed to pay him no heed, but he knew they were watching. Now and again one would be directly in his path, and, as Borel drew near, the animal would dash off a short way and then stop and eye him skittishly, as if wondering if he would pursue, for here it was that hunters lurked 'round the edges of the hunted, and this two-legged thing might be either. They were plains animals all, and so the veldt teemed with life and pursuit and occasional death. But Borel himself did not stop in this field of plenty to bring down any game whatsoever, for he would not spare the time.

Even so, he loped with his bow strung and an arrow always at hand, for large predators were numerous.

All day he trotted o'er the savanna, and when sunset drew nigh and they still had not come to a twilight border, Borel began looking for a place to encamp. For in this part of Faery, at the heels of sunset swiftly came night, a time when the bee would grow dormant, and Borel would lose his guide. He found another thorn grove, and worked his way within, Flic and Buzzer already therein and waiting in a tiny clearing nigh the center of the stand.

* * *

As they finished their evening meal, Flic looked up at Borel. "My lord, the Pooka said something I did not understand, and I would have it explained."

"Say on, Flic," said Borel, uncorking his waterskin and taking a drink, then offering the Sprite some as well.

Flic cupped his hands and drank a droplet or two, then again he looked up at Borel. "When the Pooka said that you had been as clever as any third son, just what did he mean by that?"

Borel laughed. "Ah, Flic, in many a tale told in Faery, a family has three sons: the eldest is often quite the warrior; the second son, a warrior as well, though perhaps not as puissant as the eldest; the third son is always considered the fool, and not good for much at all. In these tales, some problem besets that family.

"Usually the sire will choose one of his sons to resolve whatever ill or trouble is beleaguering the family, be it as complex as wooing a particular maiden, or as vexing as discovering a miscreant, or as simple as laying by the heels a rogue of sorts, or any number of other difficulties, setbacks, or puzzles.

"And so, the father most often sends the eldest son forth to deal with the issue, and in these stories that son utterly fails, at times merely to his embarrassment, occasionally to his complete disgrace, and still other times he falls to a deadly doom.

"Then the second son tackles the problem, customarily following directly in the footsteps of the eldest, with nearly identical results.

"Finally, the third son, fool that he is, begs the father to let him try. With his sire expecting no better results, and with his brothers—assuming they survived and returned home—demeaning him, he is allowed to go out to deal with the trouble, and no one in his family or among his neighbors or among the townsfolk—if there is a town in the tale—believes he has even the slimmest of chances.

"But what the others don't know is that he is truly quite clever, and either through stealth and guile, or through various ingenious means, he triumphs where others have failed. Oh, occasionally a third son is truly a fool, yet he succeeds in spite of himself, but a third son being an actual simpleton is the exception to the rule.

"By the bye, Flic, many tales take on this form, though mayhap only a handful are true. People, you see, find them amusing or sometimes useful to make a point, and so they embellish them to suit the occasion of the telling.

"Regardless, in all of these tales a third son is oft considered foolish when he is quite clever instead."

"I see," said Flic, grinning. "So, when you walked toward the Pooka's hindquarters saying that you had to see his teeth, you were acting as would a so-called third son, right?"

"Exactly so, my friend, and for that you can credit my sire. There is an adage he always stressed: 'Clever trumps Force nearly every time.' "

"Oui," said Flic, yawning. "As it did when Valeray dressed as an old crone of a soothsayer to fool Nefasí into showing him where Orbane's weakness lay."

"Stealth, cunning, and guile," said Borel. "My sire is renowned for all. Even so, there are times when force is the only option, and then my sire says, 'Strike first and strike hard, and if you don't get to strike first, then strike even harder.' "

"That saying does not sound like a hero's way to me," said Flic, his eyelids beginning to droop. He yawned again and added, "Oh, the last part about striking harder, that's all right. But the part about striking first, well, it seems somehow . . . low."

"Perhaps so," said Borel, "yet it's quite effective against vile foe." He paused and poked at the small fire and lay on another branch. "Let me ask you this, Flic, if faced with a hulking Troll or a vicious Redcap or a wild Ogre or even a malevolent, seven-headed Giant, if you had the means to do any one of them in, would you strike first or would you let him have the initial blow?"

Flic didn't answer, for he was sound asleep.

Borel smiled and picked up the wee Sprite and placed him on the leaf beside Buzzer, then he settled down and drifted into slumber himself.

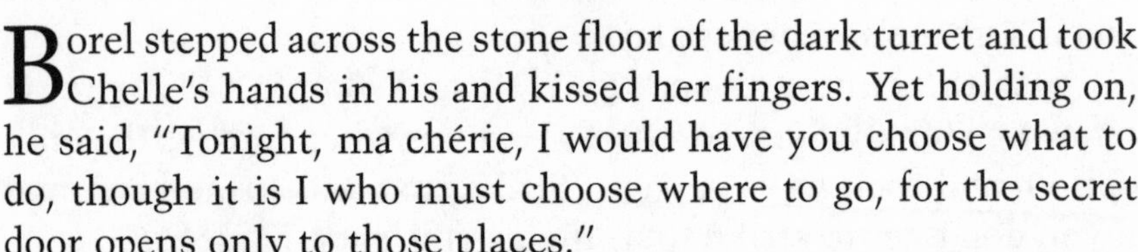

37

Échecs

Borel stepped across the stone floor of the dark turret and took Chelle's hands in his and kissed her fingers. Yet holding on, he said, "Tonight, ma chérie, I would have you choose what to do, though it is I who must choose where to go, for the secret door opens only to those places."

"As to what to do, Borel, I have enjoyed all your choices. The flight on the back of the Great Eagle was marvelous. And the strolls through the Summerwood and Autumnwood and Springwood were lovely. And I liked the lake and the boat and the island."

"Nevertheless, my darling," said Borel, "what would you have?" He released her hands and made a sweeping gesture toward the deeply shadowed wall. "Our hidden door awaits."

Chelle canted her head, her brow furrowed in thought, though Borel could not say what look dwelled in her eyes, hidden as they were by a shadowy band. "Archery," she said at last. "Either that or échecs."

"You play échecs?"

"I do."

"Très bien!" exclaimed Borel.

"My père taught me long past," said Chelle.

"So did my père teach me," said Borel, smiling. "My sisters and my brother as well. My mère plays, too, as does Camille, my soon-to-be sister-in-law. Occasionally, we have tournaments, and there is much laughter, especially when we play heartbeat échecs."

Chelle's brow furrowed. "Heartbeat échecs?"

"Oui. Each player must move within ten heartbeats following the other's move. If you and I were to play, Chelle, I would count for your moves, and you would count for mine."

"A very fast game, I see," said Chelle.

"Indeed, and with many blunders," replied Borel, grinning. "It is much fun."

Chelle smiled. "It sounds quite gay. Even so, I think I'd rather test your skill first."

"Oho! You would then duel?"

"I would," replied Chelle.

"Very well, Demoiselle," said Borel, and he bowed.

"Then, Sieur, let us have at it," said Chelle, curtseying.

"Have you a setting, Mademoiselle, where you would like to hold this contest? Perhaps I can conjure one up."

Chelle said in mock haughtiness, "I remind you, Sieur, it is a duel; I named the weapons, hence you must choose the site." Then she broke into laughter.

Borel's laughter joined hers, and he said, "Very well." He stood a long moment in thought, and then looked up and smiled and said, "I have just the place, where hunters and hunted do dwell—a site most fitting for our deadly duel."

He closed his eyes in concentration a brief moment, and then offered his arm and said, "My lady."

Grinning, Chelle hooked her arm through his and said, "Let us away, my lord."

They stepped through the enshadowed door to emerge—

—in a small clearing in a thorn grove on a savanna, where bright stars wheeled through the black sky overhead, and a narrow crescent of a waning moon rode above the far horizon. A small campfire burned bright in an earthen ring, and on the yellow grass beside the fire sat an échiquier, the pieces thereon of ivory and ebony.

"Oh, Borel, how unique. Where are we?"

"I am not certain, Chelle, but it is a wondrous place. In daylight you can see thousands of animals aroam in vast herds, with perilous predators lurking 'round the fringes."

As if to underscore Borel's words, a deep roar sounded in the distance, as of a beast enraged afar.

Chelle turned in the direction of the bellow. "A hunter?" she asked.

"Perhaps," said Borel. "Yet here we are well protected by the thorns; do not be afraid, my love."

"I'm not," Chelle replied calmly. But then she gasped. "Oh, look, Borel, a winged Sprite asleep on a leaf next to a bumblebee."

"They are my companions," said Borel. "It is the bee that the Sprite and I follow, for she is our guide."

"And where is it you are going?" asked Chelle, turning to face Borel.

He took her hands in his. "We are looking for you, my love." Before she could reply, he kissed her fingers and released her and said, "Come, let us play." Borel stooped and took up the white and black queens, one in each hand, and put them behind his back and pretended to shuffle them. He held out both hands, a queen hidden in each fist. "Choose."

"Dextral," said Chelle.

Borel opened his right fist; in it lay the ivory queen. "You move first," he said, smiling. He gave her the white queen and handed her down to the grass on the ivory side of the board, and then stepped to the ebony side and sat.

"King's spearman advances two paces," said Chelle, moving the piece.

Borel leapt his king's chevalier over the spearmen ranks and leftward one square in response. "King's chevalier two paces before king's tower," he said.

And the game was under way.

Out in the darkness of the veldt, a beast giggled in seeming glee, and Chelle looked up from the board and said, "What is that laughing creature? —And, no, my prince, I am not afraid, but instead just curious."

Borel grinned at her and shrugged. "Were I to stay here long, perhaps I would find out. Though to me it sounds rather like a mad loon's hilarity or the joy of a jackass being tickled."

Chelle broke into laughter, and as if in response the distant beast laughed with her, and Borel's guffaws joined them.

Finally Chelle sobered and said, "King's hierophant steps out four. He'll bring religion to you, my prince, with a bloody club, I add."

"Oh ho, with a club, you say. Well then, my queen's hierophant's spearman steps forward one."

Many were the moves and countermoves, her game no less reckless than his, and, with heroic spearmen butchered, hierophants brutally murdered, towers awreck, and kings taking flight but a pace at a time, at the end of these many moves, black and white pieces were lying slain beyond the borders of the board.

"It seems we are evenly matched, my love," said Borel.

"Not any more," said Chelle, and with a low throaty laugh she took Borel's remaining tower with her remaining hierophant.

"Ah, so you fell for my trap," said Borel, chuckling, and his sole chevalier cruelly took her now-unprotected sole tower in return. "Check."

"Oh, ho, so you think you've got me. Well, my arrogant prince, here—"

Of a sudden, Chelle raised her head in alarm. *"Ssst!"* she shushed. Then she whispered, " 'Ware, Borel, peril is nigh."

Borel raised his own head and listened. Beyond the thorn grove stealthy paws padded. He reached for his bow and said, "Chelle, you must leave."

"No, I will stay."

Borel growled, but set arrow to bowstring, and then faced out into the dark. And there he saw three pairs of smoldering red eyes above bared fangs adrip.

And beside him Chelle cried, "Wake up, my love, wake up!" and Borel—

—awakened to see in the dim glow of his low-burning fire the peril of his dream had come, for there in the shadows three pairs of eyes glowed crimson above slavering jaws as three spotted creatures pushed through the thorns and toward his small encampment.

38

Caravan

Borel leapt to his feet and kicked up the fire. He grabbed a sputtering brand and waved it in the air, and flames burst out anew.

But still the three large, spotted, doglike creatures came onward. They had big heads and lengthy necks and long, muscular forelegs and short hind legs, and they stood some three feet at the shoulder; formidable teeth filled powerful jaws that could easily crush bones. And the brutes shifted this way and that as they eased past long, sharp thorns on their way inward, their glowing red eyes reflecting firelight, their gazes never leaving their intended prey.

"Yahhh!" cried Borel, and he lunged forward, thrusting the flames at them.

Startled awake, Flic leapt up, épée in hand.

Even as Flic took to wing, his silver weapon glittering in the torchlight, "Yahhh!" cried Borel again, snatching up another brand, and with fire in each hand, once more he leapt forward, but this time he also snarled a word enwrapped in a growl.

Faced with an alert foe wielding flames, a foe who spoke in a tongue akin to that of the wild dog packs of the savanna, the spotted beasts turned and fled, crying out in agony as thorns pierced their flesh in the haste to get away.

Flic flew up and over the acacia grove and waved his sword and shouted at the creatures even as they ran, then returned to camp. As he sheathed his épée he said, "Well, I guess we put the rout to them, now didn't we?"

An eyebrow arched, Borel looked at Flic.

"What?" said the Sprite.

In that moment, in the predawn dark, there came the sound of insane giggling from afar.

Borel broke into laughter and threw more branches into the fire.

"Goodness," said Flic, his gaze turned toward the veldt, "who's the madman out there running about?"

Still smiling, Borel shrugged and took up his waterskin. "Perhaps it's one of those spotted beasts *we* routed, eh, Flic? —Drink?"

Flic turned and said, "Indeed. All this fighting makes me thirsty."

Neither Flic nor Borel felt the least bit sleepy, and in the nearing dawn they sat quietly by the fire. After a moment Flic said, "Say, I thought I saw you playing échecs with someone in a mask, or mayhap I merely dreamed it."

"I did play échecs in my own dream," said Borel. "Yet it is strange that you would see it as well."

"The one in the mask was Chelle?"

Borel nodded. "But it was not a mask you saw; rather it's some strange shadow across her eyes."

They sat without speaking for a while, and then Borel said, "There is more to Chelle's dreaming than we suspect, for I am able to share that dream, and now it seems you are able to share it, too."

"Not until this night," said Flic. "Even then it's as if I were asleep on my leaf and only awakened a bit to see you two at play."

"Oh," said Borel, his eyes widening. "Perhaps it's because I brought Chelle here to the thorn grove for our échecs game, and I imagined this place just as it was when I last saw it, with you and Buzzer asleep yon and the fire burning brightly. It might be that those I involve in our shared dream become involved as well."

"I think Chelle is in a *magique* sleep," said Flic. "And the *magie* affects all who share it."

"Yes!" said Borel, clenching a fist. "That is what I've been missing all along. You *must* be right, Flic. Rhensibé is a sorcière, and Chelle is held prisoner in a sleep of *enchantement.*" Borel looked at the Sprite. "Thank you, my friend, for your keen insight."

Flic frowned a moment, for his thoughts had not run that way at all, but then he straightened up and threw out his chest and said, "Think nothing of it, my lord."

They sat quietly for long moments, long enough for Flic to slump back down, and then the Sprite said, "But from what you have told me, my lord, she does not know she sleeps and dreams."

Borel shook his head. "Flic, just as she did when I was in the Troll dungeon, and now here in the thorn grove, she cried for me to wake up, hence on some level she knows it is a shared dream and she is one of the dreamers."

Flic slowly nodded then said, "Perhaps, my lord, it is only when peril comes that she realizes such."

Dawn came, and the trio broke fast. Borel then asked Flic to find the nearest water, and when the Sprite returned and said there was a shallow lakelet nearby, Borel drowned his fire and packed away his goods and strapped his rucksack to his back. With his bow strung and his quiver at hand, he worked his way out from the thorn grove.

When Borel's waterskin had been replenished, Buzzer spiralled up and took a bearing, then flew away, heading for the place where the sun would set that day, and Borel, with Flic atop the tricorn, loped after.

Long did he run throughout the morn, occasionally passing

through herds of tan grazers and those of dark brown, and now and again seeing dark-maned hunters and that very swift spotted cat. He saw a small pack of round-eared, doglike animals, and a few of the heavy-boned creatures of the kind that had tried to invade the camp.

On he ran and on, pausing occasionally for a drink of water, offering some to Buzzer and Flic as well. As for Buzzer, she had finally learned how fast—or rather how slow—Borel loped, and so she flew but a twenty-five or so of his paces in the lead, and she seemed less impatient with him.

As was their wont, they stopped in the noontide to take a meal, and they sat in the shade of a strange tree, with a fat trunk that narrowed the higher it went, with no limbs up its length except at the very top, and that's where all of the branches were, and they spread out in a flat, circular manner, rather like the roots of an oak, only these were where leaves grew.

"In shape, it looks somewhat upside down," said Flic, licking honey from his finger, then dipping it again into the bit Borel had dribbled into the jar lid. "Rather like a carrot, roots and all, turned on its head," added Flic.

Borel laughed around his mouthful of jerky and glanced at the tree above. "I agree, Flic: upside down it is."

With their noontide meal done, they were on the move again, Buzzer showing the way.

And as the sun slid across and down the sky, in the distance ahead Borel could see a trace of dust in the air. "It does not appear to be a stampeding herd," he said.

"Shall I fly forward and look?" asked Flic.

"Not yet, Flic. I think it will resolve itself soon."

And onward Borel loped.

Another league went by, and now Borel could make out what was raising the dust: "I ween it's a caravan."

And as they drew closer, indeed they could see it was a slow-moving train of trudging camels and horses awalk and men afoot and—

"What in Faery is that?" asked Flic.

"Though I've not seen one before, 'tis a tusker, I think," said Borel, for in the mid of the long line a ponderous grey creature plodded.

"It looks to have a small tent riding upon its back," called Flic.

" 'Tis a seat of sorts," said Borel. "Or so the tales tell."

"A what?"

"A seat fitted with a canopy and railing, and some have curtains all 'round."

On flew Buzzer and on trotted Borel, slowly overtaking the procession, the caravan travelling on nearly the identical heading that Buzzer flew. If both maintained course, Borel would pass on the right some twenty paces wide of the long file.

A half candlemark went by, and another league receded behind Borel as he slowly closed with the unhurried procession.

At last Borel came alongside a tassel-bedecked camel at the rear of the train. Borel called out to the rider, a black man, "Know you where the Endless Sands lie?" The man shrugged and called back that he didn't know.

To the next rider he came, and he shouted out the same question, with the same result.

Camel riders he passed, and those upon horses, and guards afoot, and riders and walkers alike were all black men. And they wore loose-fitting, colorful silks and turbans with face-veils lightly fastened 'round, and well-crafted boots shod their feet. They were armed with bows and scimitars and lances, and their mounts were gaily caparisoned, tassels and ribbons swinging with each stride.

Now Borel passed the giant grey creature lumbering serenely along; its massive head—with its broad, flapping ears and lengthy trunk—had great curving tusks, the long ivories each capped with a golden ball. A man with a hook on a staff walked alongside.

And as Borel trotted past and called out his question, a slender black hand drew aside the silken curtain of the canopied seat atop the tusker, and a dusky maiden of incredible beauty peered out, and she gasped at the sight of the handsome runner and the Sprite riding atop the man's hat.

But Borel did not pause, for none knew the answer to his question, though they did understand Common. And so he jogged on, and soon he had passed beyond the plodding train, and he ran on and on, until he was out of sight.

And the black princess called unto the nearest guard, and swiftly he came running. "What did they want?" said the princess.

"He asked after the Endless Sands, Princess."

"How odd," she replied.

"Indeed, my lady, yet even odder, he seemed to be chasing a bee."

Long did she laugh, and on the spot made up a tale of the handsome fool—with his wee companion riding atop his hat—who ran across the Endless Sands pursuing a bee . . . the fool a third son of a potentate, once rich but now poverty-stricken because of an evil djinn. Naturally, in the end the fool succeeded where his two sneering older brothers along with others had miserably failed, and, of course, having triumphed, this most handsome and clever third son married a most wise and demure and beautiful princess, much like she herself was.

Even as the sun was setting, Borel and Flic and Buzzer came to a twilight border, and as they stepped through, they came into stony green highlands with a tang of salt in the cool air, and in the distance leftward came the undulating boom of rollers breaking hard upon vertical cliffs.

39

Arrows

After making camp within a wind-twisted cedar grove down in a dip in the land, Borel left Flic on guard and in the twilight strode toward the sound of the waves. Within a furlong or two he reached the brim of high stone cliffs stretching away for miles, and they loomed above a darkling sea. The ocean itself was tumultuous, as if a violent storm raged somewhere beyond the horizon, one so powerful that its effects were being felt even here. Borel scanned the waters to the limit of his vision in the failing light, and he saw only luminous whitecaps rolling in, and no ships of any kind asail. He breathed in the bracing air laden with salt of the sea, and he reveled in the tang of it, for not often did he come to the tempestuous oceans of Faery. Finally he turned and as he did so, far to the right along the cliffs Borel could just make out a pile of stones, perhaps the remains of a tumbled-down tower, a remnant of elder days, perhaps to keep watch on the sea. Borel briefly considered walking there to see, but night was upon him, and morning would be soon enough. And so, instead, he made his way back toward the cedars, reaching there as darkness fell absolute . . . but for light from the stars above and the tiny campfire within.

Flic was yet awake by the small blaze and finishing off the

last of the honey from the jar lid. Buzzer was adoze on a nearby green-needled branch. Borel dropped down by the earthen-ringed fire, and he fished about in his rucksack for jerky and hardtack.

"Have you ever seen the wild waters of Faery?" he asked.

Flic looked up. "Do you mean the ocean?"

"Oui."

"Non," said Flic.

"Well, my wee Sprite, they lie not two furlongs yon. You might want to take them in."

"In the morning," said Flic, yawning. "All this travel makes me weary."

"What?" said Borel as if taken aback. "With you aride on my hat?"

Flic grinned but then sobered and morosely said, "You know what I mean."

Borel shook his head and frowned. "Just what *do* you mean, my friend?"

Flic shrugged. "I don't know. Or perhaps I do. It just seems that nothing happens."

"Nothing happens?" said Borel, wide-eyed in astonishment. "I suppose you mean nothing happened when we escaped the Trolls and wrecked the raft, or when we freed Hegwith the Gnome from the crack, or when the unseen creature of the swamp came, or when we found Roulan's vale turned to stone, or when we came across Lady Wyrd, or when you met Fleurette, tracked the Pooka and found three hairs, got your épée, helped subdue the Pooka, met the Riders Who Cannot Dismount, shared a dream, routed the spotted beasts, and saw a caravan with a great tusker. Is that the 'nothing happens' you meant?"

Flic sniffed. "Well, I didn't really meet the Riders Who Cannot Dismount. They bore iron, if you recall."

"But you saw them."

"Oui, yet those things you listed, they're not what I meant when I said 'nothing happens.' "

"Well, just what did you mean?"

"That we seem to be no closer to finding Chelle and setting her free."

Borel's features fell, and now his own words were morose. "Believe me, Flic: I am frustrated, too. I would that we were closer than we seem. Yet Lady Wyrd set us on this path, and we simply need to go on, for, given that aid, I am certain that we will succeed. And, as you once said, there yet seems time to do so." Borel glanced at the spangled sky and said, "A fortnight and three remain ere the moon rises full again."

"Well, I would have your lady free *now*," said Flic, peevishly.

"As would I," declared Borel, and then more softly, "As would I." Then he sighed and said, "Come, let us sleep. The morrow will see us in better spirits."

And so they bedded down, and the wind slowly strengthened, and far out to sea dark clouds crept over the horizon.

"Ah, Borel," said Chelle, "You remembered."

"My lady?"

"I see you have brought your bow," said Chelle. "Have you one for me?"

"Ah yes, archery," said Borel. "And I know just the bow for you."

"I could use yours," said Chelle.

Borel smiled. "Perhaps, though you might find stringing it difficult and the pull a bit arduous. Yet even if not, my arrows are fitted to my draw, and I think my reach exceeds yours somewhat."

He spread his arms wide, and Chelle laughed and did the same and pressed up against him and raised her face toward his and smiled. Clearly his span outreached hers by a good foot, but neither of them was thinking of such.

Borel swept her up in his arms and kissed her deeply, and she clutched him tightly and returned his kiss with fervor. At last they broke and Borel looked into her face. "My lady, methinks you a Vixen."

"And you, Sieur, a Fox," she replied. But then she grinned and said, "But I would challenge you to a contest: bow and arrow at fifteen paces."

"Your paces or mine?" asked Borel.

"Why, mine, of course," said Chelle. "—But only if you find me a suitable bow . . . and, naturally, arrows to fit."

"Very well, ma chérie, but I ask you, what be the prize?"

"Name it, my love."

"Ah, a dangerous suggestion, that," said Borel.

"It is?" said Chelle, a smile at the corners of her mouth.

"Indeed," replied Borel. *She knows not that we are in a dream, at least not at the moment, for peril is absent.*

"Where be this contest?" asked Chelle.

"I have just the place in mind," said Borel, and he offered her his arm.

They stepped through the door and—

—found themselves on the thick, grassy lawn of Summerwood Manor, where stood haycocks with a target pinned to each. And though but a fingernail-thin crescent of a moon and the stars in the slow-turning sky illumed the land below, still they could see that one target bore the outline of a buck, while another haycock held the silhouette of a Redcap Goblin, and the third sported a conventional bull's-eye.

"My bow, Sieur?"

"Here on this bale with your arrows, sweet demoiselle," said Borel. " 'Tis the bow used by Lady Saissa—my mother—when she comes to game at Alain's estate."

Chelle took up the bow and strung it and pulled. "The draw suits," she said. She nocked an arrow to string and again drew. "The arrow fits," she said, then she turned and let fly at the bull's-eye target. The shaft struck just inside the center ring.

"Hmm . . ." said Borel, reaching for an arrow of his own, "it seems I have my hands full." The shaft he pulled from his quiver was fitted with a flint point. Borel replaced that arrow and paused a moment in thought, and picked another shaft, this one with a proper head of bronze. He nocked and drew and loosed. His arrow struck just inside of hers.

"My, do you have Fairy arrows, Borel?" asked Chelle. " 'Tis not fair if so."

"Fairy arrows?"

"They are magique, my love, and only miss should a greater spell come along to deflect them."

"Non, sweet Chelle, my arrows are plain and simple, lacking magie altogether."

"Neither Fairy arrows nor those of Elves, you swear, eh?" said Chelle, grinning.

"Elf arrows?" said Borel. "This is another kind, I take it."

"Indeed, Sieur. Have you not heard of being Elf-shot?"

"Yes, though I think it but ill-founded rumor. Elves are for the most part quite honorable, whereas to be Elf-shot means to be afflicted with a spell or disease delivered by an Elf arrow."

"I know what it means, my love," said Chelle. "Nevertheless, Elves have arrows that fly exceptionally true, and so, Fairy and Elf shafts are outlawed in the contest we play." She laughed and took up another arrow and turned and drew and let fly. Her shaft struck inside Borel's.

Shaft after shaft they loosed, and it became clear that Borel was the better archer, yet Chelle's own shots were quite excellent, for the palm of Borel's hand would cover her spread, but the smaller palm of her hand would easily cover his.

As they vied with one another, the gentle breeze became a wind, and clouds rolled in, and lightning flashed afar. "It seems we are in for a storm," said Borel. "Mayhap we had better call it a night."

"While you are winning, my love?" said Chelle. "Ah, you are a Fox indeed, or perhaps I should say a Wolf."

"Would you settle for a tie?" asked Borel.

"Nay, my lord, you have won fairly and squarely," said Chelle. "Name your prize."

He took her in his arms and said, "If any be Elf-shot 'tis I, enspelled in the heart by you."

Of a sudden they were lying unclothed in the soft grass and clasped tightly in each other's arms. Their lips sought one another's, and fire ran through their loins and their hungry kisses as well. Rain came, yet they took no heed of it, and lightning flared. And still Borel kissed her as if he would consume her, and his hands caressed her body, and Chelle moaned in response, and—

CRKK! lightning struck—

BOOM! thunder roared—

SHHSSSHHH . . . ! cold rain came drenching—

And Borel—

—awakened in the downpour. And he blundered to his feet, and took up his weatherproof cloak and wrapped it 'round himself. Then he grabbed up sputtering Flic and groggy Buzzer and shoved both under his wrap.

40

Seacoast

Lightning flashed, and thunder boomed, and the wind roared, and rain hammered across the cedar grove in horizontal sheets. The drenching downpour quenched the fire, and, with Buzzer and Flic safely within his cloak, Borel dragged his goods and himself under the shelter of the cedar boughs. But then water began running into the dip in the land where stood the trees. And as it started rising around Borel's boots, "I'm going to have to find better refuge," he called to Flic.

"Where will we go, my lord, in this abysmal dark?"

"There seem to be ruins not far from here along the edge of the cliffs. Can you slip into one of my pockets and hold Buzzer?"

"No, my lord," called Flic. "We would be crushed. Instead, place me under the hood of your cloak. There will Buzzer and I ride."

When the Sprite and the now-semi-awake bee were in place within the hood and clinging to the collar of Borel's shirt, he shouldered his rucksack and quiver and bow, taking care not to crush his friends. He then splashed out from the cedar grove and up onto the land and set off through the dark, storm-hammered night.

Carefully, and with the aid of lightning flashes, Borel made his way toward the cliffs, and the storm grew fiercer as he went, and the wind battered him, and he feared for Flic and Buzzer. Yet the Sprite and the bee slid down within Borel's collar, and tiny bee feet walked upon the skin of his neck, and it was all Borel could do to keep from slapping. At last he came nigh the edge of the fall, and the savage sea below crashed into the vertical stone and spewed water high into the air, and spray drenched Borel.

Rightward he turned—*Caution, my lad. It will not do to go atumble down to the sea below*—and followed the brim toward where he'd seen the ruins, and the shrieking wind tore at him, and the raging sea thrashed him with salt-laden spray, both air and water seeming furious that he did not yield, but continued on toward the remnants of an ancient refuge.

By lightning flashes he could see the spill of stones ahead, and as he neared, he heard a wailing above that of the wind itself. And then he saw a white-gowned lady standing on the verge, her dress and hair blowing all about, and she wept and wailed and held her arms out to the sea, as if imploring, as if pleading. And then—"No!" cried Borel—she stepped over the brink, and fell down and down and down into the rage below.

Borel ground his teeth and slammed a fist into palm, yet there was nought he could do.

He came unto the ruins and cautiously stepped to the lip of the sheer fall and peered through the spray and down into the luminous churn. There was no sign of the lady in the white dress.

Borel turned and made his way into the fallen stone, and he found a sheltered corner of yet-standing walls, with remnants of beams above, and therein he took refuge, as the tempest grew in strength.

Day came, and still the storm raged, and still Buzzer and Flic resided in Borel's collar, with little bee feet yet walking about, little itchy bee feet.

"Buzzer cannot fly in this," said Flic.

"I know," replied Borel, as he moved their camp into a partial room he'd found when the dim light of morning seeped through the roiling black sky above. Within the protection of the remains, Borel had found broken lumber—the remnants of a floor—the timber but a bit damp. Using a chunk of rubble, he shattered wood, and then he cut shavings from the dry interior using his flint knife. In moments he had a small fire aflame, and Flic and Buzzer came out from Borel's shirt and took warmth beside the blaze, and Borel spent awhile scratching his neck.

Borel dropped a dab of honey into the jar lid and said, "I'm going to explore this ruin. Perhaps I can find why the woman in white leapt to her death."

"Woman in white?" said Flic.

"When we came through the storm, as I neared the ruins, a white-gowned lady jumped into the sea."

"Hmph," said Flic. "More likely a ghost, if you ask me." He gestured about. "I mean, look at this place. It's a broken shell, and hasn't been lived in for many seasons."

"Nevertheless, I'm going to look," said Borel.

"As you will, my lord," said Flic. "Buzzer and I will stay and tend the fire."

In the driving rain, Borel clambered through the ruins, yet he found nought that indicated anyone had lived therein of recent. *Mayhap Flic is right. Perhaps 'twas a spirit torn with grief . . . someone who lived in this tower long past. On the other hand, it could be a dweller from nearby, someone with a broken heart.*

Borel stepped to the brim of the precipice and again looked into the rage below. There was nothing to see but furious water achurn.

He scanned the skies. All was dark clouds for as far as his gaze could reach, both inland and asea, though they did ride along and perhaps pass through the twilight border he and Flic and Buzzer had just yester crossed.

Perhaps we should go back through the twilight and take refuge from the storm. Ah, I think not, for we are well off enough in the broken room.

He went back to the chamber where the fire burned, and he shed his cloak and sat down and added a bit of wood to the blaze, and thereafter he broke his own fast.

* * *

All day it rained, and the wind lessened greatly, though the clouds did not diminish one whit. And Borel took to pacing back and forth within the limits of the remains of the room.

"My lord, if you keep trodding to and fro you will be most weary should we set out soon," said Flic.

Borel flung himself down next to the blaze and said, "Ah, Flic, you are right, yet I cannot but know that time is fleeting, and Chelle is yet a prisoner."

"Still, my lord, we need Buzzer to guide us, and she cannot in these conditions."

Borel took a deep breath and slowly blew it out. Then he lay back and tried to rest. Yet within a quarter candlemark, once again he was on his feet pacing.

Night fell—

And still it stormed—

And Buzzer fell dormant.

Borel and Flic made ready to sleep.

With Flic tugging on his ear and hissing—"Wake up, my lord, wake up!"—Borel roused.

"Wh-what is—?"

"Shh, my lord, look," said Flic.

A ghostly figure, a weeping woman in white, descended a spiral stairway that was not there. An ethereal aura glowed dimly about her as 'round she came and down, and in her hand she clutched a letter, or so it seemed. As she came to what had once been the ground floor she let the letter flutter from her hand, and as it fell away she headed for the remnants of a doorway, her grief beyond measure. She passed straight through piles of rubble instead of climbing up and over and down. It was as if the wrack were not there, as if the floor were yet in place, and the walls and the tower still standing as it once must have been.

Weeping inconsolably, out to the edge of the cliff she went, and she cried out a name: "Valmont, Valmont, oh my beloved

Valmont." She extended her arms toward the raging waters and then stepped over the brim and fell away.

"That was your lady in white?" asked Flic, his voice yet a whisper.

Borel nodded. "It was."

"I told you she was a ghost," said Flic.

Borel stood and stepped across the chamber to a pile of rubble.

Flic added, "It seems she is a spirit doomed to, um, to relive her sorrow. —That is, if ghosts can be said to 'relive.' "

"Repeat," said Borel, lifting away stones. "She is doomed to repeat."

"Ah, yes," said Flic. "That is the word I was searching for." He watched Borel paw through the rubble, heedless of the rain falling upon him. "Speaking of searching, Prince Borel, what are you looking for?"

"Here fell the letter she was holding," said Borel. "Perhaps can we find it and burn it, no longer will she be trapped in an endless cycle."

"Endless cycle? Do you think she is in an endless cycle? Perhaps she only does this when there is a storm at sea, or maybe just during a certain time of year, or—"

"Aha!" said Borel, and he held in his hand a fragment of parchment. He stuffed it into his jacket and continued to dig through the wrack. Yet nothing else was found.

Borel returned to the fire and dried himself off with his own cloak. Then he took the vellum from his jacket. "Hmm . . . it's torn, and much is faded beyond recall, weathered, no doubt. But this I can make out:

> *. . . regret to . . . Valmo . . . at sea . . .*
> *went down . . . violent stor . . .*

"That's all," said Borel. "The rest is too weatherworn, too faded by the elements to read. Yet from what I gather, I ween that Valmont's ship was lost in a furious storm, much as is this one, and he was drowned. I think the lady in white leapt into the sea to join him. And so, my wee friend, perhaps you are right: it could be the lady only appears during a raging storm to repeat her sorrow."

"And you think if we burn the remains of the letter she will, um . . ." Flic's words faded to silence.

"Be released from her torment," said Borel, finishing the thought. Then he said, "I would we had a hierophant to tell us what to do, perhaps to bless her, yet we don't."

"Well, my lord, if I can bless a crofter's field, surely you can bless a spirit. I say we do what you suggest."

And so Borel added wood to the fire and knelt before it with the remnant of the letter in hand. "Mithras," he softly said, "let this torment end." And he thrust the letter into the flames, and it caught and burned, and its glowing ashes swirled up in the wind and flew away—

—and the rain abruptly stopped.

There was yet a good part of the night remaining, and though he did not believe he could fall asleep, along with Flic, Borel lay down to get whatever rest remained, for if the storm was truly gone, then when daylight came, they would be on their way again.

Yet his thoughts were churning—thoughts of Chelle and the lady in white and of Flic and Buzzer and their journey and of Roulan's stone vale and of pink-petaled shamrock and blushing white roses and thorn-laden blackberry vines and . . . and . . .

. . . and he drifted into slumber.

41

Dark of the Moon

"Ah, I see you brought your bow again," said Chelle. "And, Sieur, I would string it if I might."

Borel grinned and handed her the weapon.

Somewhere, just on the edge of hearing, a squeaking sounded, or perhaps it was music; it was entirely too faint to tell.

Chelle set the lower bowstring loop into the nock at the end of the lower limb. She grounded that end against the floor and grasped the upper limb and stepped her right leg in between the body of the bow and the string. Taking the upper loop in her left hand, with her right she began to bend the bow. The gap between the upper-limb nock and the loop narrowed and narrowed, yet not enough for her to set the string in place. She relaxed and looked at Borel, the smile still on his face. She blew a stray lock of her golden hair up from her forehead and took a deep breath and gritted her teeth and bent the bow again . . . and again . . . and yet again, but try as she might, she simply could not set the upper loop in place.

The squeaking grew, or mayhap the music grew, and now clearly but faintly sounded.

Borel frowned and looked about for the source, but he found nought.

Finally, after repeated attempts, Chelle laughed and relaxed and gave the bow back to Borel. "You said I might find it difficult to string, and I thought I would try."

The squeaking, the music, was no longer faint, yet Chelle seemed to pay it no heed.

Borel slung the bow by its carrying thong and said, "Well, Chérie, what would you have us do this eve? I am certain I can find a suitable setting, but I would have you choose the deeds."

In spite of the shadows, Borel could see a shade of red creeping up Chelle's face. "My lord, often have we come close to making lo—"

From below there came up the stairwell the sound of a door opening.

Now the squeaking became a squeal, or the music grew shrill, and echoed up the stairwell and down.

Chelle gasped, and glanced at one of the windows. "Oh, my Borel, you must flee."

A door closed somewhere below.

"Flee?"

" 'Tis the dark of the moon, and Rhensibé said she would come."

"Rhensibé?" said Borel. "She is here?" He unslung his bow and strung it.

Above the growing shrill music, the growing squeal, footsteps sounded, as if someone crossed a stone floor far below.

"She said she would come on the day of the dark of the moon, to gloat and tell me that there was but a fortnight and one ere the moon rises full."

Borel pulled a flint-tipped arrow from his quiver.

Now the footsteps started up the stairs.

"You cannot face her, my lord." Chelle pressed her hands against Borel's chest and pled, "Flee through your secret door."

"Let her come," gritted Borel, "for I will not take flight."

Much like a wagon wheel grown rusty and needing grease, the squealing, the music, sounded loudly, but above that shrill din the footsteps sounded even louder as they came up the spiral stairway.

Borel moved to the side and nocked the arrow and started toward the well opening, but Chelle flung herself in front of him. "My lord, she is too powerful a sorcière. I beg you to fly through the door."

"Go," said Borel, "seek safety beyond the door, while I deal with Rhensibé," and again he moved to one side, and he drew the arrow to the full and took aim at the opening where Rhensibé would first appear.

"I cannot, my love, for if I do, she will discover that very door and use it to—"

The strident screeching drowned out Chelle's words, but the footsteps thudded on upward, closer, ever closer, now just a—

—the screeching rose—

—the steps grew louder—

Chelle said softly but clearly, "Find me, Borel. Please find me. And hurry."

—and of a sudden the walls began to fade, and Borel cried out, "No! Chelle, do not take the dream away! Do not—"

—Borel jolted awake on his feet in the dawn, and in his hands he held his strung bow, with an arrow nocked and drawn to the full.

42

Lot

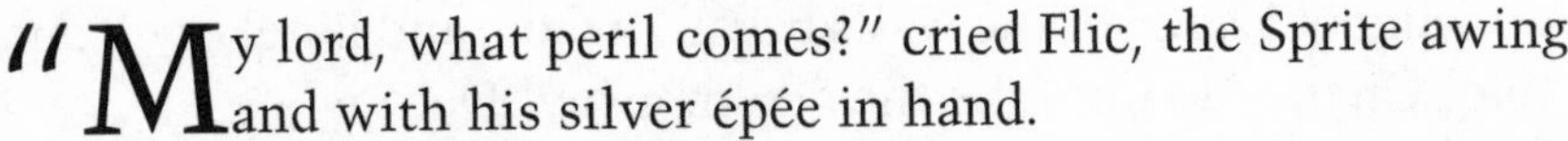

"My lord, what peril comes?" cried Flic, the Sprite awing and with his silver épée in hand.

"Merde!" shouted Borel and eased his draw and stomped about, cursing, "Merde! Merde! Merde!"

"My lord?" said Flic.

"Flic, Flic, Chelle is in the hands of Rhensibé, and I could do nought to save her."

"Are you certain, my lord? 'Tis but a dream, you know."

"Of course I am certain!" shouted Borel, and Flic, shocked, backed through the air and away.

Borel slumped to the dirt next to the fire and looked up to see the Sprite yet flying, Buzzer now hovering at his side. "Ah, Flic, I am sorry. It's just that I might have been able to slay Rhensibé."

"In a dream?"

"I don't know. Perhaps."

Flic sheathed his épée and settled down opposite the prince, Buzzer alighting as well. "Tell me this dream," said the Sprite.

Borel sighed and said, "Rhensibé was coming up the stairs of the turret, and Chelle took away the dream before I had a chance to loose an arrow at the witch."

"Rhensibé is a witch, then?" said Flic.

"Chelle called her a sorcière," said Borel.

"Ah, then, that agrees with what Charité and Maurice told us back nigh Roulan's vale," said Flic.

Absently, Borel nodded.

"My lord," said Flic, "I think Chelle did the prudent thing, casting you out of her rêve."

Borel looked up. "What?"

"Heed, Prince Borel: had Rhensibé found you in the dream, she is a sorcière and could have done you great harm through magie, whereas I think your arrow—being stone-tipped and not magique at all—would have done no harm whatsoever to her."

Borel frowned and vented a hard sigh and said, "Perhaps you are right, Flic, but, oh, I would have spitted her neatly."

"I'm sure you would have, my lord," said Flic.

Borel sighed again, this time more softly, and he said, "Chelle's last words to me were 'Find me, Borel. Please find me. And hurry.' "

Borel looked out through the stone ruins of the tower at the yet clouded sky of dawn, and he turned and rummaged within the rucksack and said, "Let us break fast swiftly, and then away, for time grows ever more short."

To make certain that they were on the correct line, they returned to the edge of the dip in the land where grew the cedar grove, and they found the stand trunk-deep in water. Buzzer flew up and, even though the just-risen sun was not visible behind the cast of the sky, she circled about and took a bearing and then shot off in the direction where the sun would set.

The prince followed at a lope, with Flic once again riding in his customary position in the prow of Borel's hat.

Across the grassy, rock-laden highlands the prince ran, the cliffs always to the left, with the ocean far below, and still the waters were aroil from the storm, great swells crashing headlong into stone.

On he ran and on, and now and again they passed an isolated farmstead with farmers at work afield and livestock grazing upon the green grass and clover. Occasionally they could see a sailing vessel far out upon the churning sea, making headway either with or against or athwart the waves in the brisk breezes yet blowing.

But then the coastline began to recede as the sheer faces of the leagues-long cliffs slowly swung away, and after a candlemark or so, Borel could no longer hear the ocean surge.

Still he ran on, and the character of the land began to change, for now he splashed through streams flowing down to the sea. Now and then a thicket came into view, and then woodlands, and Borel found himself running through a green forest, and though Buzzer flew but twenty-five or so yards ahead of the prince, occasionally she returned to make certain the slow human was yet on course.

The overcast above began to break, and soon the sky was riven by great swaths of blue. But Borel did not pause to admire the firmament, but continued the long lope.

As the sun rose into the zenith, downslope through the trees Borel espied a glimmering ribbon of water ahead. "It seems we are coming to a river," he said. "We'll take our noontide meal on its banks."

And as they ran down the long cant of land and neared the broad flow, "Uh-oh," said Flic. "Look."

Beside the run a child sat on the bank weeping.

"Take care, my lord," added Flic. "This could be another one of those Fey."

Borel laughed and trotted on down to the bank, and the child, a rather skinny, yellow-haired demoiselle, perhaps eight summers old, turned and saw him coming, and then began to wail in earnest.

"Demoiselle, why do you cry?" asked Borel, sitting down beside her.

Snuffling and snubbing, the girl looked at the prince, great teardrops welling in her light brown, almost golden, eyes, and she looked at the Sprite, and brightened only slightly, and looked at the bee, and cried, "*Eee!* Don't let it sting me."

"Hmph!" snorted Flic, but he said no more, for having been once burned, he was now twice shy.

But Borel said, " 'Tis a very tame bee, my lady, and she would not harm even a fly or a flea."

"Well, she can sting all the flies and fleas she wants," said the little girl, "just as long as she doesn't sting me." Then the child began to wail again, and gestured at the river.

"What is it, my wee demoiselle?" asked the prince, "And by the bye, I am Borel. Could I have your name?"

"M-my n-name is D-Dandi," snubbed the girl.

"And what is grieving you, my lady?" asked Borel.

Yet *snuck*ing a bit, the child got her sobs somewhat under control, and she said, "I came across when the river was low, but now, with the rain, it is quite high and swift and entirely too deep for me to wade, and—*snkk*—I do not know how to swim, and even if I did, it would—*hnk*—sweep me out to sea, and then I'd be lost and all alone—*uuu*—and probably end up on an island with monsters that eat young and tender things like little girls—oh poor me—and I'm hungry and my mother probably thinks I'm dead—poor Momma—or carried off by tigers and bears and Trolls and—*wahhh!*"

Borel put his arm about her. "Hush, hush, child. I will feed you and then carry you across, and you can then run swiftly home to your mother, and she will sweep you up in her arms and hug you and kiss you and no longer worry."

Borel fished about in his rucksack, and he gave her some jerky and a hardtack biscuit, and as she chewed, he poured some honey into the jar lid for Buzzer and Flic. He saw Dandi's pale brown eyes light up, and he motioned for her to hold out her biscuit and he dribbled a bit of honey thereon.

She gobbled it right up, and looked at Borel soulfully and said, "More, please?"

Borel grinned and set out another hardtack biscuit and drizzled honey atop.

They spent long moments sitting on the bank and speaking about this and that and the rain and the storm and the river and the drifting of the clouds leaving blue skies behind. But at last the meal was done, and Borel said, "Well, now, my girl, it's time to take you across." He turned his back and said, "Hop on, Dandi, and I'll give you a ride."

"The river is awfully deep," she said timidly.

"But I am tall," said Borel.

"The water is quite swift," she said.

"But I am strong and sturdy," replied Borel. He looked about and found a hefty stick to act as a stave. "And I'll use this to steady me. —Come, come, girl, hop on."

She climbed on his back and whispered in his ear, "I am quite afraid."

"I'll be brave enough for both of us, Dandi," said Borel. And grasping her under one knee with one hand, and with the stave in the other, he waded into the stream.

"Eeeee!" Dandi screamed.

Borel waded on.

Buzzer and Flic flew across, but then flew back and whirled and twirled in the air, trying to take Dandi's mind off the water.

But Dandi paid them no heed, and she cried "Oh, oh, I told you it was too high and swift and entirely too deep to wade."

Now up to his waist, Borel sloshed on, and Dandi began to thrash. Borel tightened his grip under her knee, but her other leg was loose and kicking frantically.

"Oh, oh," wailed Dandi, flailing about, "I do not know how to swim; we'll drown."

Borel clasped her even tighter.

"We'll fall in and be swept out to sea! *Wahhh!*"

It was all Borel could do to hold on to her, thrashing about as she was.

"We'll be captured by pirates," wailed Dandi, sobbing and floundering 'round, "and they'll throw us onto an island and we'll be eaten by monsters and then chased by tigers and bears and Trolls and—"

Struggling to maintain his grip on her, Borel finally made it to the opposite shore, and Dandi had entirely collapsed into tears. He abandoned the stave and swung her around and set her down at the foot of an oak tree. "D-dry m-my eyes," she blubbered. And Borel fished about in the rucksack and pulled out a cotton bandanna he had purchased in Riverbend. He knelt and reached forth with the kerchief.

At the very first touch, she grew tall and stood before him as a matronly mademoiselle with yellow hair and golden eyes. Somewhere nearby there sounded the clack of shuttle and the thud of batten of a loom.

"Told you," shouted Flic, sitting on a branch nearby, Buzzer at his side.

Yet kneeling, "Lady Lot," said Borel.

She nodded her head in acknowledgement.

"She Who Fixes the Present and Seals Men's Fate," he said.

Once again she nodded in agreement.

"Lady Verdandi," he added.

"Yes, Prince Borel, those are names I am known by, and by many others as well."

Borel stood and bowed deeply, and as he did so he reached out and took her hand and kissed her fingers.

"Ah, Skuld said you were quite the bold one, and now I see why. You would dare flirt with Destiny, eh?"

"If that's what it takes to free my beloved," said Borel, not a sign of guilt or fear in his eyes.

Verdandi laughed, and then sobered. "I want to thank you for freeing the lady in white at the ruined tower, for she has been throwing herself from that cliff during storms for summers beyond count. Yet the letter was left behind, and it kept drawing her back, would not let her leave this plane. Your burning it while saying a blessing was just the right thing to do."

Borel smiled. "I am pleased that I did something right, yet I seem no closer to finding Chelle. Would you help me, my lady, as did your sister Skuld?"

Verdandi sighed. "List, Prince Borel, you have already missed one chance to find the Endless Sands, but you yet have—"

"I what?" said Borel.

"I said, you have missed one chance to find the Endless Sands," replied Verdandi.

"Lady Lot, when did I—?"

"That is neither here nor there," snapped Verdandi, "for it is already woven into the tapestry of time." Then her voice softened, and she said, "Heed, you have one more chance, and I can give some small assistance, for you did aid me across the river and did not let me fall."

"He fed you, too," cried Flic from the branches above. "Just like he did Skuld."

Verdandi smiled and looked up. "Indeed he did, and with honey, too." She turned to Borel. "Even so, I cannot aid you unless you answer a riddle." She frowned in thought a moment, then glanced at the Sprite above. "You are quite the flier, I hear, swift beyond many."

"Yes, I am," said Flic, thrusting out his wee chest. "There is none among the Sprites who is better." Then quicksilver-swift his face fell in dismay and he groaned. "Oh, my, this is not another riddle concerning my abilities, is it?"

Now Verdandi laughed and said, "Indeed it is, for my elder sister said that she put you in the riddle she posed, and I would do likewise."

"Your elder sister, you say?" asked Flic. "Oh, no, we've not met Urd at all. 'Twas Demoiselle Skuld instead."

"Skuld *is* my elder sister," said Verdandi.

Flic shook his head. "Oh, no, my lady, for, as I said, she is but a demoiselle, whereas you are, um, er"—Flic searched for a polite way to say "older," and he finally said—"more ripe."

A smile flashed o'er Verdandi's face, and she said, "Nevertheless, Skuld is my elder sister, whereas Urd is my younger."

"Flic," said Borel, "it is all in how one looks at time. I will explain it later. Yet for now I have a riddle with which to contend." He turned to Verdandi. "Madame, I must warn you, I know the answer to the riddle of the Sphinx, and the riddles you and your sisters posed to Camille, as well as Lady Skuld's most recent riddle."

Verdandi smiled. "Skuld said you were honorable, and I see

she is right, but none of those things will I ask you. Instead, here is my riddle:

"If Flic were in a Spritely contest
To fly highest of his Kind,
But in some manner unknown to him
He had fallen behind—"

"What? Me fall behind?"

"Quiet, Flic," ordered Verdandi.

"But if with a furious burst of speed
He shot into the sky
What assuredly would happen to him
Should he fly much too high?"

"Oh, oh," cried Flic, waving his hand, but abruptly fell silent at a glance from Verdandi.

"He would swoon, Lady Lot," said Borel, touching the brim of his hat in a casual salute to Flic, "from lack of air to breathe."

Verdandi smiled. "Well and good, Prince Borel."

"Now the aid, my lady?" said Borel.

Verdandi nodded and said, "There is but barely time to rectify the mistake you made, yet here is what I can say:

"The king will offer five different games,
Play the one you played with your dame.
Remember true and remember well
The guiding words of your love Michelle.

"And this I will tell you for nought: ask for the High Lord's favorite horse, else you will not see the sands ere the full moon rises, yet beware, for the King Under the Hill is quite tricky, and you must recall what you know."

Borel nodded and said, "My Lady Lot, I would that you—"

But in that moment the persistent sound of the loom swelled, and then vanished as did Lady Verdandi.

* * *

As Borel trotted across another stream, Flic said, "Why must these Fates *always* say that *I* fall behind, when anyone knows that would never happen?"

Borel laughed. "Ah, Flic, ever humble, I see. Were I you, I would not question the Sisters Three."

"You're not one to talk, my prince," said Flic. "After all, she said you are the one who 'would dare flirt with Destiny.' "

Borel laughed and kept running.

After a while, Flic said, "What's all this about Skuld being the older? Why, anyone can see that she is a demoiselle, whereas Verdandi is a matronly lady."

Borel said, "Some call them the Maiden, the Mother, and the Crone, where Skuld is the Maiden, Verdandi the Mother, and Urd the Crone, for they do resemble those three. And Skuld is the one who sees the future and weaves it into the tapestry of events, yet, even as it leaves her loom, that weaving is not then immutable; for when it gets to Verdandi, whatever changes have been made through the extraordinary deeds of men and others, she alters the pattern set down by Skuld and weaves those changes into the Present; finally, Urd fixes all events forever into the Past. And so, Flic, the one who sees the events of time *first* is the one considered Eldest, and the one who sees the events *last* is the one considered Youngest."

"Ah, then," said Flic. "Skuld the Maiden sees things first, and so she is eldest of the three; Verdandi the Mother is the middle child; and Urd the Crone is the baby of the family—eh?—for things come to her dead last."

"Yes," said Borel, smiling at Flic's choice of the words "dead last."

"It still doesn't make sense, though," said Flic. "I mean, if that be the case, why wouldn't Skuld be the Crone and Urd the Maiden?"

"Because, Flic, I think they take on the visage that others give them, and most others think the Past is the oldest, and the Future the youngest."

"Well, isn't that true?" asked the Sprite, frowning.

"It's relative, Flic, and it depends on whether you think of yourself as moving through time, or whether you think of time as moving through you."

"Huh?" said the Sprite, now confused.

"I believe I'll let you ponder that, Flic, while I continue to run."

And Borel did run throughout the rest of the day, and as the sun began to set, they came to another twilight border.

"This is the third and last bound spoken of by King Arle of the Riders Who Cannot Dismount," said Borel.

Through the marge they pressed, and they came in among grassy downs. Buzzer then alighted on Borel's tricorn, for with the night drawing nigh, she would sleep.

But Flic took to wing, and up he flew and scouted among the myriad green knolls, and a quarter candlemark later, as dusk came on, he darted back to Borel.

"My lord, yon," he cried, pointing. "A light glows, just as Arle said. Therein should be the halls of the King Under the Hill."

Flic led Borel to a great grassy mound, atop which sat a dolmen, with three upright, twice-man-tall megaliths equidistant from one another, and a great flat capstone atop. And within that triangular setting a large hole yawned, with stairs and a wagon ramp leading down and in.

Flic said, "My lord, if you will, I shall stay here with Buzzer, for the Lord of the Fey is quite capricious, and if I go in he is likely to assign me some onerous and lengthy task, and I would much rather stay at your side until we have your lady free."

Borel nodded and removed his tricorn with the bee aboard and said, "Very well, Flic, I leave Buzzer with you." And he set his hat to the ground nigh one megalith of the dolmen.

Then Borel shed his rucksack and laid it beside the hat. He uncapped the honey jar and put it down, saying, "In case dawn comes ere I return." He then unstrapped the long-knife scabbard and set it there as well and said, "Even though the blade within is nought but rust, I would not take iron in any form within the High Lord's demesne."

"Remember, my prince," said Flic, "eat no food and drink no wine nor take any other form of refreshment from them . . . not even water. And remember Lady Verdandi's words, even though I cannot fathom what they might mean."

As Borel checked his bow and quiver and waterskin, all yet borne by him, Flic added, "And may Fortune's beaming face be turned your way."

Borel smiled grimly and said, "May it be so." Then he spun on his heel and strode under the capstone and into the light below.

43

Fey Lord

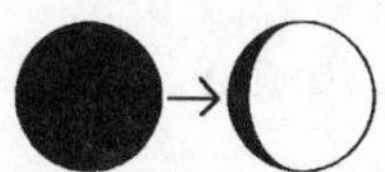

Down the steps alongside the wagon ramp went Borel, both stairs and road sweeping in wide and shallow spiral turns as into the hollow hills they went. At last Borel came to the bottom, and there to one side were stables with magnificent steeds—*For Fairy rades, no doubt*—and opposite the stables and up three steps was a long corridor leading toward light and music beyond.

Into the passageway went Borel, and he came into a great banquet hall, and therein gracefully danced men and women of exotic beauty, their faces long and narrow, their ears tipped, their eyes aslant, their forms lithe and lissome.

And as Borel entered the chamber, some turned to see this human who had come uninvited into the hall, while others simply continued their elegant dance and paid him little or no heed.

Yet from the throne on which he sat, one looked up and smiled in welcome. "Prince Borel of the Forests of the Seasons, hail and well met."

A corridor opened up among the dancers, and Borel walked through and to the foot of the dais, where he bowed low and said, "Your Highness."

Beside the redheaded, green-eyed king sat a woman of incredible loveliness, her hair raven-black, her eyes sapphire blue, her flawless skin tinged with just a hint of gold, a tint held by all the Folk within the hall but Borel.

Again Borel bowed and said, "My lady."

Both the King Under the Hill and his queen tilted their heads in acknowledgement, and the High Lord signalled for silence, and the music stopped, as did the dancers. When quiet fell, he smiled and said, "Won't you join us in banquet and ball? Let me get you a glass of wine."

As the king turned to signal a page, Borel said, "I must decline, my lord, for I am on an urgent mission, and I beg a boon."

The High Lord frowned. "A mission? A boon? Then tell me, what mission, what boon brings the Prince of the Winterwood unto my demesne?"

"My lord, I would find the Endless Sands."

"Ah, then, and you think I would know where these Endless Sands lie?"

"I have it on good authority that you do," said Borel.

The king frowned again and looked first at his queen and then among the dancers. Yet none volunteered that he or she had given the prince any guidance. "And who might that be?" he asked Borel.

"A Pooka," replied the prince.

"A Pooka? And just how did you get a Pooka to tell you that?"

"I rode him to submission," said Borel.

A gasp went up among the gathered Fey, for, even though they were Fairies all, none there had the courage to do the same.

"Ah, then, you must be quite a sportsman," said the Fairy King.

"Not really, for he almost did me in," said Borel.

"Yet in the end you triumphed?" asked the queen, her voice melodious and entrancing.

"Barely," replied Borel, grinning ruefully.

She turned to the king and said, "You must help this brave prince, my lord."

"But he has asked for a boon, and you know what that entails."

The queen nodded. She turned to Borel and said, "You must best my husband at a game ere he can aid you. Yet heed: he will try his utmost to get the better of you, for otherwise 'tis but a sham."

"A game?" said Borel.

"Yes," said the king. "A contest. And should you lose, you must dine with me and my queen. Do you agree?"

But if I dine with them, then I might suffer a fate similar to that of others who have paused to make merry with the Fairies, and a millennium might pass, and Chelle will be lost forever. And that is the terrible penalty if I lose.

Yet with her words Verdandi indicated I must play, and if I win . . .

"Lord, might I name the stakes if I win?"

"Indeed," said the King of the Fairies.

"Then this is what I would have: that you not only tell me where lie the Endless Sands, but you also loan me your very own favorite horse to get there."

"My favorite horse?"

"Oui."

The Fairy King looked at his queen and then said, "Very well, I agree."

"As do I," said Borel. "What is the game?"

"I offer you five," said the king, "for since I name the weapons, you will choose the play."

Borel canted his head in assent.

"These are the five," said the Fairy King. "Taroc, échecs, quoits, archery, dames."

Ah, just as Verdandi had said:

> *"The King will offer five different games,*
> *Play the one you played with your dame.*
> *Remember true and remember well*
> *The guiding words of your love Michelle.*

Two of these games I played with Chelle: archery and échecs. Which to choose? Oh, but wait, 'Remember true and re-

member well/ The guiding words of your love Michelle.' Did she give me guiding words? Borel frowned in thought. *I remember none whatsoever. Guiding words . . . guiding words . . . What guiding words?*

Borel unslung his bow and drew an arrow, and as he looked at the shaft, the Fairy King smiled and said, "It is archery, then?" He turned to signal an Elfin page.

"I—" Borel started to say, but of a sudden he seemed to hear Chelle's voice: *"My, do you have Fairy arrows, Borel? 'Tis not fair if so. . . . They are magique, my love, and only miss should a greater spell come along to deflect them."*

Borel looked up and said, "Non, my lord," and he placed the arrow back into his quiver and reslung his bow. " 'Tis échecs I choose."

"As you will, Prince Borel," said the Fairy King, and he signalled for an échiquier to be brought forth.

A table and two chairs were set in the very center of the chamber, and Fairies gathered 'round as the Fairy Queen held out two enclosed hands to Borel. "You are the guest within these halls, Prince Borel, and so you have first choice."

Borel drew the white, and therefore had first move.

"White king's spearman two paces forward," said Borel, moving the piece.

"Black king's spearman two paces forward as well," said the Fairy King, smiling in anticipation.

And the game began, with Fairies crowding about and murmuring after every move, sometimes *Ooh*ing, sometimes *Ahh*ing, sometimes gasping at a bold move by either player.

Borel and the Fairy King both seemed engaged in reckless play, yet it was anything but. Swiftly were moves made and countered, with pieces captured, chevaliers falling, and towers brought to crashing ruin. Hierophants fell in diagonal flight. Kings fled, and queens were slain in spite of the valiant efforts of the spearmen. A great slaughter took place on that grid-marked board, but at last the Fairy King said, "Although the material is fairly balanced, I have the advantage, and it is certain that I will win, for you cannot stop at least one of my black spearmen from reaching the final row and transforming into a black queen."

Borel studied the board. He had a king and a spearman and one tower left, whereas the High Lord had a king at one edge of the board with six spearmen at hand, all of them threatening Borel's king and his spearman.

At last, Borel said, "Tower to white king's tower's three. Check."

The High Lord said, "My prince, are you certain you want to make that move?"

"Indeed," said Borel.

"Very well," said the Fairy King. "Spearman takes tower. Check. And now you have nought but a king and a single spearman left, whereas I yet have all my pieces. Surely you must concede."

"Nay, my lord," said Borel, "I do not concede. White king to white king's hierophant's three."

"Hmm . . ." said the Fairy King. "Black spearman to black king's chevalier's five. Check."

Borel nodded and said, "I avoid the check thus: white king to white king's hierophant's four, taking a blocking black spearman."

Now the Fairy King studied the board long. "I have but one move," he said. "Black spearman to black king's chevalier's six."

Borel laughed and said, "And my lone remaining white spearman takes that black spearman. Check."

The Fairy King said, "Ah, Borel, I must make a move and yet cannot, for the only piece that is not blocked is my black king, and he cannot move to the open space nor capture your single spearman, for to do either would bring him adjacent to your white king, and, of course, that cannot be. Ah, me, I must concede." And he lay his black king on its side.

The gathered Fairies gasped, for seldom did the High Lord lose.

The King Under the Hill reached across the table and shook Borel's hand and said, "Well played, my prince. Well played."

As the gathered Fairies applauded, Borel stood and bowed.

And then he said, "And now, my lord, your favorite horse and directions to the Endless Sands."

"Won't you have some wine, Prince Borel?" asked the Fairy King. "To celebrate your victory, of course."

Borel shook his head. "Non, my lord, for I cannot delay."

"Very well, then," said the king. "Clear the floor," he called.

Fairies bore away the table and chairs and the échecs game, and all stepped to the sides of the great ballroom, and, at an elaborate wave of the Fairy King's hand, thirty-two horses came galloping in. Black horses there were, and white ones as well, and there were sixteen of each, the same as the number of échecs pieces, and the same colors as well. And they were caparisoned in stunning bridles and saddles and other accoutrements: there were tassels adangle and swaying; and brass and bronze and golden bells and jingles rang as the horses moved about; and all had stirrups of the same metals, and bits and rings as well. Splendid were the saddles with their decorated saddlebows and cantles. Reins and bridles were studded and bejewelled and aglitter. And their shoes were of silver and gold and bronze.

"My favorite is amid these," said the Fairy King. "All you must do is find him."

And the animals milled about with arched necks and high tails as Borel walked among them.

"Have you more than one favorite?" called Borel.

"Non," replied the Fairy King.

"And it is within this herd?"

"Oui," said the High Lord.

Verdandi's words echoed within Borel's mind: "*. . . ask for the High Lord's favorite horse, else you will not see the sands ere the full moon rises, yet beware, for the King Under the Hill is quite tricky, and you must recall what you know.*"

Well, the High Lord is indeed tricky, for I must choose one from among the thirty-two. Yet what do I know of Fairy horses? Nothing, I think. Nothing whatsoever.

Borel stepped among the steeds, pushing some aside to look at others.

"Recall what you know," had said Lady Lot, but what is it I know?

And then Charité's words came unto him: *"Tell him about the Fey ladies on the horses with silver bells."*

That's it! Maurice was speaking of the day Chelle came into her majority, the day she was cursed. Maurice and Charité were sitting outside and watching the procession up to the duke's manor, when the Fairies rode by on their Fairy horses.

Borel then began looking among the animals, and at last he came to a white horse adorned with silver bells. Borel continued searching, yet he found no other. Finally he strode to the only mount caparisoned with bells of silver and called out, "This is the steed I choose."

"You have chosen wisely, my friend," said the Fairy King, and with a wave of his hand the other horses vanished, for they were nought but illusions all. And they left behind the single white steed bedecked with the silver bells, for it was the true Fairy horse.

"This is Asphodel," said the Fey Lord. "Asphodel, meet Prince Borel, a mighty rider, and you will bear him where he wills."

The white horse looked at Borel and tossed his head, and Borel bowed in return.

Borel then turned to the king and said, "And where are the Endless Sands, my lord?"

"Just say to Asphodel where you would go and he will bear you there," replied the Fairy King.

"Then I must away," said Borel, preparing to mount.

"But wait, my prince," said the High Lord. "It is dark. Will you not stay the night?"

Again Verdandi's words echoed in Borel's mind: *". . . beware, for the King Under the Hill is quite tricky."*

"Nay, my lord," replied Borel, "for my mission is urgent, and I cannot wait."

"Then fare you well, Prince Borel," said the Fairy Queen, "and we wish you all good success."

Borel mounted the white horse and rode out from the great

hall and to the spiral ramp and up. And, lo! it was twilight when he emerged from under the capstone and into the air above. And a waxing, nearly full, gibbous moon rode above the horizon.

"My lord, my lord," cried Flic frantically, "there are but two days left ere the moon rises full."

"Two days? How can this be? 'Twas the dark of the moon but candlemarks agone," cried Borel, leaping down and taking up his rucksack and long-knife sheath and hat. He retrieved the honey jar as well, its contents nearly gone.

"Time runs at a different pace in the halls of the Fairy King," said Flic. "You entered a full fortnight past!"

With his gear strapped on, and Buzzer asleep on the hat, Borel leapt back on the horse and said, "Come, Flic, we must ride."

Flic took station on Borel's tricorn and held on to Buzzer, and he said, "My lord, we had better hope this horse flies like the wind, else all is lost."

Borel took the reins in hand and whispered into the ear of the Fairy horse, "To the Endless Sands, Asphodel, and hurry."

And with a jingle of silver bells, the steed leapt swiftly away.

44

Doom

And like the wind the Fairy horse did run, as away from the dolmen he sped. In a flash, it seemed, Asphodel was past the twilight border and into the stony green highlands, the ones Borel and Flic and Buzzer had come through but a fortnight ago—or, depending upon who might be asked, perhaps that very same eve.

O'er the hills and tors ran the steed, silver bells sounding the way, and straight into the woodlands he sped, slowing down not one whit, for the Fairy horse was like a zephyr weaving among the trees. Across rivers and streams he passed, silver-shod hooves leaving nought but ripples ringing outward in Asphodel's wake.

Now Borel could hear the surf booming against the leagues-long cliffs, and when the racing mount came to the sheer drop, over the rim he leapt.

Down they plummeted, down through the air, down toward the waves below, and Borel's knuckles grew white upon the reins he gripped. Yet gentle as a feather did the steed land, and o'er the combers he ran, Asphodel's heels kicking up white foam behind.

"By all the gods above," shouted Borel, "but what a wondrous steed!"

And across the waters they sped, and below the ruins of the tower high above where the white lady had died, and they saw no sign of her, but of course no storm raged. Yet even had a tempest whelmed upon sea and land, the white lady would not be there, for by Borel's hand she had been put to rest at last, or so had said Lady Lot. And on beyond the ruins they angled, and soon they were upon the open waters of the wide ocean, with land no longer in sight.

A ship they passed and then another, men adeck shouting and pointing, and the vessels changed course.

"We run like the Pooka does o'er the waves," cried Flic, shrieking to be heard above the wind of their flight.

Long did they course upon the vast sea and through numerous twilight borders, passing from roiling waters to smooth, from cold oceans to warm, from stormy seas to calm. And as they ran, the gibbous moon sailed serenely above, paying no heed to the miraculous scene below. And somewhere during this passage, Flic fell quite asleep.

Nigh mid of night and beyond another tenebrous border, a headland appeared in the distance. Up the slopes the Fairy horse sped, and to the fore mighty mountains did loom afar, and when the steed came unto them, up sheer massifs and o'er vast chasms and among jagged crags he leapt.

Over the range they passed and through another twilight marge to race across a vast bog, the steed running so lightly he left not a track therein. Finally Asphodel emerged through another bound and came to a fiery land, with the ground arumble and mountains spewing flame.

Past that land, across a great plain they ran, while the moon continued to slide down the sky. Another border they breached, and another and another, and Borel had lost all count, as over snow they raced and lakes and ponds and ice and through the streets of towns and cities and within jungles and across lands desolate of life.

The moon set, but the sun was not yet risen, and another candlemark they ran.

At last, even as the dawn graced the skies, they emerged from a woodland and crossed a grassy field to come to a twilight border, and here the white horse bedecked with silver bells halted.

And Asphodel was not breathing hard.

"We have reached the Endless Sands?" asked Borel.

With a nicker, the Fairy horse tossed his head, his silver bells ringing faintly.

Flic, awakened by the sudden stop, took to wing and passed through the border and back. "Sands as far as the eye can see," he called.

Asphodel snorted as if to say, *You doubted?*

"Do you see Roulan's estate?" called Borel.

"Non," said Flic. "As I say, nothing but sand.'Tis a desert without end."

"Noble steed, can you take us to Roulan's estate in the Endless Sands?"

The Fairy horse blew and shook his head, silver jingling.

"Can you take us to the turret where Lady Michelle is held?"

Once more Asphodel shook his head, silver bells again ringing.

"Is it because you know not where she lies?"

A whuffle, and a toss of the head was the steed's answer.

Flic hovered before the Fairy horse. "Is it because magie is involved that you do not know?"

Another whuffle and a toss of head.

Flic looked at Borel and said, "It seems we are on our own."

"I agree," said Borel, even as Buzzer took to wing and flew to hover beside the Sprite.

Borel dismounted and stepped to the fore and turned and bowed and said, "I thank you, Asphodel, marvelous steed."

Again the mount tossed his head, and as the rim of the sun lipped the horizon, the Fairy horse faded away, and neither Borel nor Flic could see ought of him. And hoofbeats receded and silver bells grew faint as Asphodel swiftly galloped off, back the way he had come.

When the bells could no longer be heard, Borel whispered, "Fare you well, noble steed." Then he turned to Flic and said, "I would see these sands," and he stepped into the twilight border, and the Sprite and the bee followed.

* * *

As they broke fast on the woodland side of the marge, Flic said, "What be our strategy, my lord? How do we go about finding what we are meant to find in yon Endless Sands? I mean, Lady Skuld would not have sent us here if there were nought to discover, nor would Lady Verdandi have told us how to reach this place before the full moon rises if there were nought to see, to do. So, what be our strategy?"

Borel took a deep breath. "Now that I've flown upon the back of a Pooka o'er Faery, and upon an Eagle in a dream, I think the best way to search for something among the sands is to fly up high and simply look about. And since you can fly . . ."

"I see," said Flic, licking honey from a finger. "I scout from above."

"Oui," said Borel, chewing a biscuit. "And there is this as well: because the boundaries of Faery are quite tricky, I would have us enter the Endless Sands, have you fly as high as is safe and look and come back down. If you've seen nought, then we'll return to this side, to move on solid ground instead of slogging through loose sand as we make our way somewhat down the marge and enter again, and repeat the process."

"But, my lord, a small move along this side of the border can shift us greatly along the other side . . . and vice versa I add."

Borel nodded. "Rightly so, Flic, yet if that be the case I can only hope that a small move on this side is a greater move on the other."

"How will we know?" asked Flic.

Swallowing a bite of jerky, Borel said, "We'll leave a marker lying in the sand here, and then come back to this side, move along the border a bit, and then go in and see. If all is well, we'll continue doing so. And by leaving markers at each crossing, we'll know if we've gone too far and need to double back."

"What kind of markers, my lord? I have nothing whatsoever to leave except Argent and his scabbard and belt, and I will certainly not abandon them. I mean, after all, my épée might be needed ere we are done. And there is this, too: if it is you who leaves something behind in the sand, and if the search is long, then you will be as naked as I ere we are finished."

Borel took a bite of jerky and chewed a moment, then said, "Right you are. What would you suggest instead?"

"I think I will be able to see a marking in the sand itself. And with your huge feet, my lord, you should be able to shuffle about and leave tracks deep enough for me to espy."

Borel laughed, then sobered. "Though the sand is quite loose and some likely to spill back in, still there is no wind, and so a mark might last long enough for us to search. Hence, with my very huge feet I'll scrape out a deep number in the sand at each crossing—*un, deux, trois,* and so on—so that we'll know if somehow the twilight borders have managed to circle us 'round."

"Circle us 'round?"

"Yes, Flic. You see, I think if we have so-called Endless Sands, then perhaps somewhere within will be margins such that when one steps through he comes to the opposite side of the sands and so they merely seem endless rather than truly being so."

"I do not understand," said Flic, taking up another finger of honey and licking it clean.

"Think of it this way, Flic: say you are in a room filled with sand, but there are two dark arches on opposite sides of the room. And when you step out through one arch, you come in through the other, thus entering the very same roomful of sand. Time after time you walk across the room and go out the far arch, only to enter the near one, and thereby enter the same room of sand. Now I ask you, wouldn't the sand seem endless?"

"Oui, my lord."

"Yet had you left a special marker in the sand—an object, a particular track, or the like—you would pass it again and again, and thereby know the sand is not truly endless, but only seems so."

Flic clapped his hands. "How clever you are, my lord."

Borel frowned. "Had I been clever, then perhaps I would know what Lady Lot meant when she said I had already missed one chance to find the sands."

"Ah, those Fates: what do they know?"

"Everything," said Borel. "At least everything in its due time."

"Pish," said Flic, snorting. "I mean, look, you answered their riddles right off."

"Ah, Flic, they posed me riddles the answers to which I already knew," said Borel. "And what's more, they knew that I knew, or knew I would cipher it out. I think they are simply bound by some unwritten law or higher power or unbreakable edict to require a service, pose a riddle, and then render aid with another riddle."

"Well, my lord, that's easy for you to say. As for me, I would have failed to answer the one about me falling behind and then passing the Sprite in second place. I mean, not that I would ever fall behind"—Flic growled—"and certainly not *twice* as the Fates would have it."

Borel smiled and said, "That may be, Flic, but again I say, the riddles were simple. The true test was in bearing them across the water."

They ate in silence for a while, but then Flic said, "Oh, my goodness."

"What?" asked Borel.

"Just this, my prince: if somehow someone were dropped into the room of sand where there were but two dark arches, and if there were no other way out, then he would be trapped forever."

"How extraordinary, Flic. Ha! And you say I'm clever?"

They ate a moment more, and then Borel's eyes widened in revelation. "I say, Flic, mayhap that's the way of the Castle of Shadows beyond the Black Wall of the World."

"My lord?"

"It would explain why Orbane is trapped, why he cannot get out."

"See?" said Flic, "I told you you were clever."

"Which way, my lord," said Flic, "right or left?"

They had finished breaking their fast, and now they stood facing the twilight border.

"In," said Borel.

"No, my lord, I mean after we come back out. Which way, then?"

"Ah," said Borel, "I suppose one way is as good as another."

"Not if we choose the wrong way," said Flic.

"Indeed," said Borel, frowning. "We'll let Dame Fortune decide." He spit in his palm and slapped two fingers into the gob. "Dextral," he said, for the spit flew rightward.

In through the twilight border they went, and Flic and Buzzer flew up beyond seeing, while Borel shuffled a long, deeply trenched 1 in the sand.

He had just finished when Buzzer and Flic came flying back. "Nought, my lord."

Out through the twilight border they went, and Borel said, "I will trot five hundred paces, and then we'll go back in." And off he loped, Flic and Buzzer atop his hat resting.

Once more they penetrated the twilight marge, and as Borel trenched out a 2, Flic and Buzzer flew high and then returned. *"Ne rien,"* said Flic.

"Nothing at all?" said Borel.

"Oh, I did see the *un* you made in the sand," said Flic, and I think it might be a bit farther away than you ran on the woodland side of the bound, though I am not certain."

Borel turned up a hand and said, "Farther or not, if it stays that way, we'll cover more ground by running on good firm ground than trying to run through loose sand."

Off they went once more, and again, and again, and again. . . .

They searched all day, twice having to backtrack because they had gone beyond being able to see the trenched number. They had only stopped for a short midday meal, and then had continued. But their search was futile, and now the nearly full moon had risen and the sun was setting.

"One day," gritted Borel. "One day is all that is left."

Flic nodded and said, "Though Buzzer cannot aid, still we can search by the light of the nearly full moon, my lord."

Borel growled and said, "We don't even know whether we are going the right way, Flic."

"Nevertheless, my lord, we cannot stop."

"Oh, I do not intend to stop," said Borel, "yet I wonder whether we should have gone leftward instead of rightward. —Regardless, let us press on."

With Flic and Buzzer back on the hat, again Borel trotted, and Flic said, "Uh-oh. Ahead, my lord."

"I see her," said Borel.

In the fore, on the far side of a wide stream, a lovely demoiselle sat in the gathering twilight.

"It might be one of those Fey, my prince."

"Indeed," said Borel, "for there is but one of the Fates we have yet to meet."

"But what if it's not her?" said Flic. "What if instead it's a deadly creature of some sort?"

" 'Tis a chance I must take," replied Borel.

"Then Buzzer and I will get off at that tree this side, my lord," said Flic, "for I would not tempt Fate by getting too close. But if it *is* a trap, Argent and I will be ready."

Even as the Sprite and the bee flew to a limb, Borel splashed across the stream and then bowed. "My lady, need you assistance?"

The black-haired, black-eyed, slender, and stunningly beautiful demoiselle sighed and said, "My slippers and hose will get wet should I cross in them. And should I remove them, my delicate feet will be bruised. Will you bear me over, my most handsome sieur?"

"Oh, indeed, Demoiselle."

Borel turned his back and said, "Hop on, my lady, and we shall hie."

Her silvery laugh answered him. "Sieur, most handsome sieur, you are no horse, and I am no rider. I would have you bear me across held ever so securely in your strong arms."

Borel turned about. "You are not afraid I will fall?"

"Oh, la!" she said, placing a delicate hand on his wrist and looking up into his ice-blue eyes with her own eyes of black depths so deep one could surely drown in them. "With you so devilishly handsome and debonair? I saw how well you carry yourself; your swagger speaks of duels fought and never lost.

You move as would a Wolf, and they are never off their nimble feet, except of course when they rest beside a mate. But since you have no mate, per se, you should take your ease by lying with a lover, *n'est-il pas ainsi?*"

"Perhaps," said Borel, grinning, and he swept the demoiselle up in his arms.

As he turned to wade across the stream, her heady perfume, almost a musk, filled him with desire. And even as he stepped into the water, somehow her hands were within his leather jacket and rubbing across his chest and down his abdomen and lower still. And her breath was sweet and her lips inviting, and her eyes were filled with the heat of passion, and she raised her mouth toward his.

"No," he said, his voice but a whisper, and he turned his head aside as he waded. "My heart belongs to another." Yet in spite of himself, he began to harden.

"Ah, but, mon chéri," she whispered, her voice husky with need, "it would be a mere dalliance, and not as if it were something serious. Will you not lie with me?"

"Non, mademoiselle," Borel replied, and he waded on.

"Do you not find me beautiful, desirable? Do you not want me?" Then she laughed, somehow her hands down in his leathers. "Ah, yes, I see you do."

"Mademoiselle, that you excite me, I cannot deny, yet—"

"She is a succubus!" shouted Flic, drawing Argent and taking to wing.

But even as the Sprite darted toward the prince, Borel reached the opposite bank and knelt to set the demoiselle to her delicate feet, and the moment he did so, she transformed into a barefoot, toothless, doddering crone in black robes, and as if from a distance, there came the sound of a loom.

Even as Flic cried out and reversed course, "Lady Doom," said Borel, yet kneeling.

In the twilight the black-eyed, wrinkled crone smiled a gummy smile and said, "Heh."

"She Who Forever Fixes the Events of Time Into the Past," said Borel.

The crone nodded but said, "More like the dustbin of history, Prince Borel."

"Lady Urd," said Borel, standing and bowing, and as he did so he took her hand and kissed her fingers.

"Heh, bold," said Urd, again grinning a toothless smile. "but I think a kiss on the hand is not nearly as thrilling as bold caresses, eh?" She cackled in glee.

Borel laughed. "Indeed not."

Sobering, Urd said, "You did very well, my lad, for you were sorely tested. Others would have certainly succumbed."

"My Lady Urd, to, um, lie with Fate seems a rather risky proposition."

"Heh. Perhaps *not* to lie with Fate is even more risky . . . a woman scorned, you see."

"Madame, as I say, my heart—"

"Yes, yes," snapped Urd, "given to another. I know."

"Lady Urd, are you here to help me?"

"Of course, and you have borne me across water, as you did Skuld and Verdandi, my two elder sisters."

"Don't forget, he fed them, too," shouted Flic, "and so my prince is well ahead in the favor game."

"Cheeky little thing, isn't he," said Urd, her mouth grinning widely, her gums showing.

"Yes, my lady," said Borel.

"Nevertheless he is right, Prince Borel: you are ahead in the favor game."

"Will it buy your help?" asked Borel.

"You have met the first requirement by doing a favor for me, but still you must answer a riddle before I can aid, for I am bound," said Urd.

"Then you do know I have the answer to the riddle of the Sphinx as well as the answers to the riddles you and your sisters posed to Camille, and those most recent riddles posed by the Ladies Skuld and Verdandi?"

"Of course, of course," said Urd.

"Then ask away, Lady Doom," said Borel.

Urd looked afar at Flic, and the Sprite groaned but yelled out, "I would not fall behind!"

"Heh," barked Urd. "Cheeky indeed. Well, here it is, young man:

"If Flic were in a Spritely contest
For several objects to find,
But in some manner unknown to him
He had fallen behind—"

—Urd looked at Flic and cackled, and Flic groaned and turned his back to her—

"And there was a single object left
Down in a dip on a dint-filled plain,
How should he go about searching
And be the one to win?"

"I *wouldn't* fall behind, I *wouldn't* fall behind, I *wouldn't*, I *wouldn't*," muttered Flic on his limb beside now-sleeping Buzzer.

"My Lady Doom," said Borel, "one way is to fly very high so as to see down into every dip on that dint-filled plain."

"Indeed," said Urd, again cackling at Flic.

"My lady, the aid?" said Borel.

"Eh, eh, yes, of course," said Urd. "Now let me see, there is something you need to know, and it is this:

"The Endless Sands run forever,
But search as you have this day,
And you will find her never,
Yet there is indeed a way:

"Seek the black oak sinister
Beside the twilight wall,
Behind it a narrow portal,
Yet beware the fall.

"And this I will tell you for nought: it lies afar and you cannot rest."

"Can you say no more, Lady Urd?" called Flic. "I mean, he fed two of your sisters, and so he is ahead."

Urd nodded, and held out her hand, and of a sudden Buzzer appeared therein, and she whispered to the sleeping bee, yet what she said neither Borel nor Flic could hear.

She handed the bee to Borel and said, "Now the scales are balanced. But I warn you: remember all you were told, else you will fail in the end."

"But which way do we go, Lady Urd?" cried Flic, yet the sound of the loom swelled, and then vanished as did the Lady Doom.

45

Sinistral

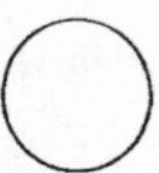

"My lord, she did not say which way to go."

"The direction is in the aid she gave," said Borel. " 'Find the black oak sinister,' she said."

"My lord?"

"Sinister, leftward, Flic. We have been going the wrong way from the outset, for we chose dextral."

Flic growled and said, "I *knew* we should never have trusted that slapped spit, for Dame Fortune oft plays dastardly tricks." Then he groaned. "All that searching we did, and all of it away from instead of toward."

"Take heart, Flic, for now we simply must find the black oak next to the twilight bound."

"My lord," said Flic, "there were no black oaks nigh the border the way we came."

"None?"

"None, my lord. It means we must go all the way back to where we started and then beyond to find Lady Urd's dark tree."

Borel sighed. "She warned us: 'And this I will tell you for nought: it lies afar and you cannot rest.' "

"Oui, my lord," said Flic, "those were her very words." Flic glanced at the gibbous moon, the orb nearly full and now some four fists above the horizon and on the rise, and he said, "And there is but a day remaining."

Borel, too, looked at the moon in the night sky. "Less than a day, my friend, for even as does the sun set on the morrow, so shall the full moon rise. We must find that black oak well ere then, for we know not what we will face in the Endless Sands."

"Daggers, my lord," said Flic, "that's what we'll face, whatever they might be."

"Oui, Flic, whatever they might be," said Borel. Then he glanced at the woodland nearby. "And you are certain that there are no black oaks between here and the place we started?"

"None whatsoever," said Flic. "Do you know what a black oak looks like?"

"Non, Flic, for I am of the Winterwood, where all trees but evergreens are barren and snow- or ice-laden. Though I do know pine and yew and fir and the like, I simply did not pay heed to the differences among the barren trees."

"No matter, my lord, for I *do* know the black oak."

Borel looked at Buzzer asleep in his hand. "Then let us hie, and as I run, you rest, sleep if you can, for Urd has said we've a long journey ahead, and I would have you afresh when we reach the place where we began."

"Oui, Prince Borel," said Flic, even then yawning. "But let us away, and now, for the moon stays not her course for any."

Borel set dormant Buzzer within the tricocked brim of his hat, and Flic took a seat there as well, and back the way they had come did Borel begin his run.

Throughout the moon- and starlit night the prince loped alongside the twilight bound, while the heavens above wheeled slowly 'round, and the moon sailed serenely on, and neither the stars nor the argent orb paused even a jot in deference to the desperate drama unfolding below. On Borel ran and on, occasionally pausing briefly for a drink at a stream or from his waterskin. All night he ran, growing ever more weary, and as first light began to grace the skies he came to the place where the Fairy horse had brought them in the dawn of the day before.

"Waken, Flic, waken!" called Borel. "I am back where we began."

Roused by Borel, Flic said, "I'm up, I'm up," and clambered to his feet. He took station in the prow and looked about as he yawned. "The sun is not yet risen," he muttered, "nor is the gibbous moon set."

"The moon will set in a candlemark or so," said Borel, "and the sun will rise shortly after. But we must press on and begin the run sinister, for Lady Doom's words tell us that I cannot rest."

"Then away, my lord," said Flic.

"Can you recognize and name trees in the dimness of dawn and the moonlight shining aglance?" said Borel.

"Though I am a Field Sprite, woodlands border meadows, and well did my mère tutor me in the lore of the verging forests, and, so, trees I know, by sunlight or moonlight or even by starlight. Hence, my lord, dally no more."

And so again Borel took up the run along the twilight bound, and the moon set and the sun rose, and Buzzer wakened, even as they came to a stream. Borel stopped for a drink, and as he gobbled down a biscuit, he uncapped the honey jar and poured a small dollop down in the brim of his hat along the cocked back. And while Buzzer and Flic broke their fast, Borel took up the run once more.

A candlemark after sunrise Borel called out, "Flic, I see a tree standing beside the border. Is it a black oak?"

Flic looked at the deep purple leaves and the smooth silver-grey bark and said, "Nay, my lord, 'tis a copper beech. Run on, my prince, run on."

And so Borel ran on, now and then momentarily stopping at a streamside for a drink, then splashing on across the flow and over the land, a marge of twilight always on his right, a woodland on his left, though no black oaks did Flic espy therein.

Just ere the noontide, Borel called out, "Flic, another tree alongside the border."

Flic eyed the green leaves and the grey-white trunk and said, "Nay, my lord, 'tis a silver maple. Run on, my prince, run on."

At the next stream, Borel gobbled down another biscuit, and once more he set a dollop of honey on the brim of his hat. And then he started running again.

Two candlemarks or so after the sun passed through the zenith, Borel called out, "Another tree, Flic, standing by the border."

"Nay, my lord, 'tis not what we seek but a golden ash instead."

As he loped onward Borel growled and said, "I'm beginning to wonder if Lady Doom has arranged this apurpose."

"My lord?"

"Three trees have we seen standing alongside the marge: copper, silver, and gold," said Borel, "a timeless progression in fables. But usually when the gold of that trio is encountered, so too is success at hand."

"That might be the case in hearthtales, my lord," said Flic, looking back, "and perhaps here as well, for each of those trees—the copper, the silver, and the gold—might signify that something marvelous lies across the border and in the sands beyond. Yet we cannot pause to see, for no black oak is nigh, and the sun ever sinks toward his setting, and the unseen moon ever nears her rise."

Borel ran onward, up slopes and down, splashing across streams and *shssh*ing through tall grasses, woodlands ever on the left, the twilight bound on the right.

And in late afternoon, "A tree alongside the border, Flic."

Flic looked at the broad limbs with their nine-lobed leaves, and the dark, dark trunk, and cried out in glee, " 'Tis a black oak, my lord, a black oak! We have come to the black oak at last!"

Weary beyond measure, Borel ran to the dark tree and stopped, and his breath came harsh and heavy. As Flic took to wing with Buzzer following, Borel glanced at the remains of the day, and his heart fell, for there was but a single candlemark left ere the sun would begin to set and the full moon begin to rise.

46

Daggers

"Come," said Borel, straightening up, "let us hurry, for time is—"

"Wait, my lord," said Flic. "Remember Urd's warning:

" *'Seek the black oak sinister*
Beside the twilight wall,
Behind it a narrow portal,
Yet beware the fall.'

"That's what she said. And so, my lord, before you go through, let me first see what lies beyond."

"Hurry," said Borel, again glancing at the sun, "we've no time to tarry."

With Buzzer following, Flic turned and darted into the twilight marge.

Long moments passed, and long moments more, and Borel could wait no longer, for the sun itself would not delay, nor would the as-yet-unseen full moon. But just as he started to step within, Flic and Buzzer returned.

"Beware, my lord. Lady Urd was right. Straight through and you'll plunge to your doom, for when I emerged out the far side,

I was in the air above a great drop. To both the left and right there are outjuts along the face of a sheer cliff, with pathways down to the sands below. Yet these are not to be trusted, for when I tried to return by flying across one of those outjuts, Buzzer and I ended above bubbling molten stone within a hollow mountain. We fled back, and I tried the other outjut, with the very same results. And so, Lady Urd was right when she spoke of the black oak: 'Behind it a narrow portal,' she said, and narrow it is. This marge is tricky, my lord, a perfect place for Rhensibé to set a trap. I would think that from this side of the bound, should you step left or right of the portal, who knows where you would end? Perhaps above that same pool of molten stone."

"Nevertheless, I must enter," said Borel.

"How, my lord? You cannot fly."

"There must be a way," said Borel. "I will try to find it." And without further delay, Borel pulled from his rucksack the rope he had purchased in Riverbend and tied one end to the tree. Paying it out, he stepped into the twilight directly behind the oak.

As Flic and Buzzer flew past, into the dimness Borel went, testing each step before taking it. Darker and darker grew the marge, and in the depths of the blackness, he came to the lip of a sheer precipice.

Down he swung on his rope, and he felt about for handholds, but the surface was smooth with no places to grip, all the way down the extent of his line. Side to side he swung, and yet there was only vertical stone.

Finally he clambered back up to the top. *Which way, I wonder, would the witch walk? Ah, yes, I know: sinister, what else?*

Hoping he would not need it, Borel left the rope behind as a marker and sidled leftward through utter darkness along the very verge of the precipice. Slowly, ever so slowly, the dimness began to lighten. And then he emerged along the flat top of a stark desert cliff two hundred feet above the Endless Sands.

A pathway led steeply down.

"My lord," cried Flic joyously, he and Buzzer circling about.

But Borel paid him no heed, for a half a league away lay a lush vale trapped between endless dunes, and in the very center a great green heap mounded up a hundred feet high or more, its length and breadth a furlong or so in each direction.

"What is it, Flic?" asked Borel.

"What is what, my lord?"

"That," said Borel, pointing.

Flic turned about. "Oh, my, there's green in the desert. How did it get here?" He turned back to Borel. "I do not know what it is, my prince. I was so concerned about you and the crossing, that I didn't see it ere now. Ah, me, some scout I make, eh?"

"I pray it be Roulan's vale carried here by the black wind," said Borel. "You and Buzzer scout ahead, Flic, while I make my way down. And be certain to look at that mound in the middle; it sits where the manse should be."

"Oui!" cried the Sprite, and away he flew, Buzzer at his side.

Down the steep path Borel trotted, and when he reached the sands he found the terrain barren and rocky, and off he loped toward the green vale with the great mound in the middle, a mile and a half away.

Before he had covered two furlongs toward the heap, he came unto the sand, and running became difficult in the shifting footing. Yet on he loped, for the sun angled down through the sky, and the moon would soon rise.

He had covered perhaps half the distance when Flic and Buzzer came winging back. "The mound: 'tis vines with thorns: great huge vines with thorns as long as your own forearms, my lord. Yet beware, for unto my Fey vision there is an aura about them, as of magie."

"Daggers," said Borel, not pausing in his run. "These must be the daggers of Chelle's dream. Did not Lady Wyrd say 'Neither awake nor in a dark dream are perilous blades just as they seem'? And these blades, these daggers, are not as they seemed, for they are instead thorns."

"We guessed they weren't really daggers," said Flic.

"Indeed, we guessed, and now we know," said Borel. "—Is there a turret within?"

"I could not tell, my lord, for the thorn vines are much too thick. Yet there is a higher place at the center where a turret could be."

Yet running, Borel said, "Lord Roulan had a turret nigh the center of his manor."

"Perhaps that is it, then," said Flic. "But there is something else, my lord: as I flew near, I could hear a squeaking coming from somewhere within . . . close to the center, I think."

"A squeaking?"

"Oui, just as you told me was in your dream, as of a wagon wheel long without grease and turning."

"Never mind, Flic. We will find what it is when we get in," said Borel.

"Oh, my lord, I think there is no way to penetrate the thorns," said Flic. "I mean, not even Buzzer could make her way through."

"There's got to be a way, else Chelle is fordone."

"But I flew all 'round," said Flic, "and I simply don't see how we can enter."

"Again I say, there must be a way, Flic, else the Ladies Wyrd and Lot and Doom would not have sent us here."

"Perhaps they did so to make certain Rhensibé is killed," said Flic. "I mean, we will avenge Chelle should worse come to worst. Surely Rhensibé will arrive to gloat if that happens."

"I will not think of such," snapped Borel, and in that moment he trotted into the green vale, and now the running eased. Onward he sped toward the massive mound and he came unto pavestones just before reaching the vast tangle of thorns.

"My lord, again I caution you, there is something of magie about the vines," said Flic. "I do not know what it might be, yet there is an enchantement upon them."

"Indeed," said Borel, "else how could they have grown so large? The entire vale must be ensorcelled, to be so green among these dry sands."

"Oui, lord, yet the vines seem somehow . . . I don't know . . . different from the rest of the vale.'Ware, lord prince, be chary."

"What kind are they, Flic? —The vines and thorns I mean."

"Blackberry, I think, my lord, though perhaps there are rose vines as well."

"Pink-blooming shamrock and blushing white roses and thorn-laden blackberry vines," murmured Borel. "I deem you are right—roses and blackberry—but these are monstrous, most as thick as my leg and more."

Cautiously, Borel moved forward along the pave. "I think this is the footpath to Roulan's gates," said Borel. "I vaguely remember such. —It has to be the way in."

"Take care, my lord," said Flic, as Borel came to the snarl of—

Of a sudden, one of the massive vines lashed out at Borel, and without thinking he snatched his long-kni— Nay! *Not* his long-knife. Instead it was the jagged remainder of the rusted sword he wrenched from his scabbard to parry the attack, even as Flic shrieked, "Look out, my lor—!"

But in that moment the blade touched the lashing thorn vine, and lo! just as had the rider, the vine withered, shriveled, blackened and fell to dust, as if it had aged a thousand years in but an instant of time.

"Hai!" cried Borel, staring at the weapon he had taken as an afterthought from the remains of one of the Riders Who Cannot Dismount. "Indeed not all perilous blades are just as they seem. Oh, d'Strait, d'Strait, your death was not in vain."

And Borel stepped forward, wading into the massive thorn tangle, striking left and right with the rusted blade at the giant lashing briars, their long thorns seeking to stab, the vines striving to grasp.

"Hurry, my lord, hurry!" cried Flic. "The sun is low and ready to set, and the full moon nigh to rising."

Hacking and slashing, onward went Borel, and attacking vines fell before him, yet with each vine turned to dust, the sword grew shorter, rust flaking away, and the farther he penetrated into the mass, the less of a blade he had.

"Mithras, be with me," cried Borel, and onward he hewed, leaving a wide tunnel through the entanglement behind. Yet Borel did not come off unscathed, for as vine after vine lashed at him, the thorns stabbed and tore at his flesh. But still he pressed on, his leathers gashed, blood seeping, and his sword diminishing with each strike.

But at last, bleeding and with no blade left, he came the remaining few feet to the end of the vines and stepped into a clear forecourt before the gates of Roulan's manor.

The portal was open and warded beyond by sleeping guards wearing blue tabards with a silver sunburst centered thereon: Roulan's sigil.

And drifting through the air from within came a strange, squeaking noise.

And the rim of the sun just then touched the horizon, and the limb of the moon peeked above the edge of the Endless Sands.

"Hurry, my lord," said Flic, "for the sun is even now setting and the full moon rising, and we must save Lady Chelle."

Borel looked at the bladeless hilt of d'Strait's sword, and he reverently laid it down, and then into the courtyard stepped the prince, Flic and Buzzer coming after. The moment Borel stepped through the gate, the squeaking became a soothing but atonal squealing flutelike sound, and Flic, entering just behind, flew past Borel and partway across the courtyard but then fluttered down to the pave, where he fell sound asleep.

Buzzer agitatedly flew about, and Borel crossed to the Sprite and took him up and set him within the rim of the tricorn. With the bee angrily circling 'round and 'round, onward Borel headed, running for the doors of the manor and the tower within.

Yet with every step taken, his own eyelids began to droop, and his mind became fuzzy, and all he wanted to do was curl up and go to sleep.

But I cannot . . . I must save . . .

An agonizing pain stabbed him in the neck and he snapped awake.

Buzzer!

The sun sank its lower limb below the horizon, and the full moon continued its inexorable rise.

Across the courtyard Borel staggered, past sleeping men and women, past sleeping Fey Folk, Fairies all. And they were dressed in finery, as if celebrating—

It was, it was . . . Oh, now I . . . I . . . Chelle's majority . . .

Lurching to the doors, he opened them and reeled into the halls beyond, sleep dragging at him. And he was so tired, so very tired, all he needed to do was lie down and—

Again the bumblebee stung Borel, and again the pain brought him awake, and the flutelike music—or was it a squeaking?—tugged at his mind.

The flute—the squealing—grew louder, and Borel jabbed his fingers in his ears, but it seemed the sound grew louder still.

And the rim of the sun sank lower, nearly a full quarter gone, and the moon rose higher, nearly a quarter up.

Now down the hallways he reeled, past sleeping men and women and Fey. He came to the stairwell, and up into the turret he tottered, and the music—the skreeking—became a discordant crescendo, and when he reached the stone floor at the top the noise was nearly unbearable, and he staggered under the burden of simply trying to remain awake, and he was losing consciousness.

But again Buzzer stung him to awareness, and there slumped against the wall lay Chelle, an overturned stool nearby. And just beyond, a spinning wheel turned, its distaff empty of wool or flax or fiber of any kind, its treadle oscillating up and down with no foot whatsoever pressing. And the wheel rotated a strange spindle, a spindle with flutelike holes along its considerable length, and from this instrument came the screeching, came the atonal music.

And now the sun was nearly halfway set, and the moon nearly half risen, and each continued its relentless advance heedless of any consequence that might ensue.

If I stop the wheel . . .

Borel stumbled toward the turning—

The moment he came to Chelle, he fell to his knees, unable to go on, and he closed his eyes and—

Again pain jolted him awake.

Once more he tried to get to the wheel, this time crawling, but the shrieking—the music—swelled even higher, and he could not go forward.

He swung about, and crawled to Chelle.

If I can just get her free . . . get me free . . . of the wheel . . .

He took her slender form in his arms, and, in an effort nearly beyond his capability, he just managed to gain his feet.

Once more Buzzer stung him, and down the stairs Borel struggled.

And the sun was nearly three-quarters gone, and the moon three-quarters up, and still they moved on and on.

Lurching, reeling, down the hallways Borel faltered with Chelle in his arms; past sleeping guests, past Lord Roulan, past Fairies, and past Lady Roulan, he staggered. He paused a moment to rest, but Buzzer stung him again.

He stumbled out through the doors and into the courtyard beyond and across, and finally he was past the gates.

And the sun was nigh set, the moon nigh risen; and the sun continued its unrelenting slide downward, its upper limb now disappearing; and the moon continued its remorseless ascent, the orb striving to reach the open sky.

Flic awakened in that moment, and he screamed, "Lord Borel, the tunnel!"

Ahead, the thorn vines were closing the hewn corridor, and Borel, now free from the spindle music, began to run through the ever-narrowing gape.

Vines lashed at him, and he held Chelle close to protect her, and he ran with speed to get her free from harm.

Through the swiftly closing gap he fled, Flic and Buzzer leading the way, and just as he thought he would be trapped forever, he burst out into the vale beyond.

Within a few more strides he sank to his knees, and, bleeding and totally exhausted, he lay Chelle to the grass.

"My lord, she does not seem to be breathing," said Flic.

"Oh, my love, you cannot die," moaned Borel. "Please, my love, please."

And he pressed his lips against hers and breathed air into her lungs, and then listened for it to escape.

And as he started to press his lips to hers again, Chelle put her arms about him and murmured, "Borel, Borel, my beloved," and she kissed him fervently.

Then she opened her incredibly blue eyes, eyes that Borel had not seen ere this moment, but for the time when she was yet a child.

Of a sudden she said, "Oh. Oh.'Tis no dream." And, completely embarrassed, she reddened.

But Borel kissed her once more, and for a moment she seemed to be utterly confused, but then she threw herself into the kiss, her passion a burning fire.

Flic smiled and looked away at the moon, just then standing full on the horizon.

47

Flight

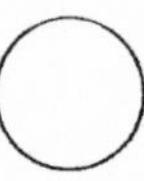

With the sun now set, twilight crept 'cross the Endless Sands, and even as Buzzer, preparing to sleep, took station upon the tricorn, Borel said, "My Lady Michelle, the kiss, forgive me for being so bold."

Chelle reddened and said, "Nay, my lord, 'tis I who must beg forgiveness."

Borel grinned and said, "Then shall we forgive one another? Or instead shall we continue to repeat the offense in the many days to come?"

Chelle laughed, and in spite of his weariness, Borel stood and offered his hand and raised Chelle to her feet.

As she stood, "My lord, you are wounded!"

"Nought but scratches," said Borel, even as he winced when Chelle reached out to touch a gash in his leathers.

"We must bandage you," said Chelle.

"When we are on the other side of the twilight border," said Borel, gesturing.

She looked about, her eyes widening in shock. "Where are we?"

"The Endless Sands, Lady Chelle," said Flic.

"Oh, my, a Sprite!" said Chelle, seeing the wee Fey for the first time.

With a flourish, Flic bowed and said, "At your service, Demoiselle. I am Flic, wielder of Argent and companion of Buzzer. I am, as well, Prince Borel's tagalong."

"Without Flic and Buzzer, I never would have found you," said Borel.

Chelle frowned. "And Buzzer is . . . ?"

Carefully, Borel removed his hat and pointed at the now-sleeping bee and said, "Our guide."

"I remember a dream," said Chelle, smiling. "But it was in among thorn trees where I saw a Sprite and a bee."

Borel nodded. "These are the same you saw there, and that was quite far from here."

Again Chelle looked 'round. "And these are the Endless Sands?"

Borel replaced his hat and said, "Indeed, Chelle."

"How did I get here, and what is that great green mound? It looks like a vast tangle of thorns."

Borel sighed. "There is much to tell, my lady, but this I will say: the greenery about is your sire's estate, and within that tangle lies your manor."

Chelle shook her head. "This cannot be Roulan Vale, not here in the Endless Sands."

"Mademoiselle," said Flic, "we believe the estate was borne here by a great black wind."

"A black wind?" said Chelle. "I remember no black wind."

"Perhaps you were already in an enchanted sleep," said Borel, "a sleep we believe was cast by the sorcière Rhensibé."

"Rhensibé?" gasped Chelle, then her eyes narrowed. "That wicked Fairy. Yes, I remember. She threw the spell during the celebration of my majority." Chelle glanced at the moon. "But it was nigh noon today, not in the twilight."

"Chelle," said Borel, taking her hands in his, " 'twas not this day the spell was cast, but in a time now gone."

"A time now gone? When?"

"As mortals would reckon, eleven years and eleven moons past," said Flic.

Chelle's hand flew to her mouth. "Eleven years . . . ?" Her words fell to a whisper even as Borel embraced her.

"And eleven moons," said Flic.

She looked up into Borel's face unbelieving. " 'Tis true," he softly said.

She rested her head against his breast for a moment, and then she said, "My père and mère, are they well?"

"Chelle," said Borel, "they, too, were enspelled by the enchanted sleep, as were all your guests and the staff."

"Where are they?"

"Trapped within that tangle of thorns in your père's manor, held by the same magie that ensorcelled you."

"We must set them free," said Chelle, pulling away and starting toward the mound.

"Non, non, my love," cried Borel, quickly catching her and drawing her back. "The thorns are enchanted and they will strike down any who come nigh."

"But you got in," said Chelle, tugging against his grip.

"Oui, yet the sword I used was special, and it is gone, destroyed in turn by the very same vines it destroyed. And the path it made through that tangle is now grown shut."

Chelle stopped resisting and cried, "Oh, Borel, we must get through and break the spell."

"Oui. But the spinning wheel yet turns the spindle, and we need find a way to counteract its magie."

"Spinning wheel?" said Flic.

"Do you remember the squeaking and the music?" asked Borel.

"Oui," replied the Sprite.

Borel said, "There is a magique spinning wheel turning an enchanted spindle, and the spindle casts the spell. That is what we must overcome."

"How did you do so?" asked Flic.

"Buzzer kept me from falling asleep—"

"Buzzer?" said Flic.

"Oui. She stung me repeatedly, and the pain barely fended away the charm."

"Aha!" said Flic. "Perhaps *that's* what Lady Urd whispered to Buzzer—instructions to keep you awake, and Buzzer did so by the only means at her command."

"That might be so, Flic, yet at the moment we are helpless. We have no way to get in, and even had we the means to break through the thorn barrier, we would need a way to counteract the wheel."

"Perhaps we can simply put wax in our ears," said Flic. "That way we won't hear the—"

A prolonged, shrill, enraged scream shattered the air, yet whence it came, they could not say.

"Rhensibé," gritted Borel, turning to Chelle. "She has discovered you are free."

Chelle gasped and said, "We must flee before she can cast a snare."

"My lord, look! Something dark and dreadful!" cried Flic, and he pointed at the moon.

Silhouetted against the silver orb, like hideous dark cloaks flapping in the wind, an eldritch black swarm came flying across the sky.

"Where can we run?" said Chelle, looking about even as she pulled a long ribbon from her hair and hiked up her dress and tied it 'round her waist.

"Back through the twilight border," said Borel, stringing his bow.

"Then let us away," said Chelle.

And so, out from the green vale they sped and into the Endless Sands, Chelle following Borel, for he knew the way, Flic flying above, Argent in hand.

And the footing was uncertain in the loose sand, yet still they made good headway toward the sheer cliffs.

Behind them, the flapping shadowy swarm reached the great entanglement of thorns and circled 'round and 'round the turret hidden within.

And still Borel and Chelle and Flic made for the high cliffs and the footpath up to the twilight wall above, for they would flee through the narrow portal in the bound.

Like great black leaves blowing in a desert wind, behind them the swarm of Shadows arrowed away from the hidden turret and raced toward those who thought to escape.

And even as Borel and Chelle and Flic came to the pathway up, the first of the Shadows overtook the fugitives. And like smothering black cloths they wrapped themselves about the heads of the runners, and Borel found he could not breathe, for the Shadow, the creature, cut off all air. And he began to suffocate.

Yet of a sudden and with a thin wail the Shadow vanished, and Flic flourished Argent and skewered another Shadow, and it vanished as well. Still another of the black creatures enwrapped itself about the Sprite, only to disappear into oblivion like its dark brethren, for 'twas silver did them in.

"Yahh!" cried Flic, and he pierced a Shadow wrapping itself about Chelle, and it perished whining.

"Run!" shouted Flic. "I will hold them off."

Up the pathway ran Borel, Chelle in tow, while all about them darted Flic, Argent stabbing and stabbing.

As they reached the top of the outjut, Borel looked back to see a vast horde of Shadows streaming from the desert and toward the cliffs, and he groaned, for there were entirely too many for Flic alone to fend away. Borel slung his bow and said to Chelle, "Come, and follow me exactly. Listen to what I say, else we'll both plunge to our doom over the cliff or into molten stone."

Chelle nodded, and Borel took her hand and said, "We must sidle along the very rim of the fall."

"Let us away, my lord," said Chelle grimly.

And so they began to edge along the brim of disaster, while Flic darted and stabbed, yet the Shadows came on.

Hand in hand, into the darkness of the border went Borel and Chelle, feeling carefully of the rim ere taking a step.

And the Shadows began to sacrifice themselves against Flic, each one wrapping about and carrying him a bit farther away ere the silver of Argent did it in.

Darker and darker became the dusky wall as Borel and Chelle sidled inward, for this place was ensorcelled to be deeply obscure instead of the usual dim twilight, and even as they reached the depths of the blackness, a Shadow enwrapped itself about Borel's head.

He could not breathe, and yet he went onward, and at last his foot encountered what he had been searching for. Down he stooped, and he managed to take up the rope yet tied to the black oak beyond the wall, and he pulled Chelle after as he followed the line outward.

The moment he stepped beyond the border, with a feeble, high-pitched shriek the Shadow vanished, for Flic had broken free of the swarm. Once more Flic stabbed, and he slew the dark creature who had enwrapped Chelle. And both she and Borel stood gasping the sweet, sweet air.

But once more the Shadows began flooding Flic, and even as he was carried away a bit at a time, and with Shadows flying about, Borel heard a horn, and in the near distance he saw a cavalcade of horses charging through the moonlit dusk.

And with horns blowing, the riders came, horses in tow, baying dogs running alongside.

A Shadow blotted out Borel's view, and once more he could not breathe. But of a sudden the black creature released him, and Shadows flew amok.

Borel heard Flic cry out in agony, and the Sprite flew away into the woods.

And then the horses thundered 'round, men with swords waving.

Again and again the Shadows tried to fly in to suffocate Chelle and Borel as well as the men on horseback and even the excited and barking dogs, but always the wraithlike creatures veered away, unable to come nigh.

And then Borel saw why: it was King Arle and the Riders Who Cannot Dismount. And they bore iron, and that was why the Shadows could not close, and why Flic flew away . . . though with his silver épée the Sprite was in no danger from the black, flapping creatures.

And dogs barked and leapt snapping at Shadows as the men on horseback milled 'round and held the black creatures at bay. Surrounded by iron, Chelle and Borel held each other and watched as the dark wraiths were repelled. Even so, the Shadows continued to try, but their attempts were in vain.

And as if from another world altogether, there came an enraged and distant scream much like the one before, and the Shadows flew back to vanish through the slot and into the Endless Sands.

Borel turned to thank Arle, and in that same moment—"No!" cried Borel—the king swung his leg over his saddlebow and leapt from his steed and strode forward and embraced the prince.

48

Troth

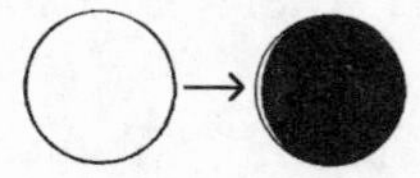

"Why didn't you tell me that you wanted to find the Endless Sands?" asked Arle upon hearing Borel's tale. "My men and I have ridden over much of Faery in the untold time since cursed. I could have saved you days."

"Oh," groaned Borel, smacking himself on the forehead. "*That's* what Lady Lot meant when she said I had missed an opportunity. Ah, me, I was so intent on finding the King Under the Hill that it simply didn't occur to me to ask."

Chelle merely smiled, but Flic said, "Had I been at your side, my lord, it would never have occurred to me either, but that is neither here nor there, for iron had driven me off."

They were sitting in a small grove a goodly distance away from the other eight riders, for Flic could only bear to be at hand if no iron were nearby. And so, Arle had shed his armor and weaponry—all but his bow and arrows—and he and Borel and Chelle had walked away from the main campsite to set up a small fire within a horn call should the need arise for the others to come or for Arle to return to his men. And then Flic had flown in, and they had patched up Borel's many scrapes and wounds from his fight with the thorns. And now they sat and supped and drank and, as requested, Borel told his story to Arle, Chelle hearing it for the first time as well.

Arle looked at Buzzer asleep in the night. "And this was your guide?"

Borel and Flic both nodded, and Arle said, *"Incroyable!"*

As Arle replenished their cups of wine, including a droplet in a tiny upturned leaf for Flic, "And you, Lord Arle," said Borel, "what is your tale?"

"Ah, my friend, we broke the curse, just as you said we would. The Fairy King's little dog leapt down of its own volition the moment we came upon a bitch in heat."

"There is more of a tale here for the telling," said Chelle.

Arle laughed. "Indeed, there is, Lady Michelle. Would you like to hear it?"

Chelle nodded, and Arle said, "You see, I am from the mortal world, and one day twelve of my chevaliers and I went ahunting. We jumped up a White Hart, and into Faery it fled, and we . . ."

". . . And so, following Prince Borel's advice, we rode into town, and stopped in the square and, frightened by our ghastly appearance, the citizens rushed to comply when we asked that they bring all the bitches in town who were in heat." Arle broke out laughing. "One of the men brought us his wife."

"Regardless, three female dogs were fetched, and nearly as soon as they came into scent range of the Fairy King's little dog, he leapt down and almost immediately—begging your pardon, Lady Chelle—almost immediately began copulating.

"We sat there and watched a moment, and then Roubaix leapt down from his horse, and lo! neither he nor his mount fell into dust, and we knew the curse was laid to rest.

"Ah, me, but it was good to get off my steed and take a bath and eat my first meal in—I don't know—in summers beyond count."

"My lord," said Flic, "you mean you didn't eat or drink or, or, um, relieve yourselves all the time you were cursed?"

"Non, for it was part of the curse that we and our mounts had no needs whatsoever while the dog was with us," said Arle.

"Well, that answers that," said Flic, looking at Borel, the prince grinning at the Sprite.

"Flic, Flic," said Arle, "That is what is so *diabolique* about the spell. You see, with no need to procure food or water or ought else, we would ride forever unless we deliberately chose to dismount. And of course, should we do that, a thousand years would catch up with us all at once."

"Oh, how dreadful," said Chelle.

They sat in silence for a moment, and then Chelle said, "But that is not all the story, surely. I mean, you now have horses with you and dogs and goods. How came you to acquire those?"

"Ah, that. There is a citadel above the town of Níone, a goodly sized *ville* just a half day's ride from here. Three years past, the former chevaliers of that stronghold rode off on a campaign against nearby Trolls and haven't been seen since. A representative of that town happened to be where we found the bitch—the dog, not the wife—and he asked us to come and be their protectors, for we have weapons of steel, and that's most certainly good enough to lay the Trolls by the heels. He gave us funds, and we bought what we would need to get us there: packhorses, supplies, other goods."

"What of the dogs?" asked Chelle.

Arle laughed. "I told the merchant I would use them to track, but the truth is I love to hunt, though I'll not pursue White Harts ever again."

"I should think not," said Chelle, laughing.

"Ah, so it is to Níone you go?" asked Borel.

"Oui." Arle looked at Borel. "You and your party are welcome to join us, my prince."

Of a sudden Chelle looked at Borel. "Are weapons of iron—of steel—such that they can break through the tangle of thorn? If so, we can rescue those within."

Borel said, "There is still Rhensibé to deal with, and the wheel yet turns the ensorcelling spindle."

"I said this before and I'll say it again: can we not simply put wax in our ears?" asked Flic. "That would shut out the sound."

Borel said, "I tried stopping my ears, Flic, but Rhensibé's spell overcame that. After all, it is magie at work here, and I think we will need a magicien in our company to cope with the arcane."

Chelle's face fell, and she glumly nodded in agreement. Then she said, "But we must find one as soon as we can, Borel."

Borel nodded and took her hand and sealed the agreement with a kiss on her fingers, and then he turned to Arle. "My lord, when we find someone powerful enough to go against Rhensibé, will you aid us?"

"Prince Borel, I and my men will aid you in any way we can, for if it were not for you, we would yet be cursed. But again I ask, won't you join us in my citadel, my friend? As I say, it is not far."

Borel glanced at Flic and then said to Arle, "My lord, because of your iron and my Spritely friend here, this I ask: how far is the citadel above the town? That is, how far away from the ville will iron be from Flic?"

Arle shrugged. "A mile more or less I was told."

Flic said, "A mile is certainly enough to allay the twist of aethyr."

Borel grinned and said to Arle, "This then I propose: We will accompany you as far as your town of Níone, yet for the sake of my Spritely friend, we will stay in the ville, while you go up to your citadel. I need to purchase a bronze long-knife, and acquire three horses and the supplies we will need to return to the Winterwood. Shortly thereafter we will ride to the Summerwood, for my brother is betrothed, and the wedding comes soon, and I would be there when that happens."

"Staying in Níone will also give you a chance to rest and heal," said Chelle.

"A minor matter," said Borel.

Chelle smiled ruefully and shook her head and said, "Men."

"After the wedding," continued Borel, "we need find a magicien or sorcière to combat Rhensibé, and then we will come and ask you for help in freeing Lord Roulan and his household from Rhensibé's curse."

"Well and good," said Arle, smiling. "We will be ready."

That night, with Flic and Buzzer on a leaf nearby, Chelle and Borel slept by the small fire well away from King Arle's camp. Borel—exhausted, drained from two full days without rest, much of it loping o'er field and stream and sand—fell aslumber the moment he lay down. On the other hand, Chelle spent much of the night watching him sleep in the illumination of the full moon, noting how the silvery radiance played o'er the planes of his face, how the argent beams highlighted the sheen of his hair. At last she sighed and lay down against his back and held him close.

The next morn, following the directions given the evening before by King Arle, Flic and Buzzer flew away, the Sprite to be far from the iron the chevaliers bore. Shortly after Flic took to wing, Arle rode nigh, dogs running alongside, and in tow he had a horse.

"André would be honored if you would ride his steed," said Arle.

"My lord, what will he ride?" asked Borel.

"One of the packhorses unladed of its goods."

"A chevalier's mount belongs to none else, my lord. Chelle and I will ride the packhorse in André's stead. Besides, 'tis easier on the animal if two ride bareback than one in saddle and the other across the withers."

"Oh?" said Chelle. "You were planning on riding on the withers, Prince Borel?"

Then Chelle broke into laughter, and Borel's guffaws joined hers.

Arle said, "Ah, a spirited demoiselle. You have chosen well, Lord Borel."

Borel's laughter stopped, as did Chelle's, and they looked at one another. "My lord," said Borel, "I remind you: but for a brief time long past, until yester we had only met in dreams. And even though my heart is most surely hers, I would court her properly."

"Ah, yes," said Arle. "I had forgotten you were not yet lovers."

Chelle blushed and Borel sighed and Arle laughed. Then the king said, "I would hear your own story, Lady Michelle, as we ride this morn."

Borel mounted the steed and gave Chelle a hand up, and with her riding behind, they rode to the chevaliers' camp and dismounted.

Over André's protests, the prince and his lady rode bareback upon a gentle gelding, and as the cavalcade wended its way toward the town of Níone, King Arle reined back until he rode alongside the pair. "Your tale, my lady?"

Chelle nodded and said, "My father—the duke—decided well in advance that on the day of my majority he would hold a gala. And so he invited many to attend—nobles, Fairies, merchants and other townsfolk. And they all came, Fey Folk on horses with silver bells, merchants in broughams, nobles on prancing steeds, and even some Fey who flew in.

"Ah, the party was splendid, with croquet and quoits and darts and blindfold tag, with music and dancing, and the food, oh the food, it was delicious—roasts and quail and breads and fruits and pastries as well as sweet candies.

"And the gifts were considerable. The Fairies gathered 'round and spoke as if their gifts had been given to me at my birth, though I don't know what those might have been.

"Regardless, one of the Fey Folk, a most gracious and beautiful lady who had somehow arrived unnoticed and unheralded, drew me aside and asked if I would see her offering. Of course I said I would, and she took me to the unused chamber at the top of the turret, and there sat a lovely spinning wheel, a gift I had not heretofore seen. And this Fairy asked me to try the treadle, to see how easily the wheel spun. I sat on the stool and pressed it but once, and it ran without needing another press, but it squeaked horribly, yet it also somehow made music. It was then that Rhensibé dispelled the glamour surrounding her, and she showed her true self to me. She laughed cruelly, and I tried to flee, yet I did not even reach the stairwell, but collapsed instead. What happened thereafter, I cannot say."

Chelle fell silent, but Borel said, "That's when the terrible black wind carried the entire vale away unto the Endless Sands, leaving a bare stone valley behind."

Chelle shook her head. "I still cannot believe that took place eleven years and eleven moons ago, as mortals would reckon time. It seems just yester to me."

Arle said, "As Prince Borel told us last eve, you were in an enchanted sleep, Lady Michelle, in which I deem all time did stop."

Chelle sighed and said, "You must be right, King Arle. But even so . . ."

They rode a moment without speaking, and then Chelle said, "Rhensibé came to me in my dreams, and she laughed in glee and told me that I was trapped. Then did I seek you out, Borel, for I knew you would come."

"And that was but a moon ago?" asked Arle.

"A few days more, my lord," said Borel. "Yet it was not until there was but a bare moon left that I knew Chelle was real and not just a dream. Then did I set out to find her."

"Hai! And find her you did, my prince, and found me and my men as well."

"But not in time for d'Strait," said André, who had been riding nearby and listening.

"He did not die in vain," said Arle, "for it was his blade allowed Prince Borel to fight his way through the thorns."

André nodded. "He would have been proud to know of that, and if his wife and children were yet alive they would have been proud as well."

"Perhaps they do know," said Arle, glancing at the skies above.

And they rode along in somber silence.

A delegation welcomed King Arle and his chevaliers to Níone, and when they discovered that Prince Borel of the Winterwood and Lady Michelle of Duke Roulan's vale accompanied King Arle, nothing would do but that the prince and his *amour* take up residence in a temporarily vacant hillside chalet owned by the mayor himself. Not only that, but he would send a cook and a ladies' maid and a valet to serve them as well.

And so it was that Borel and Chelle and Flic and Buzzer found themselves ensconced in very elegant and private quarters rather than in rooms at an inn.

A healer was sent to deal with Borel's thorn-given wounds, but Flic had already prepared tisanes and balms and anodynes, and Borel was well on the mend.

Over the next several days, as Borel healed he acquired three horses—two for riding, one to be a pack animal—and sufficient supplies to get them to the Winterwood. He had his leathers repaired, where the thorns had scored and torn and punctured them. And he sent his tricorn to the milliner to be cleaned and blocked as well. The prince obtained a bronze long-knife to replace the one he had lost during the wild Pooka ride. But when he tried to use the remaining Gnome-gifted coinage to settle with the various merchants, the tradesmen waved him away, saying King Arle had paid for all.

Each evening, in deference to Flic's intolerance of iron, King Arle shed his arms and armor and came down from the citadel to dine with them. Chevaliers took turns accompanying the king, and there were celebrations every night for a sevenday, with singing and dancing and merrymaking all 'round, as well as tale-telling, and here Flic did shine. He strutted about and waved his silver épée and—striking *en gardes* and lunging and parrying and making running *flèches*, sometimes afoot on tabletop, other times awing in air—he told of how he and Argent had routed the dreadful Shadows, also mentioning as an afterthought that King Arle and his men did help. And Arle roared with laughter at the antics of his wee friend.

And Chelle and Borel danced the bee dance, showing the townsfolk how 'twas done. And when they were asked where they had learned such a step, Borel spoke of Buzzer, and then there was nothing for it but that Buzzer had to be strutted out for display the very next day. And the townsfolk *Ooh*ed and *Ahh*ed as if they had never before seen a bumblebee. It is said that in the days after, many folk suffered stings while trying to make pets of bees.

After each gala and upon returning to the chalet, Borel and Chelle oft stood on the balcony and looked at the moon and spoke of inconsequential things as well as things substantial.

During the days, as well, they strolled about the town, and Chelle outfitted herself with boys' riding breeches and boots, for she would not go sidesaddle all the way to the Winterwood.

Borel smiled and said, " 'Tis not ladylike, my lady."

"I suppose your sisters never ride astraddle?" asked Chelle.

"Oh, they are not ladylike either," said Borel, and he broke out laughing.

Too, Chelle acquired a supply of feminine necessities she would need for the journey, and one special sheer garment for herself. Borel made himself scarce during that shopping trip, and instead chose tack and supplies for his horses, now that he knew how the Lady Michelle would ride.

And every day they strolled along the mossy banks of a burbling stream, or played échecs, or whiled away the time at other idling but oh so important tasks.

And always they remained quite circumspect, and yet . . .

On the fourth night in the chalet, as they stood before her bedroom door, Borel said, "Chelle, perhaps you do not remember, but I courted you throughout our dreams, and I tried to not take advantage, for you did not know we were dreaming, whereas I did. Yet you fired my blood, and you still do, and I often lost control in the dream, and it is all I can do to not lose control now. For I would sweep you up in my arms and—Chelle, what I am trying to say is that you have my heart and you occupy my every thought. I would court you truly if I may and if it is your will. You need not answer now, my love, and—"

Michelle silenced him with a kiss, then she quickly stepped into her room and closed the door behind.

Borel, bewildered, walked to his own chamber.

Slowly he undressed, and lay down, yet he could not sleep, Chelle filling his mind: her scent, her sweet breath, her hair, her eyes, her laugh, her slender form and grace and elegance.

In the middle of the night with the moon shining in, Borel yet lay awake when his door softly opened, and, barefoot, Chelle came padding in. Borel turned to see her standing in the moonlight, her negligee sheer and revealing.

She came and stood at the side of his bed, her blue eyes unseen, enshadowed, though not by a magic spell but by the night instead. "My love, I remember every one of our dreams," she said, her voice just above a whisper. "And in them I told you I have loved you since a time long past when I was but a child." She let her delicate gown slip away unto the floor, and with her golden hair falling across her bare shoulders, she said, "But I am a child no more."

And Borel reached up and drew her into his bed, and he kissed her soft lips and her eyes and her throat and her breasts and lower, and though she had no experience, she moaned with need and caressed Borel, running her hands along his firm muscles and across his flat abdomen and more. And they made gentle love and passionate love and wild love throughout the moonlit night.

"My, but you look chipper today," said Flic.

"Do I seem to be walking on air?" asked Chelle, scooping slices of melon onto her trencher, along with eggs and rashers and crêpes with syrup and toast with butter and a bit of cheese on the side.

"Where's Borel?" asked Flic, eyeing the enormous mound of food on Chelle's plate.

Chelle shrugged. "Perhaps yet abed," she said, taking up a bit of melon and popping it into her mouth.

Flic grinned. "Uh-huh, as if you didn't know."

Chelle smiled and looked about to see if anyone were near, and then she whispered, "Oh, Flic, it was wonderful, and we are lovers. Isn't it grand?"

"Well, it took you two long enough," said Flic.

"Long enough for what?" said Borel, walking into the room. He stepped to the sideboard and filled a plate of his own.

"Long enough to, um, plight your troth," said Flic.

Borel sat next to Chelle. "If she will have me, we are betrothed," he said. He turned to Chelle. "Will you marry me, my love?"

Chelle's eyes sparkled and she answered, but what she said neither Borel nor Flic understood, her mouth stuffed with food as it was. And both Borel and Flic looked at one another, and they shrugged and turned up their hands.

"I think she said 'No,' " said Borel, a twinkle in his eye.

"I believe you're right, my lord," said Flic, grinning.

Chelle frantically shook her head and groaned a wordless protest, and both the prince and the Sprite broke out in laughter.

Finally, Chelle swallowed and this time clearly said, "Oh, yes, my love, I will marry you." And she threw her arms about Borel and kissed him soundly.

Nine more days and nights they stayed in the chalet in Níone, and every day they celebrated their betrothal, and in the nights as well.

The evening they told King Arle, he made a public proclamation, and the entire town celebrated. And Arle toasted their good health and said, "Well, now, my friends, you have notified a king. Hence all you must do is post the banns, and, after the waiting time is over, find you a hierophant."

"In my own demesne will we post the banns," said Borel, "and in Duke Roulan's demesne as well, once we get him free, for I would have the wedding be one wherein he gives away the bride."

"Pah!" snorted Flic, but he was smiling. "You humans with your rituals."

On the fourteenth day in Níone, Borel and Chelle and Flic and Buzzer made ready to depart, and Arle came unto them and he presented Borel with a bronze sword, its edge keen, its hilt capped with a white chalcedony gemstone, and a grey leather belt and scabbard with it. He then presented Chelle with a moonstone pendant. And to both he said, "These two stones are governed by the moon, and they will remind you of the perilous times and of your lasting love."

Borel embraced the king, and Chelle hugged Arle and kissed him, and murmured her thanks.

Arle turned to Flic and held up a jar of honey and said, "This is for you and Buzzer. I am told it comes from the white moonflower and is honey rare indeed."

Flic bowed and said, "Thank you, my lord, and I thank you on behalf of Buzzer as well. She and I will both be pleased with such a gift."

On Flic's behalf, Borel took the jar and slipped it into one of the packhorse bags with the food.

Then King Arle presented Flic with a wee tiny pendant as well and said, "This stone is known as a moondrop; it is said to be moonlight itself made manifest; well do you deserve it, my little friend, whose heart is perhaps the biggest of all. Wear it to remind you of the perils you faced and the victories won."

Flic drew his silver épée and saluted the king. "Thank you, my lord. I will wear it with pride. Yet I remind you, the adventure is not finished until we free Roulan and all those entrapped by Rhensibé."

Arle looked at Flic and then Borel and finally Chelle and said, "Oh, I have not forgotten that quest, my friends. As soon as you return with the magicien or sorcière to deal with that foul witch, I and my men will ride with you."

"We thank you, my lord," said Borel, and again he and the king embraced, and again Chelle hugged and kissed Arle, and then they mounted up and watched as Buzzer flew 'round and took a sighting on the sun and then shot off toward the demesne on the generally sunward bound of the Winterwood, an adjacent realm where grew yellow daffodils and blue morning glories and red clover, all three of which Flic and Chelle identified after Borel had described them.

And so, with a packhorse in tow, out from Níone they rode, and some townsfolk stood along the street to wave them good-bye. Up the far hill they fared—Borel and Chelle ahorse, Flic on the tricorn—all of them following a beeline for a distant border. And as they topped the rise, behind them there sounded a long and resonant horn cry: it was King Arle's *au revoir*.

Borel and Chelle turned and waved good-bye, Flic waving as well, and Chelle cried out, "Au revoir, King Arle, for we will meet again."

And then they turned and rode over the hill and down the far side and away.

49

Minion

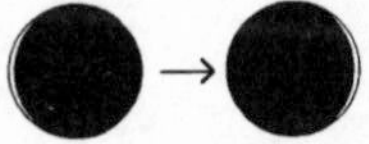

Out from Níone they rode, over hills and through forests for the entire day, Borel and Chelle talking and Flic achatter, Buzzer flying somewhat ahead, though the bee often returned to make certain they were following her line. Now and again they came to a river they had to ford, and at these flows Flic would fly upstream or down- to scout out a suitable crossing. Flic also flew whenever they came to a drop or a rise the horses could not traverse, and the Sprite would find a fitting place for the steeds to make their way onward.

And the sun rose into the sky and across and down, and when evening came, they camped in a woodland green.

The next day they crossed a twilight border, and came into a lowland of reeds and many lakes. And though Buzzer could fly a straight line over water and vegetation alike, it took the riders three days altogether to wend a passage through. And as they finally emerged from a twilight border and into a land of rock and grass and thickets, Borel looked back and said, "All it would take is one good long rain to submerge that entire realm."

"That might be so, my lord," said Flic, "nevertheless 'tis the way Buzzer knows."

Chelle laughed and said, "Let us hope she doesn't come to a place of bottomless mud, a place she could easily fly over but we could not cross at all."

"If it comes to that," said Flic, "we will simply go into a different realm and see if she can find her way from there."

"How many demesnes of Faery has she been in?" asked Chelle.

"I think 'tis a number beyond count," said Flic. "But each realm must have flowers, else it simply isn't within her ken."

"Like the Endless Sands," said Borel.

"Yes," said Flic, "like the Endless Sands."

"I saw no flowers in the place we just came from," said Chelle.

"The reeds, my lady," said Flic, "they flower in their season."

"Ah," said Chelle, and on they rode.

A twoday later, early morn found them wending their way up through a high mountain pass, and ahead at the crest of the col stood a man, as if waiting. And he held a great black sword unsheathed.

"A toll-taker, do you think?" said Chelle.

"Perhaps," said Borel. Even so, he loosened the keepers on his long-knife and sword and spurred forward to ride ahead of Chelle.

On toward the man they went, and now they could see that he was lean and tall and hairless, and he wore only a dhoti, and there was a ghastly white pallor to his skin. His fingers were long and bony, as were his legs and arms, and yet he sported a small rounded belly, as if it were swollen from lack of food.

"My lord," hissed Flic. "There is something about this creature, or so my Fey vision tells me. I think he is not a man at all, but a thing of a different sort. Just what, I cannot say."

Grimly Borel rode on, and he reined to a stop some paces short of the being.

"I have been waiting for you," said the man—the thing—his voice hollow, his words strangely accented, and he smiled a wicked smile, and his teeth were nought but fangs.

"Waiting for us?" said Borel. "How so?"

"Not you, O Man," said the creature. "You may ride on past, for it is the woman I am here to slay." Then the being looked past Borel to Chelle. "Rhensibé summoned me; she wanted you to know she had done so. And she told me to say unto you that the moment you are slain, so shall die all those enspelled in your father's manse. Know this as well, Woman: you cannot escape me, for I am of *Enfer* itself, and I am bound to Rhensibé until you are dead."

He looked back at Borel and said, "Ride on, O Man, ride on." And he stepped forward, his great black sword raised, his gaze fixed on Chelle.

Flic took to wing, Argent in hand.

"Yahh!" cried Borel, and he drew his sword and spurred his horse forward to deal the *thing* a death blow, but the creature cut the horse's legs out from under Borel, and the steed screamed and tumbled to the ground.

Yet Borel had leapt free, and with his long-knife now in his left hand and his sword in his right, he ran at the creature and swung and slashed a great deep cut across the thing's swollen abdomen.

But no blood flew. No ichor. And the being laughed, and even as he did so, the great gaping wound vanished.

Shang! Down came the creature's own blow, and Borel barely deflected it, ebon shocking into bronze with numbing force. With a backhanded sweep Borel lashed his long-knife up and at the creature's throat. But with a warding bash of its bony arm, the thing fended Borel's blade and took another deep cut, this one on its arm, but the gash healed nearly instantly.

Chelle leapt from her mount and ran to Borel's downed steed; and even as the horse thrashed about—unable to rise, for its forelegs were shorn in two—Chelle grabbed Borel's bow from its saddle scabbard and snatched up an arrow.

At one and the same time, crying "Die, Démon, die!" Flic dove down and stabbed and stabbed with Argent at the creature's head and neck and back, yet the Sprite was no more bothersome than would be a gnat.

And Borel lashed his sword upward in a slashing cut, only to find the creature's dark weapon blocking the way. Borel sprang leftward, to come at the thing's flank, but with its own back-handed blow the monster swung its black blade, and Borel barely managed to fend.

Chelle struggled with all her might to string Borel's bow, yet she could not quite slip the loop over the upper arm and into the groove.

Now Borel struck left and right with both of his blades, half of which the creature fended, yet the other half found their marks . . . to no avail, for as quickly as a cut was made, just as quickly did it heal.

And still Flic stabbed and stabbed with Argent, yet each puncture closed instantly.

Borel sprang back from the creature, his breath now coming in harsh gasps.

"Fool of a man," cried the thing, "do you not know I am a Démon, a Fiend, a *Diable,* and nothing smelted, cast, carven, or forged can hurt me?"

And then it attacked, and black rang on bronze, the Fiend driving the prince back and back, and Borel parried and riposted, blocked and counterstruck, but the Démon was mighty, and it drove Borel hindward, and now it was all Borel could do to fend the creature off.

Of a sudden—*ching!*—Borel's long-knife went flying. And moments later—*clang!*—he lost his sword. And the Diable smashed him down with a blow of its fist.

Chelle screamed, and the Fiend turned toward her. But Borel kicked out, smashing the Démon in the leg. The creature grunted, and swung back toward Borel, and raised its great black blade up for a death-dealing blow.

And as she saw the dark sword swing up, with strength born of desperation, Chelle strung the bow.

And in that same moment the Diable screamed in agony, for Buzzer had returned, and she found Flic striking and striking at a monster; without any hesitation whatsoever, Buzzer hurled herself at the creature and ran out her stinger and stabbed the Fiend in the neck.

And even as the Démon howled in anguish and slapped at the bee, Chelle set the arrow to string and cried out, "Flic, away!" and as the Sprite flew up from the Fiend, Chelle summoned strength she knew not she had and drew Borel's bow to the full of her pull and loosed the flint-tipped shaft at the Démon . . . and it struck the creature dead center in the back.

"Ygah!" cried the Fiend, and it dropped the black blade and staggered and vainly clutched at the deeply embedded arrow jutting out, black blood seeping.

And snarling a Wolflike growl of rage, Borel leapt to his feet and jerked the flint knife from his belt and stabbed the blade into the Diable's heart, and a dark ichor gushed forth.

The Démon looked with disbelief into the icy eyes of this puny man who had somehow just slain it, and Borel twisted the flint and jammed it deeper and gritted, "All perilous blades are not what they seem."

And then the Fiend collapsed, the creature dead even as it struck the ground.

50

Acolyte

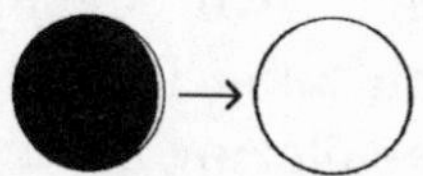

"Flint," said Borel, embracing Chelle, she yet trembling in the aftermath. "Your flint arrow and my flint knife were neither smelted, cast, carven, nor forged, and when I kicked him, I knew he could be hurt. And then Buzzer stung him, saving my life. And then you shot him with a flint-headed arrow, and I stabbed him in the heart with a flint knife . . . and both the arrowhead and the knife were knapped from stone."

"Neither awake nor in a dark dream are perilous blades just as they seem," said Chelle. "Isn't that what Lady Wyrd told you?"

"Oui," said Borel.

"Hmm . . ." said Flic, looking at his épée, "it seems a silver blade isn't always proof against creatures of darkness. Perhaps Argent isn't quite as perilous as I thought."

"Nevertheless, Flic, it slew the Shadows, and were I you I don't believe I'd throw it away," said Borel. Then he looked at the slain Démon. "By the bye, I think you should call Buzzer off. The thing is dead, you know."

Flic glanced at the bee, yet circling above the Démon just in case it was feigning death.

Chelle looked, too, and then all three broke into laughter, and it went on and on, and they could not seem to stop themselves, for after all they had just cheated death . . . they were yet alive.

But from behind came a grunt, and they turned to see Borel's horse, and abruptly the laughter stopped. Borel sighed and retrieved his long-knife and sword. The sword he sheathed, but the long-knife he kept in his hand, and he went to the steed and knelt and said, "Sorry, my friend."

And Chelle looked away as Borel put his horse beyond the reach of pain.

Borel then stepped to the Démon's side and took up the black sword, and he looked about and then walked to a large split boulder and jammed the blade into the crevice and, with a grunt, snapped the sword in two. The moment the blade broke, the shards of the weapon burst into violent flames, and Borel sprang back and flung the blazing hilt from him.

Chelle cried out, and Borel whirled to see the Démon aflame as well, with Buzzer and Flic fleeing the fire and toward Chelle. The Sprite and the bee landed on her shoulders, and all watched as both the Fiend's corpse and its weapon furiously and swiftly burned to ashes.

"My lord," said Flic, "I think next time you should be wary of breaking a Démon's sword, for, as Lady Wyrd said, neither awake nor in a dark dream are perilous blades just as they seem."

Borel saddled the packhorse and distributed the supplies between the two steeds, and Borel said, "Flic, we need find a town and get another horse."

"And me a bow with arrows to suit," said Chelle. And when Borel looked at her, she added, "I nearly didn't get yours strung, my love, and your arrows are much too long."

Flic nodded and said, "I will talk to Buzzer. Perhaps there's a ville nearby with a garden she remembers."

A quarter candlemark later, they rode down from the pass and out onto a plain, and there did Buzzer turn and take a new heading. And late in the day they came unto Arens, a modest ville with several inns and a number of stables.

ter watering the steeds, they went to bed, and Borel lay Chelle, holding her close, and they fell asleep that way.

the next day they rode, and Ice-Sprites ran before and be-and around them, the wee ice-dwelling creatures grinning lancing in glee within the frozen surfaces. And Chelle ed joyfully at their antics, while Borel looked for the Sprite ad accompanied him to Hradian's cote, but he saw it not. d over snowy ridges and down through silent valleys they some atrickle with meltwater, others with dashing ns. And Chelle was all eyes and curiosity, and she pointed e subtle colors amid the blacks and whites and greys. at night they stayed in another lodge, this cabin in a hol-long a fold of land.

accompanied by dancing and racing Ice-Sprites—ing here, popping up there, always within the ice itself—and Chelle rode through a wintry but low mountain range, erge in snow-covered vales beyond.

d the sun rode through the skies, up and across and down, longside a small river they passed, the water swift under e, air bubbles trapped in the run, though now and again were stretches of open water; and the flow sang and d on its way toward a distant sea. And as the sun set and r twilight graced the land, and with the full moon just now g above the horizon, they came into the vale overlooked nterwood Manor.

el halted and dismounted, Chelle dismounting as well. ith Sprites peering out through clear windows on the ice-ees and rocks, of a sudden Borel cupped his hands 'round outh and gave a long howl. The sound echoed and rever-d throughout the valley, and joyous calls answered, the s of many joining those of the one.

elle laughed, and as the cries died out she said, "That was ack?"

el chuckled and said, "Oui."

emember the dream," said Chelle. "We were in the Spring-

They took a room in *Le Taureau Noir*, and luxuriated in hot baths and ate delicious hot meals and downed copious glasses of hearty red wine. And Chelle and Borel slept in a real bed, and they made love.

They stayed in Arens that night and two more, resting, relaxing, eating, acquiring another horse and replenishing their supplies, and obtaining a bow and arrows for Chelle.

But when the next day dawned, they rode away from the Black Bull inn, and through the town and to a nearby hillock, and there Buzzer took a bearing, and off the bee shot on a line for the demesne along the sunward marge of the Winterwood.

Through twilight borders they fared, and across lands of Faery, but midmorn of the fifth day they emerged from an umbrous bound and came unto the realm where grew yellow daffodils and blue morning glories and sweet red clover. They had entered the stream-laden demesne adjacent to the Winterwood.

On they rode, splashing through rills and runs and streams, and nigh the noontide of the second day within this land they arrived at another twilight wall.

As Borel and Chelle dismounted, Flic and Buzzer flew through the marge and quickly back, and the Sprite came shivering. "Snow, ice, barren trees: what a dreadful realm you have, my lord, for surely it is the Winterwood."

Borel, fetching winter gear from the packhorse, grinned and shook his head. "Dreadful you say? Non. Marvelous say I, for it is both savage and peaceful, with times when the wind howls like fury come alive, flinging snow and ice in its rage, and other times of preternatural stillness, when one can hear a snowflake fall across the width of a vale. Non, my friend, 'tis a breathtaking realm for all days are different, yet somehow all the same."

"Well, you can have it, my lord, for neither Buzzer nor I can deal with the cold: she would fall dormant, and me?"—Flic grinned—"I do believe I would fall dead. Besides, now that Buzzer and I have delivered you securely to your realm, you will be safe as soon as you pass through this twilight wall."

Chelle's face fell and she said, "Surely you two are not leaving us, are you, Flic?"

Flic sketched a bow in the air and said, "I must, my lady, for, truly, neither Buzzer nor I can withstand such cold as is in the Winterwood. Ah, me . . . I am but a warm-weather friend, oui?"

"Non, my friend," said Borel, shaking out cold-weather gear. "Most certainly not."

"But where will you go?" asked Chelle, taking a winter cloak and gloves and warm stockings from Borel. "I would see you again, my friend. Besides, there's my père and mère and their guests to set free, and I would have your épée at my side."

"My lady, I will of certain be one of your chevaliers, though how I will cope with King Arle's iron, that I cannot say. But first, and most immediately, I will seek out my Fleurette, for she is waiting, and I love her as much as Borel loves you. But then—"

"But then," said Borel, pulling on his socks and then his boots, "you will come to the Summerwood, for I would have you and Buzzer attend my brother Alain's wedding."

Chelle clapped her hands even as Flic said, "Summerwood?"

"White camellias," said Borel, looking at Buzzer, the bee hovering at Flic's side. "Red, red roses, and yellow ones as well. And lilacs. —Oh, and something called hydrangea. But do not ask me more, for that is the extent of my knowledge."

"I will see if she knows," said Flic. And he and Buzzer landed on a patch of ground. After a moment of silent converse, Buzzer did a waggle dance. Then she paused and did an entirely different dance of waggles. Flic laughed and looked up and said, "She knows the Summerwood, and so we will be there. She also said that for someone as slow as you are, my lord, you seem to get about a lot." Flic broke into giggles, as did Chelle, and Borel's guffaws joined them.

Borel and Chelle pulled on gloves and fastened cloaks about their shoulders, then mounted.

Buzzer and Flic took to wing and hovered, and Flic drew Argent and saluted both the lord and his lady.

"Au revoir, my wee friend," said Borel.

"Till we meet again," said Chelle.

"See you in the Summerwood," said Fli
circled 'round and took a bearing, and both
away.

When they were beyond seeing, Chelle an
horses and rode into the Winterwood.

All the rest of that day and into the nigh
no longer needing the guide who went dorma
could press on. And the nearly full moon r
way before them.

The land was extraordinarily still, with n
and through the quiet they rode, the only
horses and the creak of leather. But then fron
the hoot of an owl, and Borel answered in k
or so, these two kept up a running conversa
one another they came, and then a sile
through the air and across and up; a snowy o

"Oh, how beautiful," said Chelle, watchi
owl rose and briefly silhouetted itself agains
vanished among the stars.

On they rode, and as the moon passed t
they came to a pine grove standing dark in t

"Here we will stay the eve, my love," said
way inward.

Midst the evergreens stood a cabin, unli
They dismounted and unladed the horses
down. Borel stepped into the tiny lodge an
blankets with which he covered the steeds.

Then he and Chelle carried their goods i
poured oats from the grain they carried into
the horses, while Chelle readied a fire. When
had a small blaze going, and Borel fetched ice
them on the irons above the fire.

"Water for the horses," said Chelle, her
question.

Borel then broke out biscuits and jerky an
block of cheese they had gotten in Arens, and

wood, and they came, and you introduced them to me, and me to them: Slate, Dark, Render, Shank, Trot, Loll, and Blue-eye."

"You remember their names," said Borel, his eyes widening in admiration.

"I could not forget them," said Chelle.

Borel threw an arm about her, and in the light of the half-risen full moon he pointed across the vale and up. "There is your mansion, my love, there atop the far bluff."

"Oh, how lovely," said Chelle, "and it sits like a great aerie atop its widespread cliff." She giggled. "My lord, with eagle eyes we will perch high above and—"

"Sstt!" hissed Borel and pointed, and Chelle could see Sprites fleeing within the ice, scattering, fear on their tiny faces.

Borel released the keepers on his long-knife and sword and whipped them from their sheaths, and in that moment the air before them began to waver, to ripple, as of heat rising from the ground, yet this ground was cold, icy, such heat not present. And then stepping through the undulance as if passing through a door, with her ebon cloak swirling about her came a tall, stark woman, her eyes dark, her hair black, her features haughty, imperious.

"Rhensibé!" sissed Chelle.

And even as Borel started to raise his sword, with a casual wave of her onyx-nailed hand Rhensibé cast a spell, and neither Chelle nor Borel could move.

"I have come to set matters straight," she said, a sneer in her voice. "You thought you could escape your just doom, my pretty and oh-so-blessed Michelle, yet you see I am here to make certain you do not, for I and my sisters—Hradian, Nefasí, and Iniquí—we four acolytes of Orbane, we each have sworn that all those who conspired to prevent my master from executing his grand plan shall suffer as have we. And among our many vows, not only will I and my sisters ultimately set Orbane free, we have pledged that Valeray and his get will agonize dreadfully.

"In the matter of you, Michelle, an oracle foretold that you would bring joy unto one of Valeray's sons, and so we took it upon ourselves not only to prevent that but to destroy Roulan, Valeray's ally.

"And so, though it is a full moon later than planned, I have come to slay you, and as an added windfall, I will let you watch as I kill this fool of a prince."

Rhensibé looked at the black nails on her hands—sharp as talons—and she smirked at Chelle and said, "All it will take is a slight prick from my beautiful, ebon, and quite venomous clutch, and he will die a most satisfying and agonizing death." And laughing in her wickedness, she reached forth with her left hand and stepped toward Borel.

Chelle tried to scream, but could not.

And sweat broke out on Borel's brow as he tried to raise his sword, yet all was in vain.

Rhensibé sneered at their futile efforts and flexed her black claws and brought them up to Borel's throat and—

—running full speed, Slate slammed into the witch, smashing her sideways and down, and racing Wolves followed and leapt upon her and their snarling and rending and tearing drowned out her terrified shrieks. Blood flew wide to stain white snow, and Rhensibé's shrill screams chopped short as Render tore out her throat, and the rest of the pack ripped her apart—hands, arms, legs, feet, viscera, her face, her head. And Borel, the paralysis long lifted, made no move whatsoever to save her, but looked on coldly instead, while Chelle turned aside and only glanced now and then.

Finally, Borel growled a word, and the pack stepped back, all but Blue-eye, who yet stood—hackles raised, fangs exposed—over the remains.

And Borel looked at the moon, just then standing full on the horizon. He took Chelle in his arms and said, "She would have killed you at the rise of the full moon; it is only fitting that she die in its light."

Chelle nodded but said nought, and Borel softly said, "Let us go."

And they mounted up and rode away, the pack trotting alongside, and they left Rhensibé's remains lying in the snow for the scavengers to find.

51

Manor

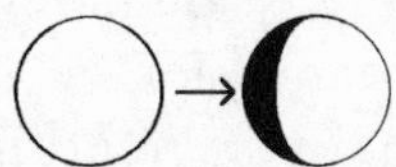

Borel and Chelle rode down the slope of the vale, their escort of Wolves ranging to left and right and fore and aft. Across the way and atop the great bluff, men bearing lanterns and arms came running from the manor and down the path. Borel grinned and said, " 'Tis Arnot and the house guard. They must have heard Rhensibé's screams."

On rode the prince and his lady, and, with hooves knelling on ice, they crossed the river at the foot of the bluff. As the men reached the base of the path and turned to cross the vale, "Bonjour, Arnot!" called Borel. "I am come home!"

"My prince, is it you? Is it truly you?" came a cry. And Borel and Chelle spurred forward, and in but moments they rode among the men, and Borel leapt down and embraced a slender, dark-haired man and said, "Arnot."

"*Grâce des dieux*, it is you!" said Arnot. "Oh, my prince, we did not know what to think. Are you hale?"

"Indeed, my friend, I am well."

A small man stepped forward and doffed the cap from his red hair and bowed, as did all the men 'round.

"Gerard," said the prince.

"My lord, we are glad you are back," said Gerard.

"I am glad to be back as well," said Borel.

Arnot then looked up at Chelle and said, "And is this the girl of your dreams?"

"In more ways than you can imagine," said Borel, smiling even as Chelle blushed.

"My Lady Michelle, may I present Arnot, steward of Winterwood Manor. Arnot, meet Lady Michelle, daughter of Duke Roulan, and soon to be mistress of this demesne."

Arnot bowed as did the rest of the men, and Chelle canted her head in acknowledgement.

"My lord," said Gerard, "the Wolves howled, and then there were screams and snarls; is there ought amiss?"

"Nothing at all any more," said Borel. "I will speak of it later. But now let us go to the manor, for we are famished." He turned to Gerard. "Has Madame Chef something for us to demolish?"

Gerard grinned. "If she has not at this moment, then soon, my lord, very soon."

Arnot turned and said, "Redieu, run ahead and tell Madame Millé that the prince has returned with Lady Michelle, and they are hungry. Notify Albert as well, for surely wine is wanted."

A skinny youth bobbed his head and bolted away.

"Come, my prince," said Arnot, "let us to the manor. The entire staff will be overjoyed to hear of your safe return."

Leading the horses—Chelle yet amount—Borel walked beside Arnot, and they and the men and the Wolves all started for the pathway up.

"Separate quarters, my lord?" said Arnot.

"Adjoining, Arnot," said Borel, "for we are betrothed, and as soon as the banns are posted and her sire is rescued, we will be married."

"What of notifying a king?" said Arnot. "I mean, your sire will no doubt—"

"Though I will also tell my sire, we have already notified a king, Arnot, and he has approved."

"Which king, my lord, if I may ask?"

"King Arle, formerly of the Riders Who Cannot Dismount, but now of Níone and the lands 'round."

Arnot's eyes flew wide in startlement. "The king of the Riders Who Cannot Dismount? But they are cursed."

"Not any more, my friend," said Borel, as they reached the beginning of the path upward. "The curse is broken."

"How, my lord?"

"Prince Borel did it," said Chelle, coming alongside on foot.

Borel turned and grinned at her, and Chelle said, "I dismounted, for I would join this converse."

And as they strolled up the pathway to the manor, Chelle told Arnot how the curse was broken, and mentioned that King Arle and his men had saved both of their lives.

"It sounds as if you had quite an adventure, my lady, my lord," said Arnot.

"I will tell you the whole of it in the days to come, Arnot," said Borel. "But you, how have you fared?"

"Lord Borel, when you went to see Vadun, and must needs pass through the cursed section and nigh Hradian's cote, we were worried. And when the Wolves returned without you, I had Jules"—Arnot gestured at the tall, dark-haired armsmaster—"organize a small warband, and they went looking for you. They found Hradian's cote burned to the ground, some stone walls yet standing, others not, and they felt that something dreadful had occurred—"

"Hradian must have set it afire herself," said Borel, "mayhap to destroy any evidence, for when last I saw it, it was yet standing." Borel turned to Jules. "Did you find my rucksack? In it was a journal I would read."

"Non, my lord," said Jules. "All was burned. —But, my lord, does that mean you were there and inside?"

"I was until Hradian came; she sent me away upon a black wind," said Borel. "But that is a tale for later telling, for I would hear yours first."

Arnot signalled for Jules to take up the tale, and the armsmaster said, "From the burnt cote we marched on to Vadun's abode, for he was who you had set out to see and have your dream divined, but the *devin de rêves* said you had not arrived, and he knew nought of your whereabouts. After speaking with him, we knew nowhere to go to seek you, for surely the Wolves would have been at your side, or would have been tracking you . . . were you to be found. But they came back to the manor instead, and if *they* did not know where to go, then neither did we."

Jules fell silent, but Arnot added: "A time later, the Wolves howled, and they sped away toward the Springwood, and Gerard and I thought you might be at the manor of Lady Céleste, and yet you were not."

Chelle looked at Borel and said, "Surely, it was our dream drew them there." She turned to Arnot and added, "I think it was an effect of the spell I was under, and it caught the Wolves as well."

"Ah, then, magie," said Arnot. Then he sighed and said, "I must tell you, my lord, Ladies Céleste and Liaze and Camille and Lord Alain are quite beside themselves with worry, missing as you are, or rather as you were. Yet none of us knew where to search. And the Lady of the Mere did not appear when Lord Alain went to ask after you, and so his question remained unanswered."

At that moment they came to the doors of Winterwood Manor, and Borel said, "We will send falcons to my sisters and brother and let them know I am safe."

Gerard sprang forward to open the door, and Borel handed off the steeds to the same gangly youth who had run ahead and now stood waiting. "Rub them down thoroughly, Redieu, and curry them and feed them and give them water, for they have served us well."

Then Borel took Chelle's hand and they stepped through the door and toward the welcoming hall beyond, and all the staff were waiting within to greet them, and when the prince and his lady stepped in, they gave a great and prolonged cheer and much applause.

Over the next fortnight and three days, Winterwood Manor was a hive of activity, for Lady Michelle needed a full wardrobe, not only for the Winterwood, but for the Springwood and Autumnwood and Summerwood as well, for the wedding in the Summerwood drew nigh, and surely afterward the lady and her prince would be visiting all the manors in turn. And so, all achatter and giddy with joy, for it seemed they had been waiting the whole of their lives for such an opportunity, the seamstresses of Winterwood Manor measured the lady herself, noting the hue of her skin, the color of her eyes, the cast of her hair, her slimness, the gauge of her bosom and waist and hips, and the lengths of feet and hands and forearms and upper arms and thighs and lower legs. And wasn't she just perfect? And she a duke's daughter, no less. A splendid match for handsome Prince Borel. On that they did agree.

When all was said, they had every measurement they could possibly have made, and Chelle not only felt treasured and admired, but by the same token she also felt like a prized piece of livestock.

And then the seamstresses insisted that Lady Michelle help with the selection of cloths and threads and sequins and beads and ribbons and other such . . . and jewellery, oh, the jewellery. The sapphires so well suited her eyes, golden beryl her hair, moonstones her skin, pink pearls, too. Emerald, amethyst, malachite, peridot, sunstone, diamond—why, it seemed there wasn't a jewel or gem in all creation that wouldn't go with this fille.

And the cobbler came, and the hairdresser, and others too many to name, and they fussed over her and primped and groomed and spruced and trimmed and fitted.

On the other hand, Prince Borel's days were given to the governance of his demesne, and he settled disputes awaiting his return, and arranged for shipments of food and other goods to a village hard hit by a blizzard. He pardoned a man wrongfully accused of stealing and slaughtering a neighbor's cow, for the animal had been found half starved several miles away. He settled a dispute concerning the rights of two miners whose horizontal shafts had met somewhere in the midst of a broad tor as each dug along the same vein of ore starting from opposite ends.

And he and Arnot and the various *commis* went over book after book of accounts, each clerk in turn stepping forward with his ledger of tallies, Arnot and Borel certifying that the tots therein of grain and livestock and goods of other sorts were properly balanced.

"I don't know why you have me do this, Arnot," said Borel. "I have yet to find even a single thing out of order."

"Nevertheless, my lord," said Arnot, "should something happen to me, you will know how 'tis done."

"But I already know how 'tis done, Arnot."

"Still, my lord . . ."

They had had this discussion every year, and always did Borel yield to his steward's wishes.

Every eve, Chelle, wearing a new dress and new shoes and stockings and linens, and adorned with different gems, dined with Borel, the prince also in finery. And afterward they vied at échecs or taroc or read to one another or danced to music played by members of the staff, other members making up the fours and eights and sixteens needed for a complete minuet or quadrille or reel.

Never had Winterwood Manor been so gay.

And in the depths of the nights, never had Winterwood Manor been so tender, so passionate, so loving, not only in the bed shared by Borel and Chelle, but in beds shared by others throughout the manse as well.

Some seventeen days after arriving at the Winterwood, again the mansion was abustle, for on the morrow the prince and his lady would leave for Summerwood Manor, the wedding of Prince Alain and Lady Camille now but twelve days hence.

Horses were gathered and the next morn were laden with what would be needed for the trek and for the gala, including much of Chelle's completely new wardrobe, and many garments for the prince as well.

And they set out in a rade, horses in cavalcade, riders on

some, goods on others, Wolves in escort, and off for the Summerwood they rode.

Sprites raced through planes of ice all along the route, and Borel did see the one who had aided him just two months, a fortnight, and three days past there at Hradian's cote. And Borel saluted the tiny being, and it bounced in glee from ice-coated tree to frozen pool to icicles galore dangling down. And Borel and Chelle laughed at its antics as it played hide-and-seek with them.

It was a leisurely ride through the winter 'scape of the woodland, and only light snow fell in the midst of the first day, and none thereafter.

They rode by day and camped by night, and midmorn of the third day they passed through a twilight border and came unto the Autumnwood.

They paused and shed their winter gear and donned clothes suited for cool days and brisk nights. Then they rode on, now accompanied by unseen gigglers down among the underbrush and running from tree to rock to tree.

Chelle was astounded by the abundance within this woodland, and when they camped that eve she simply had to see if what she had dreamed with Borel was true. And so she plucked an apple from a tree in a nearby orchard, and tied a ribbon about the particular twig whence it came. The apple itself was delectable, and within a candlemark she returned to the tree and looked at the beribboned twig, and thereon a ripe apple dangled, just like the one she had eaten. When she returned to camp, Borel looked up, a question in his eyes. "I had to make certain that I had not been befooled by a mischievous tease," said Chelle, by way of explanation.

"Mischievous tease?" said Borel, frowning, looking about, clearly perplexed. "Who might that be?"

Chelle leaned over and kissed him, but she otherwise didn't enlighten him.

All the next day it rained, and the rade went a bit slower, the footing more difficult in places along the way, and they rode with their cloaks held close and with the hoods pulled up, as the rain fell from the overcast above.

Past cascading waterfalls and along high-running streams they fared, and through woodlands adrip. And that night they camped on a bit of a knoll, for down lower it was quite wet.

The next day dawned clear, as did the day after, and onward they went, and in midafternoon of the sixth day of travel they rode past a field of grain and up the long slope, and nigh the top sat a huge man beneath an oak, a great scythe across his knees.

As the prince approached, the man stood and doffed his hat, revealing a shock of red hair, and he bowed low.

"Afternoon, Reaper," said Borel, riding past.

"Afternoon, Prince Borel," said the man, but he remained bowed.

Borel growled something unto Slate, and Slate in turn spoke the same language to Trot and Loll and Blue-eye, and that trio broke away from the escort and went hunting.

"Conies on the way, Reaper," said Borel.

"Thank you, my lord," said the huge man, but he didn't straighten from his bow until the entire cavalcade had ridden by.

"Who was that?" asked Chelle, when she and Borel were out of earshot.

"I call him the Reaper, for he scythes grain for any who need it. Yet beyond that I don't know. It seems he has always been there, sitting under that tree, and none I know can tell me his tale, and I feel it improper to ask him, for I sense there is a great sorrow involved."

They rode a bit farther, and then Chelle said, "Perhaps Camille is right, and sometime long past a bard of the Keltoi told a tale about a reaper sitting under an oak, and he has been there ever since."

"If so," said Borel, "then that would make him one of the Firsts."

"First of his Kind, you mean?"

Borel nodded and said, "And perhaps the last."

On they rode and on, and Trot and Loll and Blue-eye came

running and rejoined the escort, and Borel growled a word and Trot answered.

"Three," said Borel.

"Three?"

"Conies," said Borel.

"Your Wolves can count?" asked Chelle.

Borel frowned. "Perhaps. But I know it was three because Trot said they each caught one."

"Ah," said Chelle. "Three for the Reaper."

"Two only," said Borel. "They ate the other themselves."

As sunset drew near, they came unto another twilight marge, and they crossed over to come into the Summerwood.

The night was balmy and they changed into still lighter clothes even as they made camp.

The next morn they set out across this forest, the summer day warming, birds singing, insects humming, among them bumblebees. And Borel and Chelle looked for Buzzer, but finally Borel said, "Love, without Flic alongside, these *all* look like Buzzer to me."

Chelle ruefully grinned and said, "Me, too." Then she frowned and added, "I wonder if all Humans look alike to bees?"

Borel said, "I think Buzzer came to recognize us as separate individuals."

Chelle nodded. "We should ask Flic."

All that day they rode, and toward evening Gerard spurred nigh. "My lord," he said, "shall we press on, or instead make camp?"

Borel looked at Chelle, and she said, "If I understand the meaning beneath Gerard's question, I advise we camp, else we'll arrive at Summerwood Manor in the depths of night. I think that not appropriate for either our staff or that of Prince Alain."

"We camp, Gerard," said Borel.

The next day in midmorn they came to a long slope leading to Summerwood Manor below. Gerard sounded a resonant call on a horn, and as the cry echoed throughout the woodland, the rade progressed downward.

As they rode, Michelle studied the estate: the mansion itself stood some four or five storeys in height, though here and there it rose above even that; it was broad and deep with many wings, and even courtyards within. The far-flung grounds about the great château were surrounded by a lengthy high stone wall, with gates standing at the midpoints, at the moment all closed. Inside the wall there were groves of trees and gardens with pathways through, as well as a small lake, and—

"Oh, Borel, a hedge maze."

Borel smiled and said, "You should try it, love; to find the center is the goal, yet it is the most fun when one gets lost," and on down the slope they rode.

Several outbuildings ranged along part of one wall at the back of the manse: a stable, a carriage house, a smithery, barns for the storage of grain and hay, and various utility sheds, some large, others small.

It was a great deal like her père's estate, though on a much grander scale.

And they rode through one of the gates and along a white stone lane curving between two lines of old oaks standing sentry, their limbs arching overhead and forming a canopy. Across a stone bridge they went, a stream meandering under, with graceful black swans aswimming. They emerged from the oaken canopy, and straight ahead across a broad mead stood the great château. And waiting in the forecourt were servants to take charge of the horses.

They dismounted at a large and deep portico, and Borel offered his arm to Chelle, and into the manse they strode.

52

Vows

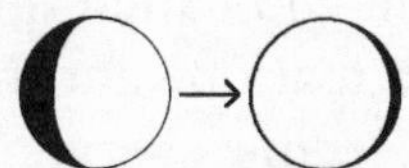

At the doorway stood a grey-haired, blue-eyed, lean man dressed in black.

"Lanval," said Borel.

"My lord," said Lanval, and he looked at Chelle and smiled.

"Lady Michelle, I present Lanval, steward of Summerwood Manor." As Lanval bowed, Borel added, "Lady Michelle is Duke Roulan's daughter, and soon to be mistress of the Winterwood, for we are betrothed."

Lanval nodded, yet this was not news to him, for messages between the Winterwood and the other Forests of the Seasons had flown back and forth by falcon.

"My lord, my lady," said Lanval. And he gestured and said, "Shall we?" And down the short corridor they stepped to come unto the welcoming hall, where on an inlaid depiction of a green oak in the center of the floor stood a man and three women; and Lanval called out, "My Lord Alain, and my Ladies Céleste, Liaze, and Camille, I present Lord Borel, Prince of the Winterwood, and the Lady Michelle, daughter of Duke Roulan and betrothed of Prince Borel."

Borel and Alain bowed, and Céleste, Liaze, Camille, and Michelle curtseyed, and then, unable to contain themselves any longer, Alain and Camille and Céleste and Liaze rushed forward, and hugged and kissed Borel and embraced Chelle, and they all talked at once and laughed and drew the Prince of the Winterwood and his truelove down the hall to a sitting room, where tea and scones and jellies awaited. And as all took seat and Camille served, Alain said, "Well, big brother, you and Michelle have a tale to tell, one we are very interested in hearing. But before you begin, I have the strangest dream to relate to you, a dream shared by everyone in this household: it seems you and a masked"—of a sudden Alain looked at Michelle and said—"Oh, my, it was you! You were the masked lady, Michelle. And you and Borel were here at a gala in Summerwood Manor, and you taught us a strange dance you called the bee dance and—"

Chelle and Borel looked at one another and broke into laughter, and Borel said, "It seems everyone we shared our shared dream with, shared the same dream with us."

Liaze frowned and said, "Frère, you speak in riddles."

Borel pushed out a hand and said, "As Chelle told Arnot, it is an effect of the spell she was under."

At a questioning look from Céleste, Borel shrugged and added, "It will become clear when we tell our tale, but for now just call it magie." He turned to Chelle and said, "Chérie, why don't you begin?"

Chelle looked at the four eager faces before her, and took a sip of tea and then said, "It was the day of my majority, and my sire the duke had invited many folk to a gala in my honor. Fairies came on high-prancing horses bedecked with silver bells, and from the nearby town of Riverbend came merchants in broughams and . . ."

The next day, as all were sitting in Camille's favorite gazebo, Scruff the sparrow suddenly began chirping, his attention focused on the grounds beyond. And across the hedge maze two iridescent-winged Sprites and a dark bumblebee came winging. And they flew to the railing and alighted—Flic and Fleurette and Buzzer—and all were as naked as the day they were born, but for Flic's épée and belt, and the moondrop pendant Fleurette now wore, the pendant given Flic by King Arle. And Fleurette was definitely female, with her wee breasts and cleft groin; she had brown hair as did Flic, though her tiny locks held pale highlights within and fell down to the middle of her back. After introductions were made all 'round, Flic said, "We have talked it over, Fleurette and I, and if rings are involved in this silly human ritual you are about to undertake, Lord Alain, Lady Camille, well, hurm, we would be honored to bear them."

The very next day, a long horn call in the distance announced the arrival of another rade, and, in cavalcade, up the length of the vale came slim, dark-haired King Valeray, his eyes piercing and grey, much as were Alain's. And at his side rode Queen Saissa—slender, dark-haired, with arresting eyes of black. How these two could produce Borel with his ice-blue eyes and silvery hair, and Liaze with her eyes of amber and auburn hair, and Céleste with her green eyes and pale blond hair, none could say, though perhaps Fairies were involved, or so went the rumor.

In Valeray and Saissa's entourage rode Hierophant Marceau—bald-headed and short and a barrel of a man and seemingly all laughter and cheer . . . when he wasn't pontificating.

And when the king and queen came into the welcoming hall, awaiting them were two sons, two daughters, two daughters-to-be, as well as two Sprites and a sparrow and a humming bee.

Once again Borel and Chelle told their stories, and when they were done, Valeray said, "Rhensibé, Hradian, Iniquí, and Nefasí: four sisters, all acolytes of Orbane. And Rhensibé came after my old friend Roulan through his daughter. How cruel."

"She also tried to prevent Borel's happiness," said Alain.

"What a terrible thing to do," said Camille. "Four sisters, acolytes all, and out to gain revenge."

Hierophant Marceau made a warding sign and said, "Mithras, protect us."

Valeray looked at the rotund priest and then turned back to the others. "I knew of Nefasí. And after Saissa's and my experience, and Camille and Alain's as well, we were certain that Hradian was one of Orbane's acolytes, too. But that there were two more . . ."

"Well, at least Rhensibé is dead, Father," said Liaze, "thanks to Michelle and Borel."

"Thank Mithras," said Marceau, making another warding sign.

"Thank the Wolves instead," said Chelle, "for they were the ones who did her in."

They sat in silence for long moments, and finally Céleste glanced at Hierophant Marceau and turned to the others and said, "Since it seems we are here to witness Alain and Camille's vows, let us all take another pledge upon ourselves: that we will do whatever it takes to rescue Lord Roulan and the others, and vow as well that we will do all in our power to stop Orbane's acolytes from setting that vile wizard free."

"Well, I do so pledge," said Chelle, "and—"

Of a sudden there came the sound of shuttles and looms, and before the gathering stood three women: Maiden, Mother, and Crone; the Ladies Skuld, Verdandi, and Urd; the Fates Wyrd, Lot, and Doom.

Borel and Alain and Valeray stood and bowed, as did Flic. And Chelle and Camille and Liaze and Céleste and Saissa curtseyed, as did Fleurette. Buzzer was asleep, and so too was Scruff, and neither bee nor sparrow stirred. Hierophant Marceau did nought, for he had fainted dead away.

"Be careful what you pledge," said the Maiden, Skuld.

"For we will hold you to it," said the Mother, Verdandi.

"If not to the letter, at least to the spirit," said the Crone, Urd.

Camille said, "*Mesdames,* when I was searching for Alain, you did tell me that if Orbane ever escaped the Castle of Shadows beyond the Black Wall of the World, he would pollute the River of Time itself. And so, any pledge to keep that from happening seems worthy."

"Indeed it is," said Skuld, with Verdandi and Urd nodding in agreement.

"My Lady Wyrd," said Borel, "since you see the future, have we a chance?"

They took a room in *Le Taureau Noir*, and luxuriated in hot baths and ate delicious hot meals and downed copious glasses of hearty red wine. And Chelle and Borel slept in a real bed, and they made love.

They stayed in Arens that night and two more, resting, relaxing, eating, acquiring another horse and replenishing their supplies, and obtaining a bow and arrows for Chelle.

But when the next day dawned, they rode away from the Black Bull inn, and through the town and to a nearby hillock, and there Buzzer took a bearing, and off the bee shot on a line for the demesne along the sunward marge of the Winterwood.

Through twilight borders they fared, and across lands of Faery, but midmorn of the fifth day they emerged from an umbrous bound and came unto the realm where grew yellow daffodils and blue morning glories and sweet red clover. They had entered the stream-laden demesne adjacent to the Winterwood.

On they rode, splashing through rills and runs and streams, and nigh the noontide of the second day within this land they arrived at another twilight wall.

As Borel and Chelle dismounted, Flic and Buzzer flew through the marge and quickly back, and the Sprite came shivering. "Snow, ice, barren trees: what a dreadful realm you have, my lord, for surely it is the Winterwood."

Borel, fetching winter gear from the packhorse, grinned and shook his head. "Dreadful you say? Non. Marvelous say I, for it is both savage and peaceful, with times when the wind howls like fury come alive, flinging snow and ice in its rage, and other times of preternatural stillness, when one can hear a snowflake fall across the width of a vale. Non, my friend, 'tis a breathtaking realm for all days are different, yet somehow all the same."

"Well, you can have it, my lord, for neither Buzzer nor I can deal with the cold: she would fall dormant, and me?"—Flic grinned—"I do believe I would fall dead. Besides, now that Buzzer and I have delivered you securely to your realm, you will be safe as soon as you pass through this twilight wall."

Chelle's face fell and she said, "Surely you two are not leaving us, are you, Flic?"

Flic sketched a bow in the air and said, "I must, my lady, for, truly, neither Buzzer nor I can withstand such cold as is in the Winterwood. Ah, me . . . I am but a warm-weather friend, oui?"

"Non, my friend," said Borel, shaking out cold-weather gear. "Most certainly not."

"But where will you go?" asked Chelle, taking a winter cloak and gloves and warm stockings from Borel. "I would see you again, my friend. Besides, there's my père and mère and their guests to set free, and I would have your épée at my side."

"My lady, I will of certain be one of your chevaliers, though how I will cope with King Arle's iron, that I cannot say. But first, and most immediately, I will seek out my Fleurette, for she is waiting, and I love her as much as Borel loves you. But then—"

"But then," said Borel, pulling on his socks and then his boots, "you will come to the Summerwood, for I would have you and Buzzer attend my brother Alain's wedding."

Chelle clapped her hands even as Flic said, "Summerwood?"

"White camellias," said Borel, looking at Buzzer, the bee hovering at Flic's side. "Red, red roses, and yellow ones as well. And lilacs. —Oh, and something called hydrangea. But do not ask me more, for that is the extent of my knowledge."

"I will see if she knows," said Flic. And he and Buzzer landed on a patch of ground. After a moment of silent converse, Buzzer did a waggle dance. Then she paused and did an entirely different dance of waggles. Flic laughed and looked up and said, "She knows the Summerwood, and so we will be there. She also said that for someone as slow as you are, my lord, you seem to get about a lot." Flic broke into giggles, as did Chelle, and Borel's guffaws joined them.

Borel and Chelle pulled on gloves and fastened cloaks about their shoulders, then mounted.

Buzzer and Flic took to wing and hovered, and Flic drew Argent and saluted both the lord and his lady.

"Au revoir, my wee friend," said Borel.

"Till we meet again," said Chelle.

"See you in the Summerwood," said Flic, and then Buzzer circled 'round and took a bearing, and both bee and Sprite shot away.

When they were beyond seeing, Chelle and Borel turned their horses and rode into the Winterwood.

All the rest of that day and into the night rode the two, for, no longer needing the guide who went dormant in the dark, they could press on. And the nearly full moon rose and lighted the way before them.

The land was extraordinarily still, with no wind whatsoever, and through the quiet they rode, the only sound that of the horses and the creak of leather. But then from far off there came the hoot of an owl, and Borel answered in kind. And for a mile or so, these two kept up a running conversation, and closer to one another they came, and then a silent shape swooped through the air and across and up; a snowy owl it was.

"Oh, how beautiful," said Chelle, watching the flight as the owl rose and briefly silhouetted itself against the moon, ere it vanished among the stars.

On they rode, and as the moon passed through the zenith they came to a pine grove standing dark in the night.

"Here we will stay the eve, my love," said Borel, leading the way inward.

Midst the evergreens stood a cabin, unlit and unoccupied. They dismounted and unladed the horses and rubbed them down. Borel stepped into the tiny lodge and returned bearing blankets with which he covered the steeds.

Then he and Chelle carried their goods inside, where Borel poured oats from the grain they carried into nose bags to feed the horses, while Chelle readied a fire. When Borel returned, she had a small blaze going, and Borel fetched ice in buckets and set them on the irons above the fire.

"Water for the horses," said Chelle, her statement not a question.

Borel then broke out biscuits and jerky and the remains of a block of cheese they had gotten in Arens, and he and Chelle ate.

After watering the steeds, they went to bed, and Borel lay with Chelle, holding her close, and they fell asleep that way.

All the next day they rode, and Ice-Sprites ran before and behind and around them, the wee ice-dwelling creatures grinning and dancing in glee within the frozen surfaces. And Chelle laughed joyfully at their antics, while Borel looked for the Sprite that had accompanied him to Hradian's cote, but he saw it not.

And over snowy ridges and down through silent valleys they fared, some atrickle with meltwater, others with dashing streams. And Chelle was all eyes and curiosity, and she pointed out the subtle colors amid the blacks and whites and greys.

That night they stayed in another lodge, this cabin in a hollow along a fold of land.

Yet accompanied by dancing and racing Ice-Sprites—vanishing here, popping up there, always within the ice itself—Borel and Chelle rode through a wintry but low mountain range, to emerge in snow-covered vales beyond.

And the sun rode through the skies, up and across and down, and alongside a small river they passed, the water swift under the ice, air bubbles trapped in the run, though now and again there were stretches of open water; and the flow sang and danced on its way toward a distant sea. And as the sun set and winter twilight graced the land, and with the full moon just now peeking above the horizon, they came into the vale overlooked by Winterwood Manor.

Borel halted and dismounted, Chelle dismounting as well. And with Sprites peering out through clear windows on the ice-clad trees and rocks, of a sudden Borel cupped his hands 'round his mouth and gave a long howl. The sound echoed and reverberated throughout the valley, and joyous calls answered, the echoes of many joining those of the one.

Chelle laughed, and as the cries died out she said, "That was your pack?"

Borel chuckled and said, "Oui."

"I remember the dream," said Chelle. "We were in the Spring-

"Better yet, have we time?" said Valeray.

Skuld turned up her hands and said, "I will not say what I have seen, only that a distant peril comes."

"This will I say," said Verdandi, "with the death of Rhensibé, you have seriously set back their plans, though you have also gained even more enmity."

"And so, take care, beware," said Urd, "for they will seek revenge."

And the sound of shuttles and looms swelled, but Flic cried out, "Wait!"

Skuld and Verdandi had already vanished, but Urd yet remained, and she looked at the Sprite, an eyebrow raised.

"Begging your pardon, Lady Urd," said Flic, "but I don't think even for some unknown reason I would ever fall behind, and so I would appreciate it if—"

But with a cackle of glee, Urd vanished as well, as did the sound of looms.

The very next day, with the sun standing at the zenith—"A very auspicious time," declared Hierophant Marceau, follower of Mithras that he was—in the flower gardens of Summerwood Manor a wedding got under way.

But for the kitchen crew, the staff of Summerwood Manor was present, for none would miss this occasion. Too, those who had accompanied Borel and Chelle from Winterwood Manor were in attendance, as well Lord Valeray and Lady Saissa's entourage. And the women stood on the bride's side of the garden, and the men stood on the groom's side.

Of Camille's kindred none were present, for they were scattered to the four winds: Camille's father, Henri, had run away with a circus and could not be found; her mother Aigrette was dead of avarice, for she had drowned in a so-called wishing well while trying to fetch coins; Camille's beloved brother Giles was ruling an isle far over the sea; and of her five sisters, Colette and Felise and the twins Joie and Gai were all very afraid of Faery and hence would not come, and besides, they were occupied raising families; while Lisette—whose very rich old roué of a husband and his panting dogs had all died on the very same night of a mysterious stomach ailment, leaving behind a vast fortune—she was entirely too busy being squired about continental cities by a bevy of young and handsome and muscular men.

And though none of Camille's kindred were there, all of Alain's were.

As to the wedding party: at the fountain and to the left of Hierophant Marceau stood Alain, with Borel as his best man, and they were dressed in grey. Liaze and Céleste stood opposite, and they were joined by Chelle, maids of honor all and dressed in blue. And Lord Valeray and Lady Saissa were at the head of the spectators, Valeray on the groom's side, Saissa on the bride's.

Scruff and Buzzer sat side by side on a limb above the fountain.

Flic and Fleurette perched on flowers—white camellias—Flic near the best man, Fleurette near the bridesmaids.

And as someone played a soft flute, Lanval walked Camille down the aisle in between, for Lanval had been like a father to her.

And she was dressed in the palest of blue, nearly white, and from a tiara a gauzy veil fell. Down the aisle she seemed to float, and Alain smiled with joy, while Borel glanced across at Chelle and smiled in joy as well.

Lady Saissa began softly crying, but she stifled her sniffles and managed a smile when Camille stepped past.

At last, Lanval delivered Camille to the hierophant, and then took his place beside Lord Valeray.

And all alternately held breath and then sighed as each vow was given and each oath taken, Hierophant Marceau leading the way, and for once he looked rather priestly, in his red robes with the golden sunburst on his chest and his tall miter atop his head.

On cue, Flic delivered the ring to Borel, and Borel in turn gave it to Alain, and he in turn placed it on a small, round, golden-sunburst pillow before the hierophant.

Likewise, Fleurette gave the ring to Michelle, and she to Céleste, and she to Liaze, who gave it to Camille, and she placed it on the pillow as well.

Marceau lifted the pillow and rings up into the sunlight and called out a blessing, and then he lowered all. And the bride and groom then took up the rings and slipped them on one another's ring finger; first Alain placed his ring on Camille's hand, and then she on his.

And Hierophant Marceau declared them officially wed.

At the gala afterward, Flic was heard to say, "What did I tell you, Fleurette? Ah, these humans and their rites."

"I thought it was rather nice," said Fleurette, and Flic could only gape in surprise.

And as the celebration went on, there were contests of archery and quoits and croquet. There were games of blindfold tag. And many celebrants went to the hedge maze and tried to find the center. Some were lost for quite a while, and some couples came out with their clothes a bit rumpled or otherwise in disarray. And the sun slid down the sky and set, and dusk darkened the land. Lanterns were lit and placed upon tables and hung among the trees, and the gala went on. But in the twilight there came a horn cry from afar, from down the valley rather than across.

The horn rang again, and Lanval sent men running to the far gate, and shortly thereafter a rider towing two remounts came galloping up that lane and toward the manor. And he reined up among the festivities. In the light of the lanterns and the rising full moon someone cried, " 'Tis a slight youth, and he wears a blue tabard with a silver sunburst!"

Chelle, standing upon the archery range, overheard and said to Borel, "My love, it is the sigil of my sire!" and she ran toward the now-dismounted rider.

And as she came in among the crowd ranged about the youth she overheard him saying ". . . dispatched throughout Faery looking for the Lady Michelle, the missing daughter of Duke Roulan. Has anyone here seen a beautiful maiden with golden hair and—"

The crowd laughed and parted, and Chelle stepped through.

"My lady, oh, my lady," said the youth, dropping to one knee. "You are alive and well, and I have found you."

"But, Phillíp, I was never lost," said Chelle. "Yet you, how come you to be here? Last I saw, you were mucking out stables. Were you not caught in Rhensibé's—" Suddenly, Chelle's eyes widened in hope. "Can it be that—? Oh, Phillíp, what of my père and mère? Are they—?"

Phillíp stood and said, "They are well. We are all well. When we awoke from the sleep, the Fairies told us that someone named Rhensibé was dead, and with her passing the spindle had stopped spinning, and the spell was broken. But we were in a dreadful desert, and thorns surrounded all. Yet the Fairies working together managed to allay the thorns and restore the vale to its proper place. But you were missing, my lady, and some thought the worst. Yet your sire sent us out to—"

Phillíp's words were cut short as Chelle screamed in delight and grabbed him and hugged him fiercely. And then she whirled to find Borel standing at hand, and she grabbed him and hugged him fiercely as well.

"Lady Michelle," said Phillíp, "your père and mère are terribly worried, and Lady Roulan paces the floor and weeps many nights. But now that you are found, I will ride at speed and—"

"We must go there, Borel," said Chelle, "for I would not have my parents think I am lost or a captive or dead."

Céleste handed Phillíp a goblet of red wine, and the youth gulped it down and said, "We did not even know that we had been in an enchanted sleep, but when the Fairies returned us to Roulan Vale, nearby steaders said—as mortals would reckon it—some twelve years had passed since we had disappeared in a great, whirling black wind."

"We know," said Céleste. "Oh, not that you had been restored, but rather that it had been some twelve years since the wind carried the vale away. —Here, have another glass of wine."

"Well things are a proper mess in Riverbend," said the youth to Céleste's receptive ear. "People thought dead, their homes and lands occupied by others, businesses taken over, wealth given to heirs, and the like. I mean, the duke's got a tangle to unsnarl, and a proper one at that." Phillíp gulped down the wine.

Borel said, "Ma chérie, we will ride out and soon, for I would ask your sire for your hand, and he must needs give you away at our wedding, wherever we hold it."

"Winterwood Manor," said Chelle. She looked at the moon on the rise and said, "And in the light of a full moon, for it has been our touchstone."

Chelle turned to Phillíp, "You will rest a day or two, and then, with fresh horses, I would have you ride in haste back to Roulan Vale, and tell my sire we are on the way."

"Oui, my lady," said Phillíp, and then he put his hand to his head. "Woo, but I am dizzy."

"Lack of food, no doubt," said Céleste. "Come, let us get some good beef and bread into you."

As Céleste led Phillíp away, Chelle and Borel kissed deeply, and that night they danced in the light of the full moon for many long hours before finally going to bed.

Four days later, after Borel and Chelle and the full of Borel's cavalcade made ready to ride away to Lord Roulan's manse, with hugs and kisses they said good-bye to Alain and Camille and Liaze and Céleste. Then they stepped to Valeray and Saissa, and Borel said, "Father, Michelle and I are to be married, and I am notifying you not only as a king, but as a father as well. And we would like your blessing, and yours, too, Mother."

"Post the banns," said Valeray, grinning widely.

And Saissa embraced and kissed Chelle and said, "I could not ask for a better daughter. And thank you, my dear, for stringing the bow you should not have been able to string; and for drawing the arrow to the full of your pull, a pull you should not have been able to draw; and for loosing the shaft upon an unwoundable thing and wounding it severely . . . and for saving the life of my son."

"But it was Buzzer who—"

"Pish, tush, Michelle, for had you not done those things the Démon would not have dropped its terrible black sword and would have used it to slay Borel the moment he got to his feet." Again Saissa hugged and kissed Chelle, and then gave her over to Valeray.

And Valeray embraced her and said, "I welcome you to the family, Sleeping Beauty, you who were ensorcelled by a magic spindle and trapped within a vast tangle of thorns and awakened by a kiss from a prince. I think such a tale will become a legend someday, and I can only hope whoever tells it gets it right."

Chelle laughed and kissed Valeray on the cheek, and then she and Borel mounted their steeds, and both slipped cocked hats on their heads; Flic and Fleurette came to land, one upon each. Buzzer flew up and 'round and took a sighting on the sun and shot off on a line. And with an entire rade following, and with a pack of Wolves ranging fore and aflank and aft, Prince Borel and Lady Michelle set out for the vale where grow pink-flowering shamrock and blushing white roses and thorn-laden blackberry vines.

Epilogue
Afterthoughts

And thus ends this part of the tale that began but three moons and seven-and-one days past, when Prince Borel of the Winterwood fell asleep and dreamt a dream—a special dream, a shared dream—upon a summer day.

In this dream he met a beautiful demoiselle with a shadowy band across her eyes. Of course, when he finally found her, there was no spellbound darkness masking, for he was seeing her in reality and not in a dream.

Perhaps the others caught in the thrall also dreamed; they were, after all, ensnared in the very same magie. Yet if they did, it appears they did not jointly dream with anyone outside the bounds of Roulan Vale there in the Endless Sands.

Only Chelle seems to have managed that, and then only with her truelove Borel. You might find that strange, but it is the way of enchanted sleep.

Neither awake nor in a dark dream
Are perilous blades just as they seem.

Afterword

If the original fairy tale, "Sleeping Beauty," did not come from the French, I do hope that those folk in the country of its origin will forgive me for seasoning the story with a French flavor, for, in addition to being a magical adventure, this tale is a romance at heart, and French is to my mind perhaps the most romantic language of all.

Lastly, for those of you who would like to see the échecs problem wherein Prince Borel defeated the King Under the Hill when all looked lost, the following is chess Grandmaster Tal Shaked's solution to that thorny knot:

You may think it strange that the King Under the Hill ended up with all but two of his spearmen (pawns) collected on one side of the board, but with their diagonal capturing ability it is not beyond reason . . . after all, both Borel and the Fey Lord seemed to be playing somewhat recklessly.

And the Fairy King said, "Although the material is fairly balanced, I have the advantage, and it is certain that I will win, for you cannot stop at least one of my black spearmen from reaching the final row and transforming into a black queen."

Borel studied the board. He had a king and a spearman and one tower left, whereas the High Lord had a king at one edge of the board with six spearmen at hand, all of them threatening Borel's king and his spearman.

At last, Borel said, "Tower to white king's tower's three. Check."

The High Lord said, "My prince, are you certain you want to make that move?"

"Indeed," said Borel.

At this point, one might think that Borel had made a terrible move, for his most powerful piece in play was certainly his tower (rook castle), and here it seemed he was sacrificing it needlessly to a lowly spearman.

Oh, well . . .

"Very well," said the Fairy King. "Spearman takes tower. Check. And now you have nought but a king and a single spearman left, whereas I yet have all my pieces. Surely you must concede."

"Nay, my lord," said Borel, "I do not concede. White king to white king's hierophant's three."

"Hmm . . ." said the Fairy King. "Black spearman to black king's chevalier's five. Check."

Borel nodded and said, "I avoid the check thus: white king to white king's hierophant's four, taking a blocking black spearman."

Now the Fairy King studied the board long. "I have but one move," he said. "Black spearman to black king's chevalier's six."

Borel laughed and said, "And my lone remaining white spearman takes that black spearman. Check."

The Fairy King said, "Ah, Borel, I must make a move and yet cannot, for the only piece that is not blocked is my black king, and he cannot move to the open space nor capture your single spearman, for to do either would bring him adjacent to your white king, and, of course, that cannot be. Ah, me, I must concede." And he lay his black king on its side.

And thus did Borel win the game of échecs.

One other note: throughout this tale, I have relied upon the phases of the moon. I used the earth's own moon cycles to do so, and I hope they correspond to those in that magical place. But perhaps I am quite mistaken in my assumptions . . . who knows? For, once you cross the twilight borders and enter Faery, strange and wonderful are the ways therein.

Lastly, I enjoyed "restoring" this fairy tale t length, adding back those things I think should h tained, but which I believe were omitted bit through the ages. I hope you enjoyed reading it.

Dennis L
Tucson, A

About the Author

Born April 4, 1932, I have spent a great deal of my life looking through twilights and dawns seeking—what? Ah yes, I member—seeking signs of wonder, searching for pixies and iries and other such, looking in tree hollows and under snowden bushes and behind waterfalls and across wooded, moonlit lls. I did not outgrow that curiosity, that search for the edge of ery when I outgrew childhood—not when I was in the U.S. r Force during the Korean War, nor in college, nor in graduate hool, nor in the thirty-one years I spent in research and develment at Bell Telephone Laboratories as an engineer and maner on ballistic missile defense systems and then telephone stems and in think-tank activities. In fact I am still at it, still arching for glimmers and glimpses of wonder in the twilights d the dawns. I am abetted in this curious behavior by Martha e, my helpmate, lover, and, as of this writing, my wife of over ty-six years.